WHY KILL THE INNOCENT

WHY KILL THE INNOCENT

A Sebastian St. Cyr Mystery

C. S. HARRIS

BERKLEY
New York

BERKLEY
An imprint of Penguin Random House LLC
375 Hudson Street, New York, New York 10014

Copyright © 2018 by The Two Talers, LLC

Library of Congress Cataloging-in-Publication Data
Names: Harris, C. S., author.
Title: Why kill the innocent: a Sebastian St. Cyr Mystery/C. S. Harris.
Description: First edition. | New York : Berkley, 2018.
Identifiers: LCCN 2017037791 | ISBN 9780399585623 (hardback) |
ISBN 9780399585630 (e-book)
Subjects: LCSH: Great Britain—History—George III, 1760–1820—Fiction. |
Saint Cyr, Sebastian (Fictitious character)—Fiction. |
BISAC: FICTION/Mystery & Detective / Historical. |
FICTION / Historical. | GSAFD: Regency fiction. | Mystery fiction.
Classification: LCC PS3566.R5877 W4786 2018 | DDC 813/.54—dc23 LC record
available at https://lccn.loc.gov/2017037791

First Edition: April 2018

Printed in the United States of America
1   3   5   7   9   10   8   6   4   2

Jacket photo © Christine Goodwin/Arcangel

For Angel,

1998—2017

So shalt thou put away the guilt of innocent blood from among you,
when thou shalt do that which is right in the sight of the Lord.

—DEUTERONOMY 21:9

WHY KILL THE INNOCENT

Chapter 1

A howling wind flung icy snow crystals into Hero Devlin's face, stinging her cold cheeks and stealing her breath. She kept her head bowed, her fists clenched in the fine cloth of her merino carriage gown as she struggled to drag its sodden weight through the knee-deep drifts clogging the ancient winding lane. A footman with a lantern staggered ahead of her to light the darkness, for Clerkenwell was a wretched, dangerous area on the outskirts of the City, and night had fallen long ago.

She was here, alone except for the footman and a petite French midwife who floundered through the snow in her wake, because of an article she was writing on the hardships faced by the families of men snatched off the streets by the Royal Navy's infamous press gangs. The midwife, Alexi Sauvage, had offered to introduce Hero to the desperate eight-months-pregnant wife of a recently impressed cooper. No one had expected the woman to go into labor just as a fierce snowstorm swept in to render the narrow lanes of the district impassable to a gentlewoman's carriage. Thanks to their presence, mother and child both survived the long, hard birth. But the snow just kept getting deeper.

"Do you see it yet?" Alexi called, peering through the whirl of white toward where Hero's carriage awaited them at the base of Shepherds' Lane.

Hero brought up a cold-numbed hand to shield her eyes. "It should be j—"

She broke off as her foot caught on something half-buried in the snow and she pitched forward to land in a deep drift on quickly out-flung hands. She started to push up again, then froze as she realized she was staring at the tousled dark hair of a body that lay facedown beside her.

The footman swung about in alarm, the light from his lantern swaying wildly. "My lady!"

"*Mon Dieu,*" whispered Alexi, coming to crouch next to her. "It's a woman. Help me turn her, quickly."

Together they heaved the stiffening woman onto her back. The winter had been so wretchedly cold, with endless weeks of freezing temperatures and soaring food and coal prices, that more and more of the city's poor were being found dead in the streets. But this was no ragged pauper woman. Her fine black pelisse was lined with fur, and the dusky curls framing her pale face were fashionably cut. Hero stared into those open sightless eyes and had no need to see the bloody gash on the side of the woman's head to know that she was dead.

"She must have slipped and hit something," said Hero.

"I don't think so." Alexi Sauvage studied the ugly wound with professional interest. As a female, she could be licensed in England to practice only as a midwife. But Alexi had trained as a physician in Italy, where such things were allowed. "She couldn't have died here. A wound like this bleeds profusely—look at all the blood in her hair and on her pelisse. Yet there's hardly any blood in the snow around her." With ten-der hands, she brushed away the rapidly falling flakes that half obscured the dead woman's face. "I wonder who she is."

Hero watched the snow fall away from those still features and felt her chest give an odd lurch. "I know her. She's a musician named Jane Ambrose. She teaches piano to"—she paused as Alexi swung her head to stare at her—"to Princess Charlotte. The Regent's daughter."

Chapter 2

$\mathcal{S}$ebastian St. Cyr, Viscount Devlin, stood at the river steps below Westminster Bridge, his worried gaze on the turgid ice-filled expanse of the Thames before him.

Never in anyone's memory had London seen a winter such as this. Beginning in December and lasting for more than a week, a great killing fog had smothered the city with a darkness so heavy it could be felt. After that came days of endless snow that buried the entire Kingdom beneath vast drifts said in some places to run as much as twenty-three feet deep. And then, yesterday, a brief, sudden thaw sent massive blocks of ice from up the Thames spinning downriver to be carried back and forth by the tide, catching in eddies and against the arches of the bridges, where they crashed into one another with a series of echoing booms that reminded Sebastian of artillery fire. Now, with this evening's plunging temperatures and new snowfall, the city had turned into a strange black-and-white world of bleak windblown drifts cut by a ribbon of darkly dangerous ice-filled waters. And still the snow fell thick and fast around him.

He was aware of a strange silence that seemed to press down on the city, unnatural enough to be troubling. Twenty years of war combined with falling wages, soaring prices, and widespread starvation had already brought England to her knees. There was a very real worry that this vicious, killing winter might be more than the country could—or would—bear.

He glanced back at the ancient stone walls of the Houses of Parliament, which rose just beyond the bridge. They seemed so strong and invincibly enduring. Yet he knew they were not.

"*Gov'nor.*" A familiar shrill cockney voice cut through the icy silence. "Gov'nor!"

Sebastian turned to see his sharp-faced young groom, or tiger, slip and almost fall as he took the icy footpath curling down from the bridge. "Tom? What the devil are you doing here?"

"I like t' never found ye, yer honor," said Tom, almost falling again as he skidded to a halt. "A message jist come to Brook Street from 'er ladyship."

"Yes, I heard she's been delayed in Clerkenwell."

"Aye, but this is a *second* message, yer honor. She's at the Queen's 'Ead near the Green, and she says you'll be wantin' t' come right away. Somebody close to Princess Charlotte's been murdered, and 'er ladyship done tripped over the body jist alyin' there in the street!"

He found Hero beside a roaring fire in the private parlor of a ramshackle old inn at the base of Shepherds' Lane. She stood lost in thought, her hands held out to the blaze. Her wet, rich dark hair lay plastered against her face; the skirts of the elegant black gown she wore in mourning for her dead mother hung limp and sodden.

"Devlin. Thank heavens," she said, turning as he entered.

"I'm sorry it took so long for your message to find me." She was one of the strongest people he knew, determinedly rational and fiercely brave. But as she came into his arms and he held her close, he felt a faint shudder rack her tall Junoesque frame. "Are you all right?"

"Yes." She drew back to give him a lopsided smile, as if vaguely embarrassed by that brief display of vulnerability. "Although more shaken than I'd care to admit."

"Anyone would be shaken."

"Not Alexi. She's gone off to treat the cook's frostbite."

Sebastian grunted. He wasn't sure anything could shock that enigmatic fiery-haired Frenchwoman. But all he said was "Tell me what happened."

He drew her back to the fire's warmth while she provided him with a crisp, calm summary. "A couple of the parish constables are guarding the body," she said. "But I made certain they sent word directly to Sir Henry at Bow Street rather than to the public office here at Hatton Garden."

"That was wise," said Sebastian. Violent deaths connected in any way with the royal family had a tendency to present the officials involved with a Faustian dilemma. And the magistrates of Hatton Garden had in the past proven themselves to be far from reliable. "Does anyone else know yet?"

"Not to my knowledge."

Sebastian nodded, his gaze meeting hers. There was no need to give voice to what both were thinking. "Good."

Sir Henry Lovejoy arrived in Clerkenwell not long after Sebastian.

The Bow Street magistrate was a small man, barely five feet tall, with stern religious views, a serious demeanor, and unshakable integrity. There'd been a time not so long ago when Sebastian had been a fugitive on the run for murder and Sir Henry the magistrate tasked with tracking him down. But in the years since then an unusual friendship had developed between the Earl's son and the dour middle-aged magistrate. As different as the two men were, they shared a fierce dedication to the pursuit of justice.

Huddled now in a heavy greatcoat with a scarf covering his lower face, Sir Henry stood outside the Queen's Head in quiet consultation with his constables while Sebastian handed Hero up into her carriage. Sebastian was watching the coachman pull away to carefully guide his team down the snowy street when Sir Henry came up beside him.

"Her ladyship is certain of the victim's identity?" said the magistrate, his eyes narrowing as the carriage's rear wheels slid sideways on the icy cobbles.

Sebastian nodded. "I'm afraid so."

"Not a good situation."

"No," agreed Sebastian.

The carriage swung around a distant corner, and the two men turned to wade through the deep drifts clogging Shepherds' Lane. The snow still fell thick and fast around them.

Two parish constables stood guard over a dark, silent form rapidly disappearing beneath the falling snow. The men had been stomping their feet and swinging their arms in an effort to stay warm, but at the Bow Street magistrate's approach, both went rigid.

"At ease, men," said Sir Henry.

"Aye, yer honor," said one of the constables, although he still didn't move.

Crouching down beside Jane Ambrose's body, Sebastian yanked off his glove and used his bare hand to brush gently at the snow that had already re-covered the dead woman's lifeless skin and dark blue lips. She'd been a poignantly attractive woman, he thought, his hand curling into a fist as he rested his forearm on his bent knee; she was probably somewhere in her early thirties, with thick dark hair, wide cheekbones, and a heart-shaped face.

The side of her head was a pulpy mess.

Lovejoy thrust his hands deep into the pockets of his greatcoat and looked away. "Did you know her, as well?"

Sebastian pulled on his glove again, his gaze returning to that still, pale face. "Only by reputation." She'd been born Jane Somerset, the daughter of the organist at Westminster Abbey. As child prodigies, she and her twin, James, had given numerous musical performances to great acclaim. But modesty required females of her class to retire from public view once they reached marriageable age. And so, while her brother James Somerset had gone on to be acknowledged as a promising young composer and one of the greatest pianists of their age, Jane had ceased to perform, married a successful dramatist named Edward Ambrose, and confined herself to such socially acceptable "feminine" pursuits as writing glees and ballads and teaching piano to the children of the wealthy. Premier amongst those students was Princess Charlotte, ebullient young daughter of the Regent and heiress presumptive to the throne behind her father.

Sebastian found himself considering Jane Ambrose's ties to the House of Hanover as he studied the pink-tinged snow around the dead woman's head. Alexi Sauvage was right: If Jane Ambrose had been killed here in Shepherds' Lane, the snow would have been drenched crimson with her blood. It was not.

"I wonder why she was left here, of all places," he said aloud.

Lovejoy hunched his shoulders against an icy gust. "Unfortunately, the wind and snow have covered any tracks her killer might have left. I suppose it's possible she was attacked somewhere near here by footpads who were then interrupted in the process of dragging the body to a less public locale."

Sebastian touched the bloodstained fur-trimmed collar of Jane Ambrose's pelisse where a gold locket still hung around the dead woman's neck. "No footpad would leave that."

Lovejoy cast a quick glance around, then crouched on the far side of the body and pitched his voice low enough to be inaudible to the constables holding back the crowds that were beginning to gather despite the freezing temperature and wind-driven snow. "And yet I fear the palace is likely to insist on saying some such thing is what happened. If we're to get a postmortem, we'd best move quickly."

Sebastian met the magistrate's gaze and nodded.

Pushing to his feet, Lovejoy sent one of his men running to the nearest deadhouse for a shell that could be used to transport the body to the surgery of Paul Gibson, an anatomist known for his ability to read the evidence left by violent death. It was when they were lifting what was left of Jane Ambrose onto the shell that Sebastian noticed the dead woman's hands, which until then had lain hidden beneath the folds of her pelisse.

They were bare.

"She's not wearing gloves," said Sebastian. "Or a hat, for that matter."

Lovejoy came to stand beside him. "How very odd." Even in the best of weather, no gentlewoman would think of appearing in public without a hat and gloves. And in this weather, it would be madness. "I'll set the lads to beating the snowdrifts to look for them. Perhaps they're lying somewhere hereabouts."

"Perhaps," said Sebastian. "But it would still be odd."

Chapter 3

*W*hile a solemn-faced Lovejoy set off to personally notify Edward Ambrose of his wife's death, Sebastian spent the better part of the next hour scouting the surrounding area and knocking on the doors of the ancient dilapidated houses that lined the crooked lane. He was hoping to find someone who'd seen or at least heard something. But the bitter cold and heavy snowfall had long ago driven the area's residents to their firesides; no one would admit to knowing anything.

Giving up, he stood for a moment and watched Lovejoy's constables, their lanterns shuttered against the driving snow as they continued to flounder about in the deep drifts looking for Jane Ambrose's missing hat and gloves or anything else that might help explain what had happened to her. The snow muffled their movements the same way it silenced the usual racket of the vast, freezing city around them. And it struck Sebastian that, so intense was the unnatural hush, they might have been in a snowy forest glen surrounded only by the unseen creatures of the night.

Readjusting his hat against the snow, he shook off the peculiar thought and turned his steps toward the Tower Hill surgery of a certain one-legged, opium-eating Irishman.

Sebastian's friendship with the Irish surgeon Paul Gibson stretched back nearly ten years, to a time when both men wore the King's colors and fought the King's wars from Italy and the West Indies to the mountains of Portugal. Then a French cannonball shattered Gibson's lower left leg, leaving him racked with phantom pains and struggling with a dangerous opium addiction. That was when he had come here, to London, to teach anatomy at hospitals such as St. Thomas's and St. Bartholomew's and to open a small surgery in the shadow of the Tower.

But when Sebastian arrived at the lantern-lit stone outbuilding used by Gibson for both official autopsies and surreptitious, illegal dissections, it was to find only the Frenchwoman Alexi Sauvage with a stained apron pinned over her gown and a bloody scalpel in one hand.

A fine-boned woman in her thirties with pale skin, brown eyes, and hair the color of autumn leaves, she looked up from the naked body that lay on the stone slab in the center of the room and said, "Ah, it's you," before going back to work on what was left of Jane Ambrose.

Pausing in the doorway, Sebastian cast one quick glance at what she was doing and turned to stare across the undulating snow-filled yard toward the ancient stone house Paul Gibson used as his surgery. Alexi Sauvage had lived with the Irishman for a year now, although she steadfastly refused to marry him. "Where's Gibson?"

This time she did not look up. "A wherry overturned trying to shoot the bridge. Some timber yard workers managed to rescue two of the three men aboard, but they were half-dead by the time they were pulled from the river, and Paul has gone to see what he can do for them." She hesitated, then added, "Given Jane Ambrose's connections to the palace, I thought it best not to wait until he returned to start the postmortem."

"That was wise. Thank you," said Sebastian, although it didn't ease his discomfort. It wasn't that he doubted either her knowledge or ability, for Gibson had assured him both were considerable. But once, four years before, in the mountains of Portugal, Sebastian had killed her lover, and Alexi Sauvage had vowed to kill him in revenge. Hero had managed to move beyond that and form a friendship with the Frenchwoman. But Sebastian still couldn't be easy around her, and he knew the feeling was mutual.

He cleared his throat. "Have you learned anything yet?"

She brushed a stray lock of fiery hair out of her eyes with the back of one crooked wrist. "I can tell you that if she was hit with something, it wasn't an iron bar or a wooden club, but something larger and more irregular in shape."

"'If'?"

"It's also possible she fell and struck her head on something. Given the location of the wound, it's virtually impossible to tell which."

"You're saying she might have died accidently?"

"I'm saying it's possible. Although it's more likely someone hit her and knocked her down. There's a bruise just below her left eye."

Sebastian brought his gaze back to the dead woman's face. He could see the faint discoloration high on her left cheekbone, the size and shape of the type of mark typically left by a man's fist. "That's recent?"

"Yes. Probably within minutes of her death."

"So it could be manslaughter. Someone struck her, she fell and hit her head, and died."

"Perhaps. Although it's possible someone struck her in the face, knocked her down, and then deliberately bashed in her skull. She also has some quite new burns on the fingers of her right hand. Not bad, but there."

"Burns?" Sebastian came closer to hunker down and study her hand. The pads of her thumb and first three fingers were all faintly blistered. "From what?"

"No way to tell."

He rose slowly. "How long do you think she's been dead?"

"It could be anywhere from four to ten hours. Given the cold, it's difficult to say with any certainty since it would depend on if she were outside in the snow all that time or kept someplace warm until shortly before we found her."

Sebastian shifted his gaze to the pulverized side of Jane Ambrose's head. "Would she have died instantly?"

"Almost, yes. She didn't run down Shepherds' Lane and then collapse, if that's what you're thinking." Alexi nodded to a nearby shelf where a small earthenware bowl held a plain gold ring and the locket Sebastian had noticed earlier around the dead woman's neck. "Are those her children?"

Conscious of a hollow sense of sadness, he went to pick up the locket. It opened to reveal miniatures of two smiling little boys aged perhaps two and five. "I don't know," he said after a moment, his voice tight. He glanced at the clothes neatly folded on the shelf nearby. Jane Ambrose's gown, like her blood-soaked pelisse, was black. She'd obviously been in mourning for someone. But when he touched the shoulder of her gown, he found it dry and unstained by traces of blood.

"I think she was wearing the pelisse when she was killed," said Alexi Sauvage, watching him. "There was no blood on anything else."

He closed the locket with a soft *click*. "As soon as the palace learns she's dead and has been brought here for a postmortem, they'll probably send someone to seize the body. They can't afford to allow even a hint of scandal to touch Princess Charlotte, which means they'll also pressure you to give them the results they want and keep quiet about anything you might have seen. You need to be prepared for that."

She gave him a strange, tight smile. "I'm just a simple midwife who is very good at pretending to be stupid when I must."

Sebastian nodded and started to turn away. She stopped him by saying, "There is one other thing that may or may not be relevant: I think she was raped. Not today, but recently. Perhaps yesterday or the day before."

Sebastian turned to look at her in surprise. "You're certain it was rape? I mean, sometimes—" He broke off, annoyed with himself for feeling embarrassed and wishing like hell Gibson were there.

The narrowing of her eyes told him she both recognized and understood the cause of his discomfiture. "It isn't simply the abrasions that suggest it. There are bruises on her wrists and thighs, as if someone held her and forced her. Bruises older than the one on her face. I'd say—"

She broke off as the gusting wind brought them the sound of a heavy fist pounding on the door of Gibson's surgery and a man's imperious voice demanding, *"Open up in the King's name."*

Hero sat curled up in one of the high-backed upholstered chairs beside the drawing room fire, her gaze on the little boy asleep in her arms. His name was Simon, and he was just days away from his first birthday. She watched the firelight play over his innocent, relaxed features, watched his little mouth pucker in a faint sucking motion as he dreamed, and she smiled. It was past time to carry him up the stairs to his nursemaid and bed. And yet she lingered.

She was still holding the child when Devlin came in a few minutes later, bringing with him the scent of frigid night air and coal smoke. "I hope you've dined," he said, going to stand with his cold-reddened hands held out to the fire.

"Long ago. Cook saved yours, if you're interested."

"Not really." He turned, his features solemn as he searched her face. What he saw there must have concerned him, because he said, "Are you certain you're all right?"

She smoothed the drooling bib beneath their sleeping son's chin. "Yes, although I fear you've caught me being rather self-indulgent. I suppose there's nothing quite like the sight of sudden death to make us want to hug those we love close."

He came to stand behind her, his hands resting on her shoulders, and she felt the faint quiver that passed through him as he said, "I know."

She let her head fall back so she could look up at him. "Discover anything?"

"Very little. Gibson was off tending some boatmen who'd been pulled from the river, so Alexi Sauvage began the autopsy herself. Which was fortunate, because she hadn't progressed very far when the Regent's men arrived to claim the body."

"Good heavens. How did the palace hear of Jane's death so quickly?"

"One of the parish officials sent them word. Madame Sauvage wasn't able to determine whether Jane Ambrose's death was manslaughter or murder. But if it was manslaughter, someone was obviously worried enough about the consequences of her death to move the body and attempt to make it look like a simple accident. She didn't arrive in the middle of Shepherds' Lane by herself. Not with that wound."

"No one in the area saw anything?"

"Nothing they're willing to admit. I suspect we'll be reading in all the morning papers about how she slipped in the snow and tragically died after hitting her head. The palace is not going to want it known that someone close to Princess Charlotte has been murdered." Of course, by "the palace" Sebastian meant Hero's own father, Charles, Lord Jarvis, the powerful Machiavellian figure behind the Crown Prince's weak regency. But there was no need for him to spell it out; Hero knew her father better than anyone.

She said, "I was never close to Jane, but I admired her greatly and would like to have known her better. She was so bright, so incredibly talented, so . . . full of life."

"Did you ever see her perform?"

"Only privately. She gave up performing in public when she was seventeen."

"How long ago was that?"

"Fifteen, maybe sixteen years ago. I've heard many considered her a finer pianist than even her brother, and he was beyond brilliant." The career of Jane's twin, James Somerset, had ended all too soon when he died of consumption at the age of twenty-three.

"Do you ever think," said Devlin quietly, "of how many great artists, musicians, scholars, and inventors have been lost to our world on down through the ages, simply because they were born female?"

She looked up to meet his gaze again and smiled. "Frequently."

He drew a gold locket from his pocket and flipped it open. "She was wearing this. Do you know if she had children?"

"I believe she did, yes." Reaching cautiously so as not to disturb the sleeping babe, Hero cradled the locket in her palm. "How terribly tragic this all is." She gazed at the miniatures of the two round-cheeked, fair-haired children in silence for a moment. "Has her husband been told?"

"Lovejoy was doing it."

She looked up at him, and something in his voice provoked her to say, "Surely you don't think Edward Ambrose himself could have killed her?"

Devlin went to where a carafe of brandy stood warming on a table near the fire. "Husbands do have a nasty habit of murdering their wives. According to Alexi, someone forced himself on Jane just a day or two ago, and I'd lay even money that was her husband." He poured a measure of brandy into a glass, then glanced over at her. "How close are you to Princess Charlotte?"

Still carefully cradling the child in her arms, Hero eased to her feet and went to ring the bell for Simon's nurse. "No one is close to Princess Charlotte. The Regent keeps that poor child shut up in Warwick House like Rapunzel in her tower."

"Except that she's not a child anymore, is she?"

"No, she's not. She turned eighteen at the beginning of the month—

although most people don't realize it because her ever-loving father refused to have the occasion marked in any way."

"Charming."

"I suspect it's because every time she appears in the streets, the
people cheer her as loudly as they boo the Regent. So he does his best
to keep her out of sight."

Devlin came to stand with her before the fire, his glass cradled in
one hand. "And then he wonders why the people hate him."

Simon's nurse, Claire, appeared then to carry the sleeping babe
off to bed. Hero waited until the Frenchwoman had gone before saying, "I am acquainted with one of Princess Charlotte's ladies—Miss Ella
Kinsworth. I could visit her in the morning. See what she can tell me
about Jane."

Devlin took a long, slow swallow of his brandy. "That would be
helpful."

Hero eased the glass from his fingers, took a sip, and handed it
back. "You think the Princess is somehow involved in Jane Ambrose's
death?"

"Charlotte herself, no. But something in Jane's life led to her being
found in the middle of Shepherds' Lane with her head bashed in. And
there's no denying that a royal court can be a deadly place."

Chapter 4

Paul Gibson sat on the edge of his bed, his head bowed as he rubbed an arnica-enriched ointment into the inflamed stump of his left leg. A single candle flame lit the small chamber with a faint, flickering glow. He could hear a distant watchman crying, *"One o'clock on a snowy night and all is well!"* But the only other sound came from the snow falling in a rush outside.

The surgeon was a slim, wiry man, thinner than he should be, thanks to an opium addiction he knew was going to kill him if he didn't master it soon. Once, his hair had been dark. Now it was increasingly threaded with silver, although he was only in his thirties. He'd just spent hours fighting for the lives of two half-drowned, broken men, and yet one of them had died anyway. He was feeling tired and old and useless.

A soft feminine hand touched the small of his back, and despite the glumness of his mood, he found himself smiling.

"You saved one," said Alexi, who frequently seemed to know what he was thinking better than he knew himself.

"And lost the other."

"It happens."

"It shouldn't."

She shifted on the bed, rising onto her knees to slip her arms around him and hold him close. He could feel the weight of her breasts through the thin cloth of her night rail, pressing against his back. "The babe I delivered today will not survive forty-eight hours."

He tipped back his head to rest it against hers. "And that doesn't bother you?" he asked, somewhat in awe. There was a side to Alexi that mystified him—a hard side that could frighten him even as it attracted him.

"On one level, yes. But the babe's mother already has three children she can't feed, and she's so starved herself that her milk will never come in. Lady Devlin left the woman money, but it won't last. Perhaps it's better that the infant die now, quickly, rather than linger to die slowly." Alexi made an angry noise deep in her throat as passion roughened her voice and accentuated her native French accent. "And then there's our charming Prince Regent, who has no problem at all finding the funds to drape his mistresses in jewels or rebuild his various palaces year after year."

Gibson knew a faint blooming of disquiet. She didn't often discuss such things. But after a year of sharing this woman's bed and going through the pattern of his days with her, he'd come to realize that she despised the British monarchy nearly as much as she hated Napoléon and his empire—and for the same reason: because at heart she was very much a fervent republican.

And then, because she always seemed to know what he was thinking, she tipped her head to nuzzle his neck. "Don't worry. I was most demure and respectful when the Prince's men came to carry away Jane Ambrose's body."

"I'm sorry I wasn't here."

"It's just as well you weren't. You like to think you're always so prudent and wise. But the truth is, you've a stubborn streak yourself."

Grunting, he set aside the ointment and lurched up to hop over to the basin and wash his hands.

She watched him, her eyes narrowing. And although he was nowhere near as prescient as she, he knew what she was going to say. "Your leg is hurting."

"The stump? Aye." He laid on his Irish burr thick and heavy. "Although not nearrrly as much as the foot that 'tisn't therrre."

"I could do something about that," she said.

He gave her a lopsided smile. "With your smoke and mirrors?"

"No smoke. Just mirrors." When he kept silent, she said, "Why not try it? If it doesn't work, then you can say, 'It didn't work.' But it might."

He didn't answer because they'd been over it all before, and in truth he was as terrified the idea might work as he was afraid it wouldn't.

Smiling faintly in a way that told him she knew his reasons only too well, she grasped handfuls of her night rail and drew it off over her head.

"You'll get cold," he said even as the heat of want surged within him.

She shook back her fiery hair, her neck arching seductively. "Then come keep me warm."

Chapter 5

Friday, 28 January

*T*he snow eased up shortly before dawn. Then a howling wind swept in from the north, and the temperatures plunged even lower.

London awoke to a paralyzed white world. Shopkeepers and servants were out early shoveling the snow from the pavement in front of their establishments, but the streets remained hopelessly blocked. Sebastian took one look at the drifts clogging Brook Street and decided to walk to Bow Street.

"You've seen the papers?" said Sir Henry Lovejoy when the two men met in a crowded coffeehouse beneath one of the ancient arcades overlooking Covent Garden Market. The air was thick with the smell of roasting coffee, hot chocolate, and wet wool.

"The *Morning Gazette* was the only one to make it through to Mayfair," said Sebastian, sliding into the old-fashioned high-backed bench opposite the magistrate. "But I assume they're all the same."

Lovejoy nodded. "The palace has announced that Jane Ambrose slipped in the icy streets and hit her head."

"Less sensational than the footpads option, I suppose."

"Decidedly." Lovejoy sipped his hot chocolate in brooding silence, then said, "I received a visit late last night from a certain Major Burnside."

Sebastian was familiar with the major, who played a key role in that legion of former military men, spies, informants, and assassins used by the Regent's powerful cousin, Lord Jarvis, to maintain his position. "And?"

The magistrate set down his cup with pronounced care and cleared his throat. "I will attempt to assist you in this where I can. But officially my hands are tied."

Sebastian met the other man's troubled gaze. "I understand."

From the piazza outside came a loud clatter, followed by a shout. Normally at this hour of the morning, Covent Garden Market was a cacophony of buyers and sellers, its stalls overflowing with fruit and vegetables brought in from the countryside to be sold to shopkeepers and the costermongers who fanned out across London. But so little produce was trickling into the city that many of the stalls hadn't even bothered to open.

Sebastian said, "You spoke to Jane Ambrose's husband?"

"Last night, yes. He appeared both shocked and devastated by the news of his wife's death. But was either emotion genuine?" Lovejoy sighed. "I honestly couldn't say. Something about his reaction seemed slightly off to me, although I can't put my finger on why."

"Did he say where his wife was yesterday?"

"No. He found it difficult even to speak of her, and finally apologized for being so distraught as to be of little assistance. I told him you were taking an interest in the case. Perhaps you'll have more success with him today."

"If he hasn't dosed himself into insensibility with laudanum."

Lovejoy nodded. "Gibson is quite certain the woman was murdered?"

"It's either murder or manslaughter," said Sebastian. "But someone definitely moved her body." He saw no reason to divulge the fact that Jane Ambrose's hurried autopsy was actually performed by an unlicensed Frenchwoman.

Lovejoy rested his shoulders against the high back of his bench and frowned. "Why leave the body in Shepherds' Lane? I wonder."

"To implicate someone else in her death, perhaps? Someone who lives in the area."

Lovejoy considered this. "Yes, that's certainly a possibility."

"How much do you know about Edward Ambrose?"

"Not much, actually. But I've set one of the lads to looking into him. The palace shouldn't object to that."

"Especially if they don't hear of it," said Sebastian.

Lovejoy rarely smiled. But Sebastian thought he caught a gleam of amusement in the dour little magistrate's eyes before he looked away. "My lads can be very discreet."

The snow was starting up again by the time Sebastian cut across the drift-filled, half-deserted market toward Edward and Jane Ambrose's house in Soho Square.

Dating to the time of Charles II, the square had once been popular with dukes and earls and even George II in his days as Prince of Wales. With the construction of new areas such as Grosvenor and Cavendish Squares, most of Soho's fashionable residents had drifted westward. But it was still home to a number of notables besides Ambrose, including Sir Joseph Banks and Franz Schmidt.

The Ambroses' narrow, well-tended house stood on the side of the square once occupied by the elegant residence of that ill-fated royal bastard the Duke of Monmouth. Sebastian's knock was answered by a young housemaid with a pale face and big brown eyes swollen with tears. When Sebastian handed over his card, she sniffed, said, "Oh, my lord, Mr. Ambrose said we was to show you right up," and led the way to a gracious drawing room, where Edward Ambrose stood before a cold hearth.

He looked drawn and haggard, as if he hadn't slept much the night before. He was a tall man, perhaps five or six years older than his dead wife, and of a surprisingly muscular build. His features were even and attractive, his golden hair just beginning to recede from his high forehead. The son of an impoverished Middlesex vicar, he had enjoyed only modest success as a playwright until around the turn of the century, when his opera *Lancelot and Guinevere* took the town by storm. He still wrote the occasional play, but none was as popular as his operas, which were always enthusiastically received.

He stood now staring up at a large canvas that hung above the mantel. Following his gaze, Sebastian realized it was a portrait of Jane Ambrose and what looked like the two children from her locket.

"Thank you for seeing me," said Sebastian as Ambrose turned, his features ravaged by grief. "My sincere condolences for your loss."

Ambrose nodded and swallowed hard, as if momentarily too overcome by sorrow to answer. "Please, sit down," he said, indicating a nearby seat. "I'm told it was Lady Devlin and a friend who discovered Jane's body. How perfectly ghastly for them. I hope the ladies are all right."

"They are. Thank you," said Sebastian, taking one of the delicate Adams-style chairs. "I'd like to ask you some questions, if I may?"

Ambrose stayed where he was. "Yes, of course. I'll help in any way I can."

"Can you tell me when was the last time you saw your wife?"

"Yesterday morning." Ambrose brought up one hand to rub his forehead in a distracted gesture. "At breakfast."

"Do you know how she planned to spend the day? Did she say?"

He nodded briskly. "Her Monday and Thursday mornings were always devoted to the Princess."

"Did she actually attend Princess Charlotte yesterday?"

Ambrose looked vaguely confused, as if the question surprised him. "I suppose. I mean, I don't know for certain, but . . . why wouldn't she? The snow didn't become worrisome until midafternoon."

"Where would she have gone after her lesson with the Princess?"

"I expected her to come home."

"She didn't?"

"I don't believe so, no. None of the servants saw her."

"You weren't here?"

"I was, yes. But I'm working on the libretto for a new opera. It's giving me fits at the moment—as they usually do at this stage." His lips twitched as if he almost smiled. Then the smile tightened with what looked like pain. "Jane knows—knew—to leave me alone when I'm like that. I shut myself up in the library."

"You weren't concerned when she wasn't home by evening?"

"Not overly much, no. Jane had her own life. I don't—didn't—keep a tight rein on her activities. It wasn't until I realized just how late it was getting that I even gave it a thought. And then I assumed she must have decided to stay someplace until the storm passed. God help me, I was even mildly annoyed with her for not bothering to send a message telling me she'd been delayed."

"Do you have any idea what your wife might have been doing in Clerkenwell yesterday?"

"No. I understand that's where she was found, but I can't imagine why she would go there."

"Who do you think killed her?"

A spasm passed over the playwright's features and he gave a half shake of his head in denial. "The magistrate who was here last night—Sir Henry—suggested she'd been murdered. But this morning the papers are all saying she simply fell and hit her head."

"Given her connection to Princess Charlotte," said Sebastian, "you do understand why, don't you?"

Ambrose's gaze met his. Then he looked away and nodded silently.

Sebastian said, "Do you know of anyone who might have wanted your wife dead?"

"Jane? Good heavens, no."

"No one?"

"No."

"Can you tell me more about her?"

"What is there to tell? She was a brilliant, beautiful, talented woman. Why would anyone want to kill someone like that?"

Sebastian glanced again at the portrait of Jane Ambrose above the fireplace. She held the younger boy—in this painting a laughing babe of perhaps eighteen months—on her lap, while the more pensive older child leaned against his mother's knee. Rather than looking outward at the viewer, Jane had her head turned, her attention all for her children. A gentle, loving smile softened her features. Sebastian found it profoundly disturbing to be given this glimpse of her as she'd once been—so warm and glowing with life and love—and then remember the way he'd last seen her, a cold, bloody cadaver on a stone slab in a surgeon's dissection room. And he knew a powerful surge of fury directed at whoever had robbed her of her future and left her as only a memory.

"Your children?" asked Sebastian, keeping his voice steady with difficulty.

Ambrose followed his gaze. "Yes." He sucked in a quick breath that shuddered his chest. "That was painted seven years ago. They're both dead now. We lost Benjamin last summer, and Lawrence in November."

Oh, Jesus, thought Sebastian, his heart aching for this man's tragic series of losses. "I'm sorry."

Ambrose swiped one hand across his face and nodded.

Sebastian said quietly, "Did your wife have any family?"

"Not really. Jane lost her mother when she was still quite young, while her father passed away ten years ago or so—not long after Jane's twin, James. And then her sister, Jilly, died two years ago. Consumption, same as James. A dangerous weakness to the disease seems to run in the family."

"How long has Jane served as Princess Charlotte's piano instructor?"

Ambrose looked thoughtful. "It must be nine or ten years, at least. Why?"

"So she knew the Princess well?"

"She did, yes. But surely you don't think her death could have anything to do with Charlotte?"

"At this point, I don't know. Did she talk much about the Princess?"

"Not really. You don't stay with the Princess long if you talk about her—or even get too friendly with her. If Prinny could have his way, that poor girl would be attended only by deaf-mutes who hate her."

The rough anger in the man's voice didn't surprise Sebastian. There were few in contact with the Prince Regent who didn't come away with sentiments ranging from contempt to disgust. "Who else did your wife teach?"

Ambrose frowned. "She's had various pupils over the years. But the only one I can name off the top of my head is Anna Rothschild."

Sebastian knew a flicker of interest. "The daughter of Nathan Rothschild, the German financier?"

"Yes. Jane's been teaching Anna for three or four years now. Or, at least, she did until several weeks ago, when Rothschild suddenly dismissed her."

"He dismissed her? Do you know why?"

"No. All I know is that Jane was extraordinarily upset by it. Rothschild's daughter, Anna, was a talented pianist, and Jane was disappointed to lose her as a student. Although . . ." Ambrose's voice trailed off.

"Although?" prompted Sebastian.

Ambrose drew in a quick breath that flared his nostrils. "She refused to talk about it—she actually became angry with me when I tried to press her on it. But to be honest, I'd say she was more than upset or disappointed. She was frightened. Don't ask me to explain it because I can't. But that's the only word I can use to describe it.

"I don't know why, but Jane was definitely frightened."

Chapter 6

"*I* didn't sleep well again last night," announced the Prince in a petulant, accusatory voice that informed everyone present that he considered them personally responsible for his sufferings.

His Royal Highness George Augustus Frederick, Prince of Wales and Regent of the Kingdom of Great Britain and Ireland, lay sprawled in naked, bloated splendor in the six-foot-long copper tub that was the focal point of the Moorish-tiled bathing room he'd had installed at enormous expense in his palace of Carlton House. Once he'd been a handsome prince, beloved of his people and cheered everywhere he went. Now in his fifties, he was monstrously overweight, endlessly self-indulgent, notoriously dishonest, and reviled by the same populace that had loved him so long ago.

A half circle of prominent, proud men stood around him, summoned so that he might berate them for their failings: two of his personal physicians, Drs. Heberden and Baillie; the Prime Minister, the Earl of Liverpool; the High Chancellor, Lord Eldon; and the Prince's distant but extraordinarily powerful cousin, Charles, Lord Jarvis. Only Jarvis remained silent and watchful as the other men rushed to murmur platitudes of sympathy and sycophancy, for Jarvis knew his prince, knew the calculated, manipulative games he played on everyone around him, knew that this whining complaint was mere prologue to something else that had nothing to do with his night's rest or his health.

When one of the doctors ventured to suggest that a simple solution might be for the Prince to moderate his food and alcohol intake to avoid aggravating his gout, the Prince roared, "It wasn't because of the port and buttered crab, you fool! I lay awake all night fretting about that Brunswick bitch. She is plotting against me again. I know it."

This announcement was met with embarrassed discomfort, for "that Brunswick bitch" was the Regent's wife, Caroline, Princess of Wales.

"I tell you, she is determined to destroy the monarchy of this country," fretted the Prince. "It has been her intention for nineteen years now, and she will not rest until she has achieved her goal."

His listeners exchanged knowing glances. It was beyond ridiculous to suggest that Caroline—niece of the current King of England, great-granddaughter to his predecessor, and mother of the young woman who would one day be queen—might nourish any such ambitions. But the Prince of Wales had been convinced of his wife's perfidy and malignant intentions for years, and no one had ever been able to persuade him otherwise.

When his audience remained awkwardly silent, the Prince shifted in the tub, sloshing sudsy water over the high sides to splash against the tiles. "I blame the Privy Council. Twice the cowards have been given the opportunity to rid me of her, and twice they failed. Twice! We now see the result. She's scheming to destroy everything I have planned, and she has everyone from Henry Brougham and Earl Grey to that rat Lord Wallace intriguing with her—God rot their souls. In a better-regulated society, they'd all be hanged, drawn, and quartered for treason."

The assembled men exchanged glances again. There was no denying that Brougham, Grey, and Wallace—all prominent Whigs—had taken the Princess's side in her long, painful struggles against her husband. But in no sense could they be accused of anything treasonous.

"I don't think—," the Prime Minister, Liverpool, made the mistake of trying to say.

"That's because you don't know! You don't know the blackness, the evil that lives inside that vile hell's spawn of a woman. She actually makes effigies of me from wax and sticks pins in them, like some African voodoo queen! I tell you, she will stop at nothing to destroy me unless I destroy her first."

This last statement was accompanied by a fierce stare directed at Jarvis, who, unlike the other men present, knew precisely which plans most concerned His Highness.

Jarvis gave a low bow. "We have the matter quite in hand, Your Highness. You may rest easy."

"Well. At least someone understands the gravity of the situation," grumbled the Prince. "Perhaps you should bleed me, Heberden," he added in a plaintive voice to the nearest physician. "I feel my pulse beginning to race."

"Of course, Your Highness."

As the other men bowed and backed from the royal presence, Liverpool shot Jarvis a quick questioning glance and said quietly, "What the devil was that about?"

"The Princess," said Jarvis.

"The Big P or the Little P?" asked the Prime Minister—the "Big P" or "Big Princess" being the Regent's wife, Princess Caroline, while the "Little Princess" was their daughter, Princess Charlotte.

"Both," said Jarvis with a smile. "And neither."

Chapter 7

*R*othschild.

Sebastian found himself turning the financier's name over and over in his head as he slipped and slid his way across the freezing, paralyzed, miserable city toward the financial district in the east.

The son of a minor Frankfurt coin dealer turned banker, Nathan Rothschild had appeared in England just fifteen years before. At first he'd focused on skimming money off the Manchester cotton industry before transferring his unsavory but undeniably brilliant talents to the London Exchange. In just a few short years, he'd managed to become one of the richest men in the Kingdom.

But Rothschild was more than a financier. Like many of his peers, he was also heavily involved in smuggling, and at that level smuggling was a deadly serious, highly lucrative, and dangerous business. If, in the process of teaching Anna Rothschild, Jane Ambrose had accidently overheard or stumbled upon something she wasn't supposed to know, Sebastian could see Nathan Rothschild or his associates ordering her killed.

Quietly and efficiently.

At this time of day, Nathan Rothschild could typically be found at his station in the Royal Exchange, a massive arcaded baroque building that stretched between Cornhill and Threadneedle Streets and that was the center for buying and selling and all kinds of deal making. Given the weather, Sebastian wouldn't have been surprised to discover Rothschild's position deserted. But the financier was there, leaning against his customary pillar on the eastern edge of the Exchange's vast open quadrangle.

A short, stout figure in a threadbare greatcoat and a misshapen top hat he wore pulled low over his eyes, he looked more like a tradesman or shopkeeper down on his luck than the kind of man who lent money to kings and emperors. He stood with his hands in his pockets, his expression, as always, utterly unreadable. When Sebastian paused before him, Rothschild simply blinked and turned his head to stare at the arched arcade on the far side of the snow-choked courtyard.

"Go avay. You're bad for business."

Sebastian cast a significant glance around the largely deserted quadrangle. "The Exchange isn't exactly booming at the moment."

"All the more reason for you to go avay."

Sebastian tipped his head to one side. "Now, why wouldn't you want to talk to me? I wonder."

Rothschild fixed Sebastian with a deadened glare. An extraordinarily ugly man with a big round head, protruding cleft chin, and large pouty lips, he looked to be somewhere in his late forties or fifties, his red hair already fading to gray. But he was actually still in his thirties, just five years older than Sebastian himself. "You think I don't know vhy you're here?"

"Actually, I assumed you did." The Rothschild family—which included four other brothers strategically placed in Paris, Vienna, Frankfurt, and Naples—was said to maintain a magnificent network of spies, informants, and courtiers that rivaled or perhaps even exceeded those of powerful statesmen such as Jarvis and Metternich.

The financier's eyes narrowed with what looked like a cross between annoyance and animosity. "Jane Ambrose ceased to function as my daughter's piano instructor veeks ago."

"So I'd heard. Why? I wonder."

"Do you, indeed? And yet I fail to see vhy I should answer any of your decidedly impertinent questions."

Sebastian let his lips pull back into a smile. "I suppose the answer to that depends on how much you have to hide."

A sound that might have been a laugh shook the other man's fleshy frame. "Are you threatening me? Seriously? *Me?*"

"You find that statement threatening?"

"Have you by chance spoken vith your father-in-law?"

"No. Should I have? I'd no notion Jarvis was involved in the selection and dismissal of your children's music instructors."

Rothschild shrugged. "Jane Ambrose vas no doubt an excellent pianist. Unfortunately, my daughter Anna has exhibited little interest in music and even less talent. Hence the decision to terminate our arrangement."

"Really? That's odd."

"Odd? Vhat? Vhy?"

"Because I'm told Jane Ambrose considered your daughter an unusually promising student."

"I can only assume that if Mrs. Ambrose did indeed say such a thing, then she vas simply being kind. Despite a father's inevitable prejudices, even I must admit that my little Anna vas a vaste of Mrs. Ambrose's time."

"And your money."

"Obviously."

"What I find particularly curious is that Jane Ambrose wasn't simply upset by her dismissal. She was frightened."

Rothschild pursed his full lips. "She told someone that? Who?"

"Not in so many words. I gather it was more along the lines of an observation."

"Mmm. Curious. I know of no reason vhy the woman should have been frightened. But I assure you, it had nothing to do vith me."

"When was her last lesson with your daughter?"

Rothschild shrugged. "Surely you don't expect me to recall precisely? It was near the end of the Great Fog. The lessons were always on a Tuesday."

"And when did you terminate your arrangement with her?"

"That afternoon."

"You spoke to Jane Ambrose yourself?"

"As it happens, I did, yes."

"And she didn't seem upset at the time?"

"She expressed disappointment. But she acknowledged that given Anna's lack of talent, there vas little sense in continuing."

"I see. And your daughter is how old?"

Rothschild hesitated a moment, as if the response required some calculation. "Ten."

"Would you mind if I spoke to her?"

"I'm afraid that's impossible. The poor child is naturally grieved by the death of someone she both knew and respected. I vouldn't vant to do anything that might upset her further."

"Of course," said Sebastian, settling his top hat lower on his forehead. "Thank you for your assistance."

Rothschild simply inclined his head and dug his hands deeper into his pockets.

Sebastian started to turn away, then paused to glance back and say, "You wouldn't by chance know what might have taken Jane Ambrose to Clerkenwell yesterday, would you?"

"Hardly. I vas scarcely acquainted vith the woman."

"Yes. So you said."

Sebastian was aware of the rich man's gaze following him as he crossed the quadrangle toward the main entrance with its ornate looming clock tower. And it came to him as he pushed his way through the small knot of shivering Barbadian, Jamaican, and Spanish traders congregated around a brazier there that for someone who claimed he had no explicable reason to be interested in Jane Ambrose, Nathan Rothschild was nevertheless curiously well informed about the true nature of her death. Because Sebastian would never have been here asking questions if Jane hadn't been murdered—and Rothschild obviously not only understood that, but he hadn't been surprised by it.

Not only that, but for reasons Sebastian couldn't explain but certainly intended to discover, Rothschild had likewise taken it for granted that her death involved the Regent's powerful cousin and Sebastian's own father-in-law, Charles, Lord Jarvis.

Chapter 8

*H*er Royal Highness Princess Charlotte Augusta of Wales, grand-daughter of King George III, only legitimate issue of the Prince of Wales, and heiress presumptive to the throne of the United Kingdom of Great Britain and Ireland, lived with her attendants in a cramped and decrepit seventeenth-century brick structure known as Warwick House.

Lying on the far side of a narrow lane to the southeast of the Prince's own palace of Carlton House, Warwick House had served as Princess Charlotte's home ever since her father—in the grip of one of the endless remodeling schemes for his grandiose palace—had cast covetous eyes on his daughter's apartments and decided to move her out. She'd been eight at the time.

Charlotte had lived alone ever since, with no one in the house who wasn't paid to be there with her. Her mother had been banished years before and was seldom allowed to see her. Her father, the Prince, visited even less. Her care was entrusted to the oversight of a succession of aging noblewomen who held the honorary title of Governess to the Princess. The current holder of that position was the middle-aged Dowager

Duchess of Leeds, an ostentatiously *grande dame* with annoying airs of condescension—and a long-winded, boring fixation on her own health—who typically put in an appearance at Warwick House between the hours of two and five. Assisting the Duchess were two live-in ladies, also gently born but considerably more impoverished. Although officially styled as subgovernesses, they essentially functioned as minders. The Princess's actual education was managed by the Bishop of Salisbury, a humorless, pretentious prelate who oversaw an array of specialized tutors and instructors.

The previous year, as her seventeenth birthday approached, Charlotte had dreamed of throwing off her fusty old governess, replacing the subgovernesses with true companions styled as ladies-in-waiting, and finally being free to attend balls, dinners, and the theater like any other young lady her age. That ambition was ruthlessly squashed by her father, the Regent.

Charlotte then looked at her aging, unmarried aunts, the daughters of George III who were living out their wasted lives shut up at Windsor Castle in what Charlotte had long ago nicknamed "the Nunnery," and panicked.

Hero arrived at Warwick House midway through the morning. Unable to use her carriage in the snow-filled streets and scorning sedan chairs, she pulled on demi-broquins of fine morocco lined with fur, wrapped herself in a fur-trimmed pelisse with a matching Swedish hat fastened up on one side, and walked.

It was a shockingly outré thing, to call on a royal princess *on foot* and stomp snow all over the cracked tiles of her dilapidated entrance hall. But then, Hero hadn't come to visit Princess Charlotte. Hero was here to see her friend Miss Ella Kinsworth.

A tall, angular woman with graying dark hair, Miss Kinsworth had in years past enjoyed the kind of adventurous, independent life a younger Hero had once envisioned for herself. The unmarried daughter of an admiral, Miss Kinsworth had lived abroad for decades with her widowed mother and supported herself by writing books. But the wars eventually made continued residence on the Continent dangerous, and the death of her mother had diminished her income. Now in her late fifties, alone and impoverished, Miss Kinsworth was reduced to serving a royal family not known for endearing itself to retainers. For seven years she had held the position of companion to George III's foultempered Queen before being appointed to serve as one of Princess Charlotte's subgovernesses. In a spirited, daring rebellion, Miss Kinsworth had honored the young Princess's wishes by insisting on being called a "lady companion" rather than a "subgoverness." It was a tribute to both the force of her personality and the respect in which she was held that she'd been allowed to get away with it.

"This ferocious weather!" said Miss Kinsworth as she whisked Hero up to her small private sitting room on Warwick House's first floor, not far from the Princess's bedchamber. "You should have let me come to you, my lady."

"Nonsense," said Hero, ridding herself of ice-encrusted mittens, hat, scarf, and pelisse. "The walk was"—she paused, searching for the right word as she sank into a chair beside the sitting room's fire, and finally settled on—"bracing."

Miss Kinsworth took the seat opposite, the smile in her gray eyes fading. "Don't tell me you're here because Jane Ambrose was murdered."

Hero looked up from holding her cold hands out to the blaze. "What makes you think it was murder?"

"I didn't think it before. But I'm not vain enough to believe you tromped through the snow on a day such as this simply to pay me a social visit. *Was* Jane murdered?"

"I'm afraid she probably was, yes."

Miss Kinsworth's face quivered and she looked away. "Ah. Poor Jane."

Hero studied the older woman's tightly held profile. "How well did you know her?"

"I've known Jane for years. She used to teach piano to Princess Amelia when I was with the Queen, and she's been Charlotte's instructor since the girl was quite small." Miss Kinsworth drew in a deep, shaky breath. "Needless to say, Charlotte is devastated. Jane was with her longer than almost anyone except perhaps her personal maid, Mrs. Louis. The Prince is constantly dismissing the Princess's servants, you know, as well as her governesses, subgovernesses, and tutors."

"Why?"

Miss Kinsworth turned her head to meet Hero's gaze. "Do you want to know the truth?"

"Yes."

"It's because he wants them to be loyal to him and him alone, and to unhesitatingly enforce his most arbitrary and heartless decrees. But Charlotte is a sweet, generous, likable soul who quickly wins the hearts and allegiance of those who are around her for long. And when that happens, the Prince dismisses them."

"Beastly man," said Hero.

"You can say that, my lady. Unfortunately, I cannot. At least, not aloud."

Hero gave a soft laugh. "So, was Jane Ambrose here for the Princess's lesson yesterday?"

"She was, yes. She left as usual shortly after twelve o'clock—just as the snow was beginning to fall. I remember because I happened to look out the window and saw her crossing the courtyard toward the gate."

"Do you know how she planned to spend the rest of the day?"

"Sorry, no. I assumed she was going home, but I don't know for certain. I saw her when she first came in and said good morning, but that was about all."

"Did she seem nervous or frightened in any way?"

"Frightened? I don't think so, no. Although I did sense a certain . . ."

Miss Kinsworth hesitated. "I don't quite know how to put it. We've all been under a bit of strain lately, and she did seem preoccupied by something. She was trying to put a cheerful face on it, but I had the feeling her thoughts were elsewhere."

"You've no idea what might have been troubling her?"

"No. Sorry."

Given that Jane had been raped a day or two before her death, Hero suspected her preoccupation might well have been tied to that. But it was awkward to discuss such things in polite company. To even address the subject was a delicate exercise to be wrapped up in all sorts of polite euphemisms such as "interfered with" or "an act too infamous to be named." Hero said bluntly, "She never mentioned anything about someone forcing himself on her?"

Miss Kinsworth's face went slack. "Good heavens, no. You think that's what happened to her? Is that why she was killed?"

"It's possible. Or it could be completely unrelated."

"Oh, poor Jane." The older woman's lips parted. "She never said anything to me."

Hero wasn't surprised. Women who were raped usually didn't talk about it if they could help it. For most, their rape was a dark, shameful secret to be hidden and dealt with in private, if at all. It was also possible that Edward Ambrose had violently forced himself on his own wife. In that case, under British law such an act would not have been considered rape or illegal in any way.

Hero cleared her throat. "Jane had children?"

"She did, yes: two boys. But both died last year. She lost the younger child first, to the flux, and the other, Lawrence, just last autumn to consumption."

"How unbearably tragic," said Hero.

"It was, yes. Music and those children were Jane's world. When she lost the boys, it was as if a light went out of her life."

"Was she happy in her marriage, do you think?"

Miss Kinsworth smoothed a hand over the skirt of her sensible worsted gown. "To be honest? I wouldn't say she was, no. But it's sometimes hard to tell, isn't it? We never discussed it."

"What makes you think she might not have been?"

"It wasn't anything she said precisely. But I sometimes suspected she had a certain measure of resentment toward her husband."

"Resentment? Do you know why?"

"No. Although sometimes I wondered . . ." The other woman paused.

"Yes?" said Hero.

Miss Kinsworth looked troubled. "I've sometimes wondered if she didn't in some way resent Edward Ambrose's success as a composer. I hesitated to say it because that makes her sound like a petty, jealous person, and she wasn't that way at all. She was good and kind and giving—a truly warm, caring person. And yet . . . you know what it's like for women. She was forced to give up performing even though she was every bit as talented and accomplished a pianist as her twin brother. She was also an amazing composer who could have produced pieces much grander than the glees and ballads and simple chamber music she was known for."

"So why didn't she?"

"I asked her that once. She said it's one thing to write an opera or symphony but something else entirely to find an orchestra willing to perform a piece composed by a woman."

"Ah, yes, I can see that."

"When her brother James was alive, he actually published some of her pieces as his own. She said he hated that she didn't get credit for them, but he thought they deserved to be performed and he knew that was the only way it would happen."

"I've heard Mozart did the same for his sister, Maria Anna."

"I suspect it's far more common than anyone would like to admit," said Miss Kinsworth. Hero nodded, and the two women sat in companionable silence, quietly sharing a lifelong cold anger at the limitations society placed on their sex.

After a moment, Hero said, "Do you have any idea who might have wanted to see her dead?"

"Who might have killed her, you mean?" The older woman pressed the fingers of one hand to her lips.

"There is someone, isn't there?" said Hero, watching her.

Miss Kinsworth thrust up from her chair and went to stand at a narrow-sashed window looking out over the snow-covered city, her arms crossed and her elbows held close to her chest. After a moment, she said, "This is very delicate, given the circumstances, but . . . there is a gentleman attached to the Dutch embassy—van der Pals is his name, Peter van der Pals."

"Yes. I met him recently when I was visiting my father," said Hero. "I understand he's become quite popular with London's hostesses in a surprisingly short time."

"He has, yes. He's an extraordinarily handsome, charming man. At one point he was quite friendly with Jane."

"Meaning?"

"Oh, nothing serious. Please don't misunderstand me. But he did single her out, and I think she was flattered by his teasing attentions. What woman would not be? He is very attractive."

"So what happened?" prompted Hero.

"It turned out he was simply trying to cajole her into spying for him."

"Good heavens. On Princess Charlotte, you mean?"

"Yes."

Hero had no need to ask why a member of the Dutch ambassador's entourage would be interested in spying on Princess Charlotte. It was an open secret that the Prince Regent was eager to see his daughter married and that the needle-thin, awkward, and decidedly unattractive

William, Hereditary Prince of Orange—nicknamed Slender Billy—was his favored suitor. For his part, Orange was said to be more than eager to wed the woman who would someday reign as Queen of England. "When was this?"

"That Jane realized what he wanted? One day last week—last Thursday, I believe. Needless to say, she refused. He then tried to bribe her. And when that failed, he turned ugly. Quite ugly."

"How do you know this?" said Hero.

"Because Jane came to me the next day and told me. She thought I needed to know in case he should approach other members of the Princess's household. It seems that when she refused, he threatened her."

"Threatened her how?"

"He warned her not to tell anyone, and said she'd be sorry if she did." Miss Kinsworth turned to face Hero, her arms still hugged close to her chest. "She was quite shaken."

"Did you tell anyone else about van der Pals?"

"No."

"Not even the Duchess of Leeds?"

Miss Kinsworth grimaced. "Technically, I suppose I should have. But I thought it best to keep it to myself."

"Could Jane herself have told someone?"

"Perhaps. Although I warned her not to."

It was a statement that spoke volumes about the degree of mistrust, suspicion, and backstabbing in the Princess's household. Hero said, "Would it be possible for me to ask Princess Charlotte about her last lesson with Jane?"

Miss Kinsworth made a scoffing sound deep in her throat. "Not if Lady Leeds has anything to say about it." She looked thoughtful a moment, then said, "Charlotte and I frequently go for walks in the afternoon. If I sent you word, perhaps you could contrive to come upon us . . . quite by accident, of course."

Hero smiled. "Yes, I believe I could manage that."

Chapter 9

The Dutch courtier Peter van der Pals had arrived in London the previous December in the train of his good friend William, the Hereditary Prince of Orange. A strikingly handsome man with a strong jawline, softly curling auburn hair, and a wide boyish smile, the courtier was—like Orange—quite young. His English was extraordinarily good, for he had attended Oxford with his prince and also, like Orange, served as aide-de-camp to Arthur Wellesley. Yet he had chosen to remain in London when Orange returned to the newly liberated Netherlands. At the time, Hero had wondered why.

Now she thought she understood.

On leaving Warwick House, she turned her steps toward the residence of the Dutch ambassador, intending to make inquiries there into the young courtier. But as she neared the ambassador's stately town house, she was fortunate enough to find van der Pals himself carefully descending the embassy's icy front steps.

At the sight of Hero, he drew up, a faint expression of puzzlement crossing his handsome features before being hidden away behind a courtier's practiced smile. "Lady Devlin," he said, his elegant bow somewhat spoiled by his refusal to let go of the railing beside him. "You are beyond courageous, venturing out in this weather. Unfortunately, His Excellency the ambassador is not at present here."

"That's quite all right," said Hero, smiling. "As it happens, I was actually looking for you. Shall we go inside for a moment? I'd like to ask you some questions."

Van der Pals hesitated the briefest instant. But one did not rebuff the daughter of the most powerful man in the Kingdom. He bowed again. "Of course."

Nodding to the liveried footman at the door, he ushered her into a small overheated withdrawing room just off the grand entrance hall. "Please, my lady, do take a seat. Shall I ring for tea?" His recitation of the requisite polite formalities was everything it should have been— except that the courtier made no attempt to remove his greatcoat and simply stood inside the door, his hat in his hands in a none-too-subtle message.

"Neither will be necessary. Thank you." Hero eased open the throat latch of her fur-trimmed pelisse as the heat of the room enveloped her. "I assume you know why I'm here."

The courtier gave a startled laugh. "Actually, no. I fear you find me quite at a loss. Should I?"

"When a man threatens a woman who later turns up dead, he must surely expect to be the object of scrutiny."

Van der Pals shook his head in a credible show of confusion that Hero might have assumed was real if she hadn't known his type as well as she did. "I don't understand," he said. "What dead woman?"

"Jane Ambrose."

"Ah." He raised one hand to pinch the bridge of his nose as if overcome by distress. "But Mrs. Ambrose's death was caused by a fall. It was in the papers this morning. The streets have become beyond treacherous with all this snow and ice."

"They have indeed. Yet Jane Ambrose did not slip on the ice and hit her head. It appears that she was in all likelihood murdered. Quite viciously."

"Murdered?" His expression of shock was everything it should have been—and potentially every bit as false as his earlier show of confusion. "How perfectly ghastly. But I still don't understand what any of this has to do with me."

The heat from the room's fireplace was becoming overwhelming; Hero quietly tugged off her fur-lined mittens. "Perhaps I should explain that we know you tried to charm Jane Ambrose into spying on Princess Charlotte for the House of Orange. When charm failed, you attempted bribery. And when that, too, was unsuccessful, you warned her that if she told anyone of your overtures you would make certain that she— How did you put it? Ah, yes, you said she'd 'be sorry.'"

"Who told you this?" he hissed. He was no longer smiling.

"You don't seriously expect me to answer that, do you?"

"Yet you expect me to respond to these absurd accusations?"

Hero raised one eyebrow. "You deny the encounter took place?"

"Of course I deny it!"

"So you're suggesting—what? That Jane Ambrose made up the entire tale out of whole cloth?"

"Either Mrs. Ambrose or whoever regaled you with this nonsense, yes."

"And precisely what would be the purpose of such a deception?"

"Presumably to discredit me—and, by extension, the House of Orange."

"Oh? And why would Jane Ambrose wish to discredit you or your prince?"

The Dutchman's eyes narrowed. "Forgive me, my lady, but why are you here asking these questions? As Lord Jarvis's envoy? Or for some other reason?"

It was an astute question and one that forced Hero to be more honest than she would have liked. "I am here because Jane Ambrose's association with Princess Charlotte precludes a more formal investigation of her murder." She gave him an icy stare. "Is there a reason you're avoiding answering my questions?"

Van der Pals went to stand facing the room's fireplace, one fist resting on the mantel, his gaze on the blaze on the hearth. After a moment, he said, "This is a trifle delicate, but the truth is that Mrs. Ambrose and I enjoyed a light flirtation. Nothing serious, you understand. But I fear she must have read more into my gallantry than was intended, for when she chanced one day to see me laughing—quite innocently, I assure you!—with Lady Arabella, she flew into a frightful rage. It was really quite shocking."

He glanced up at Hero in a way that caused a boyish shock of hair to fall over his forehead. He was an extraordinarily attractive young man, and he not only knew it, but was accustomed to using his looks to disarm and cajole.

Hero was not easily disarmed. "Who is Lady Arabella?"

"Lady Arabella Osborne, daughter of the Princess's governess, the Duchess of Leeds. The Duchess recently introduced her to Warwick House in the hopes of providing the Princess with a friend close to her own age. But the girl is still quite young and rather unsure of herself, so I sought to try to put her at ease. I never imagined Jane would react so . . . violently."

His use of the dead woman's given name was both suggestive and, Hero suspected, deliberate. She said, "You would have me think that you and Jane Ambrose were lovers?"

His wonderful white teeth flashed as he gave an embarrassed laugh. "Good heavens, no. Ours was a flirtation only, as I said—although Jane obviously thought things more serious than I had intended." He tipped his head to one side as if struck by a sudden thought. "Have you considered that she might have been killed as the result of a lovers' quarrel?"

"You're saying Jane Ambrose had a lover? Who?"

"I've no idea."

"Yet you have no difficulty suggesting that she might have one?"

He spread his arms wide as if in surrender. "It wasn't my intention to offend you, my lady—simply to give you a hint as to the nature of the woman we're discussing."

"You mean that she was the type of woman who might have been unfaithful to her husband?"

Rather than answer, he glanced significantly at the clock on the mantel and gave a faint, startled exclamation, as if suddenly becoming aware of the passage of time. "I fear you must excuse me, my lady; I've an appointment I cannot miss."

Hero drew on her mittens with quick, jerky movements. "Yes, of course. Thank you for your information."

He sketched another of his elegant bows. "Please do not hesitate to let me know if I can be of any further assistance."

"Oh, don't worry. I shall," she said with a smile.

It was when he was escorting her to the door that van der Pals said, "Have you by chance spoken to Valentino Vescovi?"

She paused to glance over at him. "The musician? No. Why?"

"He teaches the harp to Princess Charlotte, you know."

"No, I didn't know. Is there a particular reason you think I should speak with him?"

Van der Pals scratched one cheek as if in some embarrassment. "Actually, yes. You see, he and Jane had quite an angry confrontation just this past Monday."

"How do you know this?"

"Because they were unwise enough to engage in an undignified shouting match beside the canal in St. James's Park. Vescovi is an ice-gliding enthusiast, and he's been going there every afternoon to take advantage of our current freezing conditions." When Hero remained silent, he added, "A number of others were present, and the argument was quite heated. I doubt I was the only one who saw them."

"And what was the nature of their quarrel?"

"I fear I couldn't hear well enough to understand what was being said. Although—" He broke off.

"Yes?"

"I did hear Vescovi tell her she needed to be careful."

"About what?"

"That I didn't hear. Only 'you need to be careful.'"

"Perhaps Vescovi was warning her about you," suggested Hero, and had the satisfaction of seeing van der Pals's self-satisfied, confident smile slip.

Chapter 10

The Prince Regent's powerful cousin Charles, Lord Jarvis, was smiling faintly as the men carrying his sedan chair staggered through the deep drifts that continued to render even such vital streets as White-hall, Cockspur, and Pall Mall impassable to anything except foot traffic.

The snow was undoubtedly a nuisance. But Jarvis—who'd had a busy morning and was heading back to Carlton House after a meeting at Downing Street—was concerned with far weightier matters, namely the looming, inevitable defeat of Napoléon and the enormous task of restructuring Europe. Things were going well in that quarter. Quite well indeed.

Carlton House had been home to the Prince of Wales for more than three decades, and His Highness had spent every one of those years altering, expanding, and refurbishing it into something he considered more befitting the heir to the throne of the greatest kingdom on earth. As his dear, trusted cousin, Jarvis generally encouraged him, despite the onerous cost. The Prince's preoccupation with art, architecture, fashion, and jewels allowed more serious—and mentally stable—men to go about the business of actually running the Kingdom.

They were approaching the palace now, and the chairmen were laboring hard, for Jarvis was well over six feet tall and increasingly fleshy as he headed toward his sixtieth year. When they turned in through the ornate classical screen that separated the forecourt of Carlton House from Pall Mall, he noticed with revulsion a ragged, skeletal woman clutching what looked like a dead child in her arms as she leaned against the base of the row of columns. He made a mental note to have her removed.

Some minutes later, having finished giving his instructions to the guards, he was walking toward the palace's entrance when he became aware of the tall, leanly built figure of his daughter's husband, Viscount Devlin, crossing the forecourt.

Jarvis ignored him.

"I was hoping I'd find you here," said Devlin pleasantly.

Jarvis kept walking. "I wish I could say I'm delighted not to have disappointed you, but I fear that would be beyond even my considerable powers of dissemblance."

The Viscount gave a huff of laughter and fell into step beside him. "I think you underestimate yourself."

Jarvis grunted. "What do you want?"

"You mean, besides Jane Ambrose's body?"

"You're sadly behind the times, I fear. The inquest was held this morning—"

"Already? Without the testimony of those who found her?"

"—and the lady's corpse delivered to her husband in Soho Square."

"Along with a warning not to allow it to fall into my hands again, I assume."

"Edward Ambrose is no fool."

The footmen flanking the palace's magnificent classical portal jumped to open the doors wide and bowed as Jarvis swept past them.

Devlin said, "Why are you so determined to prevent any real investigation into what happened to her?"

Jarvis crossed the hall toward the imposing main staircase, his boot heels clicking on the polished marble floor. "You think her death should concern me, do you?"

"You consider the murder of a young woman on the streets of London of no importance?"

"She was not murdered. But even if she were, when her death is set beside affairs of state, it is beyond insignificant."

"That still doesn't explain why you're blocking any investigation."

Jarvis drew up at the foot of the stairs. "Really, Devlin? Are you truly such a fool, or are you simply determined to play one? The last thing the Regent needs at the moment is to have Princess Charlotte's name bandied about in conjunction with that of a woman unwise enough to get mixed up in something as tawdry as murder."

"'At the moment'? And why is this moment any different from all the others?"

Jarvis pressed his lips together and began to mount the sweeping marble steps.

Devlin kept pace with him. "I had an interesting conversation this morning with Nathan Rothschild. He asked if I'd spoken to you. Why is that? I wonder."

"Stay away from Rothschild."

"Oh? Why?"

Jarvis paused and swung to face him. He kept his voice low, his words coming out clipped and deadly. "You think because you are married to my daughter, you are safe? You're not."

Devlin didn't even blink. "I never made the mistake of imagining I was. But it does raise the question: Why are you so anxious to keep me away from Rothschild?"

Jarvis continued up the stairs. "Curiosity is a dangerous weakness. You should strive to overcome it."

"This isn't about curiosity. It's about justice for a vital, talented young woman left in a snowy street with her head bashed in."

"Justice." Jarvis rolled the word with distaste off his tongue. "This maudlin obsession of yours with vague and essentially useless philosophical constructs is beyond tiresome. Justice comes from God."

"So do you believe that what is morally good is commanded by God because it is morally good? Or is it morally good because God commands it? Because if the latter, then all justice is arbitrary. But if the former, then morality exists on a higher plane than God."

"Don't try to argue Plato with me. That's a false dilemma and you know it."

"Is it?"

"Apart from which, you're simply wrong. Jane Ambrose's death has nothing to do with Rothschild."

"So certain?"

"It has nothing to do with Rothschild and nothing to do with Princess Charlotte."

"Then why are you afraid of what an investigation might discover?"

"These are delicate and dangerous times. You would cause more harm than you know."

"Oh? So explain it to me."

Jarvis made a rude noise deep in his throat. "You've been warned."

Then he walked into his chambers and shut the door in his son-in-law's face.

Chapter 11

Frozen solid and milky white under a cloudy sky, the canal in St. James's Park was crowded with skaters of all ages.

Hero bought a cup of hot cider from one of the booths pitched near the lake's snow-encrusted banks and strolled along the edge of the ice, her gaze moving over the laughing, shouting mass of skaters. A few were well-dressed young bucks—mainly Scottish by the sounds of it— who belonged to skating clubs and obviously took their sport seriously. But most were considerably less practiced, either creeping cautiously along with shiny new blades strapped to their boots or else striking out in ungainly rushes that inevitably ended in spectacular crashes.

It didn't take her long to spot the Italian harpist Valentino Vescovi. A lanky, craggy-faced man dressed in black with a red scarf tied around his neck, he was in a class by himself, gliding effortlessly across the ice as he executed an intricate pattern of graceful figures reminiscent of a courtly dance.

She stood for a time watching him. But after throwing one or two glances in her direction, he finally skated straight toward her, stopping with a flourish just offshore by leaning back on his heels with the acorn-tipped fronts of his skates pointing into the air.

He was a man somewhere in his thirties or forties, with dark hair and an expressive, mobile face. He'd come to London perhaps a dozen years before via Amsterdam—which was presumably where he'd learned ice-gliding. *"Bene!"* he said, his breath coming fast from the recent exercise. "I'd like to think you're focused on me because you admire my skating. But that's not it, is it? You are here because of Jane Ambrose, yes?"

Hero choked on her cider. "How did you know?"

His dark eyes gleamed with what might have been amusement. "You were at Warwick House this morning, Lady Devlin. And the walls there have ears."

"Evidently."

He said, "What I don't understand is why you wish to speak with me."

"I'm told you had an argument with Jane Ambrose last Monday. A very public argument. Here, by the canal."

"Ah." He climbed carefully off the ice to perch on a nearby bench and set to work unstrapping the skates from his boots. "I did, yes. It was so public, in fact, that I see no point in attempting to deny it."

"Your honesty is refreshing."

He glanced up, the first skate loose in his hand, and bobbed a self-deprecating little bow. *"Grazie."*

"Care to tell me the subject of your disagreement?"

He bent over his task again. "A certain personage told Mrs. Ambrose something about me. Something . . . unflattering. And no, I have no intention of spreading the information any further by telling you what it was."

"Was it true?"

"As it happens, yes, it was true. But I managed to convince her it wasn't as serious as it sounded."

"And which 'personage' told this 'unflattering' truth about you?"

He lifted one shoulder in a very Italian shrug as he tugged at the leather straps holding the second skate to his boot. "I do not recall."

"I don't believe you."

At that he laughed out loud. "No? Well, believe this: If I were ever to decide to kill someone, it would be the *figlio di puttana* who was spreading such tales of me." He looked up, his face now utterly serious. "Not Jane Ambrose."

An older man and a little girl sailed past on the ice, the man skating, the grinning child simply holding on to the tails of his coat and gliding along in his wake. Hero said, "What do you know about the friendship between Jane and the Dutch courtier Peter van der Pals?"

The harpist's expressive face twitched into a frown as he pursed his lips. "I don't think I'd go so far as to call it a 'friendship.'"

"What would you call it?"

He gave another shrug that could have meant anything and nothing. "Van der Pals played the gallant, and I suppose she enjoyed having a handsome, well-connected young man seem to find her interesting and attractive."

"That's all?"

He threaded the straps of his skates together and fastened the buckles. "That's all. And then he began to make her uncomfortable."

"How?"

Vescovi pushed to his feet. "Presumably because he began expecting favors she was unwilling to grant him."

Hero studied the harpist's bony, wide-featured face. "Were they lovers?"

"Goodness gracious, no."

"So certain?"

"Yes."

"Did she have a lover, do you think?"

He looped the skates over one shoulder. "It's hardly the sort of thing we discussed."

"No? Yet you know van der Pals wasn't her lover and that he made her uncomfortable?"

"Oh, yes."

Hero handed her cup to the booth's boy and turned with Vescovi to walk up the packed icy footpath that ran along the canal. Hero said, "I was told Jane became jealous when van der Pals transferred his attentions to another woman."

"Who told you that?"

"It's not true?"

"Hardly."

"So was van der Pals flattering Jane in an attempt to convince her to spy on Princess Charlotte for him?"

Vescovi's brows twitched together, but he kept staring straight ahead and remained silent.

"That is it, isn't it?" said Hero.

The Italian let out his breath in a long, pained sigh. "Princess Charlotte might be young and tucked away in her own crumbling, cramped establishment separate from the rest of the royal family's various palaces and castles. But her household is still part of the royal court." He grimaced. "And show me a court that isn't alive with intrigue and spying."

"Is that why you warned Jane to be careful?"

"That was part of it, yes."

"Only a part?" Hero studied the Italian's bony, troubled profile. "Who do you think killed her?"

"I wish I knew, believe me."

"Why should I believe you?"

"Why?" He drew up and swung to face her, his dark eyes intense and shadowed. "Because I teach Princess Charlotte to play a musical instrument, just as Jane Ambrose taught the Princess to play an instrument, and now Jane is dead." His face went oddly bleak, as if he were maintaining his composure with effort. "You think I'm not afraid?"

"You think she might have been killed by someone you both knew? Someone who might also be a threat to you?"

"I see it as a possibility, yes. You do not?"

"So exactly whom do you have in mind?"

"No one in particular."

"No one? If you're afraid, why not be more honest with me?"

"I have told you nothing that isn't true."

"Perhaps. Yet I suspect there is much that you could tell me but have not."

He stared off across the white, undulating expanses of the park, its bushes and hollows now reduced to anonymous snow-covered mounds and dips. "The truth is frequently more dangerous than a lie."

"Then tell me who you are afraid of," Hero said quietly.

"Ah." His lips twitched into a self-deprecating, unexpected smile. "But that would be the most dangerous of all."

Chapter 12

The ancient cobbled lane that separated young Princess Charlotte's dilapidated residence from the gardens of her father's grand palace was known as Stone Cutters' Alley. On leaving Carlton House, Sebastian had to pass through the classical colonnade that guarded the palace's forecourt from the street, turn right, and walk past four tall houses before turning right again into the narrow lane. At one time the Prince of Wales had sought to seize the lane in order to expand his palace. But Stone Cutters' Alley provided the only public approach to St. James's Park from Pall Mall, and so great was the popular outcry that he was forced to give up the scheme.

When he reached the surprisingly dilapidated brick wall that sheltered Warwick House's Renaissance courtyard from the lane, Sebastian paused, his eyes narrowed against the snow. The fresh white blanket gave the scene a simple, peaceful air. But he knew that was deceptive. The young Princess was separated physically and in almost every other way from her father, the Regent, yet her position as second in line to the throne made access to her both rare and coveted. And corridors of power were always dangerous.

He tipped back his head, his gaze scanning the brick house's upper floors, and saw a curtain move at one window. It shifted for only an instant and then hung still. But he knew someone had been watching him.

The sound of the house's front door opening and closing carried clearly in the snowy hush. Sebastian heard the crunch of footsteps crossing the snow-filled yard toward him. The solid wooden gate's heavy iron latch twisted with a creak and the gate jerked inward to reveal an older man in an exquisitely tailored cassock and old-fashioned periwig.

He looked to be in his late sixties, with swooping heavy brows that drew together in a fierce frown. "What precisely do you think you are doing?" demanded the prelate, his long, prominent nose twitching. "I don't know who you are or why you are here, young man, but you'd best move on before I—"

"The name is Devlin," said Sebastian, calmly handing the man his card.

The prelate broke off, his thin-lipped little mouth going slack as he took the card. "Ah. My lord." Mouth tightening, he gave a curt, begrudging bow. "I beg your pardon. I did not recognize you." He sniffed. "Allow me to introduce myself. I am the Bishop of Salisbury, Preceptor to Her Royal Highness the Princess Charlotte."

"Bishop," said Sebastian with a polite bow. He had heard of the Right Reverend Doctor John Fisher, Bishop of Salisbury. With a reputation as a humorless, vain, self-important clergyman, Salisbury had coordinated the Princess's education for nearly ten years. He had an affected manner of speaking and a strange way of pronouncing the word "bishop," so that it came out sounding like "bish-UP." Sebastian had heard that Charlotte, who heartily detested the humorless man and possessed a gift for mimicry, had long ago nicknamed him "the Great Up."

The Great Up sniffed again. "I noticed someone loitering in the lane and thought it best to move them along."

"Oh?"

"Can't be too careful, what?" said the Bishop. "Not when one considers what happened to Mrs. Ambrose."

"So you don't believe she simply slipped on the ice?" said Sebastian.

"Oh, no, no, of course I believe it." The Great Up gave an incredulous scoff that told Sebastian the Bishop knew only too well why Sebastian was here. "To suggest otherwise would be ridiculous."

"Would it?"

"But of course!"

"Did you see her yesterday?"

"I did, yes. We encountered each other in the entrance hall just as she was leaving."

"What time was this?"

"Must have been shortly after noon, I suppose."

"You spoke to her?"

"Briefly. We exchanged a few pleasantries, nothing more."

"Do you know where she planned to go after leaving Warwick House?"

"Sorry, no; I couldn't say." The Bishop gave an exaggerated sigh. "Shocking to think that only a few hours later she was dead. A timely reminder to us all to be prepared to meet our Maker at any moment."

Sebastian was beginning to understand why the young Princess found the prelate so annoying. "Do you know if she had any enemies?"

"Enemies?" The Great Up drew back his head in an exaggerated gesture of disbelief nicely combined with obvious disapproval. "Of course not."

"No?"

"She was a pianist!"

"Pianists don't have enemies?"

The Bishop's full cheeks darkened. "Jane Ambrose slipped in the snow, hit her head, and died. To suggest anything more nefarious is at work here is not only frivolous, but it is also irresponsible and—given the woman's relationship to the Princess—dangerous nearly to the point of sedition."

"Sedition? Seriously?"

The Great Up glared at Sebastian in righteous silence.

Sebastian touched his hat. "Thank you, Bishop. You've been . . . most helpful."

The prelate responded with a stiff bow, took a step back, and closed the old heavy gate with a reverberating crash.

Sebastian stood still for a moment, the snow falling gently around him. He was about to turn away when he became aware of an elegant young woman in a fur-trimmed pelisse and a jaunty Swedish hat emerging from the public footpath that wound up from St. James's Park. She was an extraordinarily tall woman, nearly as tall as he, with strong, handsome features and the aquiline nose of her father, Lord Jarvis.

"Good heavens," said Hero, blinking against the falling snow as she came up to him. "What are you doing here?"

"I was about to ask you the same question."

"I've been watching an Italian harpist ice-skate."

"And that's an explanation?"

She linked her mittened hand through his proffered arm and smiled. "It is."

They turned their steps toward Brook Street while she told him what she had learned from her friend Miss Kinsworth and her subsequent conversations with the Dutch courtier and the harpist Valentino Vescovi.

"So, which of the two men do you think is telling the truth?" Sebastian asked, his gaze on her profile. "Van der Pals? Or Vescovi?"

She shook her head. "I'm not convinced either of them is. Although if I had to put money on one or the other, I'd pick the Italian harpist over the decorative Dutch courtier any day."

"Because what he told you agrees better with what you heard from your friend Miss Kinsworth?"

"Partially. But I suspect it also has something to do with my profound aversion to handsome young men who believe themselves so charming that no female can resist them."

"Ah."

Hero looked troubled. "Could van der Pals have killed Jane simply because she'd exposed his attempts to convince her to spy on Princess Charlotte? He did say she'd be sorry if she betrayed him."

"I wouldn't put it past him. Except, how did he know Jane told someone? Unless of course your Miss Kinsworth wasn't actually as silent as she claims."

Hero gazed off across the snow-filled intersection of Piccadilly and Bond Street, her features troubled.

"What?" he asked.

"I just wish I were more convinced that Ella Kinsworth was being completely honest with me. Don't misunderstand me—I believe her to be a good, honorable woman. But when you serve as lady companion to a princess, you can't always be as truthful as you'd like."

The snow was coming down harder now, filling their world with a whirl of white. "I can't believe the Regent is seriously considering marrying his daughter to Slender Billy," said Sebastian, squinting up at the heavy sky.

She glanced over at him. "Orange was with Wellington in the Peninsula when you were there, was he not?"

"He was."

"So you knew him?"

"I did."

"And van der Pals as well?"

Sebastian nodded. "The two were inseparable."

"Meaning?"

His gaze met hers. "Meaning a great deal. But I'm afraid it's not something one can discuss in the middle of Bond Street—even if most of the shops are shuttered because of the snow."

"Oh, dear. And does it have anything to do with why you were at Carlton House seeing my father?"

"Ah. You figured that out, did you?"

He told her then about his meeting with Jane's bereaved husband and the pianist's puzzling dismissal by Nathan Rothschild.

He did not tell her that Jarvis had essentially threatened to have him killed.

"For a simple musician," said Hero as they turned up a snow-filled, strangely silent Brook Street toward home, "Jane Ambrose lived an unexpectedly dangerous life."

"When you deal with people like the Rothschilds and the royal family," said Sebastian, "life is never simple."

It was late in the afternoon by the time Sebastian met with his friend Paul Gibson at the surgeon's favorite tavern near the Tower.

"Sorry I wasn't there to help with the inquest last night," said Gibson, the pupils of his Irish green eyes noticeably small despite the dimness of the ancient Tudor tavern. "With both Alexi and me working, we might have found something before the palace came to seize the body."

"I doubt there was much more to find," said Sebastian, taking a deep drink of his ale.

"So, have you discovered how that poor woman came to be lying in the middle of a snow-filled lane?"

"No." Sebastian leaned back in his seat, aware of a growing sense of frustration, of having spent the entire day grasping at the insignificant outer edges of Jane Ambrose's life without ever coming close to capturing the essence of the woman she was or understanding why she was dead. "As far as we know, the last person to see Jane Ambrose alive was one of Princess Charlotte's women, who chanced to look out a window of Warwick House around midday and see Jane crossing the courtyard toward the gate. But after that . . ." Sebastian paused. For some reason he could not explain, that moment haunted him. He kept imagining the slender, sad young woman, dressed in mourning for her dead children, walking across a neglected courtyard as the snow began to fall and going—*where?* Where the hell had she gone? And why?

"Nothing?" said Gibson.

"Not a bloody thing. I don't know where she was killed, when she was killed, or basically anything that happened to her from the time she left Warwick House until Hero and Madame Sauvage stumbled over her body in Shepherds' Lane. I can't even figure out what the hell she was doing in Clerkenwell." Sebastian took another deep drink. "Clerken-well, of all places."

"Alexi says she was wearing her pelisse when she died."

Sebastian nodded. "Which means she was probably outside when she was killed. Although since she wasn't wearing a hat or gloves, it's also possible she was simply preparing to go out—or had only recently come inside. As to why or how she burnt her fingers . . . I've not the slightest idea."

Gibson shook his head. "Who would want to kill a thirty-three-year-old pianist?"

Sebastian grunted. "More people than you might expect. At the moment my list of suspects includes her husband, an Italian harpist, a Dutch courtier, and Nathan Rothschild."

"Rothschild? You can't be serious?"

"I wish I weren't. I was inclined to doubt it myself until a certain royal cousin warned me quite explicitly that looking too closely into the German financier's affairs would be hazardous to my health."

Gibson drained his ale and set the tankard aside with a dull *clunk*. "Bloody hell. You think Jarvis himself could be involved in this?"

Sebastian met his friend's worried gaze. "I'm afraid so."

"Does her ladyship know?"

"Not yet."

Gibson shook his head and said again, "Bloody hell."

Chapter 13

That evening, the snow continued to fall in big fat flakes that hurtled down out of a hard sky.

As was their habit of late, Hero and Sebastian gathered in the drawing room before dinner with Simon, fresh from his bath and ready for bed. "What's this?" asked Sebastian, turning the page of a wooden book painted with barnyard animals as he sat beside his son on a low ottoman.

"Mm-ga-ga-gee," said Simon, pointing to a shaggy billy goat.

"Sounded like 'goat' to me," said Hero with a smile. "Your son is brilliant."

"Of course he's brilliant. He has a very brilliant mother. And what's that?" Sebastian asked as the boy turned the next thick wooden page himself.

Simon smashed a fat finger down on the fluffy black lamb. "Mm-ga-ga-gee."

"Alas, they're all mm-ga-ga-gees," said Sebastian, just as a knock sounded at the distant front door. He looked over at Hero. "Expecting someone?"

A stranger's voice could be heard below, mingling with that of their majordomo, Morey. "No," she said.

Tiring of his book, Simon scooted off the ottoman and tottered over to the long-haired black cat curled up in one of the cane chairs near the bowed front window. "Mm-ga-ga-gee."

The big cat looked at the boy through slitted green eyes and lashed his magnificent long, thick tail—a movement that was not generally a sign of either affection or pleasure.

"Careful there, young man," said Sebastian, rising to his feet as Morey appeared in the doorway.

"A gentleman to see you, my lord," said the majordomo. "A Mr. Liam Maxwell. He says it's about Mrs. Ambrose."

Sebastian exchanged a quick glance with Hero. "Show him up."

Hero moved to retrieve the fallen book and thrust it in a drawer. "Do you know who he is?"

Sebastian shook his head. "I've no idea."

The man who entered looked to be in his late twenties. Of medium height and slim build, he was respectably rather than fashionably dressed, with fierce dark eyes and windswept dark hair that glistened with wet from the snow. It was obvious he was laboring under barely suppressed emotions, his features pinched with what looked like profound grief. "Lord and Lady Devlin," he said with a perfunctory bow. "My apologies for interrupting you at this hour."

"That's quite all right," said Sebastian. "Please come in and sit down, Mr. Maxwell. How may I help you?"

Their guest made no move to take a seat but continued to stand just inside the door, his hat in his hands, his posture stiff enough to be almost hostile. "I'm here because of Jane—Jane Ambrose."

Sebastian walked over to the small table where a decanter of brandy and glasses were warming by the fire. "You knew her?"

Maxwell hesitated just a shade too long before saying, "I've known her for years. Her brother and I once published a newspaper together."

Sebastian looked up, the brandy decanter in one hand. "I'd no notion James Somerset was involved in journalism."

Maxwell shook his head. "Not her twin, James. I meant her younger brother, Christian. He and I were in school together at Westminster."

"Christian Somerset is Jane's brother?" said Hero, as if the name meant something to her. Sebastian himself had no idea who Christian Somerset was, but Hero was staring at Liam Maxwell as if she now understood something that had escaped her before.

Maxwell nodded. "I'm told your lordship is looking into the circumstances surrounding Jane's death, which doesn't make sense if she truly slipped on the ice the way the papers are saying."

Sebastian poured a healthy measure of brandy into two glasses. "There will be no official inquiry into Jane Ambrose's death because the palace will never allow any hint of scandal to touch the Princess. But Jane did not slip in the snow and hit her head. It's not clear whether her death was murder or manslaughter, but she didn't die in the lane where she was found. Someone moved her body there after she was already dead."

"Dear God."

Sebastian held out one of the brandies, and after a moment's hesitation, Maxwell took it and drank deeply. "I want to help find whoever is responsible for this."

"You have an idea who might have killed her?" asked Hero.

Maxwell glanced over at her, the features of his face tightening with what looked very much like animosity. "Not exactly."

"But you have some suspicions?" said Sebastian.

"To be frank, I thought you might suspect me."

"Oh? Should I?"

A muscle jumped along the man's clenched jaw. "Jane and I were very close."

"Were you lovers?"

The abrupt frankness of the question seemed to take Maxwell by surprise. Rather than answer, he cast another glance at Hero, only this one was more embarrassed than hostile.

The meaning of that look was not lost on her. Stooping to swing Simon up onto her hip, she said, "If you'll excuse us, Mr. Maxwell, young Simon here and I will say good night."

He gave a curt bow. "Of course, my lady."

The boy began to fuss in protest as they moved toward the stairs, and Sebastian could hear her saying softly, "Let's count the steps, shall we? One, two, three . . ."

"So, were you lovers?" Sebastian asked again.

Maxwell went to stand before the hearth. "No; we were not. But I can understand how someone might think we were. Jane was . . . very dear to me."

"Was the feeling reciprocated?"

Maxwell turned his gaze to the flames. "We were old friends. Nothing more. Nothing."

Sebastian studied the man's half-averted face. In the distance he could hear the low murmur of Hero speaking to Simon's nurse, Claire, followed by the whisper of her footsteps coming back down the stairs and slipping into the adjoining morning room. "Do you think Edward Ambrose suspected that his wife was being unfaithful to him?"

Maxwell's head came up, his nostrils flaring. "But she wasn't!"

"Yet he could have suspected it, couldn't he? If, as you say, you were close enough that some might think it."

Maxwell hesitated a moment, then nodded.

"Which means he had a reason to kill her."

"Ambrose didn't need me as an excuse to kill Jane. Their marriage had long ago turned into something more closely resembling an armed truce than a marriage. The deaths last year of Benjamin and Lawrence— Jane's two children—ended what little good was left between them."

"Did Ambrose ever hit her?"

Maxwell nodded again, his nostrils pinched. "He gave her a black eye at least once that I know of. And several times he left a mark on her face, just here—" He touched his fingertips to his left cheekbone at exactly the same place where someone had struck Jane moments before she died.

"She told you he hit her?"

"No. She always came up with some tale to explain the marks— she'd even laugh at herself for being so clumsy. But she wasn't clumsy. She wasn't clumsy at all. I could never understand why she protected him the way she did."

"Perhaps she was ashamed."

Maxwell turned abruptly to face him, his hand tightening around his glass. "Why the devil should she have been ashamed? He's the one who hit her!"

"Some women are ashamed when their husbands or lovers beat them. I'm not saying I think they should be, because they shouldn't at all. But that doesn't alter the fact that it's a common response." Sebastian took another slow sip of his brandy. "When was the last time you saw her?"

Maxwell dragged a hand down over his haggard face. "The day before yesterday. I have a printing shop off Fleet Street and she . . . came in."

"Why?"

"No particular reason. She was in the area and stopped by to see me."

It was a simple offhand statement that told Sebastian a great deal about just how close Maxwell's relationship with his old friend's sister had been. "Did she ever mention Anna Rothschild to you?"

"I know she was upset when she recently lost her as a student. Why?"

"Do you know of any reason why her last encounter with Nathan Rothschild might have frightened her?"

"Frightened her? No. Why? What are you suggesting?"

"Nothing, at this point. Any idea what she was doing in Clerken-well yesterday?"

"No. I can't imagine."

"She didn't say how she planned to spend yesterday afternoon?"

Maxwell shook his head. "I don't believe she had any lessons on Thursday afternoons—although she'd recently been to see Lord Wallace, so she may have scheduled something."

"Phineas Wallace?" said Sebastian, sharper than he'd intended. Phineas Wallace, the second Baron Wallace, was a prominent Whig politician and one of the Princess of Wales's closest advisers.

"Yes. Why?"

"Just wondering. When you saw Jane on Wednesday, how did she seem?"

The younger man looked as if the question confused him. "What do you mean?"

"Was she happy? Nervous? Afraid?"

He thought about it a moment. "Well, she was worried about the Princess. But then she's been upset for weeks now on account of this bloody betrothal the Regent forced on Charlotte. The poor girl is in a panic, and Jane has been beside herself because of it."

"What betrothal?" Sebastian said.

Maxwell's eyebrows pinched together in a vaguely puzzled frown. "Don't you know? To William, the Hereditary Prince of Orange. They're keeping it quiet because Orange wants to make certain his position in the Netherlands is secure before the betrothal becomes known. But it's all been arranged since before Christmas. As soon as he's confident they have control of the situation there, it will be made public."

"You know this for a fact?" Sebastian had a sudden, distinct memory of Jarvis saying, *The last thing the Regent needs at the moment is to have Princess Charlotte's name bandied about in conjunction with that of a woman unwise enough to get mixed up in something as tawdry as murder.* He now understood what was so critical about "the moment."

Maxwell threw down the rest of his drink. "I wouldn't have said anything about it except I assumed given her ladyship's relationship to

Lord Jarvis that you already knew. Truth is, there's some would think me more than a bit daft coming here, her ladyship being Jarvis's daughter and all."

The statement did much to explain the animosity Maxwell had shown toward Hero before. "I wouldn't be looking into Jane Ambrose's death if I were Jarvis's tool," said Sebastian. "If that's what you mean."

"No, I don't suppose you would."

"You said the betrothal has been arranged since before Christmas. So did something else happen at the court recently?" Sebastian asked. "Something that might have disturbed Jane when you saw her on Wednesday?"

Maxwell hesitated a moment, then said, "Not that I'm aware of, no. I think she was simply angry with the lot of them—with the Regent for caring more about his grand vision for rebuilding London than about his own daughter's happiness, and with Lord Jarvis for having pushed the Orange marriage in the first place. It's all his scheme, of course. They're going to turn the Dutch Republic into a monarchy and vastly expand its territory with the idea of making it into a powerful bulwark against the French—with poor Princess Charlotte as the hapless plum on the top of the pudding."

"Charlotte agreed to this?"

"She did, yes. That bloody father of hers, he told her that if she didn't marry he'd keep her locked up with stodgy old governesses and subgovernesses until the day he died. She held out for a while, but she knew he could do it to her—hell, look at all those old maid aunts of hers. In the end, she met Orange just once at a dinner party and agreed that very night to marry him. Jane told me she regretted it almost instantly." Maxwell set aside his empty glass with a soft *clink*. "But there's no turning back for her now, poor girl."

"Another brandy?" offered Sebastian.

"Thank you, but no. I must go. You needn't ring for a footman. I can find my own way out."

Sebastian walked with him to the top of the stairs. "When I asked Edward Ambrose about his wife's family, he never mentioned a brother named Christian. In fact, he led me to think she had no family left alive. Why was that, do you suppose?"

Maxwell paused with his hand on the banister. "Probably because he wishes Christian Somerset actually were dead."

"Any particular reason?"

His lip curled. "Royal patronage is important for a playwright, isn't it? I imagine it's more than a tad embarrassing for Ambrose, having a former radical journalist as a brother in law—particularly one who spent the better part of two years in Newgate for calling the Prince of Wales a fat spendthrift who persecutes his wife and oppresses his people."

"When was this?"

"That we were in prison? From the fifteenth of January 1808 to the twenty-second of December 1809." Maxwell huffed a rough, humorless laugh. "They were kind enough to let us out a few days early for Christmas."

Sebastian understood now why Hero had recognized the names of Christian Somerset and Liam Maxwell. Sebastian himself had been off fighting the Hanovers' wars at the time and had been only vaguely aware of the trial.

Sebastian said, "I take it Jane didn't share her husband's attitude toward her brother?"

"Jane was no radical herself, if that's what you're asking—far from it, in fact. But she wasn't ashamed of us. Ambrose was always trying to get her to stay away from everyone in her family, but she wouldn't do it. When Ambrose gave her that black eye, it was over Christian."

"Where does he live now?"

"Christian? In Paternoster Row, over his bookstore and printing shop. These days he publishes mainly travel guides and romances, along with the usual odd printing jobs."

"So you're no longer in the newspaper business?"

"I am. But not Christian. A spell in Newgate definitely has a way of dampening some men's passion for espousing reform."

"Not yours?"

"Some of us are wiser than others." Maxwell gave a sad smile that had the effect of making him look both younger and considerably more relaxed. "Jane always did say I'm more pigheaded than most."

"Were brother and sister close?"

"Always." He turned his hat in his hands. "If there is anything—anything at all I can do to help—you will let me know?"

Sebastian studied the younger man's dark, haunted eyes. "I will, yes."

After Liam Maxwell had gone, Hero came from the shadows of the morning room to stand beside Sebastian at the top of the stairs.

"How much of that did you hear?" he asked as the front door closed behind their interesting visitor.

"I missed the first part. So, were he and Jane lovers?"

"He says they were not."

"Do you believe him?"

"When it comes to murder, I have a tendency to believe very little of what anyone tells me." He went to stand for a moment beside the front window and watched as their visitor walked away, head down, through the driving snow. "So exactly how radical are Christian Somerset and his friend Mr. Maxwell?"

"Not as radical as some. Their newspaper advocated for reform rather than revolution."

"For which they spent two years in prison," said Sebastian as Liam Maxwell turned the corner and disappeared into the cold night.

"They did. I understand Christian Somerset has moderated his verbiage considerably since his release."

"And Liam Maxwell?"

Her eyes narrowed with a faint smile. "Not so much."

Sebastian kept his gaze on the now empty, snow-blown street below. "Given her brother's politics, I'm surprised the Regent allowed Jane Ambrose anywhere near the Princess."

"I believe Jane was Charlotte's teacher even before Christian Somerset's arrest. And at one time Prinny was pretending to be a Whig, remember?"

Sebastian turned to retrieve his brandy and take a deep swallow. "That he was." Because the Prince's father, King George III, was a Tory, the Prince of Wales had once publicly associated with the Whigs. But as soon as he became Regent, he repudiated his old friends and allied the monarchy closer than ever with the most conservative and reactionary of the Tories—a cynical move that embittered the Whigs even more.

Hero said, "You think her brother's politics could have played a part in what happened to Jane?"

"It doesn't sound like it. But her brother's old friend Mr. Maxwell? Perhaps."

"He didn't need to come here tonight and draw attention to himself."

"No. But I would have become aware of his existence soon enough. He might have thought it wise for him to make the first move." Sebastian came to stand beside her at the fire. "How much do you know about him?"

"Maxwell?" She shook her head. "Only what was in the papers at the time of the trial, and I suspect that was biased against him. Most journalists at the time were anxious to be seen as currying favor with the Prince."

He slipped an arm around her waist to draw her closer. "Fess up now: Did you know Princess Charlotte was already betrothed to Orange?"

"I did not. Although it certainly helps explain why Peter van der Pals was so anxious to get Jane to spy on the Princess—particularly if Charlotte is now regretting having given her consent to the match."

She shifted to loop her arms around his neck. "Speaking of which, you never did tell me precisely what it was about Orange and van der Pals you didn't find it proper to discuss in the middle of Bond Street."

"Let's just say that if there were no need for Orange to beget an heir, I seriously doubt he would ever marry."

Her eyes widened. "You're certain?"

"Yes."

"Do you think the Regent knows?"

"Oh, he knows, all right. Orange has always surrounded himself with attractive, ambitious men like van der Pals. I suspect the real question is, does Charlotte know? And if she doesn't, how would she react if she found out?"

Hero's gaze met his. "Not well, I suspect. That poor girl."

Sebastian nodded. "I can see someone killing Jane Ambrose if they thought she'd learned the truth about Orange and was planning to tell the Princess." He didn't add that the person most likely to order such a killing was Hero's own father.

But then he saw the stricken look in her eyes and knew that she had guessed it anyway.

Chapter 14

$\mathcal{S}$ebastian began the next morning with an unfashionably early call on Phineas Wallace, second Baron Wallace, the notorious Whig politician mentioned by Liam Maxwell as someone Jane had recently visited.

Wallace had first entered the House of Commons as a young man of only twenty-two, freshly down from Cambridge. Brilliant, opinionated, and self-confident to the point of abrasive arrogance, he was the fourth son of a famous general known for his ruthless prosecution of war against everyone from Jacobites and American rebels to the French. As a younger son, Wallace never expected to inherit his family's modest holdings in Northumbria. And so he had poured his energies and considerable talents into Whig politics, championing everything from the abolition of slavery and Catholic emancipation to public education and electoral reform.

Wallace's elevation to his father's newly created peerage had come about unexpectedly when his three elder brothers died childless. In contrast to his brothers, the second Baron was the father of a prodigious number of offspring: eight sons and seven daughters by his wife, plus a young woman he claimed as his little sister but who was known by everyone to be the result of a torrid long-ago affair between Wallace and Georgiana, Duchess of Devonshire, the beautiful, tragic Whig hostess.

He was close to fifty now, still trim and attractive in a very English way, with a sharp nose, a small thin-lipped mouth, and shrewdly analytical eyes. Sebastian knew him slightly through Hendon—who heartily despised the arrogant, outspoken Whig. There was no denying that on a personal level, the man could sometimes be abrasive, although Sebastian himself couldn't help but admire Wallace's intelligence and dedication to reform. But what interested Sebastian most about Jane Ambrose's recent visit to Phineas Wallace was the fact that, like his colleague Henry Brougham, Wallace had for years served as adviser and protector of the Prince's estranged wife, Caroline.

"Frightfully cold morning," said Wallace with a grimace when he received Sebastian in the simply furnished drawing room of his Mount Street home. "May I offer you some wine?"

"Please," said Sebastian, going to warm himself before the fire.

"I saw Lady Devlin's recent article on climbing boys," said the Baron, pouring wine into two glasses. "She does excellent work. If she were a man, I'd recommend she run for Parliament." He laughed when he said it, as if the idea of a woman in Parliament were a ridiculous notion.

"I've no doubt she would be extraordinarily effective there," said Sebastian, accepting the glass held out to him. "Even as a woman."

"Yes, well . . ." Wallace took a judicious sip of his own wine. But over the rim of his glass, his eyes were watchful and assessing. "I'm told her ladyship had the misfortune of coming upon Mrs. Ambrose's body in the street the other day. Dreadful business, that. I trust she suffered no ill effects?"

"You knew Jane Ambrose?" said Sebastian.

"Not really, no."

"Oh? I was under the impression she came to see you recently."

"She did, yes. When one is the father of fifteen sons and daughters, it seems one is constantly looking for music instructors, dance instructors, tutors—it never ends."

"She taught your children?"

"She was considering it, yes." His lips relaxed into a self-conscious smile of paternal pride. "My wife and I like to think our Elizabeth is exceptionally talented. But nothing was ever formalized, and now the poor woman is dead."

"Except that Jane Ambrose didn't simply die," said Sebastian. "She was killed. It's unclear yet whether it was manslaughter or murder, but her death was not the innocent accident the palace would have the public believe."

Wallace's eyes bulged in a credible display of shock. "Good heavens. How terribly disturbing. Is that why you are here? Because you think I might shed some light on what happened to her? I wish I could be of some assistance, but the truth is, I barely knew the woman."

"Who recommended her to you?"

"Ah," said the Baron. "That was Princess Caroline."

"So the Princess of Wales knew Mrs. Ambrose?"

"She did, yes. Caroline has always loved music—especially the piano."

"How close were they?"

"That I'm afraid I couldn't say." He gave a faint smile that came nowhere near touching those watchful eyes. "Sorry."

"When precisely did you say she came to see you?"

"I don't believe I did say, actually. But it was a week ago this past Wednesday. Why?"

"Are you familiar with Christian Somerset?"

Wallace stiffened. "I know who he is, obviously. But I don't consider him a friend, if that's what you're suggesting. Your father, the Earl of

Hendon, may not see a difference between the Whigs and the Radicals, but there is one, believe me."

"Is Somerset still a radical?"

"Perhaps not so much anymore. But are you familiar with his former associate Liam Maxwell?" The older man's features twitched with revulsion.

"Just how radical is he?"

"Maxwell? Radical enough that he belongs back in prison, if you ask me." Wallace indicated Sebastian's glass, which was still half-full. "May I offer you more wine?"

Sebastian set the glass aside. "Thank you, but no."

"Sorry I couldn't be of more assistance," said Wallace, walking with him to the stairs. From the upper floors of the house came the sound of children's laughter and running feet.

"Do you know the names of Jane Ambrose's other pupils?" asked Sebastian, pausing.

Wallace shook his head. "No, sorry. I can't help you there."

And that, thought Sebastian as the stony-faced butler closed the door behind him, was Wallace's most obvious lie. Because what man of the Baron's standing would consider engaging a music instructor for his child without investigating her other students? Even if she were recommended by a princess.

Sebastian had no idea why Jane Ambrose had visited Princess Caroline's close confidant a week before her death. But he was fairly certain it had nothing to do with lessons for young Miss Elizabeth Wallace.

Increasingly troubled, Sebastian decided to take his questions about the politics of Jane Ambrose's brother and his journalist friend to the well-known political philosopher William Godwin.

He chose Godwin partially because he had a passing acquaintance with the man and he admired the writings of Godwin's controversial first wife, Mary Wollstonecraft. But geography also played a part, for Godwin lived on the edge of Clerkenwell, not far from where Jane Ambrose's killer had left her body.

This was a section of Clerkenwell that in times past had been dominated by the skinning trade and the great herds of livestock driven from the countryside in toward Smithfield Market. Now rows of new, small brick terrace houses stood amidst the older timber-framed dwellings dating from Tudor or even medieval times. The vast open expanse of Spa Fields lay nearby, the walkways and ruined arbors of its abandoned old gardens hidden beneath a clean white cover of fresh snow.

Godwin, who once had been as famous and influential a thinker as Edmund Burke and Thomas Paine, now lived above the children's bookstore and publishing house he kept with his second wife. When Sebastian pushed open the front door with a jingle of its bell, the writer himself was straightening a stack of Greek and Roman fables displayed on a table beneath the frost-covered front window. He was in his late fifties, his hair graying and receding, his once sharp features softened by the slow accumulation of pounds. He looked up as Sebastian shut the door against a gust of frigid air, and frowned. "I assume you're here for a reason."

Sebastian carefully knocked the snow off his hat. It wasn't a particularly promising beginning. "I have some questions I'd like to ask you, if I might have a moment of your time?"

Godwin grunted and returned his attention to the display table. "Now, why would the son and heir of the great Earl of Hendon be wanting to speak to me?"

"A woman named Jane Ambrose was found dead near here, in Shepherds' Lane."

Godwin nodded with a sigh. "Yes, I know. Sad, isn't it? The streets have been most treacherous lately."

"They can be. Except that Jane Ambrose didn't slip and hit her head. She was already dead when someone dumped her body in the snow."

Godwin gave up straightening the display and turned to face Sebastian, his hands dangling limply at his sides. "You can't think I had
anything to do with that."

"No, I didn't mean to imply that. I'm here because I'm interested in
what you can tell me about the newspaper Liam Maxwell used to publish with Jane Ambrose's brother, Christian Somerset."

Godwin began shifting a pile of children's atlases from a crate onto
a nearby shelf. "Why? That was long ago. Surely you can't think it has
anything to do with what happened?"

"At this point, I don't know. What was the paper called?"

"The Poor Man's Advocate."

"Was it stamped?" The required stamp tax added four pence to a
newspaper's cost, which was a staggering sum for papers targeting anyone but the affluent. As a result, papers aimed at the lowest classes were
typically sold illegally, unstamped.

"Oh, it was stamped, all right, which obviously had the effect of lim-
iting its circulation—the poor of England seldom having excess coins to
spend on reading material. But then, that's precisely why our benighted
government puts such a high tax on newspapers in the first place, isn't it?
Can't have the masses discovering that others not only share their discon-
tent but are advocating radical solutions to the nation's problems."

"How radical was it?"

Godwin gave a slow smile. "Compared to what? They argued that
Parliament should be representative of the entire Kingdom rather than
a tool of the privileged and maintained that England's true strength lies
with the labor of her people rather than the activities of our rapacious
aristocracy."

"So what sort of reforms were they calling for? A republican government?"

Godwin finished straightening the atlases and leaned back against
the counter, his arms folded at his chest. "I've no doubt it's what both
men wanted. But they never called for it, if that's what you're asking.

They mainly focused on things like secret ballots and manhood suffrage—and freedom of the press, of course."

"Such as the right to call Prinny a fat bastard without landing in prison for two years?"

"Something like that, yes."

"And Maxwell now publishes a different paper?"

"At least one—or so they say. He's the publisher of *The Intelligencer*."

Sebastian nodded. *The Intelligencer* printed unvarnished but careful reports of parliamentary debates and government acts, leavened by sensational accounts of the city's most gruesome crimes and accidents. "And the other?"

When Godwin simply pursed his lips and remained silent, Sebastian said, "Anything you tell me will go no further. My sole purpose is to understand how and why Jane Ambrose died."

Godwin gave a pained sigh. "Word on the street says he's also responsible for *The Pigs' Trough*."

"Good Lord," said Sebastian. *The Pigs' Trough* was a truly radical unstamped periodical calling for everything from the abolition of the monarchy to the redistribution of property. Typically hawked in alleys at night, its name was an irreverent reference to Edmund Burke's fondness for the phrase "the swinish multitude."

"I'm not saying the rumors are true, mind you. How would I know? I simply write, publish, and sell children's books."

"What about Somerset?" asked Sebastian. "Is he involved with *The Pigs' Trough*?"

"Christian? Not likely. These days he confines his publishing business to romances, guide books, and floral stationery. He does still write occasionally for the *Chronicle*, but he's careful what he says."

Sebastian studied the older man's gentle, troubled face. "Did you know Jane Ambrose?"

Godwin drew a ragged breath that jerked his chest. "Of course I knew her. She taught my daughter Mary piano for years."

"She was still teaching her?"

"Yes. Why?"

"On what days?"

"Friday afternoons."

"Is it possible Jane could have been coming here on Thursday evening?"

"I don't think so. Why would she?"

Sebastian could think of several reasons, but all he said was "How long have you known her?"

"Ten years or more. I met her through Christian."

"So you knew her well?"

"Oh, yes. She frequently lingered after my daughter's lessons to argue philosophy with us. She reminded me in some ways of my first wife when she was that age—bright and quick, with a rare courage and strength of character. Except, of course, that Jane's thinking wasn't anywhere near as unconventional."

"She believed in monarchy?"

"She did, yes. I asked her once how she possibly could, given her familiarity with the Prince of Wales."

"And?"

"She said that however great Prinny's failings as an individual—and she acknowledged that his failings were indeed great—she still believed he was dedicated to the interests of his Kingdom in a way mere politicians rarely are. I told her a man who has his subjects' best interests at heart does not run up millions of pounds in debt on self-indulgent fripperies while his people starve."

"What was her reply?"

"She insisted that Princess Charlotte would be a different kind of ruler—that unlike her father, she truly is kind and caring, as illustrated by the fact that she actually supports both Catholic emancipation and Irish independence."

"She does?"

"Oh, yes, she's quite the Whig. Jane also insisted that Charlotte is sincere in her beliefs—unlike her father in his salad days."

"Did Jane ever say anything to you about Prinny's plans for his daughter's marriage?"

"Not really. I asked her recently if the rumors we're hearing about a possible Orange alliance are true, but she pretended to know nothing about it."

"What makes you think she was only pretending?"

Godwin's lips twitched into a ghost of a smile. "Jane was always an appallingly bad liar. The truth was writ all over her face." The smile faded away into something bleak and sad. "And now she's just . . . dead "

"Who do you think killed her?"

Godwin went to stand at the bowed front window, his features solemn, his gaze on the wind-driven snow collecting in the corners of the mullions. After a moment, he shook his head. "I've no idea."

"She never spoke to you of any enemies?"

"Jane? I wouldn't have said she had any." He gave a heavy, pained sigh. "I've always believed that men are not innately evil—that the evil we see in the world around us is the result of our age's benighted social conditions and archaic institutions rather than some inherent human flaw. But my Mary never shared my belief in the perfectibility of mankind."

"And Jane?"

"Jane told me once that her heart agreed with me, but her head suspected Mary was probably right."

"Did she read your late wife's works?"

"She did, yes—although only quite recently. I've sensed a change in her these last few months, as if she were questioning some of her earlier beliefs, searching for new answers. The loss of her two boys last year, one right after the other, hit her hard. I think she was still finding her way toward understanding and accepting it."

Sebastian shook his head. "How can anyone understand or accept such a loss?"

"Perhaps one cannot."

Sebastian settled his hat on his head and turned toward the door. "Thank you for your assistance."

"Have I been of assistance? I hope so. It's a dreadful thing, if what you say is true. She was such a talented, good-hearted young woman. Why would anyone want to kill her?"

Sebastian paused with a hand on the latch. "What do you know of her relationship with Liam Maxwell?"

"I assume she knew him through her brother—although he was always far more radical than even Christian, let alone Jane."

"Yet he and Jane were close friends."

"Were they? I didn't know that. I've always been better acquainted with Somerset than with his former partner. Maxwell's far too much of a rabble-rouser for my taste. I've never believed in initiating change through violence—even before the French Revolution showed us just how ugly that approach can be."

"But Maxwell does?"

"He does, yes—although he'll tell you he favors the American model over the French version."

Sebastian found himself remembering Maxwell's bitter words on the House of Orange and the destruction of the Dutch Republic, and knew a deep disquiet. "What's the man's background?"

"Maxwell? I believe he spent his early years in India. His father was in the East India Company, and his mother was raised there. But both died when he was still a lad. He went to Westminster as a King's Scholar."

"That can't have been easy."

"No. I've always suspected it contributed more than a bit to his radical philosophies."

"Probably."

Godwin gave him a hard look. "Why do you ask?"

"I'm simply trying to understand Jane better. Did you happen to speak with her last week when she was here for your daughter's lesson?"

Godwin shook his head. "She didn't come. She sent a message saying she wouldn't be able to make it."

"Did she do that often?"

"No. Truth is, I can't remember her having done it before. Ever."

Chapter 15

*J*arvis was at breakfast in Berkeley Square when his daughter, Hero, walked into the room and closed the door behind her.

"Did you kill Jane Ambrose?" she asked without preamble, jerking at the ribbons of her black velvet hat.

Jarvis cut a piece of ham. "I did not."

"Obviously I don't mean personally."

Jarvis calmly chewed and swallowed. "The answer is still the same."

"Do you know who did?"

"I do not. And unless her death should somehow threaten affairs of state, nor do I care." He reached for the stout ale that always accompanied his breakfast. "Would you like a plate?"

She shook her head. "I've already breakfasted. Thank you." But she did push away from the door and come to sit at the table.

She was Jarvis's only surviving child. Once he'd had a son, a sickly, peculiar lad named David who'd died and been buried at sea years ago. All the other infants his late, tiresome wife, Annabelle, had managed to carry to term had either been born dead or died soon after. Annabelle herself had been dead four months now, and Jarvis had already dispensed with his black sleeve riband.

Hero still wore full mourning.

He had never thought his daughter a particularly attractive woman. She was too tall, her features too masculine, her gaze too direct and unabashedly intelligent. But she did look good in black, and he had to admit that marriage and motherhood had improved her. "How is my grandson?" he asked.

"Endlessly curious and fiercely determined."

"Good."

She placed her hands flat on the table and leaned into them.

"Is it true that Prinny has forced Charlotte to agree to marry William of Orange?"

"No one 'forced' her. The Princess made the decision of her own free will."

"When given a choice between marrying Orange and being immured with a bunch of foul-tempered old women until she dies, you mean."

"Well, at least until the Prince of Wales dies. At that point—assuming her poor old mad grandfather is also dead—she will be Queen and thus free to do as she pleases."

"Both of Prinny's parents are still alive. He could live another thirty or forty years."

"He could."

She fixed him with a fierce gaze. "Orange can't be a proper husband to her and you know it. Such a marriage would make her life wretched."

"This isn't about Charlotte's happiness. It's about what's good for the Kingdom—not to mention the future of all of Europe."

"And you think a miserable union between our future queen and a man known to prefer handsome courtiers will be good for England? Did the disastrous marriage of Prinny and his poor wife teach us nothing?"

"Charlotte may be stubborn, but like her father, she understands her duty and will do it."

"Prinny only agreed to 'do his duty' and marry Caroline because he was drowning in debt and he thought it would convince Parliament to grant him a higher allowance. And when he realized that wasn't the case, he pitched a fit and refused to go near her again."

"Yes. Well, fortunately Charlotte has been raised to be considerably less devoted to her own self-interest. She quite clearly understands that not only will a United Netherlands serve as a useful check against the French and form an important bridge between Hanover and England, but it will also separate France from an increasingly strong Prussia. With the Dutch Fleet jointed to the Royal Navy, our domination of the seas will be unchallengeable. Holland will be far more stable once it is turned into a monarchy—"

"Ah, yes: because the fates of Louis XVI and Marie Antoinette certainly illustrated for all just how stable a monarchy can be," said Hero dryly.

"—and nothing will keep this new, more powerful Dutch kingdom tied to Britain better than a marriage alliance," he finished with a repressive frown.

Hero had never been the least troubled by his disapproval. "And if the Dutch people object to having their two-hundred-year-old republic replaced by a monarchy?"

Jarvis shrugged. "A few judicious whiffs of grapeshot will quiet any objections."

Hero regarded him with a thoughtful expression that told him just how well she knew him. After a moment, she said, "There's more to this than what you're telling me."

He laughed out loud and reached for his ale without answering her.

The opening of the dining room door brought Hero's head around, her features carefully wiped of all emotion when she saw the dainty woman who paused there with one hand on the knob. "Cousin Victo-ria," said Hero, rising to her feet.

"Hero!" Mrs. Victoria Hart-Davis came forward with a warm smile to take Hero in an affectionate embrace. A stunningly beautiful widow in her late twenties, she was a distant cousin of Hero's dead mother and had been visiting at the time of Annabelle's death. Because Jarvis's own mother, the Dowager Lady Jarvis, was too old and arthritic to leave her rooms much these days, Cousin Victoria had kindly offered to stay and help run the household until someone suitable could be found.

Jarvis was in no hurry for her to leave.

She was so tiny that even when she stood on tiptoe, her kiss didn't quite reach Hero's cheek, and she laughed good-naturedly. "What a pleas-ant surprise. You're joining us for breakfast?"

"Sorry, no," said Hero, reaching for her hat. "I can't stay."

"You and Devlin must come for dinner. Perhaps one evening when this wretched cold snap has passed?"

"Yes," said Hero. "That would be lovely."

After she had gone, Victoria came to stand behind Jarvis's chair and slip her arms around his neck. "Does she know?"

"Not all of it," he said, and smiled when she playfully bit his ear.

Chapter 16

*L*ong the haunt of booksellers and literary men, Paternoster Row was an ancient, gloomy thoroughfare lying just to the north of St. Paul's Cathedral. The narrow gable-fronted residence of Jane's brother, Christian Somerset, stood not far from Ave Maria Lane. Its ground floor was given over to Somerset's bookstore and bindery, while his printing press operated from a workshop that opened onto a small court at the rear. Sebastian found the shop busy, with several men working two modern, iron-framed presses while young apprentices leapt to ink the blocks and then peel off the fresh, wet pages and hang them to dry. A slim, quietly dressed man stood near the front window, frowning as he held a proof sheet up to the light. When Sebastian pushed open the door from the snow-filled courtyard, the man glanced up and said, "May I help you?"

Sebastian closed the door against the icy cold and breathed in the thick atmosphere of linseed oil, lampblack, and sweat. "You're Mr. Christian Somerset?"

The man's hand trembled slightly as he set the sheet aside. "I am, yes." The family resemblance was there in the finely drawn features and elegant bone structure Somerset shared with his dead sister. But if Sebastian hadn't known the man was younger than Jane, he never would have guessed it, for Somerset's dark hair was already laced with gray, and life had etched early lines of strain and disillusionment in his gentle face.

Sebastian held out one of his cards. "I'm Devlin."

"Ah." Somerset nodded as he took the card. "Liam Maxwell told me you might be paying me a visit." He cast a quick glance at the men working the presses and said in a lowered voice, "Please, come this way."

He led Sebastian to a small, untidy office warmed by a rusty stove and filled with stacks of invoices, reams of paper, and crates of unbound books ready to be shipped. Most publishers sold their books in plain paper wrappers with temporary sewing, for permanent bindings were typically left to booksellers or to private buyers who took the books to their own binders and had them covered in leather to match their personal libraries. But Sebastian could also see stacks of inexpensive guidebooks bound in plain cloth covers, which was something of an innovation.

Somerset nodded to the bench of an elegant pianoforte, which stood like a calm in the midst of a storm. "Have a seat. Please."

"I should probably stand," said Sebastian, swinging off his greatcoat. "I'm rather wet."

Somerset pressed one splayed hand against the top of his cluttered desk as if bracing himself for what he was about to hear. "Is it true, then? Jane was murdered?"

"It's either murder or manslaughter. It's difficult to say which."

"Oh, dear God." His voice cracked, and he swiped a hand across his mouth and looked away, blinking. "Poor Jane."

Sebastian said, "When was the last time you saw your sister?"

Somerset sighed. "I'm afraid it's been some time—perhaps as much as ten days. She came here."

"For any particular reason?"

Somerset nodded. "I publish her music. She brought a collection of new ballads she'd written."

Sebastian glanced at the piano. "You play?"

Somerset gave a wry, self-deprecating smile. "I do—for my own pleasure. But I'm nowhere near Jane's level, if that's what you're asking. Growing up with Jane and James ahead of me was rather intimidating, I suppose. Besides, I always wanted to be a writer."

"Do you still write?"

"Oh, yes. Although I'm careful these days what I say and how I say it. I spent two years in prison for the sin of speaking my mind, and it's not an experience I care to repeat."

"Did Jane share your political views?"

"Jane?" Somerset gave a huff that wasn't quite a laugh. "She taught piano to Princess Charlotte—and to Princess Amelia before she died. What do you think?"

"I think one can take advantage of the prestige afforded by instructing members of the royal family and still quietly nurture radical ideals."

"Not Jane. Oh, there's no denying she loathed the Regent—a free Englishman can still say that, can't he? But she was a firm believer in the institution of monarchy."

"Did she ever talk to you about the Princess?"

"I know she had a genuine affection for the girl."

"She didn't say anything to you about Charlotte's betrothal?"

"Is she betrothed? I hadn't heard that."

"It's not well-known," said Sebastian. It was telling, he thought, that Jane had discussed her concerns about Charlotte's betrothal with her brother's former partner but not with her brother himself—although he suspected that said more about her relationship with Liam Maxwell than anything else. "What about her other students? Did she talk about any of them?"

"Not that I recall, no."

"Not even Anna Rothschild?"

"No, sorry. I know she taught her, but beyond that . . ." His voice trailed away and he swallowed hard. "She was typically very discreet when it came to her pupils."

Sebastian went to stand beside the frosted window overlooking the snow-filled court. From here he could see the narrow passage that opened onto Paternoster Row. "Do you have any idea what could have taken Jane to Clerkenwell on Thursday?"

Somerset thought about it a moment, then shook his head. "I understand that's where they say she was found, but I can't imagine what she was doing there."

"Any friends or relatives in the area?"

"Well, the Godwins live there, and I know Jane teaches their daughter—taught their daughter," he corrected himself softly. "Perhaps that's where she was going."

"Except that Jane's lessons with Mary Godwin were on Fridays, not Thursdays."

"Ah. I didn't know that. Then sorry. I've no idea why she was in Clerkenwell."

"Did your sister have any enemies?"

"Jane? I don't think so, no."

"She never spoke to you of the intrigues at court?"

Somerset's face hardened. "You think that's why she was killed? Because of something to do with the royal family?"

"It's one possibility. Did she ever mention a Dutch courtier named Peter van der Pals?"

"No. Never."

"What about an Italian harpist named Vescovi?"

"You mean Valentino Vescovi?"

"So she did mention him?"

"Not that I recall. But I have heard of him. He's a brilliant musician."

"What about the Prince of Orange? Did she ever talk about him?"

Somerset shook his head. "No. But as I said, she tended to avoid talking about the royal family around me. She knows—knew—my political opinions."

"So they haven't changed? Your political opinions, I mean."

Somerset huffed another soft laugh, only this one contained little real humor. "Two years in prison might make a man more circumspect about voicing his thoughts, but it's not likely to kindle within him warm feelings for the system that put him there, now, is it? My wife died while I was in Newgate. She's the one who set up the bookshop and started publishing novels and guidebooks in an effort to make ends meet while I was in prison. She was amazingly successful at it, but in the end, it all got to be too much for her. She died six weeks before I was released."

"I'm sorry," said Sebastian, letting his gaze travel again around the office. It did much to explain the shift in Somerset's printing business; he had simply picked up where his dead wife had left off. "I gather your sister was quite close to your former partner, Liam Maxwell."

Somerset was quiet for a moment, as if carefully choosing his words. "I know what you're implying, but you're wrong. Liam and I have been friends since we were schoolboys, and he and Jane got to know each other particularly well during our time in Newgate. But our father was a profoundly religious man who brought up his children with strict Christian precepts. Most of his teachings didn't stick so well with me, but they did with Jane. She was a sincerely devout woman who took her marriage vows seriously. She would never have been unfaithful to her husband."

"Did you know that Edward Ambrose used to hit her? Hit her hard enough to leave bruises?"

Somerset gave a faint shake of his head. "I didn't know for certain, no. But I'll not deny I suspected it." His jaw tightened. "That bloody bastard. If he were to be found dead in the middle of the street, I wouldn't shed a tear. I can tell you that."

"I gather your relationship with Ambrose is strained."

Somerset grunted. "Now, there's an understatement. I can assure you that if I were found dead, you wouldn't see him shedding any tears, either."

"Was he faithful to his wife?"

Somerset hesitated.

"Was he?" said Sebastian.

Somerset sucked in a deep breath. "I've heard he's involved with some actress or opera dancer. Although that could be nothing but talk."

"Did Jane hear it?"

"I never said anything to her about it, if that's what you're asking. And if she heard it from someone else, she never mentioned it to me."

"Would she, do you think?"

"Mention it to me?" He paused for a moment, then shook his head a bit wistfully. "Probably not. We were close in many ways, but I don't think she'd tell me something like that."

From the workshop behind them came a clatter, followed by a boy's laughter. Sebastian said, "Do you think the rumors are true? That Ambrose is involved with someone?"

Somerset met his gaze, his features drawn and tight with what looked like anger. "Yes. Yes, I do."

Chapter 17

By the time Sebastian left Somerset's workshop, dark, ominous clouds were once again pressing down on the city. He turned his steps west, toward the theater district of Covent Garden, intending to make some inquiries there about Edward Ambrose. But as he left Ave Maria Lane for Ludgate Street, he began to suspect he was being followed.

The cold had driven enough people off the streets to make the man behind him particularly noticeable. Short and stocky, with sandy hair and a slouch hat pulled low over his eyes, he looked much like a respectable tradesman. He stayed perhaps twenty feet behind Sebastian—close enough to keep him in sight without being too obvious. But when Sebastian quickened his step, the man walked faster; when Sebastian allowed his pace to slacken, the man likewise slowed.

The slouch-hatted shadow followed Sebastian up Ludgate to Fleet Street. After another two blocks, Sebastian swung about to stride rapidly back the way he had come.

Slouch Hat paused and turned as if in rapt admiration of the parasols displayed in the bow window of the shop beside him.

Sebastian walked right up to him. "So who the hell are you and why are you following me?"

The man gave an exaggerated start of surprise. "Yer honor?"

"You heard me. Who are you working for?"

"I wasn't fol—"

Sebastian grabbed the man's shoulder and swung him around to slam his back against the soot-stained brick wall beside them. "I suggest you don't try my patience," he said, enunciating each word carefully. "A brilliant young woman is dead, and I am in no mood to play games. Who set you to following me?"

"I don't know what yer talkin' about."

The man tried to pull away, but Sebastian hauled him back and wedged a forearm up beneath the man's chin. "Not so fast."

The man squirmed in his grasp. "Oye! Let me go!"

"When you tell me who—"

Sebastian broke off as he caught the crunch of snow-muffled footsteps coming up behind him, fast. The man's gaze shifted for one telltale instant to something over Sebastian's shoulder just as Sebastian heard the unmistakable *snick* of a blade being drawn from its leather sheath.

"Bloody hell," swore Sebastian. Grabbing Slouch Hat by his coat, he pulled the man away from the wall and swung around just as a tall, lanky man with a scarf wrapped around the lower half of his face lunged at Sebastian with a dagger.

Such was the speed and force of the attack that the assassin was unable to break away. Sebastian felt the man in the slouch hat shudder under the impact of the blade. Blood poured from the man's mouth as he pitched forward to knock Sebastian off his feet and land on top of him.

"Jack!" shouted the lanky man, trying to yank the dagger from his friend's back as Sebastian fought to shove the stricken man away. Over the folds of his woolen scarf, the assassin's gaze met Sebastian's. Filled with murderous rage, the man's eyes were oddly mismatched, one noticeably larger than the other and not quite on the same plane. Then the killer abandoned his knife and ran.

Sebastian scrambled out from under the dying man.

"Who sent you?" said Sebastian, raising the man's head so that he wouldn't choke on his own blood. *"Who sent you, damn it!"*

The man's mouth worked. Sebastian bent over him, only to jerk back his head as the man tried to spit in his face. Then the light of rage and hatred faded from the man's eyes, leaving nothing but the cold, vacant stare of death.

"So who is he?" asked Sir Henry Lovejoy sometime later as the two men stood side by side, staring down at the dead man at their feet. The snow fell around them in a sibilant rush.

"'Jack,' according to the man who accidently killed him," said Sebastian. "But beyond that, I've no idea. I've never seen him before, and he's not carrying any identification."

"And his companion?"

"Was likewise unknown to me—as far as I could tell. He had a scarf covering most of his face, but his eyes were definitely memorable."

Lovejoy frowned at the spreading pool of crimson snow around the dead man. "You'll need to testify at the inquest, of course."

"Yes."

"Any idea who might want to have you killed?"

"None."

Lovejoy pursed his lips. "Well, at least Bow Street can get involved in this death. I don't see why the palace should object."

"Unless of course the palace sent him," said Sebastian.

The two men's gazes met. But rather than say anything, Lovejoy simply burrowed his fists deeper into his pockets and blew out a harsh breath that rose in a white cloud to freeze on his eyelashes.

Hero was buttoning the tucked bodice of a fine black wool carriage gown when Sebastian came to stand in her dressing room's doorway. She glanced over at him, then went back to her buttons. "So is that your blood all over you, or someone else's?"

He walked over to inspect his face in the mirror above the washstand. "Someone else's." He reached for the pitcher and poured water into the bowl. "Two men just tried to kill me in Fleet Street. One of them got away. The other didn't."

"He's dead?"

"He is. Unfortunately, he died without revealing whom he was working for."

She watched him dab at the streak of blood on his cheek with a wet cloth. "Any idea who that might be?"

"Not really. At the moment the most likely suspect in Jane's death is probably her own husband, Edward Ambrose. But he doesn't know that I suspect him, so why would he try to kill me?" He glanced over at her. "Where are you off to?"

"Clerkenwell. Coachman John thinks he can get me there in the sleigh, so I've had Cook pack a basket of food."

"For the cooper's wife who gave birth on Thursday?"

"Yes." She reached for her hat and pivoted back to her dressing table to position it just so. "I'm also taking a sack of coal. I don't know how the poor of the city are surviving with everything either impossible to find or dreadfully dear." She turned to face him again, her gray eyes troubled.

"What?" he asked, watching her.

"It's just that I have the most lowering reflection that I'm doing this simply as a pitiful sop to my own conscience. In the grand scheme of things, what does it matter if I help one desperate mother and her children when thousands more are starving and freezing to death?"

"It's a beginning." He went to take her face in his hands and gently kiss her mouth. "Be careful, will you?" he said, his gaze locking with hers.

"I'm not the one somebody just tried to kill. You be careful."

Chapter 18

*I*t was still snowing when Sebastian reached Covent Garden, big, soft flakes that drifted lazily down on the city.

This was a part of London he'd known well as a young man just down from Oxford, when he'd fallen hopelessly in love with a brilliant, unknown young actress named Kat Boleyn. At the time he had expected to spend the rest of his life with her—have children with her, grow old with her. Then a series of well-intentioned lies tore them apart and very nearly destroyed him.

It had been a dark period in his life, one he didn't like to remember. But in time he'd learned that a powerful and enriching love can come into a man's life more than once. And gradually his affection for Kat had shifted from something passionate and desperate to something warm and good, as if she were indeed the half sister he'd once believed her to be.

Now the most acclaimed actress of London's stage, Kat was currently starring in the title role of *Queen Boudica* at Covent Garden Theater. And it was there that he found her, sorting through a motley collection of dusty stage props in the warren of frigid rooms below the stairs. She was in her mid-twenties now, a beautiful woman with rich auburn hair, her father's vivid blue eyes, and a wide mouth that curled into a welcoming smile when she turned and spotted him picking his way toward her through piles of battered shields and wooden swords jumbled together with papier-mâché horse heads and a stuffed raven.

"I was wondering when I'd be seeing you," she said.

"Oh? Are you becoming prescient?"

"I've no need to be. No one in the theater can talk of anything other than Jane Ambrose's death and your interest in it." She set aside the elaborate headpiece of beads, tarnished wire, and feathers she'd been trying to straighten. "So it's true? Was she murdered?"

"It was either murder or manslaughter." He tripped over a crate of masks and collided with a rusty suit of armor. "Did you know her?"

Kat reached out to steady the rocking armor. "I did, but not well. I've no idea who could have killed her, if that's what you're asking."

He found himself next to a big old wooden chest and promptly sat on it. It was cold enough down here that he could see his breath. "What about her husband, Edward Ambrose? Do you know him?"

"Ambrose? Of course. His plays and operas are brilliant. I've been in half a dozen or more of them over the years."

"What about the man himself? What do you think of him?"

She took her time in answering. It was one of the things she had in common with her natural father, the Earl of Hendon—this tendency to think carefully and weigh her words before speaking. "He's well liked in the theater—which is unusual, because not many writers are. He has a reputation for being affable and easygoing."

"You say that as if you disagree with the general consensus."

"Oh, I won't deny he comes across as quite pleasant. But I've never been entirely convinced it's genuine."

"Any particular reason?"

"I don't know if I could point to any one thing. It's probably more a feeling I've had." She shivered and clutched the thin shawl she wore tighter around her shoulders. "You think he killed his own wife?"

"He's certainly on my list. There's a rumor he has a mistress—possibly an actress or an opera dancer. Do you know if that's true?"

"I've heard whispers. But I don't know for certain, no."

"Could you find out?"

"I can try." Another shiver racked her frame, chattering her teeth together.

He shrugged off his greatcoat and dropped it around her shoulders. "How about if we continue this conversation over a nice hot cup of tea?"

She laughed. "I think that's a wonderful idea."

They sought refuge in a nearby coffeehouse with a roaring fire and the welcoming aroma of freshly baked scones. She was on her second scone when she said casually without looking up, "There's something else you wanted to ask me about, isn't there?"

He smiled, because she had always known him so well. Dropping his voice, he leaned in closer over the table. "I need to talk to a smuggler familiar with Rothschild's operation in the Channel. I don't mean one of his confederates, but a competitor—someone who would be willing to tell me what I need to know."

The request might have struck a casual listener as beyond bizarre. But then, few in London knew that as a fierce Irish patriot, Kat had once passed information to the French, or that she was the widow of a flamboyant ex-privateer who'd dabbled in smuggling himself.

"You think Rothschild could be involved in her death?"

"It's possible. Can you find someone?"

A flicker of something unidentifiable crossed her features. But all she said was "Give me a few days."

After that, they talked for a time of Simon's coming birthday and

Hendon's recent attack of the gout. Then Kat fell silent, her face thoughtful.

"What?"

"I was remembering one of the reasons why I'd come to doubt Edward Ambrose's reputation as a genial man. About a year or so ago, when we were doing his *Fool's Paradise*, his wife was at the theater helping organize the costumes. He got into a disagreement with her over something, and I saw him take hold of her wrist and twist it hard enough that she gave a small gasp."

"It was deliberate?"

"Oh, yes. And what made it particularly chilling is that he was smiling all the time he did it."

"Lovely."

She nodded. "I saw him do something similar just a few days ago."

"When?"

"Tuesday evening. I was walking past the Opera and noticed them standing at the top of the steps, beneath the portico. It was raining, and I wasn't near enough to hear what they were saying, but it was obvious the conversation was tense. He grabbed her by both arms and shook her—quite hard. And then she pulled from his grasp and ran away. It was beginning to get dark, but I could see her face well enough as she passed to know that she was crying."

"Bloody hell," said Sebastian.

Kat met his gaze, her features solemn. "If he did kill her, I hope you can prove it."

Sebastian took a swallow of his tea, found it cold, and pushed the cup aside. "Believe me, I'm trying."

Sebastian turned his steps once more toward Soho Square. The snow was falling now in windblown swirls, a billowing curtain of white lit by a strange light that seemed to come from everywhere and nowhere.

It was only midday, but he found himself walking through nearly deserted streets, the ice stinging his cheeks, his breath a frozen mist that hovered around him. Where did they all go? he found himself wondering—the tradesmen and cart drivers, costermongers and paupers whose voices normally echoed through the narrow, canyon-like streets of the city? For how long could they continue to seek refuge from a winter too brutal to be borne before they began to starve, go mad, die?

He walked on, his shoulders hunched against the driven snow as he tried to put together the puzzle of Jane Ambrose's death with three-quarters of its pieces still missing. In the last forty-eight hours his grasp of the woman she once was had begun to strengthen, the reality of her life and the way she'd lived it emerging like a shadowy form still half hidden by a storm. He saw a talented musician denied the brilliant career that could have been hers had she only been born male, and a devout, loving mother, faithfully honoring her religion by enduring an unhappy marriage only to then be devastated by the loss of both her children.

How could such a woman come to terms with that blow? he wondered. Impossible to do, surely, without questioning every assumption, every platitude by which she had always sought to live. Jane's brother swore she'd taken her marriage vows too seriously to ever think of leaving her husband or taking a lover. But had that remained true? Would Christian Somerset know if it did not?

Jane's husband had made a practice of hitting her. Hurting her. What would a man such as Edward Ambrose do if he discovered his wife's infidelity—or suspected it? Hit her in the face? Rape her?

Kill her?

Chapter 19

The body of Jane Ambrose lay in a silk-lined coffin set up on two straight-backed wooden chairs before the dining room windows overlooking Soho Square. Her face was like wax, her body shrinking in on itself so that she looked diminished, so much less than the vibrant woman she'd been in life. The laying-out woman had dressed her in a high-necked gown of simple black muslin with a black lace-trimmed bonnet that effectively hid both the shattered side of her skull and the exploratory incisions from Alexi Sauvage's abbreviated postmortem examination. The strange, inexplicable burns on her hand were covered by fine black gloves. Any other secrets her body might have had to tell were hidden and would never be known.

Edward Ambrose stood beside his dead wife's coffin, his gaze on her still, pale face. His shoulders were slumped, his cravat askew, and he looked up at Sebastian's entrance to show an unshaven face with eyes swollen as if from lack of sleep. He gave all the appearance of a man devastated by the death of a wife he loved. But then, Sebastian had seen men weep inconsolably at the gravesides of women they'd killed.

"My apologies for the intrusion," said Sebastian, pausing just inside the dining room door, his hat in his hands.

Ambrose nodded, his lips pressed together tightly. "I understand it's necessary."

"Is there a place we can talk?" asked Sebastian.

He saw a flicker of something in Ambrose's bloodshot eyes that was there and then gone. "Yes. Of course."

The playwright led the way to a crowded library dominated by two pianofortes. Sheet music lay scattered everywhere, along with stacks of books, several violins, and a flute. "Have you discovered something?" he asked, turning to face Sebastian. He did not invite him to sit.

"Actually, yes. I'm hearing reports that you have a mistress. Is that true?"

Ambrose's head jerked back. "Good God, no!"

Sebastian studied the other man's suddenly high color and tightened jaw. "Let me give you some advice: When it comes to murder, it's never a good idea to lie. It makes you look guilty."

Ambrose straightened his shoulders, his nostrils flaring wide as if he were working to keep his temper in check and his voice even. "I do not keep a mistress."

"If you do, I will find out about it eventually. You do realize that, don't you?"

"I do not keep a mistress and I did not kill my wife. That is what you're insinuating, isn't it?"

Sebastian let his gaze drift around the room, taking in again the multiple musical instruments, the basket of mending beside the hearth. It looked very much like a space Jane had shared with her husband rather than the private retreat he had insinuated the last time Sebastian had spoken with him. "You had a quarrel with Jane late Tuesday on the steps of the Opera—a quarrel that ended with you shaking her and her in tears. And don't even think about trying to deny it because you were seen by someone I know and trust."

Ambrose walked away to stand looking out the window at the nar-row snow-filled garden to the rear of the house. "Husbands and wives quarrel. Why should I deny it?"

"What was the quarrel about?"

"If I tell you, you must assure me that it will go no further."

"Within reason, of course."

Ambrose hesitated, then said, "I was angry because Jane had paid a visit to the Princess of Wales."

Whatever Sebastian had been expecting, it wasn't that.

Caroline, Princess of Wales, was the Regent's estranged wife and mother to Princess Charlotte. Once she had been highly sought after by members of the *ton*, an enthusiastic hostess famous for giving un-usual, amusing dinner parties frequented by everyone from men of letters such as Lord Byron and Walter Scott to the painter Thomas Lawrence and Whig politicians like Brougham and Wallace. But when the Prince of Wales became Regent, most of Society dropped her cold. Few cared to alienate the Prince, who was now both head of state and head of the royal family—and who had a reputation for holding a grudge forever and exacting petty revenges.

"The Regent's patronage is important to a man in my profession," Ambrose was saying. "You know the way he treats those who dare have anything to do with Caroline. What husband in my position wouldn't have been angry?"

"When did Jane visit Charlotte's mother?"

"I don't recall precisely. Sometime last week."

"Why?"

Ambrose looked as if the question puzzled him. "I've no idea. What does it matter why she went? Do you imagine the Prince cares what her motives might have been?"

"It matters if it had something to do with her death."

Ambrose brought up a hand to rub his forehead. "Oh, yes, of course. I wasn't thinking of that."

"No. I can see you weren't."

A faint flush touched the other man's cheeks, but he remained silent.

"Did you know Lord Wallace was planning to employ Jane to instruct one of his daughters?"

"Wallace?" What looked like a habitual kind of fury hardened the other man's eyes. "No. She didn't tell me. Good God, what was she thinking?"

"To deal with someone who has made himself such a public enemy of the Prince, you mean?"

"Yes!"

"Perhaps she didn't care."

"Obviously."

"Any chance she was romantically involved with another man?"

Ambrose let his hand drop, his jaw tightening. "You can't be serious. What are you suggesting now?"

The playwright was either oblivious to his wife's friendship with Liam Maxwell, or very good at hiding uncomfortable truths he didn't want known. Rather than answer, Sebastian said, "A day or two before she was killed, your wife was raped. Did you know?"

Ambrose stared at him. "No."

"She didn't say anything to you about it?"

"Good Lord, no."

"It wasn't you by any chance, was it?"

Ambrose took a hasty step forward, his hands curling into fists. "I should call you out for that."

"I wouldn't advise it," said Sebastian dryly.

"Get out. Get out of my house. Now."

Sebastian inclined his head and turned toward the door. But he paused to glance back and say, "One more thing: You told me you were here on Thursday afternoon. But I don't recall your saying where you were that evening."

Ambrose stayed where he was, his breath coming in hard, angry pants. "I was still here, damn you."

"In your library working on your libretto?"

"Yes!"

"Alone?"

"Of course."

In a household such as this, without a butler or footmen, the door was typically answered by a housemaid with numerous other duties, which meant that Ambrose could easily have left the house and come back hours later without any of the servants knowing.

Sebastian said, "I'm curious as to why you led me to believe Jane's family was dead when her brother Christian Somerset is still very much alive."

"Why do you think? For the same reason I objected to her visit to Princess Caroline."

"Yes, of course. And how did you learn of that visit, by the way?"

"Jane mentioned it to me."

"On the steps of the Opera?"

Ambrose hesitated a moment too long, then said, "Yes."

"Without also mentioning why she went?"

"I told her I didn't want to know."

"Oh? Why is that?"

Ambrose gave a short, bitter laugh. "You should know as well as anyone the swirl of intrigue that surrounds Caroline."

"Are you suggesting Jane was involved in that?"

"I don't know and, frankly, I don't care to know. If you think it so important, I suggest you ask the Princess yourself."

"I intend to," said Sebastian.

Ambrose simply stared back at him, his jaw set hard and his eyes now hooded.

Chapter 20

Wrapped in a warm carriage robe and with a hot brick at her feet, Hero crossed the frozen city in a horse-drawn sleigh. The farther east she traveled, the more wretched were the snow-filled lanes and courts, the more desperate the bleak eyes raised to watch her pass. This part of the city had long been a crumbling, overcrowded morass of grinding, soul-destroying poverty and aching want. Now, after endless paralyzing weeks of cold, life there was becoming unbearably grim. Near St. Giles, a water main had broken during the night, flooding the street with what had become a thick sheet of ice. Those few lucky children with shoes were running and sliding across the frozen surface, arms windmilling, voices shrieking with laughter. But their mothers stood watching solemnly, faces tight with fear, for a broken main meant no water in addition to no food and no heat.

Jenny Sanborn, the cooper's wife Hero was coming to see, lived at the end of a noisome alley in a miserable one-room hovel that looked as if it had been built as a lean-to shed for animals. When they drew up before the shed's rough door, Hero could hear the muffled sounds of a woman weeping within. Exchanging a quick glance with her coachman,

Hero looped the handle of her food basket over one arm and went to knock on the door.

The door was opened by a skinny, ragged girl of about six whom Hero remembered from the other night. "Hullo," said Hero, crouching down until she was level with the child. "You're Sarah, aren't you? I've brought your mum a present." Then Hero looked beyond the little girl to where the mother, Jenny Sanborn, lay curled up in a ball on the room's only pallet.

The woman was as thin as a fence board, with limp fair hair and a face swollen and blotched with tears. She was probably no more than thirty, although she looked fifty or more. Her newborn babe lay beside her, and Hero didn't need more than a swift glance to tell her the child was dead.

"When?" Hero asked.

The woman dragged in a ragged breath that shuddered her thin chest. "Last night."

Hero rose slowly to her feet, her throat so tight she couldn't seem to force out any words.

"Is all that food for us?" asked the little girl, her eyes round.

"Sarah—," began her mother.

"It is, yes," said Hero, summoning up a smile that trembled a bit around the edges as she handed the basket to the girl. "And my coachman's got a bag of coal for you, as well."

"Gor," breathed one of the girl's brothers, coming to stand beside her.

"I don't rightly know how to thank you," said Jenny Sanborn, pushing herself up with difficulty. "Your ladyship has already done so much for us. We'd never have made it through this dreadful cold spell without you."

Hero wanted to say, *Please don't thank me. For a sack of coal and a simple basket of food I will never even miss? Do you have any idea how guilty I feel, knowing that women like me will never be in danger of seeing our husbands snatched off the*

streets and forced to serve in a war that means nothing to them? Knowing I'll never
need to worry about my son growing up to someday suffer the same fate? I should be
here begging your forgiveness—we all should, although no one ever will.

Except of course she could say none of those things. So she said
instead, "This freeze can't last much longer." And it sounded so weak
even to her own ears that she wished she'd said nothing at all.

"You did what you could," Alexi said later that afternoon as she and
Hero walked beside the frozen moat of the Tower of London.

Hero shook her head, her exhalation billowing around her in the
cold air. "It wasn't enough."

"No. But we can only try. One woman, one child at a time."

Hero turned to stare out over the masts of the ships frozen fast in
the river below London Bridge. "This blasted war. Sometimes I think it
will never end. For how many years can the nations of Europe continue
fighting each other? Some of the men dying today must be the grand-
sons of those who fell two decades ago."

"What a horrid thought."

"It is, isn't it?"

They walked on in silence, each lost in her own thoughts, the air
heavy with the smell of woodsmoke from the fires lit in an attempt to
keep the Tower's lions and other exotic animals alive. The surrounding
streets were nearly deserted, the battlements of the castle walls stark
and empty against the heavy white sky. But Hero was becoming increasingly aware of a creeping feeling of unease that she finally realized
came from a sense of being stared at—although when she looked around
she could see no one.

"What is it?" Alexi asked when Hero looked behind her for the
third or fourth time.

"I don't know. I have the oddest sensation—as if someone were watching me."

Alexi let her gaze drift over the rows of ancient houses pressing in on the castle. "I don't see anyone."

"Nor do I. I'm probably being fanciful."

"*You?* That I find impossible to believe."

Hero smiled.

"How is your article coming?" asked Alexi.

"Honestly, I've barely given it a thought."

Alexi squinted up at the heavy clouds pressing down on the city. "Are you still interested in interviewing the wives of men who've been impressed?"

Hero glanced over at her. "I am, yes. You know of another woman?"

The Frenchwoman nodded. "A young girl named Amy Hatcher. She's originally from Devon, but after her baby was born she came up to London, hoping to trace her husband. If you want to talk to her, we'll need to hurry."

"Why? Is she ill?"

Alexi's lips flattened into a hard line. "She's in Newgate. She was arrested before Christmas trying to steal a ham and is scheduled to hang on Tuesday."

Sebastian arrived back at Brook Street to find Hero seated at his desk and calmly cleaning the brass-mounted flintlock pistol given to her years before by her father. It was a small weapon of a type known as a "muff gun," designed to be carried concealed in a woman's fur muff.

"Is this routine maintenance?" he asked, watching her. "Or did you shoot someone?"

Hero carefully replaced the barrel and locked it in place. "I think someone might be following me. I don't know for certain because I didn't see them. But under the circumstances I thought it best not to take any chances."

Sebastian tried to keep any sign of the raw panic he felt flare within him from showing on his face. "I'll assign two of the footmen to—"

"No," she said, setting the pistol aside and wiping her hands.

"But—"

She gave him a long, steady look. "Someone tried to kill you earlier today. Do you intend to take two footmen with you wherever you go from now on?"

He found himself smiling. "Point taken. But you will be careful?"

"I suspect I'll be far more cautious than you," she said, returning his smile.

And he realized that was another point he couldn't argue.

That night, unable to sleep, Hero stood at her bedroom window as a fresh fall of snow hurtled down from out of a heavy white sky. She thought it must be near dawn, although it had been hours since she'd heard the watch's cry. She hoped the old man had retreated to his box for warmth. Either that, or he'd frozen to death.

She clutched her cashmere wrap tighter against the cold radiating off the frosted glass. Frustration and sorrow swirled within her, along with a healthy dose of raw, throbbing anger. She heard the shifting of the mattress behind her, felt Devlin's arms slide around her waist to draw her back against his warm, hard body. He kissed her hair and said simply, "Hero."

She tipped her head back against his shoulder, her throat so tight it hurt. "I've always thought of myself as a fiercely rational being, driven by intellect rather than emotion and sentimentality. But I'm beginning to wonder if perhaps I don't know myself quite as well as I've always believed."

Any other man would assume she was spooked at the thought that someone was following her. But Devlin knew her well. He pressed a kiss against her neck. "Discovering that a babe you fought so hard to save has died anyway would be enough to overset most people."

"But I'm not supposed to be like most people," she said with a wry smile. The smile faded. "Alexi warned me the baby would die, that he was too tiny, too poorly nourished in the womb to survive. But I'd hoped if I could help his mother . . ."

He nuzzled his face against her neck. "I know."

"It's not right, what we do. Kidnapping men and carrying them off as essentially slaves to serve on our warships, all without a thought to the wives and children they leave behind to starve. As if their hopes and dreams—as if their very *lives*—matter not at all. We killed that baby—everyone who has ever kept silent about impressment, who accepts it as just or even an unfortunate necessity. We killed him."

"That's why you're writing this article."

She felt tears sting her eyes. "I fear it won't do any good."

"Not right away, no. But it's a start. If no one criticizes or even questions the wrongs of our society, it will never change."

"Sometimes I wonder if I'm simply tilting at windmills."

"Only sometimes?"

She gave a soft gurgle of laughter and turned in his arms to hug his naked male body close. "You'll catch cold," she said, sliding her splayed hands over the now icy flesh of his back.

"I'm tough."

She lifted her head to meet his gaze. He had the most beautiful eyes, a rich tawny gold, with an animal's ability to see clearly in the dark and over great distances. Strange, feral eyes that had captivated her from the moment she first saw him.

She said, "Make love to me."

Wordlessly he took her hand and drew her to the fire's side. There, in the warm glow from the coals, he cradled her face in his palms. Tenderly he kissed her eyelids, kissed cheeks wet with tears she hadn't even realized she'd let fall. Then his mouth took hers, gentleness giving way to a growing hunger and carnal urgency. She was dimly aware of the shawl slipping from her shoulders as his hands swept over her. She pressed herself against him, one leg coming up to wrap around his thigh.

With a groan, he bore her down before the fire, his body covering hers. Her world filled with firelight gleaming golden over hot sweaty flesh, catching breaths, and an exquisitely tightening spiral of pleasure. It was a desperate affirmation of life in the face of death, of love in the face of selfish indifference and greed.

And afterward, as he cradled her in his arms, she slept.

Sunday, 30 January

The next morning dawned clear and calm but paralyzingly cold.

Hero ate a simple breakfast, then took refuge with Simon beside the fire in the morning room. "Who's the birthday boy?" she cooed, bouncing the baby up and down on her lap.

"Mm-ga-ga-gee," he gurgled, reaching out a hand toward the big black cat that sauntered up to sit tantalizingly just out of the boy's reach.

"Shame on you, Mr. Darcy," said Hero as the cat flicked his magnificent tail back and forth, his slitted green eyes on the child. "You are a heartless tease."

"Mm-ga-ga-gee," said Simon again.

Hero stared at the cat as enlightenment dawned. "Good heavens. Mr. Darcy. He's 'Mm-ga-ga-gee'?"

"Mm-ga-ga-gee," agreed the boy, squirming now to get down.

"One year old and *beyond* brilliant," said Devlin, joining her with a cup of tea in his hand and the look of a man whose morning ablutions had been less than satisfactory. "Calhoun tells me the water pipes to the house have frozen. I suppose we should be thankful they didn't break."

"Not yet." Hero set Simon on his feet and watched the boy totter over to the cat. "According to the footmen who went out this morning to fetch water, the river has frozen so solid that some brave souls are venturing out onto the ice and the bridges are packed with people watching them. Unfortunately, they told this tale within the hearing of the scullery maid, who immediately fell into hysterics, convinced it's never going to warm up and we're all going to die."

"Lovely," said Devlin, his eyes narrowing as Simon plopped down beside the cat. Mr. Darcy stretched to his feet and butted his head against the baby's hand with an uncharacteristically loud purr.

Mr. Darcy virtually never purred.

Hero's gaze met Devlin's, and they both laughed.

She watched as he set aside his teacup and pushed to his feet. She said, "You're going to ask the Princess of Wales about Jane?"

"I am." Swooping down, he swung his squealing, laughing son high in the air. "Hopefully with the better part of the city's population ogling the river, there will be no one to see me put myself beyond the pale by paying a visit to Her Ostracized Highness."

Chapter 21

*A*new bank of heavy white clouds was beginning to roll in over the city as Sebastian drove the sleigh out to Connaught House, the current residence of the Prince of Wales's estranged wife.

She'd been born Caroline of Brunswick, daughter of the late Duke of Brunswick—an enlightened Continental ruler who was also a famous and respected German general—and his somewhat silly wife, Princess Augusta, sister of Britain's own George III. At the age of twenty-seven, Caroline had been sent to England to marry her first cousin, whom she had never seen.

Things had gone badly from the very beginning.

In a move that was surely deliberately calculated to humiliate his bride, the Prince had sent his mistress, Lady Jersey, to meet Caroline's ship. He'd further shown his contempt for his new wife by taking Lady Jersey along on their honeymoon and forcing the Princess to accept his mistress as her Lady of the Bedchamber. Simple, good-natured Caroline—homesick and lonely and not particularly wise—was no match for the exquisite, brilliant, and thoroughly nasty Lady Jersey. Sebastian thought it a tribute to Caroline's fortitude that she'd not only survived her husband's mistreatment but managed to win the love and support of the British people. Of course, the more they loved Caroline, the more the people hated the Prince of Wales. It became one more thing her royal husband held against her.

They had lived apart now for seventeen years. At first the Prince had allowed Caroline to see her daughter once a day. Then he'd restricted their visits to once a week, then once a fortnight, then every three weeks. Frequently the visits were suspended entirely for months at a time, while correspondence between mother and daughter was strictly forbidden. Sebastian suspected it was one of the main reasons Princess Charlotte's tutors, servants, and ladies were always being sacked— because they were suspected of smuggling letters between the lonely young Princess and her mother.

Caroline's newest residence, Connaught House, lay on the northern side of Bayswater Road, overlooking the ancient hanging site of Tyburn and the rolling expanse of Hyde Park beyond that. "Gor," said Tom, his face tight and solemn as he stared at the former location of the infamous scaffold. "I wouldn't want t' look out me window every mornin' 'n' see that."

Sebastian handed his tiger the reins and dropped to the ground. "Perhaps princesses aren't as intimidated by gallows as the rest of us." Although even as he said it, it occurred to Sebastian that this particular princess probably had more reason to fear than most. If the Prince of Wales—with Jarvis's assistance—could have connived it, Caroline would have been dead long ago.

Given Sebastian's connections to Jarvis, he wouldn't have been surprised if she had refused to receive him. But after a few minutes' wait, he was shown up to a small, light-filled room with a row of tall windows overlooking a snowy rear garden. Caroline—wearing a plain old fustian gown and a decidedly ratty mobcap—stood at a low table near the windows and was busy sculpting a man's head out of clay.

"I hope you don't mind if I keep vorking," she said, grinning as she held up hands stained with clay. Despite being the descendant and niece of British kings and a resident of England herself for almost nineteen years, Caroline's German accent was still quite heavy.

"Your Royal Highness." Sebastian executed a low, courtly bow. "Thank you for agreeing to see me."

She gave a loud, hearty laugh. "If you knew how few visitors I receive these days, you vould not be as surprised as you appear."

Sebastian found himself smiling. There was nothing arrogant, pretentious, subtle, or subdued about Caroline. She had never been a beauty, although most people acknowledged that in her youth she was pretty, with a fresh complexion, deep-set blue eyes, and fine fair hair. But the intervening years had coarsened her figure and ground down her once sunny, effervescent good humor beneath the endless pressures of heartache, loneliness, boredom, frustration, and fear. Prinny had twice tried to divorce her by unsuccessfully charging her with adultery—the penalty for which would have been death.

Now her eyes narrowed as she looked Sebastian over with a frankly assessing and openly curious gaze. "Vhy are you here?"

His answer was as blunt as her question. "Jane Ambrose was found dead on Thursday, Your Highness. All indications are that she was killed, but because she was Princess Charlotte's piano instructor, the palace will not allow her death to be investigated."

"It vas murder? *Mein* God," whispered Caroline, her hands stilling on the bust. "Poor Jane."

"Did you know her well?"

"Yes, of course. I've known Jane for years." Caroline herself had a reputation for playing the piano extraordinarily well. In fact, when she was younger, in Germany, she'd studied with a number of famous masters, practicing faithfully four and more hours a day. Now her eyebrows drew together in a troubled frown. "Vhy vill the palace not allow an investigation?"

"Ostensibly their motive is to prevent any hint of scandal from touching the Princess. But it's also possible they're hiding something."

Caroline was silent for a moment, her attention seemingly all for her sculpture again. She might have been an unexpectedly simple woman, but she was not stupid. And she'd been dealing with Prinny's plots, machinations, lies, and schemes for the better part of two decades. Her gaze still on her work, she said slowly, "You've heard that fat pig of a husband of mine tricked Charlotte into agreeing to marry Orange?"

"I heard the Regent had pressured her."

"Oh, he more than pressured her. He *tricked* her. He likes to say he promised never to try to force her into a distasteful marriage. But vhat do you call it when a father shouts at his daughter, calling her an obstinate, silly fool vhile threating to shut her up for life if she doesn't marry?"

"Would he do that to her?"

"Of course he would do it. He cares for no one but himself—and that nasty mother of his, I suppose," she added as an afterthought.

When Sebastian refrained from comment, she said, "Last December he made Charlotte agree to meet Orange at a dinner party at Carlton House and then pushed her into promising she'd give him an answer about the match that very evening." Her nostrils flared with indignation. "Who does that?"

"So what happened?"

"Charlotte saw Orange for two hours—two hours!—at a dinner attended by a number of others including Liverpool and his vife. And then, vith everyone still there, Vales pulls her aside and says, 'Vell, vhat do you think of him?'"

"What did she think?"

"How could she know, after such a short time as that—and her just seventeen years old? She vas still considering how to form her answer vhen Prinny says, 'Vhat? He vill not do?' And my poor girl, she says, 'I don't say that. I like his manner—from vhat I have seen.'" Caroline shook her head, the muscles in her cheeks bunching as she thrust her

jaw forward in disgust. "Now, does that sound to you as if she vas agreeing to the match? Of course not. But Vales, he's a clever one. He throws
his arms around the child and exclaims, 'You make me the happiest person in the vorld!' Poor Charlotte is still stuttering, trying to tell him she
meant no such thing, vhen that nasty, sly bastard calls over Liverpool
and announces that she has agreed! And then he brings over Orange
himself, joins their hands, and gives the couple his blessing."

Sebastian had no difficulty imagining the scene. It was just the sort
of dishonest manipulation for which Prinny was famous.

Caroline made a decidedly ungenteel noise. "Needless to say, Charlotte is in a rage vith him. But it's done, isn't it? She can't back out after
that—not vith her father telling the Prime Minister and Orange himself
that she's agreed. And to make matters vorse, not twenty-four hours
later she discovers that Orange intends to require her to leave England
and live in Holland. Prinny was aware of the scheme all along, of course,
but vas careful not to let her know."

Sebastian stared at her. "Live abroad? The heiress presumptive to
the throne?"

Caroline nodded. "It's the real reason the Prince vants this particular
marriage for her—to get Charlotte out of the country." Her breathing
had become agitated, her full, heavy breasts heaving above the shockingly low-cut bodice of her gown. "Part of it is because she's so much
more popular than he and he's jealous. But it's also because he thinks
that vith Charlotte gone, I vill leave, too, so that he vill finally be able to
push through his divorce. Then he vill marry again and have a son—a
new heir to the throne who vill dispossess my daughter." She gave a derisive snort. "Not that he has much chance of that. He could barely con-
summate our marriage nineteen years ago. And look at him now!"

It had long been whispered that Prinny's sexual performance on his
wedding night had been far from satisfactory and that Caroline had
handled her bridegroom's bruised *amour propre* with all the sensitivity to
be expected of a woman who'd just been forced to sit down to her wed-

ding feast in the company of her husband's beautiful, waspish mistress. Prinny had never been able to bear being humiliated, and he held his grudges forever.

"That fat old goat vill never be able to sire a son," Caroline was saying, "however much Jarvis might vish it." She cast Sebastian a sideways glance that told him she wasn't nearly as simple as she liked to appear. "You vant to know who killed poor Jane, you talk to Jarvis. He's behind everything that happens in this country—especially if it's underhanded and dirty."

Sebastian said, "Why would Jarvis kill Jane Ambrose?"

"Vhy don't you ask him?"

"I did, actually. He denies having anything to do with it."

"Ach." She waved one plump, clay-covered hand through the air in a dismissive gesture. "He lies almost as much as the Prince—except, of course, he's better at it."

Sebastian watched Caroline frown down at her sculpture and realized she was executing an extraordinarily skilled likeness of her brother, the current Duke of Brunswick.

He said, "I'm told you recommended Jane Ambrose to Lord Wallace as an instructor for his daughter Elizabeth. Is that true?"

Caroline kept her attention focused on the bust's hairline. "I may have. To be honest, I do not recall."

The evasiveness of the answer was telling. He said, "Did Jane bring a message from Charlotte when she came to see you last week?"

"Huh. Vhat kind of man not only prevents his daughter from seeing her mother but refuses to allow them even to correspond with each other? Hmm? Vhat kind of man?" When Sebastian kept silent, she said, "But you're wrong about Jane. Charlotte never asked her to carry letters."

"But she did come here?"

"Oh, yes—to visit vith me. Is that so impossible for you to believe?"

"No, Your Highness. But it doesn't explain why you think Jarvis might be behind her death."

Caroline rolled one round shoulder in a dismissive shrug. "Perhaps I'm wrong."

It was obvious that she would tell him no more. And one did not press the Princess of Wales, even if she was banished from court.

But it occurred to Sebastian as he bowed himself out that, however uninhibited, unsophisticated, or careless of her dress Caroline might be, she was still very much a princess born and bred, the future queen of England, and mother of the heiress presumptive to the throne. She'd known exactly what she was doing when she'd agreed to speak to Sebastian, and she had told him the sordid tale of Charlotte's betrothal for a reason.

She was leaving it up to Sebastian to discover for himself what that reason was.

Chapter 22

Sebastian came out of Connaught House's snow-blanketed front gardens to find his tiger walking the chestnuts as far from the site of the old execution scaffold as he could get and still be within hailing distance.

At the sight of Sebastian, the boy swung the sleigh around with a swish that sent up an arc of fine snow crystals. He was just reining in before the house when Sebastian spotted Signor Valentino Vescovi's lanky figure coming through the Tyburn turnpike to stride purposefully toward Princess Caroline's gate.

"Hang on a minute," Sebastian told Tom, and shifted to intercept the harpist.

The Italian had his head down, his attention all for the task of minding his footing on the slippery footpath. He remained utterly oblivious to Sebastian's presence until he said cheerfully, "Good morning."

The harpist's head jerked up, one hand flashing out to grab the railing of the garden's iron fence as his feet slid sideways in opposite directions. "*Santo cielo!* You startled me."

Sebastian thought the man looked more frightened than startled, but all he said was "You're Vescovi, aren't you? I heard you play at one of Lady Farningham's musical evenings last September. I'm Devlin."

Vescovi licked his lower lip. "If this is about *Signora* Ambrose, your wife has already spoken to me. Yesterday."

"I know." Sebastian threw a significant glance toward Caroline's tall stuccoed house. "What are you doing here?"

Vescovi swallowed. "Teaching the Princess of Wales to play the harp?" The excuse might have sounded more believable if the rising pitch of his voice hadn't turned what should have been a statement into a question.

"Indeed?" said Sebastian.

"She is very musical, you know."

"As is her daughter."

The Italian nodded vigorously. "Yes, yes."

"How convenient that mother and daughter share the same instructors. It must make it so much easier for them to pass letters back and forth with none the wiser."

Vescovi stared at him in silence, his dark eyes watering and the tip of his long, thin nose red from the cold.

Sebastian said, "Do I take it Jane Ambrose also carried messages for Princess Charlotte?"

Vescovi blew out a harsh breath and looked unexpectedly troubled. "Not to my knowledge, no."

"And would you know?"

"I think so, yes."

"So why was Jane here last week, visiting Caroline?"

"Was she? I've no notion." He tried to sidle around Sebastian toward the garden gate but had to draw up again when Sebastian shifted to cut him off.

Sebastian said, "Tell me what happened last week between Jane Ambrose and the Dutch courtier Peter van der Pals."

He thought the Italian might try to deny all knowledge of the incident. Instead he frowned and said, "Why?"

"Because there's a good possibility it may have something to do with Jane's death. Was she in love with him?"

"Jane? Of course not. I suppose she was amused by him at first. He's a clever, witty young man, and he made her laugh. But if he believed her to be captivated by him, he was mistaken. She was shocked when he tried to coax her into spying on Charlotte."

"How do you know this? Did she tell you?"

The harpist's thin, bony body swayed from side to side as he shifted his feet in the snow. "It's . . . complicated."

"Court intrigues generally are," said Sebastian.

Vescovi nodded and sighed. "Jane Ambrose was a talented, good-hearted woman. But she was too naive, too trusting to survive at court. She made the mistake of telling one of the Princess's subgovernesses about the entire incident with van der Pals."

"You mean Miss Ella Kinsworth?"

"Yes."

"And Ella Kinsworth told you?"

"*Signorina* Kinsworth? Ah, no. That woman is as determinedly upright and fiercely loyal as *Signora* Ambrose. But they weren't as careful as they should have been. They were overheard."

"By you?"

Vescovi gave a sharp shake of his head. "Me? No. By Lady Arabella."

"Who the blazes is Lady Arabella?"

"The Duchess of Leeds's daughter."

"And this Lady Arabella told you about the conversation between the two women?"

"Yes."

"Why?"

Vescovi looked confused. "Pardon?"

"Why would Lady Arabella pass this information on to you?"

"Because I am teaching her Italian."

Sebastian studied the harpist's thin, bony face. "That doesn't explain why she would think you'd be interested."

Vescovi brought up one hand to scratch his forehead with the seam of his thick woolen mitten. "She knew I'd be interested because in addition to everything else, Jane told Miss Kinsworth that Peter van der Pals said I spy for Caroline."

"Why would van der Pals tell her that?"

"Because Jane was so shocked by what he was proposing that he laughed at her. Called her a fool and told her everyone at Warwick House spies for someone." Vescovi scowled. "He illustrated that point with me."

"So whom does Ella Kinsworth spy for?"

Vescovi shrugged one shoulder. "The Regent assumes she is his creature, but she's not. Her loyalty is to Charlotte."

"As yours is to Caroline?"

Vescovi's eyes narrowed. "I serve both Princesses."

"And if their interests don't align? Who do you serve then?"

Vescovi remained silent.

Sebastian said, "You do realize you've just admitted you had a motive to kill Jane Ambrose."

The Italian's jaw sagged. "Me? What? But . . . how?"

"She knew you spy for the Princess of Wales, and she told Charlotte's subgoverness."

"But I didn't hold that against her!"

"No? You resented it enough to have words with her about it. I assume that was the subject of your quarrel by the canal in the park?"

Vescovi was breathing hard, his chest jerking with his agitation. "I simply wished to make certain she understood the situation."

"And what is the situation?"

"I pass letters between the Princesses and help keep Her Highness informed about her daughter. That is all. All!"

"You explained this to Jane Ambrose?"

"I did, yes. So you see, I had no reason to kill her." Vescovi stared back at him owlishly. "None."

"Then you should have no difficulty in telling me where you were Thursday afternoon and evening."

Vescovi focused his attention on neatening the bright red scarf he wore wrapped around his neck.

"Signor?" prompted Sebastian.

The Italian carefully aligned the ends of his scarf. "I was in my room at the Percy Arms in Red Lion Square. I—I was unwell that day."

"I can check on that, you know."

"Sicuro," said the harpist with solemn dignity.

But Sebastian noticed his hands were now shaking so badly that he gave up trying to arrange his scarf.

As they drove away from Connaught House, Sebastian said to his tiger, "Valentino Vescovi claims he was in his room at the Percy Arms on Red Lion Square all afternoon and evening last Thursday. After you take care of the horses, why don't you go around there and see if you can find someone to verify that?"

Tom sat up noticeably straighter, his eyes shining with pride. "Aye, m'lord."

"So van der Pals was the *'figlio di puttana'* who told Jane some 'unflattering truths' about Valentino Vescovi," said Hero as she and Devlin joined the crowds walking across Blackfriars Bridge to stare down at the frozen Thames.

"Apparently." Devlin paused, his gaze on the snow-covered river below. Most of the spectators were content to watch from the safety of the bridge. But a few of the braver—or more foolhardy—were venturing out onto the ice itself, laughing and calling to others to join them.

"What a hideous hotbed of spying and backstabbing that household is. Poor Princess Charlotte. Imagine growing up alone in such an environment."

"Poor Charlotte, indeed."

Hero glanced over at him. "Do you believe Caroline's tale? That Prinny tricked his daughter into agreeing to this vile betrothal?"

"It sounds like him, doesn't it?"

"It does, rather." She was silent for a moment. "Just when you think you can't despise Prinny any more, you learn one more disgusting detail about his treatment of his wife and daughter."

"When a prince pays people to stand up in court and swear to a vile collection of lies about his own wife, I suspect there is little he wouldn't do."

Out on the ice, a bagpipe player began to play a jig, and a laugh went up along the bridge as a man near him began to dance. Hero said, "How deeply involved in this tangled mess do you think Jane Ambrose was?"

Devlin shook his head. "I'm not sure. But her visit to Caroline last week is more than a bit suggestive. First Caroline, then Lord Wallace."

Hero watched an acrobat turning handstands in the middle of the river. "I wonder what else my friend Miss Kinsworth didn't tell me."

"If she's protecting Charlotte, it could be a great deal."

Chapter 23

 $\mathcal{P}$ rincess Charlotte's noble governess, the Dowager Duchess of Leeds, typically attended her charge between the hours of two and five. The exception was on Sundays, when Her Grace put in an appearance between noon and three—which was how she came to be crossing the entrance hall when Hero arrived at Warwick House that afternoon.

"Ah, dear Lady Devlin," said the Duchess, intercepting her with a tight smile. "What a pleasant surprise. Unfortunately, Princess Charlotte is at present indisposed, so that neither she nor Miss Kinsworth will be able to come down. But do say you'll join Arabella and me for tea?"

"That would be lovely, thank you," said Hero with an equally false smile as she allowed herself to be shepherded into the dilapidated drawing room that lay just off the entrance.

"Have you met my daughter? Lady Arabella Osborne."

"Lady Devlin." The slender young girl rising from the room's threadbare silk settee was so lovely it was hard not to stare. Just sixteen years old, she had flawless alabaster skin, a perfect nose, and a trembling pink rosebud of a mouth that seemed to smile shyly. But when Hero met her eyes, she found them a shrewd, icy gray, as hard and unfeeling as granite.

"I do hope there's nothing seriously wrong with Charlotte," said Hero, taking a lumpy high-backed chair by the fire.

Lady Arabella gave a pretty little frown. "What?"

"Her sudden illness."

"Oh, no, not too serious," said the Duchess, settling beside her daughter and reaching to pour the tea.

Born plain Miss Catherine Anguish, she had begun life as the daughter of a barrister from the middling gentry. She owed the coup of her splendid marriage to her beauty, which in her youth was said to have rivaled her daughter's. Now in her forties, she was still an attractive woman, although tiresome, with a tendency to tell long-winded, boring tales about her own health. She'd also allowed her elevation to the rank of duchess to go to her head, acquiring a well-deserved reputation as an insufferable snob who treated anyone she considered her inferior with ostentatious condescension. And she considered anyone not from a ducal or royal family her inferior.

"Truth be told," said the Duchess, handing Hero a cup, "the child has the constitution of an ox. I, on the other hand, have been most dreadfully plagued all winter by a severe inflammation of the lungs. Why, just yesterday the Regent sent his own dear Dr. Heberden to check on me. 'Your Grace,' he said to me, 'your sufferings would crush the spirit of nearly anyone, yet you bear it all with the fortitude and determination of a saint. A saint!'"

"How . . . admirable," said Hero, resigning herself to an excruciatingly detailed recital of Her Grace's shortness of breath, the pinched nerve in her back, the phantom pains her numerous physicians feared might mean gallbladder problems. Finally, after some ten minutes of this, Hero managed to stem the recitation of ills long enough to turn to young Lady Arabella and say, "I understand you're learning Italian."

"I am, yes," said the girl, carefully settling her teacup into its saucer.

The Duchess beamed. "She is quite the linguist, you know. She was already fluent in French, and she recently learned German, as well."

"German? An unusual choice," said Hero.

"Mmm. The Princess and Miss Kinsworth are both fluent in it, you see, and had taken to conversing in the language so that no one else could understand what they were saying. Unfortunately, as soon as Arabella mastered German, they switched to Italian."

"Cheeky of them," said Hero.

Lady Arabella threw her talkative mother a warning frown that appeared utterly lost on the Duchess. "You've no idea," she continued. "Charlotte is *quite* the little hoyden. Just last week she locked poor Arabella in the water closet for a quarter of an hour and refused to let her out."

"Oh? Why?"

"Why? Well . . . *you know*," she said vaguely. "The girl does that sort of thing all the time, I'm afraid. She shakes hands with men as if she were a man herself, strides about with all the boisterous energy of a general reviewing his troops, and laughs nearly as loudly as her mother. One would think no one had ever taught her how to behave *en princesse*. But believe me, Lady Devlin, I have tried."

"I've no doubt you have," murmured Hero. *Between the hours of two and five—or twelve and three on Sundays.*

"Have I ever! She's horse mad, of course. Gallops all over the place when she's out at Windsor. No one can stop her—not even her grandmother the Queen. The way she sets her horse at any jump she sees, it's a wonder she hasn't broken her neck."

"She must be an excellent horsewoman."

The Duchess sniffed. "I suppose she is. I wouldn't know; I myself do not ride."

Hero took a slow sip of her tea. "I wonder, did you happen to see Jane Ambrose the last time she was here?"

"Oh, no. I don't come during the week until two o'clock, you know."

"Do you have any idea why she died?"

"She slipped on the ice and hit her head, of course."

"Except that she didn't. Not really."

The Duchess met Hero's gaze for one telling moment, then looked away. "I'm afraid I don't know what you're talking about."

Hero raised one eyebrow. "You aren't concerned that her death might have something to do with Princess Charlotte?"

The Duchess froze with her cup raised halfway to her lips. It was left to her precocious daughter to give a trill of artificial laughter and say, "Mercy, no. Whatever gave you such a notion?"

"Mainly Peter van der Pals's recent attempts to convince Jane to spy on Charlotte for the House of Orange."

Mother and daughter exchanged glances again. Then the Duchess crimped her lips into a tight, supercilious smile. "Dear Lady Devlin, I've no idea who told you such a thing, but I fear they were 'having you on,' as the young gentlemen like to say." She set aside her teacup with an awkward clatter. "Now, do tell me you and Lord Devlin are planning to attend my alfresco breakfast this Thursday. I'm calling it 'A Winter Wonderland in Kensington Gardens,' and it promises to be something quite out of the ordinary. The Queen herself has promised to put in an appearance, you know."

"We hope to be there, yes," said Hero, who had intended to decline the invitation due to her state of mourning for her mother. Now she wasn't so sure.

"Lovely," said Her Grace.

Hero set aside her own cup and rose to her feet. "The weather should make it . . . interesting."

The Duchess gave another of her brittle smiles. "I think we can all contrive to keep warm. The snow will make it unique, don't you agree? Like our own exclusive Frost Fair."

"Quite," agreed Hero, thinking Lady Leeds's inflammation of the lungs obviously wasn't severe enough to keep her from braving the elements in her quest to give a party that would be the talk of the *ton*.

"I did see something recently that made me wonder about Mrs. Ambrose," said young Lady Arabella, walking with Hero to the door.

"Oh?" said Hero. "What was that?"

"I was here earlier than Mama one day and happened to glance out the window just as Mrs. Ambrose was letting herself out the gate. There was a carriage waiting for her in the lane. I thought it odd enough that I paused to watch, which is how I happened to see a gentleman step forward just as she was closing the gate behind her. They spoke for a moment. Then he helped her into the carriage and climbed in after her."

"When was this?"

"Two weeks ago last Thursday."

"Do you remember anything about the carriage?" asked Hero.

"It was a nobleman's barouche. I know because I saw the crest on the door—a gold chevron against an azure background, with a rampant lion below and two castles above." The girl gave a slow, knowing smile that came perilously close to being a smirk. "Perhaps you're familiar with it?"

"Yes," said Hero, who had grown up with the Jarvis coat of arms. "I believe I am."

Chapter 24

"'Then the Lord put forth his hand and touched my mouth. And the Lord said unto me, Behold, I have put my words in thy mouth.'"

Jarvis ostentatiously bowed his head as the glorious Stuart-era poetry of the King James Bible echoed around the soaring interior of the sixteenth-century chapel. He'd never been a particularly devout man, but he had a healthy appreciation for the role religion played in maintaining order and the hierarchy of being. And so he was careful to be seen attending services every Sunday, for it was important that members of the ruling class set a good example for the ignorant masses below them.

He often worshipped here, at the Chapel Royal in St. James's Palace, both because its schedule was set to accommodate the late-rising habits of His Highness the Prince Regent and because he appreciated the exclusivity of its congregation. Attendance today was sparse, owing no doubt to the severity of the weather. But one of the few worshippers present was that abrasive Whig politician Phineas Wallace. And because Jarvis knew it would irritate the man, he found himself faintly smiling as the reading continued.

"'See, I have this day set thee over the nations and over the kingdoms,
to root out, and to pull down,
to destroy, and to throw down,
to build, and to plant.'"

Unlike Jarvis, Phineas Wallace was not known for his regular church attendance. But the fiery Whig orator had been trying without success to arrange a meeting with Jarvis for days. And so Jarvis was not surprised when the Baron fell into step beside him as they left the chapel at the end of services.

"I take it you wished to speak to me?" Jarvis remarked pleasantly.

"I know about your scheme," said Wallace, his voice pitched low.

Jarvis paused to extract his snuffbox from his pocket and flip it open. "I never imagined that you did not."

Wallace threw a quick glance around and leaned in closer. "It's madness, all of it. Why tie Britain to the Dutch in a way that will obligate us to come to their defense? The people of this land are on their knees after more than two decades of war; they need peace and prosperity, not more war. The cost of defending the Netherlands would break us in every way imaginable. Break us!"

Jarvis lifted a pinch of snuff to one nostril and smiled. "The Bourbons will not move against the House of Orange."

Wallace gave a harsh, breathy laugh. "You genuinely believe that the French will meekly accept the Bourbons back on the throne? After twenty-five years of *liberté, égalité,* and *fraternité?*"

"After twenty-five years of *liberté, égalité,* and *fraternité,* there are scarcely enough Frenchmen left alive to sing *'La Marseillaise,'* let alone object to anyone we should choose to place at their head."

"It won't always be so."

Jarvis closed his snuffbox with a snap and stepped out onto the snowy flagway. "Then when that day comes we shall have our dear allies the Dutch as a bulwark against a resurgent republican France."

Wallace kept pace with him. "This isn't actually about the Dutch or even the French, is it? It's about Prinny's bloody crusade to rid himself of his wife. He thinks that with Bonaparte defeated and Charlotte forced to live most of the year in the Netherlands, Caroline will leave England for the Continent, and then he'll finally be able to push through a divorce."

"Do you blame him?"

Wallace's thin nose quivered with his disdain. "She is his lawfully wedded wife and has borne nothing but insult and abuse from him since she first landed on our shores."

"And you think that excuses her behavior, do you? What of the opprobrium he has borne as a result of her conduct?"

"Oh, please. Everyone with any sense knows he paid that Douglas woman to stand up and swear she saw the Princess give birth to an illegitimate son."

Jarvis calmly slipped his snuffbox back into his pocket. "Are you so certain she did not?"

"When three different physicians who treated her during that period, her dresser, and the chambermaid who changes her sheets all swear it never happened? When the friends who saw her every week laugh at the possibility? When the Prince is now paying Lady Douglas a tidy pension for life? Don't be ridiculous."

Jarvis gave a negligent shrug. "Yet many people do believe it. In the end, that's all that counts."

"And the truth?"

"The truth has nothing to do with it."

Wallace shook his head, his jaw set hard. "Charlotte knows of her father's intentions. She will never allow herself to be forced to leave the country. She has been warned of the consequences to both her mother and her own position as heiress presumptive to the throne. And because she knows her father and the way he lies and feigns affection to get what he wants, she will insist that safeguards are written into the marriage contract before she signs it."

"She'll sign. She's already agreed to the betrothal; these clever little machinations of yours are all too late."

"It won't be too late until the vows are said."

"Perhaps. But they will be said. Make no mistake about that."

"Not if I can help it," said Wallace curtly. "Good day to you, sir."

Jarvis smiled faintly as Wallace strode angrily away up St. James's Street.

He was still smiling when his daughter, Hero, came to stand beside him.

"I thought I'd find you here," she said.

"Oh?" They turned together to walk down Cleveland Row. "Do I take it from your scowl that you've learned something? Something you believe does not cast me in what you consider a flattering light?"

"You sent one of your men in a carriage to pick up Jane Ambrose as she was leaving Warwick House exactly two weeks before she was killed. Why was that?"

"And if I told you the woman was spying on Charlotte for me?"

"I wouldn't believe you. Not unless you were forcing her to do so against her will." When Jarvis remained silent, she said, "So were you?"

He kept his gaze fixed straight ahead.

Hero's nostrils flared on a quick intake of air. "I would think you have enough spies around the Princess—including a certain very beautiful duke's daughter with a gift for languages and the lethal instincts of a barracuda."

"One can never have too many informants."

"Perhaps not. Especially when you're plotting to maneuver Princess Charlotte out of the country so that the Regent can replace Caroline with a new wife and beget a new heir."

"Now, wherever did you hear that?"

"From Caroline."

"Really? Interesting."

"She's no fool."

"That's debatable."

"She says Prinny was virtually impotent nineteen years ago—which is quite believable given the rumors one hears about his current so-called mistresses."

When Jarvis remained silent, she said, "If what she says is true, the chances of the Prince producing a male heir at this point are decidedly slim."

"Slim, perhaps, but not impossible."

"What's wrong with Charlotte? She's far more stable, responsible, and just plain likable than her father. And the people love her—they cheer her every time they see her."

"She is a woman."

"So was Queen Elizabeth."

"Queen Elizabeth lived in a far different age."

"Are you suggesting the Elizabethan era was more enlightened than our own? Or simply less challenging?"

Jarvis drew up and turned to face her. "The last thing the nineteenth century needs is a woman on the British throne—especially one who believes in Catholic emancipation and Irish independence."

"Ah. So young Charlotte actually is a Whig, is she?"

"Fervently so. Her becoming queen would be an unmitigated disaster."

"And so you're marrying this innocent eighteen-year-old to a foreign prince with a known preference for handsome courtiers? How can you do that to the poor girl?"

"I'm not interested in what's best for Charlotte. My concern is what is best for Britain."

Hero studied him through narrowed eyes. "Why would someone kill Jane Ambrose?"

"I've no idea."

He was aware of Hero's gaze still hard upon him. "I don't believe you," she said.

At that, Jarvis laughed out loud and looped his arm through hers. But all he said was "So are you planning to bring your son to see your grandmother this afternoon? I've no doubt she'll complain that he's interrupting her nap and fatiguing her in every way known to man, but I doubt she'll live to see many more of his birthdays. . . ."

Chapter 25

That evening Alistair James St. Cyr, the Fifth Earl of Hendon and the man known to the world as Sebastian's father, paid a visit to Brook Street.

He came to wish young Simon a happy birthday and to present the boy with a mechanical turtle, which the child adored. Afterward, Sebastian set up the chessboard on a table by the library fire and the two men sipped fine brandy while an icy wind howled around the house. There'd been a time not so long ago when Sebastian had believed the breach between them would never be healed. But things were easier these days. Not exactly the way they had been before, but easier.

It didn't take Sebastian long to realize that the Earl's mind was not on his game. After Hendon lost first a rook, then his queen in careless moves, Sebastian said, "Somehow I don't think you came here simply to see Simon and play a game of chess."

The Earl drew his pipe from his pocket and leaned back in his chair as he began to fill the bowl. He was a big man, with thinning white hair and a heavy-featured, jowly face. Lately he'd begun to shrink as his shoulders rounded. But as Chancellor of the Exchequer he was still a force to be reckoned with in the government. Like Jarvis, he was a strong Tory. He was also one of the few men in London sometimes willing to stand up to the King's powerful cousin.

"Stephanie came to visit me yesterday," said the Earl, tamping down the tobacco with his thumb.

Sebastian took a long, slow swallow of his brandy and felt it burn all the way down. Stephanie was one of Hendon's two grandchildren by his firstborn child, Amanda. The nineteen-year-old's marriage the previous September to the handsome, dissolute, and deadly Viscount Ashworth had troubled everyone who had the girl's best interests at heart. "And?"

Hendon sighed. "Officially her child is due in June. But anyone who sees her must surely know she'll be lucky to make it to March."

"She'll hardly be the first."

"True." Hendon bit down on the stem of his pipe and thrust up from his seat to reach for a spill. He sucked on the pipe, then cast the spill into the fire. "She had a bruise on the side of her face. Claims she did it falling on the ice, but you and I both know better."

The two men were silent for a moment. Sebastian said, "I can try talking to him. But the man doesn't frighten easily. And the truth is, short of killing him, I'm not sure what I can do."

Hendon sighed. "I know. It's just so damnably frustrating. She'll never leave him, no matter what he does to her. She can't. You know the law— if she did, she'd have to leave the child with its father."

"Yes."

Hendon sank back into his chair. He stared at the chessboard for a moment, then struck out with his arm to sweep the pieces from the board with an explosive *"Bloody hell!"*

It was a startlingly uncharacteristic display of frustration and temper. He looked at the scattered pieces sheepishly. "I beg your pardon."

"It's quite all right."

Hendon rubbed a big blunt-fingered hand down over his face. "I hear you've involved yourself in the death of this pianist."

"Yes," said Sebastian.

Hendon had spent the last three years complaining about his son's participation in murder investigations. But now he simply shook his head and said, "It's troublesome."

Sebastian rose with the Earl's empty glass and went to refill it. "Why? What do you know?"

The Earl's jaw tightened. "You've heard of the Orange alliance Jarvis and the Prince are pushing?"

"I have. Are you suggesting it could have something to do with Jane Ambrose's death?"

"I don't know what I'm suggesting. But she is the niece of Richard Sheridan."

Sebastian paused with the brandy carafe suspended above the Earl's glass and swung around to look at him. "She is?"

Richard Sheridan was best known as a brilliant playwright and poet, and the former owner and manager of both Covent Garden Theater and Drury Lane. But he was also until recently a longtime member of Parliament and a fiercely vocal reform-minded Whig. Although no longer in office, he had not been silent about his opposition to the idea of an alliance with the House of Orange. And along with Whigs like Henry Brougham and Lord Wallace, he was a well-known ally of the Princess of Wales in her struggles against the Regent.

"By marriage at any rate," Hendon was saying. "His first wife was one of Thomas Linley's daughters, as was Jane Ambrose's mother." Thomas Linley had been a famous tenor, music teacher, and composer whose numerous musical children were legendary.

Sebastian set the carafe aside. "That throws an entirely different light on everything."

Hendon met his gaze. He was not smiling. "Yes, I rather thought it might."

Chapter 26

Monday, 31 January

At ten o'clock the next morning, Hero and Alexi Sauvage passed through the forbidding portal of Newgate Prison and asked to see young Amy Hatcher. No one questioned their interest in the condemned girl, for earnest, devout gentlewomen—eager to save souls for Christ—frequently visited Newgate to pray with prisoners on the eve of their executions. Hero saw no reason to enlighten the authorities as to their true purpose.

Hero had never considered herself a particularly sensitive person. Yet there was no denying that when the heavy, barred door clanged shut behind them and the prison's foul stench and endless cries of despair enveloped her, she felt her breath catch and her stomach heave. Everywhere she looked she saw dirty faces pressed against bars and filth-encrusted hands reaching out to her for succor.

"It's medieval," she whispered through the scented handkerchief she held against her nose as their escort led them down a dank, noisome passage to a small, frigid room empty except for a crude table and benches.

"I suspect it hasn't changed all that much in the last five hundred years," said Alexi, her own voice pitched low.

Hero waited until the turnkey left to fetch the doomed prisoner, then said, "You've met this girl before?"

Alexi nodded. "I try to come every week or two to visit the women and children here and provide what medical attention I can. Needless to say, they don't care if I'm officially licensed or not; they're simply thankful for any help they can get. Amy hasn't been at all well, and she's so terribly frightened."

"How old is she?"

"Seventeen."

Hero stared up at the room's single small barred window, which looked out onto a soot-stained brick wall. "Dear God. That's so young to die."

"One of the worst parts is that because she's from Devon, she has no family or friends here. She's utterly alone."

"Whatever possessed her to come up to London?"

"Ignorance and desperation, I suppose."

The turnkey came back then with a heavy tread, pushing a thin slip of a girl ahead of him with a harsh "Get in there, then. Don't want to keep the ladies waiting."

The girl, Amy Hatcher, walked awkwardly, thanks to the heavy leg irons she dragged. She was pasty white with fear and ill health, her hair hanging in unkempt clumps, her dress a filthy, tattered rag. In her arms she held a tiny infant that mewed faintly as the young mother clutched the child tight. Then her terrified gaze slid over Hero to the Frenchwoman, and her haunted blue eyes lit up with hope.

"Oh, Mrs. Sauvage, it's you. They didn't tell me it was you."

Alexi went to take the girl's arm and draw her over to one of the benches. "Here; sit and eat. I've brought you bread and ham."

The girl tore into the food as if she were starving—which she doubtless was, for provisions in Newgate were notoriously meager. While she ate, Alexi introduced Hero and explained her interest in the girl's story.

Hero began by asking about Amy's family—her parents were dead—and about her life in Devon. Then, slowly, she worked around to the night Amy's husband was captured by the press gang.

"They got him one evening when he went to meet some friends at the pub," Amy said. She'd finished eating now and was simply holding her baby with her head bowed. "I'd heard the press gang was in the village and begged him not to go out. But it was his best mate's birthday. He swore he'd be careful. Only, he never came home. It wasn't until I went out the next morning looking for him that I found out what'd happened. They got Mic Tiddler—his mate—too." The girl fell silent, her gaze on the infant in her arms.

"How old is your baby?" Hero asked quietly.

"Four months."

Hero had thought the babe much younger, for the child was painfully thin and wan-looking. But Hero smiled and said, "She's lovely." The girl's answering smile cut Hero to the quick. "When was your husband impressed?" she asked.

Amy Hatcher sucked in a quick, painful breath that shuddered her chest. "Last July. We'd only been married a few months. After he'd gone, I didn't know what to do. So once Hannah here was born, I came up to London looking for him. I know now it was foolish, but . . ."

"You walked all the way from Devon to London? Carrying your baby?"

"Yes, m'lady. I didn't have no money for the stage. Sometimes a wagoner would stop and give me a ride, but not often." The girl's face crumpled, her lips quivering as they pulled back in a rictus of fear and gut-wrenching pain. "My baby's gonna die, isn't she? Without me to feed her and hold her and take care of her, Hannah's gonna die."

For one uncomfortable moment, Hero's gaze met Alexi's. What could they say? *Your baby might survive?* Everyone knew the death rates for children thrown on the parish ran as high as sixty percent, if not more. For an infant this young, already ailing, the chances were slim to none.

"I'll leave money with the Keeper," said Hero. "You'll have good food and a bed tonight."

The girl murmured her thanks. But Hero could tell they were half-hearted, for Amy Hatcher was moving beyond concerns for such earthly comforts.

"Last night," said the girl, "they took us into the chapel and made us sit in the Black Pew with a coffin on the table in front of us while the chaplain read our burial service and told us how we're being punished for our sins just the way God says we should be."

The girl sucked in a quick, frightened breath. Hero thought it a senselessly cruel thing to do, to force condemned prisoners to listen to their own funeral service and a bloodcurdling description of the flames of hell awaiting them.

"I always used to believe in God," the girl was saying. "But I don't no more. Why would a God who's truly good and kind let that press gang take my Jeremy away from me like that? We were so happy. We thought we had our whole lives ahead of us." Tears began to slide down the girl's dirty cheeks, but a rush of what looked like raw anger now glittered in her eyes and hardened her features. "I don't care what the chaplain says. I won't pray to God and ask him to forgive me. For what? For trying to keep my baby alive? Why should I have to ask God's forgiveness for that? If there is a God and he did this to us—to my Jeremy, to my Hannah—then I don't want to see him. I don't want to go to heaven and live with somebody who's that cruel and uncaring."

She looked from Hero to Alexi, as if searching for an answer. But Hero felt her throat close up as the words of comfort she sought proved elusive. How do you console a seventeen-year-old mother who is about to die at the hands of her own government?

The truth is, you can't.

Chapter 27

The day was turning increasingly cold. By the time Sebastian knocked at the small ramshackle brick house on Savile Row now inhabited by Richard Sheridan, a fierce wind was howling down the street.

One of his generation's most successful dramatists and a respected member of government, Sheridan had been the toast of London for decades. But he'd taken a massive financial loss when both Drury Lane and Covent Garden burned within just a few years of each other, and he'd always had a tendency to live beyond his means. With the recent loss of his parliamentary seat thanks to an ugly quarrel with the Regent, he'd now become exposed to his creditors.

Even a few weeks in debtors' prison were hard on someone in his sixties. The thin, hunched man who invited Sebastian into his nearly empty parlor looked haggard and ill, his nose red and his eyes watering. He clutched an old blue-and-red horse blanket around his shoulders for warmth and had a nightcap pulled down over his long silver hair, presumably for the same reason.

"Please, have a seat," he said, indicating one of the two chairs drawn up before the fire. They were the only pieces of furniture in the room. "My creditors have taken the settees and carpet and a lovely old table that belonged to my late wife's mother. But, fortunately, the stout lad who delivers coal next door was kind enough to hide the chairs in the attic when we saw the bailiffs coming." The playwright grimaced as he settled again before the fire. "Unfortunately, I've no doubt they'll be back. It'll be a damnable nuisance, sitting on the floor at my age. But at least they can't rip out the fireplace." He fussed with the tails of his coat, then frowned up at Sebastian. "What the devil are you doing here, anyway?"

"I'm told Jane Ambrose was your niece."

"She was, yes." Sheridan's eyes narrowed. He might have been impoverished and ill, but his mind was still quick and clever. "Word on the street says she was murdered. I take it that's true?"

"It was either murder or manslaughter. She didn't fall and hit her head in the middle of Shepherds' Lane. That's for certain."

"Well, well," said the old man, shaking his head.

"When was the last time you saw her?"

"Jane? Just last Tuesday."

"She came here?"

"She did. Does that surprise you?" He gave a bark of laughter that ended in a cough. "I still had the settees then."

"Did she come to see you often?"

"Often enough. Even rescued me from the Marshalsea last November. It's the worst part about losing my seat in Parliament, you know—having all these bastards hounding me night and day."

"How did she seem when you last saw her?"

"How was she? She was bloody furious—that's how she was. Seems someone told her that His Most Serene Highness the Hereditary Prince of Orange is extraordinarily fond of his more attractive male friends and manservants, and she wanted to know if it was a tale or not."

"What did you tell her?"

"The truth, of course."

"Where had she heard about Orange?"

"She never said. She was all afret about how Princess Charlotte would react, should she find out." Sheridan exhaled his breath in a huff. "You've seen Orange—skinny as a straw, and those teeth! They don't come much plainer-looking or more awkward. According to Jane, the only thing Princess Charlotte likes about the fellow is that she believes him to be direct and honest—unlike that worthless lying cad of a father of hers. Jane said it would devastate the girl, if she ever realizes how she's been taken in by the lot of them."

"She will find out. Eventually."

"Oh, undoubtedly."

Sebastian studied the aging playwright's sagging features. His skin was slack and pale, and he needed a shave. But the ghost of his youthful good looks was still there in the strong nose, finely molded lips, and cleft, rounded chin. "Did you encourage Jane to tell the Princess?"

Sheridan stared back at him. "I did not."

"Yet I assume you are opposed to the match with Orange."

"Of course I am. But I didn't advise Jane to tell Charlotte. What would be the point, at this stage? The girl will never be allowed to back out of the betrothal now." Sheridan shifted uncomfortably in his chair. "You think that's why Jane was killed? Because of Orange? But that makes no sense. There must be dozens in London who know the truth."

"Yes. But how many have Charlotte's ear?"

Sheridan blew out a troubled breath. "There is that." He sat for a time with his gaze on the fire, his brow furrowed with thought.

Sebastian said, "Who do you think killed her?"

Sheridan looked up. "You mean besides that worthless husband of hers?"

"Was he faithful to her?"

"Ambrose? What do you think?" The vehemence of the old man's words caught Sebastian by surprise. "Of course he wasn't. He's one of the most successful dramatists working today, which means he has opera singers and dancers falling all over themselves to convince him to give them a part—and he's not the sort of man who'd fail to take advantage of that."

"Did Jane know?"

"I assume she did. How could she not? But she never said anything to me about it, if that's what you're asking."

"Was she faithful to him?"

Sheridan gave a derisive grunt. "You think she'd tell me? Her aged, decrepit uncle?"

"What do you know about Liam Maxwell?"

"Maxwell? He's a firebrand." A slow smile spread across the man's unshaven face. "I might have alarmed the palace in my day with my support of Catholic emancipation and Irish independence, but Maxwell! Even after two years in Newgate, he's still about as radical as they come—unlike poor Christian. Prison broke him, I'm afraid. Now he publishes rubbishy romances about vampires and dark, mysterious counts." He gave a derisive snort. "Can you imagine? He actually brought me one a couple of weeks or so ago. Me! Fortunately, the bailiffs took it."

Sebastian found himself smiling. "Jane went out to Connaught House last week to see the Princess of Wales. You wouldn't happen to know why, would you?"

The old man looked visibly, genuinely startled. "She went to see Caroline?"

"Yes. That surprises you. Why?"

"I suppose it shouldn't, but . . ." He hesitated, his jaw hardening. "Have you spoken to Jarvis about this?"

"As it happens, yes, I have. You're something like the third person to ask me that."

Sheridan cocked one eyebrow. "Suggestive, wouldn't you say?"

Sebastian studied the clever elderly playwright's wily, unreadable face. "There's something you're not telling me."

"Me?" Sheridan laughed out loud. "What could I possibly have to hide?"

"A great deal, I suspect."

But Sheridan only laughed again and refused to be drawn further.

Chapter 28

*I*t was shortly after her return from Newgate, while Hero was changing clothes and scrubbing the prison stink from her skin, that she received a message from Miss Ella Kinsworth, alerting her to the Princess's plans to venture down to the Thames that afternoon to observe the strange spectacle of Londoners walking on their river.

"You weren't entirely honest with me," Hero said to Miss Ella Kinsworth as they strolled along the terrace of Somerset House overlooking the frozen river. Her Royal Highness Princess Charlotte of Wales, clad in white fur trimmed with red ribbons, raced ahead with her dog, an elegant white Italian greyhound.

"I told you what I felt I could," said Miss Kinsworth, her gaze on the laughing girl and joyously barking dog. "It wouldn't have been right to repeat the Dutch courtier's words about Valentino Vescovi. I mean, what if the accusations weren't true? I would simply be helping to spread false rumors about an innocent man."

"I'm not sure anyone could describe Valentino Vescovi as an innocent man."

The older woman's eyes crinkled with amusement. "Probably not."

Hero watched Charlotte chase after her dog, then whirl laughing as the greyhound cavorted around her. The girl might have only just turned eighteen, but she looked more like twenty-five, with a well-developed figure and mature features. In many ways she resembled both her mother and her father, with the typical big-boned Hanoverian build and long nose, although she managed to be considerably more attractive than either parent. Her lips were beautifully molded, and she had an open, honest expression that was gentle without being insipid.

Yet Hero had to admit that the Duchess of Leeds was right in one sense: There was nothing either elegant or princess-like about Charlotte's ways. She was boisterous and loud and overflowing with boundless energy and good cheer. And while she carried herself with that innate self-confidence unique to those who are born and bred royal, as far as Hero could see, she was utterly lacking in conceit or condescension or an overweening sense of haughty self-importance. Lady Leeds might condemn that tendency, but Hero found it both admirable and refreshing.

"So why did the Princess lock Lady Arabella in the water closet last week?" Hero asked her friend.

Miss Kinsworth pressed the fingers of one hand to her lips to hide a smile. "It's wrong of me to laugh because it was a shocking thing to do, but I can't help it. It was such a well-deserved retribution. Lady Leeds tells everyone that she introduced her daughter into the household as a favor to Charlotte, to provide her with a companion closer to her age. But Charlotte despises the girl. She's always finding the little sneak in her bedchamber with no good excuse for being there, or listening at keyholes and creeping about where she has no business to be. That's why Charlotte and I began speaking to each other in German—although that didn't work for long." The older woman shook her head. "There's no denying Lady Arabella is clever; she learned German with enviable facility. So we switched to Italian, and now she's learning that. I fear I'm running out of languages—and unlike Her Grace's daughter, I do not acquire new ones easily."

"Latin?" suggested Hero with a laugh.

"I suspect her little ladyship's Latin is already better than mine." Miss Kinsworth's smile slipped. "It didn't occur to me she might be eavesdropping on my conversations with Jane Ambrose, too. How can someone so young be so conniving?"

"It must be innate. What I don't understand is, why all the spying on Charlotte?"

"I suspect it's because both the Regent and Orange are afraid she will try to back out of her betrothal."

Hero watched the Princess form a snowball and throw it for her dog. "Would she do that?"

"If she learned the truth about Orange? I think she might try. She's already furious over the plans to force her to leave England, and honesty is so very important to Charlotte."

Hero glanced over at her friend in surprise. "You know, then?"

"About Orange's disinterest in women? Oh, yes—at least, I do now. Unfortunately, I didn't know last December. Otherwise I would have cautioned her before she agreed to meet him."

"Did you tell Jane Ambrose?"

"About Orange? No."

"*Toby! Come!*" called the Princess. The two women watched together as the girl waded through the snow to the edge of the terrace and stood staring out at a smooth section of the river that was thick with ice-skaters.

Miss Kinsworth said, "It's horrible, what Prinny is doing—marrying her to Orange without telling her the truth. After the miserable, lonely childhood she's had, she wants desperately to find love and happiness in her marriage. But there's no chance of that with him as her bridegroom."

"It sounds as if Prinny's keeping any number of truths from her." The dog was frolicking at the Princess's feet, wanting to run. But Charlotte stood transfixed by the intricate maneuvers of a pair of experienced ice-gliders. "Does she know her father is plotting to divorce her mother as soon as she's out of the country?"

"She doesn't know for certain, but there's no denying she fears it. It's why she's fighting so hard over the marriage contracts—to try to insert a clause saying Orange won't be able to force her to leave England against her will."

"Do you think she'll succeed?"

Miss Kinsworth looked troubled. "I don't know."

They watched as Charlotte reached down to scratch the happily panting dog behind its cropped ears. Hero said, "The greyhound is lovely."

"She is, isn't she? She used to belong to Napoléon's Empress, but was taken aboard a French ship we captured."

"So she's a prisoner of war?"

Miss Kinsworth laughed. "I suppose in a sense she is. The captain sent her to the Prince, except of course Prinny hates dogs, so Charlotte rescued the poor creature."

Hero looked over at her friend. "What kind of man hates dogs?"

"Dogs don't like him. They growl and snap at him."

"The wisdom of animals," murmured Hero as the Princess turned to come running up to them, the dog at her heels.

"Oh, I wish I could try skating," she said, laughing. "Do you think Papa would permit it, Miss Kinsworth?"

"You could ask him," said Miss Kinsworth in a voice that didn't hold out much hope for success.

The Princess pulled a face at her, then turned to Hero. "Do you skate, Lady Devlin?"

"I never have. Although if this weather keeps up, I fear we all may need to learn."

Charlotte laughed again, then grew serious. The carefree child who'd been playing with her dog disappeared, her features schooled into a sober expression that gave a glimpse of the splendid queen she would one day be. "Miss Kinsworth says you wished to ask me about Jane Ambrose—about our lesson the day she died."

"You're the last person known to have had any meaningful interaction with Jane that day. Can you remember anything about that morning—anything at all—that might shed some light on what happened to her?"

"Sorry, no. Believe me, I have gone over our conversation in my mind. But I can't think of anything."

"Do you know where she planned to go after she left Warwick House?"

"I assumed she would be returning home, although I don't believe she ever actually said. We spoke of the cold, and she told me she'd heard the Cambridge stage was snowed up for eight hours before they managed to pull it out with most of the passengers nearly frozen to death. But I can't recall our discussing anything of a personal nature."

"Did she seem worried or troubled to you?"

The Princess considered this a moment, then shook her head. "I don't think I would say she was troubled. But there was something different about her I can only describe as a sort of fierceness. As if—" She broke off.

"Yes, Your Highness?" prompted Hero.

"It was as if she had finally made up her mind about something and was both relieved and determined to carry through on her decision." Charlotte gave a rueful smile. "I know it sounds an odd, fanciful thing to say, but I can't think of any other way to describe it. And it's no use asking me what she'd made up her mind about, because I've no notion at all."

"It could mean nothing," Hero said to Devlin later, after she'd related the conversation to him. She was leaning against the doorway of his dressing room and watching him tie a rough black cravat around his neck. The cravat was black for the same reason his breeches were worn and his shirt frayed: Kat Boleyn had arranged for him to meet a smuggler named Archibald Potter at a tavern called the Cat and Fiddle near Ratcliff Highway, and one did not venture into an area such as Whitechapel dressed like a Bond Street beau.

Devlin met her gaze in the mirror. "I wouldn't be too quick to dismiss Charlotte's observations. When you grow up at court surrounded by toadies, scheming courtiers, and a family as uniformly peculiar as the Hanovers, you learn to read people early—and well."

"True," said Hero. "But what does it mean?" She pushed away from the doorframe to go stand at the window overlooking the snow-filled street. "I feel as if we aren't getting anywhere. We just keep going round and round the same people and incidents, learning perhaps a bit more each time and yet never really discovering what we need to know."

He glanced over at her, his eyes crinkling with a hint of a smile. "That's because we're missing something. Something important."

"But . . . what?"

He reached for a battered, low-crowned hat with a jaunty red feather in the band and settled it on his head. "I don't know yet."

She frowned. "How will you recognize this Archibald Potter?"

"I'll know him by his cocked hat and green striped waistcoat, and he'll know me by this decidedly garish red feather—with our identities further confirmed by a prearranged conversation about my supposed recent travels to Jamaica."

"Sounds decidedly insalubrious. You will be careful."

Devlin checked the knife he kept sheathed in his boot, then slipped a small double-barreled flintlock into his pocket. "You keep saying that."

She came to tug at the brim of his hat. "And you never listen."

Chapter 29

The Cat and Fiddle was a smoke-fouled, ramshackle old half-timbered structure on John Street, not far from the vast warehouses of the East India Company. Sebastian selected a high-backed booth in a quiet corner, ordered a tankard of ale he had no intention of drinking, and settled in to wait.

Archibald Potter, when he appeared, looked more like a comfortable middle-aged shopkeeper than a smuggler. Somewhere in his late forties, he had full, ruddy cheeks, bushy side-whiskers, and a round, knobby nose. The combination could have made him look jovial and soft. It did not. His clothes were typical of an older generation, his waistcoat long and striped with green, his coat square-cut with broad lapels and large pockets. In place of a cravat he wore a stock, and he had a cocked hat perched above a periwig. He stared at the red feather in Sebastian's hatband, then walked up to stand stiffly with his fingers tapping on the scarred tabletop. He was not smiling.

"I hear you're just back from Jamaica," he said in guttural French with a strong Kentish accent.

"The weather's much better there than here," replied Sebastian in the same language.

"Huh. Where isn't it?" With a grunt, the free trader slid into the opposite bench. "Miss Kat says you want to know about smuggling in the Channel—with a particular emphasis on the activities of a certain Frankfurter we all know but few love. Says it's got something to do with that lady found with her head bashed in up in Clerkenwell."

"Yes."

Potter stared at him long and hard. "She swears I can trust you."

"You have my word."

The free trader turned to call for a tankard of ale before resting his shoulders against the bench's high back, his thick, bushy brows drawing together in a frown. "I've only ever known one other fellow with yellow eyes, and he wasn't somebody I'd care to mess with. See well in the dark, do you?"

"Yes."

Potter nodded. "So did this fellow. I met him in Dunkirk."

"I take it you spend a fair amount of time in France."

"I was born there, for all that my parents were from Dover. Still got a sister in Gravelines. She takes care of the French end of the business, while I deal with things over here."

"Convenient."

Potter waited while a young barmaid slapped an overflowing tankard of ale on the table before him. "It is that."

"Gravelines, you say?"

He took a deep swallow of his ale, then wiped the foam from his lips with the back of one hand. "That's right. It ain't like in the old days, when we used to have to collect our contraband either in the Low Countries or off neutral ships in the Channel."

"So what's changed?"

"Few years ago, Napoléon got clever. He realized that if he worked with us smugglers—made it easy for us to do business with France—he could use us to get French goods into England while at the same time keeping control over what we were bringing into France. So he issued this imperial decree, officially opening up a couple of French ports—first Wimereux and Dunkirk, then Gravelines—to smugglers. He even built special warehouses for us. Keeps them filled with lace, silk, leather gloves, brandy—whatever we want."

"That was indeed clever. So what do you take to France—besides the usual spies, of course?"

Archibald Potter grinned and leaned forward. "Letters. English newspapers. Escaped prisoners of war. And gold. Lots of gold. They even built a special quarter just for us in Gravelines—they call it the 'ville des smoglers.'"

"You're saying the entire operation is officially sanctioned by the French government?"

"It ain't just sanctioned—it's controlled. Organized. They got the Ministers of Police, Finance, Interior, War, and What-have-you, all writing reports and procedures and the like. You know the French. Ain't nobody like 'em for security passes, articles, rules, regulations, and any other kind of government paperwork a body could dream up. They've got something like seventy merchants and bankers in Gravelines officially designated to deal with us."

"'Us' being the smugglers?"

"That's right."

"How many vessels are we talking about?"

"Hundreds. Most of 'em are small—under ten tons, with some of 'em smaller still. Smugglers like galleys, you see—especially for gold smuggling. They're light and easy to build, they don't need a lot of rowers, and they're fast. Plus, you can turn a galley and row it into the wind if you're unlucky enough to stumble upon the bloody Water Guard."

Sebastian ran one finger up and down the side of his tankard. "Tell me about Rothschild."

Archibald Potter hunched his shoulders and leaned in closer, dropping his voice lower. "They call them 'the Family,' you know. Ain't nobody more active in the Channel than them. Lots of other London merchants and bankers finance operations. But the Rothschilds, they run their own bloody ships, specially constructed with secret compartments. They don't just use kegs with false heads and hollowed-out pigs of iron hidden under the ballast. They've got secret drawers built into the binnacles that open by springs, false ceilings—anything you can think of and probably more than a bit you can't. And they're all flying flags with that Rothschild red shield and gold eagle."

"So they don't get stopped," said Sebastian. The Rothschilds paid a number of officials in various countries to look the other way. And even those who weren't paid off were frequently too afraid to tangle with such a powerful, wealthy family.

"They don't get stopped very often—that's for sure. And if they do get caught with contraband, all Nathan Rothschild needs do is claim he doesn't know anything about it—just lays the blame for any illicit cargo they find on the crew and captain. That way the ship's not forfeit, and it's the crew that gets hauled off into custody."

"I wouldn't think they'd keep quiet."

"They do if they've any sense. A revenue cutter stopped a Rothschild ship just a few weeks ago—the *Viking*—with a secret cargo of guineas in her stern. The revenuers took the captain and crew into custody, but a few days later they just"—Potter fluttered his hands through the air like a conjurer doing a trick—"disappeared. Everyone knows Rothschild's got friends in high places—people who make sure anything he wants to happen, happens."

Sebastian felt a quickening of interest. "When did you say the *Viking* was stopped?"

Potter shrugged. "First part of the month—during that nasty Great Fog we had."

According to Nathan Rothschild, Jane Ambrose's final lesson with little Anna Rothschild had taken place on a Tuesday at the end of the Great Fog. It could mean nothing, of course. But then again . . .

He became aware of Archibald Potter studying him with renewed interest. "You got Scottish in you?" asked the free trader suddenly.

Sebastian shrugged. "Some. Why?"

"You remember that fellow I was telling you about—the one with the yellow eyes?"

"Yes."

"He had a Scottish name, for all he was a French colonel."

Sebastian kept his hands steady by pressing them flat on the table. "Oh? What was his name?" he asked, his voice sounding convincingly casual.

"Mac-something. Can't recall exactly. But he looked more than a bit like yourself—except older, of course. Old enough by now to maybe be your father, I reckon."

"Interesting," said Sebastian, his features carefully schooled into an expression of polite boredom even as he felt the blood coursing through his veins hard enough that for one pulsing moment he heard a roaring in his ears.

Leaving the Cat and Fiddle, Sebastian turned his steps toward the river, his gaze on the heavy white clouds pressing down on the city. But his thoughts were in the past.

He was the third son and fourth child born to the marriage of the Earl of Hendon and his beautiful, restless wife, Sophia. He'd always known he was different from his brothers, Richard and Cecil—different in looks, interests, talents, and temperament. And so very, very different from their father, the Earl. He'd grown up feeling like an outsider in his own family, wondering why his eyes were a strange feral yellow rather than the startling blue that was such a strong characteristic in the

St. Cyr family and wondering at the anger and disappointment he often glimpsed in the Earl's face when he gazed upon his unsatisfactory third son. But somehow it had never occurred to Sebastian to wonder if he were really Hendon's child.

He'd learned the truth only recently in a series of devastating revelations that had come close to destroying him. Even after all these months, even after the long-delayed reconciliation with Hendon, he still felt a stranger to himself. For if he wasn't Hendon's son, then who was he? Half of his history, half of *himself*—his unknown father's half—remained an enigma to him, a murky, mysterious world populated by the shadowy men and women from whom he was descended and yet about whom he knew nothing.

Nothing.

Looking out over the jumbled ice of the frozen river, he told himself the free trader's tale of a French colonel with a Scottish name and yellow eyes meant nothing. Yes, yellow eyes were rare, but they were not unique. And while a Welsh cavalry officer—along with an English lord and a Gypsy stableboy—had been amongst those named as Sophia Devlin's possible lover, no one had ever mentioned a Frenchman with a Scottish surname.

He told himself that one of these days he was going to need to make peace with the mystery of his origins and accept that he would probably never learn what he was so desperate to know.

He told himself these things. And still hope thrummed within him, undeniable and irrepressible.

Chapter 30

*A*fter leaving the river, Sebastian went first to the Admiralty, where he made inquiries into the fate of a certain Rothschild galley. Then, pondering what he'd learned, he turned his steps east again, toward the Bank of England and the Exchange.

Nathan Rothschild lived in the same modest brick residence from which he operated his businesses. Situated on a drab court off St. Swithin's Lane, just a stone's throw from the Bank of England, the Stock Exchange, and the official residence of the Mayor of London, the house was as squat and ugly as the warehouse that stood beside it. Dressed as he was for his meeting at the Cat and Fiddle, Sebastian half expected the middle-aged manservant in rusty livery who opened the door to turn him away. But before Sebastian had a chance to present his card, the man bowed and said, "Lord Devlin, yes? If you will kindly step into the book-room, I will apprise Mr. Rothschild of your arrival."

Sebastian was shown to a small, frigid room lined with shelves stuffed with dusty ledgers and crowded with three tall desks. None of the desks had a stool, and there were no chairs in the room. He was standing at the narrow window overlooking the court and watching a couple of workmen transfer wooden crates from the back of a wagon to the warehouse next door when he heard Rothschild's heavy tread coming down the stairs.

"Vhat the devil do you vant now?" the financier demanded as he drew up just inside the doorway. His drab old-fashioned frock coat was frayed at the hems; the overlong graying red hair fringed a balding pate.

Sebastian turned to face him. "Tell me about the *Viking*."

Rothschild's full lower lip jutted out, and he closed the door behind him with a snap. "Vhat about it?"

"I'm told it was caught smuggling gold guineas."

"That had nothing to do vith me."

"Do you seriously expect me to believe that?"

Rothschild snorted. "I don't care vhat you believe."

From somewhere up above came the sound of a child's laughter; then someone began playing the piano with exquisite skill. Sebastian glanced toward the sound. "According to the Admiralty, the *Viking* was seized in the Channel on the night of January third. Given the excellence of your family's intelligence apparatus, I suspect it's more than likely that you received word of the *Viking*'s fate the very next day—which coincidently happens to have been the last Tuesday of the Great Fog and the date of Jane Ambrose's final visit to this house. So what happened? Did she overhear something she wasn't supposed to hear? A conversation in which you betrayed your prior knowledge of the galley's illegal shipment, perhaps? Is that why she was frightened? Not because you terminated your arrangement with her, but because you threatened her—perhaps even threatened to kill her if she told anyone what she had heard?"

Not a single trace of emotion showed on Rothschild's face—not surprise, alarm, fear, or anger; he remained utterly inscrutable. "Vas Jane Ambrose here on the fourth? I do not recall."

"You know she was."

Rothschild shrugged. "And if your supposition vere true—vhich of course I in no way concede—do you seriously suppose that I would admit to it?"

Sebastian gave the man a hard, tight smile. "Actually, no. I'd expect you to react precisely as you have—scornfully dismissive, arrogant, and utterly unconcerned with the death of a talented, innocent young woman you knew."

Rothschild made a rude noise. "I did not kill that voman."

"What about the two men who attacked me the other day in Fleet Street? Did you send them?"

For the first time Sebastian saw the faintest hint of a reaction in the man's pale protruding eyes, quickly hidden by lowered lids. "I haven't the slightest idea vhat you are talking about."

"Of course you don't." Sebastian picked up his hat from where it rested on the nearest desk.

Rothschild opened the door for him. "As for the *Viking*, you don't understand the importance of vhat you have bumbled into. Take my advice and stay out of it."

"Oh? Or you'll—what?" said Sebastian. "Send someone to kill me? You already tried that, remember?"

Something flickered again in the financier's pale eyes. Something angry and brutal. But Sebastian noticed that he didn't deny it.

"You think Rothschild is the one who sent those men to kill you?" Gibson asked.

"I wouldn't be surprised," said Sebastian as the two men sat drinking mulled wine beside Gibson's kitchen fire. "Unfortunately, I doubt I'll ever be able to prove it."

"And Jane Ambrose? Did he kill her, too?"

"I'd be inclined to think so, except . . ."

Gibson glanced over at him. "Except?"

Sebastian rocked back on his bench and crossed his arms. "I don't know. Something feels wrong about it. Either that or I'm just missing something—something important."

"When's the fellow's inquest?"

"Tomorrow morning."

Gibson pushed up to go throw more fuel on the fire. "You heard Alexi and Lady Devlin are going to that poor girl's hanging tomorrow? The one who came up to London after her husband was impressed."

Sebastian stared at him. "No. Why?"

"Her ladyship thinks they owe it to the girl to be there, and Alexi agreed." Gibson paused. "It's gonna be ugly."

"Yes," said Sebastian, his heart heavy for his wife. "But then, they know that."

"Aye," Gibson admitted. "So they do."

Later that evening, now dressed in elegant knee breeches, a linen shirt, and a finely tailored greatcoat, Sebastian tucked an elegant walking stick under one arm and trolled the expensive pleasure haunts of the West End. He was looking for Viscount Ashworth, the handsome but deadly Marquis's heir who had married Sebastian's niece the previous September. Since securing the hand of Miss Stephanie Wilcox, Ashworth had reverted to his old habits, which meant spending his evenings in London's more notorious gaming establishments and brothels. Sebastian knew because he'd been keeping an eye on the man ever since that fateful September day.

Sebastian eventually spotted his quarry in a noisy hell near Leicester Square. But rather than directly approach his niece's husband, Sebastian simply hung back and watched. He watched Ashworth shift from EO table to faro to *rouge et noir*, drinking freely and laughing with friends, before casually tupping a black-haired whore against the wall in a darkened corner. Then he called for his greatcoat and hat and, whistling softly, set off alone toward the Haymarket.

The night was so cold every sound seemed magnified—the crunch of Sebastian's boots in the snow, the *clip-clop* of horses' hooves, the tinkling notes of a piano underscored by men's voices and a woman's gay laughter. With each breath, the exhalation billowed around him to hang motionless in the coal smoke–scented air.

Oblivious to his shadow, Ashworth turned purposefully into Piccadilly. When the Marquis's son approached the dark, yawning mouth of an alley, Sebastian increased his pace. Coming up behind the man in a snow-muffled rush, he reached out to grab the Viscount's upper right arm at the same time he shoved hard against Ashworth's left shoulder.

The force of the blow caused the man to pivot toward the entrance to the alley just as Sebastian let him go. Ashworth staggered forward several steps, off-balance, then tripped on the walking stick Sebastian thrust between the man's legs.

With a startled grunt, Ashworth went down hard on his stomach, his hands flung out at his sides in the snow. He was still collecting himself when Sebastian calmly planted his boot on the fallen man's right hand.

"What the hell are you—," Ashworth began, then broke off to suck in a quick breath when Sebastian slid the stiletto from his walking stick and held the sharp tip against the bastard's cheek.

"Shut up and listen," hissed Sebastian.

Ashworth went utterly still, the whites of his eyes shining clearly in the moonlight as his gaze focused on the naked steel held against his face.

"It's terrible, how easy it is to have an accident," said Sebastian softly. "I'm told your wife had an 'accident' recently, as well. You do remember, don't you? The bruise on her cheek?"

Ashworth blinked. His breathing was perhaps more rapid than normal, but other than that he seemed remarkably calm. "I take it this display of calculated barbarism is intended to intimidate me?"

"You could say that."

"I seem to recall you expressed the hope last September of seeing my lovely bride a widow by year's end. That didn't happen, did it?"

"Not yet."

Ashworth gave a low laugh. "Are you planning to take up murder now? And here I was under the impression you hold the practice in exaggerated repugnance. That is why you indulge in that peculiar pastime of yours, is it not?"

"There are ways to destroy a man besides killing him."

"True. But unless you are willing to ruin your own dear niece in the process, the number of options narrows considerably."

"Narrows. But does not disappear," said Sebastian, leaning into the stiletto ever so slightly.

Ashworth blinked again but remained silent.

Sebastian said, "Just remember: I'm watching you. Give me the faintest glimmer of an excuse, and I will take it. Without hesitation."

"You can try."

Sebastian gave a slow smile. "I seem to recall your late friend Sir Francis Rowe expressing a similar sentiment . . . right before he died."

"Rowe was a fool."

"And you think you're not?" Sebastian subtly increased the weight on Ashworth's hand as he drew a thin, bloody line across the man's cheek with the tip of his blade. "Hurt my niece again and you'll regret it."

Sebastian stepped back and sheathed his sword. "You've been warned."

Chapter 31

*T*he next morning, Hero rose before the sun and dressed in a somber carriage gown, warm socks, and heavy broquins. She was settling a veiled, low-crowned hat on her hair when Devlin came up behind her to put his hands on her waist.

"Ever been to a hanging before?" he asked softly.

She turned to face him. "No."

"The crowds can get rough."

"Alexi warned me. Tom offered to come with us, but I didn't think that would be fair." Tom's brother, Huey, had been just thirteen when he was hanged as a thief.

Devlin said, "If I didn't have this damned inquest—"

She brushed his lips with hers. "I know."

His gaze met hers, and she saw the worry he was trying to hide. He said, "Why do this? Why force yourself to watch that poor young woman hang?"

"Because she has no family in London, and someone should be

there for her." She reached for her gloves and drew them on with swift jerking motions. "What kind of society steals a man away from his pregnant young wife to send him off to war and then hangs her when she steals to try to keep herself and her child alive?"

"One with its values in serious need of realignment."

"Will it ever change, do you think?"

"Perhaps."

She gave a faint smile. "You don't sound convinced."

"Armies will always need cannon fodder. And shopkeepers and merchants will always have more clout than starving women and children."

"I keep trying to imagine what she must be going through, but it seems unbearable."

"I suspect it is."

The day dawned clear but bitterly cold despite the golden sunlight that spilled across the awakening city.

Hero thought the frigid temperatures might reduce the number of spectators at the hanging, but she was wrong. She and Alexi arrived at the Old Bailey—the street before Newgate Prison where hangings were held—to find a surging, raucous, malodorous crowd of thousands: men, women, and children, their shouts and laughter joining into a roar. The atmosphere was that of a fair, with pie sellers and broadside hawkers and a flotilla of dirty, ragged urchins who darted through the milling throng to pick the pockets of the unwary.

"It's probably because they're hanging a woman," said Alexi, her face tight with suppressed emotion as they pushed their way through the crush of onlookers toward the ramshackle old house from which they had arranged to watch the hanging. "The crowds are always larger for women, especially when they're young. Women and highwaymen and notorious murderers."

The house they'd selected lay almost directly opposite the scaffold and, like most of the other buildings overlooking the street, rented out its windows for hangings. As they reached the door, the slow, mournful tolling of a bell began somewhere deep inside Newgate. The bell would continue tolling until the last of the day's condemned prisoners was cut down, dead. Hero thought it must be hideous, living within the sound of that bell.

"Hear that?" said the portly house owner, pocketing their money. He jerked his balding head toward a steep, narrow staircase behind him. "That means the condemned've already been brought into the yard to have their irons struck off. Best hurry."

"How many hangings have you attended?" Hero asked Alexi as they climbed the worn ancient steps.

"Just one. A friend of mine was hanged not long after I arrived in London. I promised I'd be there for him, and I was."

Hero suspected there was more to the story than that, but she had no intention of asking for details. There was much about this French-woman that remained a mystery to them all.

The wide casement window of their chosen chamber looked down on the scaffold across the street. Essentially a large wooden platform draped with black cloth, it reminded Hero of a stage—which she supposed in a sense it was. The scaffold was always erected just outside the prison's lodge, directly in front of what was known as the Debtors' Door, so that the condemned would not be seen by the crowd until they mounted the steps to the platform itself. A small roofed shelter with chairs stood at the rear of the scaffold for important officials, and soldiers with pikes were stationed around the perimeter, guarding it. It struck Hero, watching the nervous way the men clutched their pikes, that beneath the crowd's typical air of excitement and anticipation lay something else, something hostile and angry.

"Who else is being hanged today? Do you know?"

"Three men. Poachers, I think," said Alexi.

It did much to explain the mood of the crowd. Murderers and their like were usually greeted with jeers and catcalls, and often pelted with rotten food or even stones. But most of the people in the street were desperately poor themselves; their sympathies would lie with those about to die.

The bell of the nearby church of St. Sepulchre joined the Newgate bell and began to toll, sounding the death knell. Alexi thrust open the old-fashioned windows and cold air rushed in, bringing them the roar of the crowd and a chorus of more distant shouts that rose up from within Newgate: The prisoners in the cells fronting the yard were calling farewells and encouragement to the condemned on their way to the lodge.

Alexi said, "They're coming."

There was a noticeable stirring in the crowd below. The sheriff and undersheriff of the City of London emerged from the covered stairway first, their eyes narrowing as they came into the strengthening daylight. Clothed in long, fur-trimmed robes with the heavy chains of their offices around their shoulders, both held ceremonial silver-tipped staves and solemnly took their seats along with a scattering of other officials.

The Ordinary, or prison chaplain, came next, his head bowed over his prayer book. A hush of anticipation fell over the crowd, so that Hero could hear his deep, mournful voice intoning the burial service. "'O God, whose days are without end and whose mercies cannot be numbered: Make us, we pray, deeply aware of the shortness and uncertainty of human life . . .'"

Hero curled her hands over the windowsill in front of her and leaned forward, sucking the cold, foul air deep into her lungs. She knew a strange sense of unreality, as if a part of her somehow refused to accept that this was happening, that she was watching the bizarre spectacle of her government setting about deliberately murdering four desperately impoverished human beings with a degree of pomp and solemnity that suddenly struck her as obscene.

A turnkey appeared at the top of the stairs, and Hero said, "She's first."

Amy Hatcher reached the last step, stumbling and blinking at the brightness as she emerged into the light. She had the heavy hemp noose that would be used to kill her draped around her shoulders, and in her arms she clutched a small bundle that Hero realized was her baby.

"Oh, Lord," Hero whispered, watching the poor girl stagger on the rough planking. Terror distorted her red tear-streaked face, and her chest jerked visibly with each rapid, shallow gasp of air. At the sight of the heavy beam above her, she tried to shrink back, her head shaking from side to side as she pleaded, "Oh, please, no. Please, no."

"Why is she still holding her child?" said Hero.

"It's probably the only way they could get her out here without dragging her."

The three condemned men who came behind Amy had their hands tied together in front and their elbows pinioned tight against their torsos. All moved awkwardly without their leg irons, as if they had become so accustomed to their weight that they now found it difficult to walk without them.

A roar went up from the spectators. "Hats off! Hats off so we can see!" The men in the crowd whipped off their tall hats.

Hero found herself watching the watchers. Not only was the street below crammed with a surging, shoving crowd, but every window overlooking the space was occupied by gawkers affluent enough to pay for a better view of the spectacle. On the roof of a nearby house she could see a man with a telescope trained on the condemned; a well-dressed young woman with a pair of opera glasses leaned out a window of the inn next door. Judging by the faint smile curling the woman's lips, she was not here to support any of those doomed to die. Then a turnkey snatched the child from Amy Hatcher's arms, and the condemned girl began to scream and struggle against the hands that reached out to hold her.

"My baby! Oh, God, no, please don't take her! Give me just one more minute with her. Oh, please don't do this."

The sheriff tightened his hold on his staff, his lips pressing into a thin line of distaste, as if there were something unseemly, something un-English about a young mother objecting to her own murder and what would surely be the inevitable death of her orphaned babe. The condemned were expected to cooperate, to "make a good end" and die repenting their sins and commending their spirits to God. Amy Hatcher was not supposed to create a scene, screaming and crying and half fainting, so that two turnkeys had to hold her up, one at each side, while her wrists were bound with cords and her elbows pinned to her body. The rope was taken from her thin shoulders and affixed to one of the black butcher's hooks in the heavy beam above while the noose was slipped over her head.

"'Lord Jesus Christ,'" prayed the Ordinary, his voice booming, as if he could somehow drown out her hysterical pleadings, "'by your death you took away the sting of death: Grant to us your servants so to follow in faith where you have led the way. . . . '"

The baby was wailing now, too, her thin, reedy cry intertwined with the mother's frantic pleadings. *"Oh, please—"*

A hush had fallen over the watching crowd, their upturned faces rapt as the three condemned men were led onto the trapdoor beside Amy and carefully positioned on the marks chalked there. One of the men was older, perhaps in his late thirties. But the other two were heartbreakingly young, still boys: a man and his two sons. All three were doing their best to "die game," their heads held high and grim half smiles plastered in place. But Hero could see their legs shaking, see the sweat that glistened on their pinched pale faces despite the cold.

The sheriff said something, and one of the turnkeys stepped forward to bind the woman's skirts around her legs with a strap to keep them from billowing up immodestly as her body fell. Because heaven forbid, thought Hero, that the multitude gathered to watch her die a hideous, painful death should be given a glimpse of her ankles.

"'. . . receive them into the arms of your mercy, into the blessed rest of everlasting peace and into the glorious company of the saints in light,'" prayed the Ordinary, closing his prayer book. "Amen."

All four condemned prisoners were now in place, the nooses around their necks, and the executioner stepped forward to yank the white hoods down over their faces. Then, at the sheriff's signal, the hangman pulled the lever that slid back the timbers supporting the long trapdoor. One of the doomed boys shouted, "Lord, have mercy on me!" as the trap fell with a loud crash that echoed around the street.

Four bodies dropped with an ugly jerk. But the distance they were allowed to fall was short—just eighteen inches. And so, rather than breaking their necks, the ropes simply began to strangle them. Slowly.

"Oh, no," whispered Hero as the dying prisoners writhed in agony, twisting and twitching helplessly, the men's legs kicking out spasmodically. Do the Morris dance on air, they called it. Dance the hempen measure, and cut a caper on the way to hell. All were euphemisms for hanging, cynical descriptions of the macabre jerks and gyrations performed by the condemned in their death throes.

There had been a time, when executions used to take place out at Tyburn, when the doomed prisoners' friends and loved ones could grasp the dying men's and women's legs and pull, thus speeding their deaths. But that was no longer allowed. Now those who could afford it paid the hangman to do basically the same thing. But such a luxury was beyond the means of a desperate woman condemned for stealing food or three poor poachers. And so the executioner simply stood with his arms crossed at his chest and watched them suffer.

"I should have left her money for the hangman," Hero said, stricken. "I didn't think."

Alexi sucked in a shaky breath. "Neither did I."

An eternity later, Hero said, "*My God.* How much longer can it go on?"

"Sometimes it can take as long as four or five minutes. It's a horrible way to die—strangling. That's why the French instituted the guillotine."

The young poachers' bowels and bladders had released, staining their breeches. And still the dying fought to live, uselessly, hopelessly.

Finally, one after the other, they ceased to struggle, until all four dangling bodies simply swayed heavily at the ends of their ropes. They would be left hanging like this for an hour before being cut down. St. Sepulchre's bell gave one final clang and fell silent. The prison bell tolled on and on.

The gathering of dignitaries beneath the pavilion rose to their feet and filed off the platform in a solemn procession. They would now retire to the Keeper's house, where they would consume the traditional post-hanging breakfast of deviled kidneys.

With the departure of the officials, the crowd of spectators pressed forward. Many would pay the hangman a shilling to touch the hands of the dead, which was believed to be a cure for warts and tumors and other growths. An executioner could make quite a tidy sum out of a hanging, since he would also be allowed to sell the clothes of the dead and to cut the ropes used to kill them into short lengths to sell as souvenirs.

Hero glanced over at Alexi and was shocked to see the Frenchwoman's face wet with tears. "It's barbarism," said Alexi, her accent unusually heavy. "How can anyone think this is right? To kill a starving seventeen-year-old girl for stealing a ham? A *ham!*"

Reaching out, Hero grasped her friend's hand, tight. And for a long moment, the two women simply held on to each other as the crowds dissipated below and the cold golden sun slid behind a new bank of clouds.

Chapter 32

"*H*is name was Jack Donavon," Sir Henry Lovejoy told Sebastian as the two men stood side by side, staring down at the ashen naked corpse of the man killed in the Strand.

The body lay facedown on an old door propped up on two empty whiskey barrels in the taproom of the Black Swan on Fleet Street, for the viewing of the body of the deceased was an important part of any inquest. The jurors who'd been called to serve were still milling about, along with a number of curious onlookers. By law, any sudden, violent, or unexplained death required an inquest. And because there were so few places capable of holding the kinds of crowds gruesome dead bodies could attract, the proceedings typically were held in a public house or an inn.

"So who was he?" asked Sebastian, his eyes narrowing as he studied the purple knife wound in the dead man's back.

"A generally unsavory character from the sounds of it, although by all accounts not a simple thief. I suspect he wasn't after your purse."

"I didn't think he was."

Sir Henry nodded. "Unfortunately, we've no idea who he was working for or who his companion—and inadvertent murderer—might have been."

"Lovely."

Sir Henry shivered. A fire had recently been kindled on the enormous old-fashioned hearth, but the blaze was meager, and the room was still cold enough that few of those present were inclined to remove their great-coats. "You've no idea who might have an interest in seeing you dead?"

"Not really."

A commotion near the door foretold the imminent arrival of the cor-oner. Sir Henry glanced behind them, then lowered his voice to say, "One of my lads did learn something you might find of interest: Edward Am-brose is in debt."

"Did your lad manage to discover why?"

"The usual: mainly gambling, along with an unhealthy addiction to Bond Street tailors and high-end jewelers such as Rundell and Bridge."

"Any sign of a mistress?"

"My lads say there is talk, but they've yet to verify it." The magis-trate pursed his lips in thought. "The debt obviously reflects poorly on Mr. Ambrose's character. But unless he's planning to acquire a new rich wife, I fail to see how it constitutes a motive for murder."

"It doesn't—if Jane was murdered. But if Ambrose struck her in an-ger and accidently killed her, the debt might explain the nature of their quarrel."

"There is that." Sir Henry shivered again and drew a handkerchief from his pocket to blow his nose. "You've seen the frozen river?"

"Yesterday afternoon. Amazing, is it not?"

Sir Henry nodded, although he looked more troubled than impressed. "There's talk of setting up a Frost Fair. Personally, I fail to see the attrac-tion of freezing in a tent pitched on ice simply to experience the dubi-ous pleasure of drinking expensive beer or purchasing a useless trinket at twice its worth so that one may afterward boast that it was acquired on the Thames."

Sebastian laughed just as a constable came bustling into the tap-room, clapped his hands loudly, and said, "Right, then, let's get this started, shall we?"

As expected, the inquest returned a verdict of homicide by person un-known.

Afterward, Sebastian joined Lovejoy for a ploughman's lunch in the inn's public room. The pub was crowded with a motley assortment of hangers-on from the inquest—shopkeepers and tradesmen, costermon-gers and apprentices, all loud and boisterous with lingering excitement from the morning's entertainment.

"I'll never understand it," said Lovejoy, nibbling without much ap-petite at a heel of bread. "Why would anyone want to deliberately look at the bloody corpse of a murdered man?"

"Presumably for the same reason they attend hangings," said Sebas-tian, his thoughts on the ordeal he knew Hero was going through.

"I've never understood that, either. We hang felons in public as a warning to all potential lawbreakers; the spectacle is intended to put the fear of God into them. But in reality, all we do is provide the city's pickpockets with a distracted crowd enjoying a free show."

Sebastian found himself smiling. "You're suggesting public hangings might not work as a deterrent?"

"One would deduce. As for hanging a man—let alone a woman or child—for stealing a handkerchief or a pheasant? I fear future genera-tions will conclude we place little value on the lives of England's poor."

Sebastian drained his ale and set it aside. "Future generations will be right."

Sebastian spent the next hour trying to find Edward Ambrose.

The playwright's nervous servants claimed ignorance of his whereabouts. In the end, Sebastian tracked Jane's widower to a low tavern on Compton Street. From the looks of it, the place dated back to the last years of the seventeenth century, with low, dark beams overhead and sawdust on the floor and a wide hearth beside which Ambrose sat slumped. He had one hand wrapped around a bottle of cheap Scotch, and he looked up lazily when Sebastian slid into the opposite bench.

"Ah. It wanted only that," said Ambrose, raising the bottle to his lips without bothering to use the glass that stood near his elbow.

"Bit early, isn't it?"

"Is it?"

"So, are you drowning your sorrows or assuaging your guilt?" asked Sebastian.

"You say that as if the two were mutually exclusive."

When Sebastian remained silent, Ambrose took another drink, then wiped his wet lips with the back of one hand. "I was a rotten husband to her. She was brilliant and beautiful and giving, and I took it all without appreciating any of it."

"And you hit her."

Something flared in Ambrose's eyes, something that was hidden when he dropped his gaze to the bottle again.

"Exactly how deeply in debt are you?" said Sebastian, then added when Ambrose's head jerked up, "And don't even think about trying to deny it."

Ambrose slumped back in his seat. "How the devil did you discover that?"

"Did you think I would not?"

Ambrose shook his head and swallowed hard.

Sebastian said, "How deep?"

Ambrose's face twitched. "Nearly five thousand pounds. A large but not insurmountable sum for a man in my position. Theoretically."

"Theoretically."

"I did not kill my wife," said Ambrose, his lips pulling away from his teeth as he enunciated each word carefully. "That is why you're here, isn't it? You think my debts somehow implicate me in her death. Well, believe me, you couldn't be more wrong."

"Why the bloody hell should I believe you?"

"Why?" Ambrose gave a ragged laugh. "Because only a fool would kill the goose that lays the golden eggs." He leaned forward, his voice dropping. "You don't understand, do you? Oh, I had a couple of plays produced before Jane and I married, but their reception was only luke-warm. It wasn't until I turned my hand to opera that I had real success. *Lancelot and Guinevere* opened a week after our first wedding anniversary."

"You're saying—what? That Jane was your muse?"

Ambrose gave a ringing laugh. "My muse? God, that's rich. For all intents and purposes, Jane *was* Edward Ambrose. Oh, I wrote some of the libretto. But the music—that glorious music was all Jane's. Not mine. Jane's."

Sebastian watched the playwright bring the bottle to his lips and drink deeply, a rivulet of alcohol escaping to run down the side of his chin. "Did no one ever suspect?"

Ambrose set down the bottle with studied care. "Her twin, James, knew the truth. She couldn't hide it from him; he knew the instant he heard that first opera that the music was hers. She never told Christian, but I think he pretty much figured it out, too." He brought up trembling hands to rake the disheveled hair from his face with splayed fingers. "So you see, I'm the last person who'd ever want Jane dead."

"Unless she threatened to leave you."

Ambrose froze with his elbows still spread wide, his gaze on Sebastian's face.

Sebastian said, "I can see a certain kind of man who owed his success—his very livelihood—to a woman becoming enraged if she threatened to leave him."

"Jane would never have left me."

"She would never leave you when walking out on her marriage meant losing her sons. But now? If she found out you were drowning in debt and spending the money she'd actually earned on a mistress? I can imagine her at least threatening to leave you. And I can see you flying into a rage and hitting her, the way you'd hit her so many times in the past. Only this time she struck her head on something when she fell and she didn't get up again. And when you saw what you'd done, you wrapped her body in—what? A carpet? A blanket? An old greatcoat?—and carried her out into the snowy night to leave her in Shepherds' Lane."

Ambrose stared at him, jaw slack, nostrils flaring with alarm. "No."

"The only thing I don't understand is, why Shepherds' Lane? Did you mistakenly think her lessons with Mary Godwin were on Thursdays rather than Fridays?"

"I didn't kill her, damn you."

"I don't believe you."

Ambrose might be drunk, but he wasn't too drunk to know that men had swung on flimsy conjectures such as this. His tongue flicked out to wet his lips. "You . . . you were asking me the other day about the Rothschild girl Jane was teaching."

"Yes." Sebastian frowned. "Why?"

Ambrose leaned forward. "Jane had an aunt who was married to Sheridan—Richard Sheridan. Sheridan and I never exactly got along, but he came to see me last night. Spun some crazy tale about Rothschild and gold shipments to France, and wanted to know if Jane had ever talked to me about it."

"Had she?"

"No. I'd never heard any of it before. But Sheridan was damnably upset about it all. I can tell you that. Went away muttering under his breath. I couldn't catch most of it, but he was saying something like 'I blame myself.'"

"'I blame myself'?"

Ambrose nodded. "I did tell you I thought her strangely frightened by her last meeting with Rothschild. Didn't I tell you?"

"You did."

"So you'll look into it?"

"I will." Sebastian pushed up from the table. "Why would Jane tell her late aunt's husband what was frightening her but not her own husband?"

Ambrose's head fell back as he stared up at Sebastian. "What do I know of the government's gold policy? Sheridan spent decades in Parliament."

"That he did," said Sebastian, reaching for his hat.

But Edward Ambrose only tipped his head and frowned, as if the larger implications of his statement eluded him.

Richard Sheridan was feeding scraps to a colony of stray cats in the noisome alley behind his house when Sebastian came to stand with one shoulder propped against a nearby corner.

"How'd you find me?" asked the old man without looking up. He was wearing a tattered greatcoat, scuffed boots, and the same nightcap Sebastian had seen on him before. Gray stubble shadowed his unshaven face.

"Your housemaid."

"Ah, Lizzy. She's a treasure. Poor girl hasn't been paid in months, but she won't give up on us. Don't know what we'd do without her."

Sebastian said, "Why didn't you tell me your niece tangled with Rothschild over a shipment of smuggled gold?"

"Been talking to Ambrose, have you?"

"Yes."

Sheridan reached down to pet a gray tabby rubbing against his legs. "It all happened so many weeks ago, I frankly wasn't even thinking about it when you were here before. I was focused on the last time I'd seen her. It wasn't until after you'd gone I started wondering if Rothschild might have had a hand in what happened to the poor girl."

"I take it she overheard something in his house she wasn't meant to hear?"

The old man nodded. "It's frightening, isn't it? The simple, seemingly inconsequential decisions we make that can shift the entire course of our lives. She went to use the water closet after her lesson with the child and was coming down the stairs when she heard Rothschild consulting with one of his men. I suppose he thought she had gone. There was little in Jane's world beyond music—and her boys, of course, when they were alive—so she didn't know the background of what she was hearing. I suspect if Rothschild had simply smiled at her and let her go on her way, she probably wouldn't have given it another thought."

"What did he do instead?"

"He came the ugly—threatened her with all sorts of dire repercussions if she told anyone and then ordered her never to come near his house again." Sheridan shook his head. "The man might be a wonder when it comes to manipulating markets and turning this nasty war to his advantage, but he's a poor judge of people. He thought he was frightening her—and he did frighten her. But he also put up her back. She went home, thought about it all for a while, then came to ask me to explain it to her."

"So Rothschild knew about the gold guineas hidden aboard the *Viking*?"

The old man gave a rude snort. "Of course he knew. He's been smuggling gold out of England for years. Last December alone he shipped something like four hundred thousand guineas' worth."

"Good God," said Sebastian.

The exportation of gold from Britain had been illegal for almost twenty years, ever since a disastrous run on gold stocks that took place shortly before the turn of the century. At the same time Parliament outlawed gold exports, they'd also made it illegal for the Bank of England to issue gold coins, forcing them to use only nonconvertible paper notes.

"The problem is," Sheridan was saying, "thanks to this blasted war, the value of the pound has been going down at the same time the price of gold has skyrocketed. It's a situation ripe for gold speculators, and the most successful speculator of them all is Nathan Rothschild. He buys gold in London with devalued British banknotes and then sells it on the Continent at a profit of twenty percent or more."

"How . . . patriotic."

Sheridan huffed a scornful laugh. "Oh, he's that all right. And he's not the only one, not by a long shot. Look at the Hopes' bank! They helped arrange the bloody loans that enabled the United States to buy Louisiana from France, thus injecting millions of pounds into Napoléon's war effort against us. How is that not treason? How? If there were any justice in this world, the lot of them would be tried and hanged. Instead, their descendants will be wealthy beyond the wildest dreams of avarice, while the poor women and children of this land starve in the streets and their menfolk are used for cannon fodder."

"Speculators always manage to profit from war."

"Yes, but this goes beyond mere speculation. What's most disturbing about that gold shipment on the *Viking* is where it was headed. Rothschild used to send most of his gold to Amsterdam, Vienna, and Frankfurt. Now it's all going to France, and the shipment on the *Viking* was only one of many he's sent there this month. He has agents stationed at Gravelines to collect it and quickly send it directly to his brother in Paris."

"You told this to Jane?"

The old man let out his breath in a pained sigh. "Some of it. I didn't know it all at the time. I had to look into it a bit."

"Do you think Jane might have told someone else about what she heard?"

"I did warn her not to."

"So why do you blame yourself for what happened to her?"

Sheridan squinted over at him. "How do you know I do?"

"Ambrose said he heard you mumbling to yourself as you walked away."

"Ah." The old man rasped one hand across his beard-roughened chin. "I warned her not to tell anyone about what she'd heard, but it occurs to me that in the process of looking into it I may have accidently betrayed her. I mean, Rothschild knows I'm her uncle. What if someone told him I was poking around, asking questions? The man could easily have put two and two together."

"And had her killed?"

Sheridan shook his head, although it was in uncertainty and confusion rather than in denial. "I don't know. Would he do that, you think?"

"You said he threatened her. Threatened her with what?"

"He said if she breathed a word about what she'd heard, he'd break every bone in her body."

"That sounds pretty specific to me."

Sheridan looked up at him with troubled bloodshot eyes. "Yes, it does, doesn't it?"

Chapter 33

*T*he brightness of the sun bouncing off the snow-covered pavement hurt Sebastian's eyes as he drove toward the City, guiding his horses through treacherously icy streets, past silent shops draped with glistening icicles and half-buried behind piles of shoveled snow. The sun might be out, but there was no warmth in it, and the few people he saw were bundled up and walking briskly. The air was cold and still, the smoke from the city's chimneys rising straight up to smudge the blue sky. He could hear the squeaking crunch of the chestnuts' hooves in the snow and the bark of a dog somewhere in the distance, the sound carrying with unnatural clarity. But all the normal racket and bustle were eerily absent, as if London were as frozen and unmoving as its river.

He was only vaguely aware of the silent, snow-plastered facades sliding past, the classical pilasters, bow windows, and pediments of Mayfair giving way to the soot-grimed red brick of an earlier age as he neared the financial district. There was a heaviness in his heart, an ache that was part sorrow but also part anger. He felt an absurd, useless wish to reach back in time to that fateful Thursday afternoon and stop Jane

Ambrose as she crossed the ancient bricked courtyard of Warwick House with the snow falling around her. If only he could call her name or somehow turn her away from whatever she was walking into.

Where had she been headed that day? he wondered for what felt like the thousandth time. To see Rothschild? Why then, in such dreadful weather? How had she then ended up in Clerkenwell?

Where, why, how?

He understood Jane better now. But he knew he still wasn't seeing her clearly. For she was more than a grieving mother mourning her lost children. More than a deeply unhappy wife married to a profligate, abusive man who claimed her glorious music as his own. She was also the kind of person willing to stand as a loyal friend to a troubled young princess.

And through no fault of her own she had found herself in possession of dangerous information about powerful, ruthless men.

Nathan Rothschild was striding up the narrow medieval lane of St. Swithen, the hem of his worn greatcoat flaring in the bitter wind, when Sebastian fell into step beside him. The financier cast him one swift glance, then stared straight ahead. His pace never slackened despite the treacherous icy footing.

Sebastian said, "I've discovered a few things since our last conversation."

"Oh? And do you expect me to applaud your cleverness?"

"Not yet."

Rothschild grunted.

Sebastian said, "According to my sources, you've been smuggling hundreds of thousands of guineas a month to the Continent for years, with most of it going to Napoléon's old allies. But the gold that was found aboard the *Viking* on the third of January was bound for France itself. For bloody *Paris*."

"I take it this shocks you?"

"On the fourth of January, you were discussing the *Viking's* interception with one of your agents when you realized your daughter's piano instructor was still in the house and had overheard everything you said. That is why you dismissed her. It's also why she was afraid—because you threatened to break every bone in her body."

Rothschild drew up abruptly and swung to face him, pale eyes glittering with animosity. "You are dabbling in affairs about vhich you know nothing. Nothing!"

"True. But I am slowly discovering more and more."

"Yet you still obviously have much to learn. Vhy do you think the *Viking's* captain and crew were let go?"

"For the same reason your crews are always released. You bribed someone."

The financier cast a quick look around the snowy street before leaning in close and lowering his voice. "The shipment aboard the *Viking* vas indeed headed for Gravelines, from vhence it would have been sent on to Paris. But vhat you do not seem to understand is that its ultimate destination vas Vellington's army in the Pyrenees."

"Wellington?" Sebastian stared at him for one incredulous moment, then threw back his head and laughed.

Rothschild's jaw tightened. "You laugh, but it is true. That shipment vas simply the first part of six hundred thousand pounds bound for Vellington so that he may meet his payroll and pay the Spanish and French merchants for his army's needs."

"I don't believe you."

Rothschild gave a dismissive shrug. "Ask your own father. He is the Chancellor of the Exchequer, after all. He vas there vhen the agreements vere signed."

"Then why all the lies?"

"Vhy do you think? Transactions of this nature are complicated and require great secrecy. Do you seriously imagine that Napoléon vould allow the transfers to continue if he knew their ultimate destination?"

Sebastian studied the financier's homely, undecipherable face. "Did you kill Jane Ambrose?"

"I did not."

"I don't believe you."

"And you think that should concern me?"

Rothschild started to turn away, but Sebastian put out a hand, stopping him. "What about Jarvis? Did you tell him that Jane Ambrose knew about the shipments to Paris?"

"I did."

"So it's possible he killed her."

Rothschild glanced toward the Exchange as the bells in the clock tower began to chime, ringing out "See, the Conquering Hero Comes." "Many things are possible. All I know is, you are delaying me. Good day to you, sir."

And with that he strode off, a stout, homely man in threadbare clothing with the morals of a cutpurse and wealth that could beggar kings.

Chapter 34

"*It* pains me to have to admit it," said Hendon as he and Sebastian walked beneath the rows of snow-shrouded plane trees in St. James's Park. "But Rothschild is telling the truth."

Sebastian looked over at him. "You can't be serious."

"I wish I weren't. You'll never convince me there wasn't another way to get that money to Wellington—a way that wouldn't have included Rothschild pocketing nearly four times as much as Wellington is receiving."

"How much?"

"You heard me. Rothschild is earning two million pounds out of the transaction."

"That's obscene."

"Oh, yes. Without a doubt." Hendon paused, his jaw tightening as he stared out over the snowy, undulating park. "The people of England are freezing and starving to death by the tens of thousands, and this man is being paid a premium to do what he's been doing against our laws in secret for years. The entire damn family has grown enormously rich by financing both sides of this interminable war, and now Jarvis has given their London representative the opportunity to pretend he's a patriot."

Hendon huffed a mirthless laugh. "If he were a patriot, he'd be transferring the money for nothing rather than making a fortune out of it."

"And Napoléon suspects nothing?"

Hendon shook his head. "Napoléon may be a brilliant military strategist, but he has a soldier's understanding of finance. He doesn't believe in either paper money or government debt, and he's convinced that a country's economy is only strong when it has strong gold reserves. That's why he's been willing to allow his bankers to cooperate with London's gold speculators. He's convinced that Rothschild and those like him are weakening England."

"But they are, aren't they?"

"They are. Although not as much as Napoléon believes." Hendon walked on in silence, his hands clasped behind his back, his face troubled. "You think Rothschild killed that woman?"

"It's looking increasingly likely. Either Rothschild or Jarvis."

"Jarvis, more likely. The Rothschilds might keep one of our age's greatest intelligence networks, but I don't think they're anywhere near as fond of assassins as your father-in-law."

"They might make an exception for someone who threatened a windfall of two million pounds."

"True." Hendon sighed. "It's a damnable business, this war financing. I've heard Napoléon likes to say that when a government depends on bankers, the bankers control the government. I fear I'm beginning to agree with him."

"Only beginning?" said Sebastian, and the Earl looked over at him and laughed.

A light snow was falling again by the time Sebastian climbed the hill to Brook Street. He found Hero sitting cross-legged on the hearth rug before the library fire, her head bowed as she focused on petting Mr. Darcy, who lay curled up nearby.

"They hanged her?" Sebastian asked quietly, going to pour himself a brandy.

Hero nodded. "Along with a man and his two boys. It was beyond ghastly. How can anyone possibly watch something like that for fun?"

"I don't know. But tens of thousands do."

She rested her hands on her knees as the cat stood and stretched. "Surely, you haven't been at the inquest all this time?"

He shook his head. "The inquest was little more than a formality." He came to sit in one of the upholstered armchairs beside her and told her of his discussions with Ambrose, Sheridan, and Rothschild.

"And Hendon confirmed this?" she said when he had finished.

"He did."

She stared at the fire beside her. "Jarvis's name keeps coming up. First with regard to Orange, and now this."

"It does. But then, little of importance happens in this Kingdom that he's not involved with in one way or another."

"You think he killed her?"

Sebastian hesitated, then said, "It's certainly a possibility."

"Dear God." She pushed to her feet and went to stare out the window at the quietly falling snow. "You've spoken to him?"

"Not yet."

"I will," she said.

He felt a heavy weight of sadness settle over him. Hero's love for her father was deep and powerful, and Sebastian wasn't sure what it would do to her if she were to discover Jarvis's hand at work in this. But all he could say was "If that's what you want."

She turned her head to meet his gaze, her eyes dark and hurting. "It's what I want."

Jarvis was seated at the elegant French desk in his chambers in Carlton House when Hero arrived. According to his clerk, he'd only recently returned from the Foreign Office and was reading a report from Castlereagh. But he set the papers aside at the sight of her.

"I know about the gold, Rothschild, and Jane Ambrose," she said without preamble.

He leaned back in his chair. "Oh?"

"That's why you sent your carriage for her several weeks ago, isn't it? Not because she was spying for you, but because she had accidently stumbled upon the details of the gold transfers through the Rothschilds. You had her brought here so that you could threaten her. Scare her."

"Under the circumstances, do you blame me?"

Hero went to stand with her back to the window, her gaze on his face. "Our warships control the Channel. You'll never convince me you couldn't send that gold directly to Spain."

"To Spain, yes. But Wellington is over the Pyrenees and into France now. The French bankers are insisting on heavily discounting our government notes to such an extent that Wellington was getting desperate. Sending the gold through Paris was easier, quicker, and, believe it or not, cheaper."

"Cheaper?"

"Yes, cheaper. These things are complicated."

"Obviously." She kept her gaze hard on his face. "You told me you didn't kill her, and I believed you."

Jarvis pushed to his feet. "As it happens, I did not kill her. I won't deny that if I had felt it necessary to eliminate her, I would have done so. But I had no reason to kill her. She had already told her uncle Sheridan about the gold, but I convinced her that she would be signing the death warrant of anyone else who heard about it from her. She wisely saw the importance of keeping quiet."

"So who did kill her?"

"I've no idea."

"Rothschild?"

Jarvis shrugged. "It's possible."

"But you don't care?"

"Is there a reason I should?"

She watched him walk over to pour wine into two glasses. "I've heard it said Rothschild brags that whoever controls Britain's money supply controls the Kingdom—and you and I both know that he controls Britain's money supply."

Jarvis smiled. "Rothschild is an extraordinarily clever, ruthless, and unprincipled financier. But I could wipe him out just like that—" He raised one hand and snapped his fingers. "If he doesn't realize it, he's a fool."

She tipped her head to one side. "So certain?"

"Yes." He held out one of the glasses, and after a moment she took it.

She said, "Someone tried to kill Devlin in Fleet Street."

"So I had heard."

"Was that you?"

Jarvis took a sip of his own wine. "He told you I warned him?"

"As it happens, no; he did not."

"Interesting."

Hero waited a moment, then said, "I notice you didn't say it wasn't you."

"Not this time."

"I hope that was said in jest."

Jarvis reached out to touch her cheek in a rare gesture of affection. "I did not try to kill your tiresome husband. Not yet." He hesitated a moment, his expression vaguely troubled, or perhaps simply confused. "Why do you continue to take such a personal interest in this woman's death? Simply because you happened to be the one to find her?"

"That's part of it, I suppose. But it's also because . . ." She paused, searching for a way to put her thoughts into words. "If I were to simply go on with my life, forgetting about her and how she died, then it would be as if I myself had had a part in killing her."

"This is nonsense. You barely knew the woman."

"You think that should matter?" She searched his face, but found none of the reassurance she so desperately needed to see there and gave a faint shake of her head. "This is the fundamental difference between you and me, isn't it? The Kingdom and its monarchy mean everything to you, and you will do anything to serve and protect them. Yet the people—the hardworking, poor, everyday *people* who form the bedrock of what Britain is and always has been—are to you nothing more than the coal beneath our soil or the timber in our forests: a resource to be exploited and, if necessary, destroyed."

"Oh, I care about the people of Britain. But on an individual level? No, of course not. That would be ridiculous."

Hero shook her head. "I can't understand that way of thinking."

"A defect you obviously share with your husband," said Jarvis.

But at that, Hero only smiled.

Chapter 35

*S*ebastian was cleaning his pistol at his desk when he heard a distant door slam, followed by a shout. He looked up as Tom came skidding into the room.

"I got what ye wanted, gov'nor!" exclaimed the tiger, ignoring Morey's loud hiss from the entrance hall. "I been askin' around the Percy Arms about that Italian cove yer interested in, and I finally found a chambermaid says 'e went off about midday last Thursday. 'E come back fer a bit t' change 'is clothes and get 'is 'arp, but then he went off again."

Sebastian carefully replaced the pistol's flint. "She's certain about the day?"

"Aye. Says it was the day they got their chimneys swept, and the sweep's boy got stuck up the one in Vescovi's room for hours. Only Vescovi never knew it 'cause he didn't come in till late!"

A respectable eighteenth-century redbrick inn with white sash windows and a tidy, symmetrical facade, the Percy Arms lay on Red Lion Square in Holborn. When Sebastian pushed open the street door and turned toward the public room, a warm atmosphere heavy with the smells of coal and tobacco smoke, roasting meat and spilled ale enveloped him. He ordered a tankard and then went to pull out the opposite chair of the table where Signor Valentino Vescovi sat eating a plate of sausages beside the fire.

The Italian froze with his fork halfway to his mouth. *"Per l'amor di Dio.* What are you doing here?"

"What do you think?" said Sebastian, settling himself comfortably.

"But I've told you everything I know!"

Sebastian took a slow sip from his tankard and set it on the table between them. "I think not."

Vescovi thrust a large chunk of sausage into his mouth and chewed in silence.

Sebastian said, "You can begin by telling me where you really were last Thursday. And don't even think of trying to convince me you were here all day, because I now know that for a lie. I did warn you, did I not?"

The Italian swallowed his half-chewed sausage, his eyes going wide.

"Where were you?" Sebastian said again.

"With the Big Princess—Princess Caroline of Wales," said Vescovi, his voice hoarse.

Sebastian sat back in his chair and folded his arms at his chest. "You do realize I will check, don't you?"

"Yes, yes—of course. But I was there. I swear it."

"All afternoon and evening?"

The harpist twitched one shoulder. "Late afternoon to evening. Before that, I was skating."

"Why so long?"

"Pardon?"

"Why were you at Connaught House so long? You were obviously there for something more than a simple music lesson."

Vescovi sat up straighter and said with an assumption of great dignity, "Her Highness was hosting a dinner party, and I provided the music."

"Oh? And who was at this dinner party?"

Vescovi frowned. "I'm not convinced I should tell you that."

Sebastian met the man's gaze and held it. "Actually, I rather think you should."

The Italian's gaze faltered away. "Brougham. Henry Brougham was there. Whitbread. Earl Grey. Some others."

"Phineas Wallace?"

"No. Not him. He was supposed to attend, but he canceled at the last minute."

Interesting, thought Sebastian. Aloud, he said, "I've been slowly piecing together a picture of Jane Ambrose's last days. On Thursday, the twentieth of January—exactly one week before she died—Peter van der Pals attempted to cajole Jane into spying on Princess Charlotte for him and then threatened her when she refused. The following day she told Miss Kinsworth of the incident, unaware of the fact that the Duchess of Leeds's nasty young daughter was listening at keyholes again. So when did Lady Arabella talk to you?"

Vescovi slumped in his seat and looked miserable. "The following Monday."

"And Jane confronted you beside the canal in St. James's Park that same day?"

"Yes," said Vescovi again, obviously not seeing where this was going. "Why?"

"Because the following afternoon—Tuesday—Jane went to see a certain gentleman of her acquaintance to ask about Orange's sexual interests. So far I haven't been able to discover who told her about Orange. But given the timing, I'm beginning to think it was you." Sebastian hesitated. "Am I right?"

Face tight with worry, Vescovi set down his fork with a clatter and pushed his half-eaten plate away.

Sebastian said, "*Signor?*"

The Italian drew a pained breath and nodded. "I was . . . angry. We both were. She made a number of unjust accusations about me, and I told her she was naive—that she didn't understand the situation at all."

"That's when you told her about Orange?"

Vescovi nodded. "But she didn't believe me. At least, she said she didn't."

"She may not have believed you at first. But she was concerned enough about what you said that she sought out someone she thought could confirm it."

Vescovi swiped his hands down over his face. "And this person she went to see, did he tell her the truth?"

"He did."

"*Dio mio,*" he whispered. "You think that's why she was killed? Because someone was afraid she might pass on what she'd learned to Charlotte?"

"I think it's a distinct possibility."

"*Dio mio,*" he said again.

Sebastian studied the musician's haggard, troubled face. "The Orange alliance is important to a number of powerful people, none of whom are the sort to take kindly to having their ambitions thwarted."

Vescovi brought up a shaky hand to cup his mouth.

"What?" asked Sebastian, watching him.

The musician cast a quick look around, then leaned forward and dropped his hand. "Those pushing for the Orange alliance are extraordinarily ruthless and powerful. But some of those working to prevent the marriage—while less powerful—can also be dangerous."

Sebastian frowned. "But Jane was against the marriage herself. Why would they be a threat to her?"

"You must understand that those working against the alliance do not all share the same motivations, nor do they all have the Little Princess's best interests at heart. Some wish simply to protect Charlotte from a miserable future and are opposed to the marriage for that reason, while others would like to prevent the Dutch entanglement but not at the cost of harming the Princess. Yet there are those who will do anything to prevent the alliance and they don't care if Princess Charlotte is hurt in the process."

"That doesn't make sense. How might she get hurt? If anything, it's in her best interests if the marriage is called off."

"That depends on why it's called off, does it not?"

"Meaning—what?"

"Please." Vescovi's voice turned into an agonized whisper. "Don't ask me. I cannot tell you."

Sebastian studied the other man's drawn, frightened face. "You might be safer if you did."

"I cannot."

And with that, the Italian pushed up from his chair and walked quickly away, his head bowed and the fingers of one hand sliding nervously up and down his watch chain.

Chapter 36

Sebastian stood beside the stone balustrade of Blackfriars Bridge and stared out over the uneven frozen plain that had once been the River Thames. Two straggly parallel lines of gaily painted booths and tents were beginning to form, with roving vendors selling everything from gingerbread and tea to gloves and hairbrushes. Troops of jugglers, acrobats, and tumblers performed for the growing crowd, while close to one of the arches of the bridge someone was roasting a sheep over a large iron pan full of coals and charging sixpence to watch or a shilling for a slice of mutton. The air was heavy with the scent of roasting meat, hot chestnuts, and ale.

There hadn't been a Frost Fair on the Thames since Sebastian was a boy. In his memories it loomed as a magical thing, a marvel of music and laughter and fanciful sights that seemed far more exciting than those of more humdrum fairs such as Bartholomew's or Southwark's. He supposed the wonder had something to do with a Frost Fair's ephemeral, spontaneous nature, as well as the inevitable spice of danger that came from knowing the ice could at any moment crack and give way, plunging everyone into the frigid waters below.

There were tents for drinking, eating, and dancing; toy stalls and skittles alleys; even a Punch and Judy show. And near the roasting sheep, a couple of apprentices were helping their master set up a printing press in a booth decorated with gaily colored streamers. The apprentices were unknown to Sebastian, but he recognized the printer. It was Liam Maxwell.

A young mother and two small children, all wrapped up warmly against the cold, were picking their way across the ice toward Maxwell's booth. For a moment the younger boy paused to gaze in wide-eyed wonder at a juggler tossing flaming torches high into the air, and Sebastian found his thoughts spinning away, inevitably, to Jane Ambrose's last days.

He suspected that, near the end, she must have felt something like a juggler herself, desperately trying to control the dangerous men who threatened her world. One of them had eventually killed her. If Sebastian could figure out how and where, it might tell him which one. But at the moment his thoughts were all up in the air, going round and round in an endless, useless whirl.

He was still staring thoughtfully out over the growing fair when a slim, elegantly dressed courtier came to stand beside him, the breeze rising off the ice to ruffle the artful curls that framed his handsome face.

"A curious level of excitement, this," said Peter van der Pals, his gaze on the bustle below. "One would think they'd never seen a Frost Fair before."

"They don't happen here often."

Van der Pals shifted his posture to lean one hip against the snow-covered battlement and face Sebastian. "I'm told you've been making inquiries about me."

"I have. I don't appreciate it when people lie to my wife."

The Dutch courtier stiffened. It was considered a grave insult, calling a gentleman a liar. "I beg your pardon?"

Sebastian kept his voice even and pleasant, his gaze on two men setting up a swing below. "When you claimed Jane Ambrose was jealous of your attentions to Lady Arabella, that was a lie. Her anger was actually provoked by your attempts to convince her to spy on Princess Charlotte. When she refused, you threatened to make her 'sorry' if she told anyone. But she did tell someone, and now she's dead. All of which makes you a prime suspect in her murder."

A weak sun peeked out through a break in the clouds, and van der Pals's eyes narrowed against the glare off the ice. "No one murdered Jane Ambrose. She slipped and fell."

"Someone certainly made a rather clumsy attempt to give that impression."

"So you're suggesting—what? That I killed her out of spite? For daring to tell some dried-up old spinster on me?" The Dutchman gave a ringing laugh. "Surely you know that everyone around Charlotte spies for someone?"

"Perhaps. Except that as a result of your rather crude overtures, Jane Ambrose learned a certain troublesome secret about the Prince of Orange. And that secret gives you a second—and considerably more powerful—motive to kill her."

The smirk remained on the courtier's face. "Do you realize how many men in England—not to mention on the Continent—know this supposedly powerful and dangerous 'secret'? Yet no one is killing them. To my knowledge, Mrs. Ambrose's death remains a singularity."

"Jane Ambrose's access to Princess Charlotte was also rather . . . singular."

Van der Pals twitched one shoulder in a dismissive gesture. "At this point it doesn't matter whether Charlotte learns the truth or not. It's too late for her to back out."

"Perhaps. But it does rather beg the question: If your Prince is certain of his future bride's constancy, why were you so eager to place a spy in her household?"

"Security. There are those who would like nothing more than to see the betrothal ended before it is announced."

"Oh? Such as?"

"Charlotte's mother, the Princess of Wales, obviously—and those who champion her cause."

"Namely?"

"Wallace. Brougham. You know as well as I with whom Caroline associates."

"Who else?"

The courtier raised one haughty eyebrow. "How would I know?"

"Because it's your business to know." Sebastian studied the courtier's handsome smiling face. "The betrothal's announcement is being delayed because Orange fears he has yet to adequately solidify his position in the Netherlands. That tells me there are forces within your own country that are as opposed to the match as Caroline and her associates. So who amongst the Dutch in London might be working to prevent the alliance?"

"None, to my knowledge. Apart from which, why would any of them want to kill Jane Ambrose? The woman was against the betrothal herself."

"So she was. Although I wonder how you came to know that."

"She told me."

"Oh? When did she tell you this?"

"The last time I saw her."

"Which was—when?"

"You seriously think I recall?"

"You claim to recall what she said."

Van der Pals pushed away from the balustrade to stand with his hands dangling loosely at his sides, his chiseled jaw set so hard he was practically spitting out his words. "That makes twice you have insulted my honor by calling me a liar. It is only my respect for what is owed the dignity of my Prince that prevents me from calling you out here and now. But I will not be so forbearing next time. Good day to you, my lord." And with that he strode off, the hem of his elegant caped great-coat flaring in the icy wind.

After he had gone, Sebastian remained on the bridge, his gaze on the makeshift booths and tents below. Of all the Whigs gathered around the Princess of Wales, Lord Wallace was probably the most likely to stop at almost nothing if he thought he could scuttle the projected alliance between Britain and the Netherlands. But did that include murdering a talented pianist?

Perhaps. The problem was, *Why?* In what way could Wallace have seen Jane as a threat to his machinations? Jane was every bit as opposed to the proposed Orange marriage as Wallace. Vescovi had hinted at something hidden, something sinister. But what?

What?

Playing a hunch, Sebastian drove to Lord Wallace's house on Mount Street. Only, instead of knocking at his door, Sebastian stayed with the horses and sent his tiger, Tom, to question his lordship's house servants and grooms.

Unassuming, subtle, and beguilingly cheerful, Tom was very good at eliciting information without raising a whisper of either understanding or alarm.

Sometime later, Phineas Wallace was crossing the snowy forecourt of the House of Lords when Sebastian fell into step beside him.

"Now what the devil do you want?" demanded the Baron as they turned onto Margaret Street toward Whitehall.

"I'm wondering where you were the afternoon and evening of Thursday, the twenty-seventh of January."

"Really? Why on earth would you want to know that?"

"That's the day Jane Ambrose was killed."

Wallace drew up abruptly and swung to face him. "You can't be serious."

"I'm afraid I am." When the Baron continued to simply stare at Sebastian, he said again, "So where were you?"

Wallace turned and kept walking. "You think I remember? That was a week ago."

"Not quite. As it happens, Her Highness the Princess of Wales gave a dinner party that evening. All your friends and close associates—Brougham, Whitbread, Earl Grey—were there. But you weren't. Why was that? I wonder. And before you claim to have been at home, I should warn you that your servants say otherwise."

"My God. Have you stooped to suborning a man's own servants?"

"Not suborning. Merely questioning." Sebastian studied the Baron's tightly held face. "It's no secret that you are strongly opposed to the marriage Prinny has arranged between his daughter and the House of Orange."

Wallace threw a quick look around and lowered his voice. "Of course I am opposed to this ridiculous alliance. But what has that to say to anything?"

"I don't think Jane Ambrose came to see you about music lessons for your daughter. I think something else was involved—something linked to either Princess Charlotte or her mother. Or both."

Lord Wallace paused at the kerb. "Did it ever occur to you that you are wrong? That Jane Ambrose simply slipped on the ice, hit her head, and died? That her death, while tragic, is not part of some grand and nefarious international conspiracy?"

Sebastian shook his head. "Jane Ambrose didn't die alone in the middle of Shepherds' Lane."

"That doesn't mean her death necessarily had anything to do with the Princesses." Wallace turned his head to stare thoughtfully up the snowy street, his eyes narrowing against the glare. "I'm told Jane Ambrose was as much against this marriage scheme as anyone. If you are right and she did not simply die by accident, then I suggest you look for her killer amongst those dedicated to seeing the alliance go through. Not amongst those who are opposed to it."

"Perhaps. Except for one thing."

"What's that?"

"Jane Ambrose would never do anything that might harm Princess Charlotte. Can you say the same?"

"Don't be ridiculous," scoffed the Baron, and walked away.

But Sebastian noticed he didn't deny it.

Chapter 37

That evening, Sebastian and his Viscountess wrapped young Master Simon in a fur-lined robe, sturdy boots, and a thick woolen cap and mittens, and set off to visit the Frost Fair.

The fair was a magical place after dark, with torches flaring up golden bright against a clear, glittering black sky and strings of colored lanterns dangling between parallel rows of makeshift booths and stalls. They'd dubbed the main thoroughfare "the City Road," a grand promenade that snaked down the frozen river from Blackfriars to London Bridge. Scores of tradesmen whose businesses were suffering from the cold and snow had seized the opportunity to reach new customers, with everyone from barbers to shoemakers setting up shop on the ice. There were gaming tents with EO tables, wheels of fortune, and *rouge et noir;* drinking tents where gin and ale flowed freely; cook stalls selling mutton pies and baked potatoes and gingerbread; and amusements such as knock-'em-downs and merry-go-rounds for the children. Their shrieks and laughter echoed across the ice, mingling with the wail of bagpipes, the screech of fiddles from dancing tents, and the quavering voices of ragged little girls singing ballads for a penny.

Rather than being smooth, the icy surface was rough and undulating, for the Thames had not frozen in a single sheet. And so the "streets" of the fair twisted this way and that, winding around jagged, snow-covered hillocks formed by the massive ice chunks that had floated down from upriver and collided into one another, allowing the river to freeze between them.

Liam Maxwell's booth was only one of half a dozen or more printing presses operating on the ice, although his appeared to be the most popular, thanks perhaps to the doggerel verse printed on his cards:

> *Amidst the arts which on the Thames appear,*
> *To tell the wonders of this icy year,*
> *Printing claims a place that at one view*
> *Erects a monument to it and you.*
>
> *You who walk here and do deign to tell*
> *Your children's children what this year befell,*
> *Come buy this print and it will then be seen*
> *That such a year as this hath ne'er been.*

Sebastian handed over his shilling for a souvenir card. "Clever."

"Thank you," said Maxwell, pulling the "devil's tail" on the press. Unlike the more sophisticated presses in Somerset's publishing house, this one was made on a wooden frame, with a simple platen and rounce handle.

"I need to ask you some questions. It's important," Sebastian added when the printer kept his attention on the press.

Maxwell hesitated a moment, then signaled one of the apprentices to take his place.

"You've discovered something?" he asked, wiping his ink-stained hands on a rag as they stepped away from the booth.

"Nothing definite, unfortunately. But I am curious about something:

When I asked you what Jane might have been doing in Clerkenwell the day she died, you said you had no idea. Why didn't you tell me she taught piano to William Godwin's daughter? Surely you knew."

Maxwell frowned as he stared at one of the booths on the far side of the row. "But Jane's lessons with Mary Godwin were on Friday afternoons. Not Thursdays."

"So they were," said Sebastian, following Maxwell's gaze to where Hero had paused with Simon before a display of colorful whirligigs. "How much did Jane tell you about her last lesson with Anna Rothschild?"

Maxwell turned his head to fix Sebastian with a hard, steady stare. "You asked me that before, and I told you she was upset to lose Anna as a pupil."

"She didn't say anything to you about secret gold shipments?"

"Gold? You can't be serious."

"I wish I weren't."

"Bloody hell." Maxwell kicked angrily at the loose snow at his feet. "I knew she was keeping something about the incident from me—I even tried to press her on it more than once. But it upset her so much I gave up." His eyes narrowed. "Are you telling me Rothschild had her killed? Because she somehow found out about his bloody gold smuggling?"

"You know about that?"

"Oh, I know. Don't ask me how, but I know. Only, Jane didn't tell me, if that's what you're asking." Maxwell threw another glance at Hero and lowered his voice. "He was watching her, you know—Jarvis, I mean. Had his men following her for weeks before she died. I thought it was because of Princess Charlotte. But now I wonder . . ."

"Jarvis says he didn't kill her."

Maxwell made a disbelieving noise deep in his throat. "Well, he would say that, wouldn't he?"

Sebastian kept his gaze on the younger man's face. "Do you know why Jane went to see Princess Charlotte's mother the week before she died?"

Maxwell's gaze met his for one telling moment, then slid away. "Jane has known—knew—the Princess of Wales for years. Most people think of Caroline as half-mad and half-foolish, but she's actually a very serious, accomplished musician."

"That doesn't explain why Jane went to see her."

"Doesn't it? I rather thought it did."

"Yes and no. You told me Jane was upset over Charlotte's betrothal to the Prince of Orange. And no one is more opposed to the Orange alliance than Caroline and the Whigs who've championed her cause."

Maxwell snorted. "You think the likes of Brougham and Wallace have championed Caroline's cause? I'd say they simply use her to advance their own causes."

"Perhaps," said Sebastian. "But that doesn't alter the fact that both Caroline and the Whigs are united in their opposition to this marriage. So I can't help but wonder at the timing of Jane's visit. Did you know one of Orange's courtiers tried to get her to spy on the Princess for him?"

"What?" Maxwell's mingling of shock and outrage were too visceral to be anything except genuine.

"She didn't tell you that, either?"

Maxwell's jaw tightened. "No. No, she didn't." He rested his hands on his hips and stared off to where a group of ragged boys was playing a game of football on the far side of the crowds of merrymakers thronging the rows of tents and booths. His features were drawn and hard with thoughts and emotions Sebastian could only guess at.

Sebastian said, "You claim you want to help catch Jane's killer. But there's something you're not telling me."

Maxwell silently shook his head. But he didn't deny it.

"Has a date been set for her funeral?" Sebastian asked.

"Tomorrow, at St. Anne's, Soho. Ambrose didn't tell you?"

"No, he didn't."

Maxwell's lips tightened into a sneer. "He's already let it be known that if I dare show my face there, he'll have me thrown out."

"He's aware of your friendship with Jane?"

"How could he not be? Christian and I have been mates since we were at school together."

"Will Ambrose allow him to attend the funeral?"

"Christian? I've no doubt Ambrose would like to keep him away. But it wouldn't look good, would it—barring Jane's brother from her funeral? And Ambrose is all about being seen to do the right thing."

"*Mr. Maxwell*," called one of the apprentices. "We need more paper!"

Maxwell cast a quick glance back at his booth. "I must go."

"Of course," said Sebastian. "Thank you."

Sebastian was still standing there, watching the printer bustle about preparing a new ream of paper, when Hero walked up with Simon clutching a square of warm gingerbread in his mittened hands.

"Do you believe what he told you?" she asked quietly.

"Some of it," said Sebastian, his gaze still on the printer. "But not all."

As they turned to leave, Maxwell stepped in front of his booth to clap his hands and shout, "Step right up, friends, and seize your chance to support the freedom of the press! After all, what can be a greater example of liberty than a genuine souvenir of the Frost Fair, printed right here in the middle of the Thames?"

They drove home through nearly deserted streets that glowed a ghostly blue-white in the waning moonlight.

"What do you think Maxwell is hiding?" Hero asked suddenly, as if she had been quietly pondering his recent conversation.

Sebastian shook his head. "I wish I knew. I'd also like to know how the devil he found out about Rothschild's gold shipments—and Jarvis's involvement in it all. He claims he didn't learn it from Jane, and that's one of the few things he's said that I'm inclined to believe."

"Yet he didn't know about Jane's problems with van der Pals?"

"Evidently not."

Hero stared out at the shuttered shops of Bond Street flashing past. It was so cold the fresh layer of powder squeaked beneath the horses' hooves. "You think Maxwell and Jane were lovers?"

"I'm not sure. He knew her lessons with Mary Godwin were on Friday and not Thursday—which is interesting, given that her own husband claims to be ignorant of her students. Of course, if—"

He broke off as the coachman shouted, *"Whoa there!"* and the carriage came to a shuddering halt, the horses snorting and plunging.

"What the devil?" said Sebastian, leaning forward.

A man lay crumpled at the turning into Brook Street. A lanky middle-aged man with a long red scarf that trailed behind him like a line of blood in the snow.

Chapter 38

$\mathcal{B}$y the time Sebastian reached him, Valentino Vescovi was struggling to prop himself up on his elbows, his breath coming in short, painful gasps.

"Where are you hurt?" said Sebastian, kneeling beside him in the snow.

The Italian's harsh features contorted with pain. "*Bastardo* . . . Stuck a knife in my back."

"Who? Who did this?"

"Don't know. Couldn't see. Most of his face was hidden."

Sebastian looked up to find one of his young footmen staring at them, his mouth slack with horror. "Don't just stand there, damn it! Run to the house and get some men to help carry him inside."

"Y-yes, my lord," stammered the footman, and took off running.

Vescovi coughed, and Sebastian carefully eased one arm beneath the man's shoulders to raise his head and support his weight. "Why would someone want to kill you?"

"I was coming to see you. Tell you about the . . . about the letters."

Vescovi's eyes started to slide closed, and Sebastian tightened his grip on the man's shoulders. "Hold on. As soon as we get you into the house, I'll send—"

But Vescovi's eyes were no longer sliding closed; they were still and staring, and Sebastian knew he was dead.

Sometime later, Sebastian stood with Sir Henry Lovejoy at the snowy intersection of Bond and Brook Streets.

"A second of Princess Charlotte's music instructors found dead in the street?" said Lovejoy, his shoulders hunched against the cold as he stared down at the dead man in silence. "Why?"

"I wish I knew."

Lovejoy shook his head in bewilderment. "The palace will never be able to quiet the speculation this time."

"That doesn't mean they won't try."

"No," said Lovejoy with a sigh. "No, it doesn't."

They sent the harpist's body off to Paul Gibson's surgery. Then, at Sebastian's suggestion, they took a couple of Lovejoy's constables and went to search Valentino Vescovi's room at the Percy Arms in Red Lion Square.

The innkeeper muttered and grumbled about being dragged from his fireside for something that could just as easily have waited until morning. He was still grousing about being disturbed when he threw open Vescovi's room. Then he broke off to clutch at his nightcap as it started to slide. "Merciful heavens," he said, his voice rising into a squeak. "What is this?"

The room had been ruthlessly searched, the mattress dragged from the bed and slit open, drawers emptied and their contents strewn about the floor. Even the Italian's spare clothes had been slashed, as if the searcher thought something might have been hidden in their seams and linings.

"Whatever were they looking for?" said Lovejoy, pausing in the doorway.

Sebastian went right to the Italian's harp. The instrument's beautifully worked frame had been hopelessly smashed. "I've no idea."

They searched the room themselves anyway, on the off chance Vescovi's killer had missed something in his haste.

They found nothing.

Wednesday, 2 February

Dawn was spilling a weak golden light down the snowy canyon of Brook Street when Hero came to stand in the doorway to the library, a cup of tea held in one hand. "Did you sleep at all?" she asked Devlin.

He looked up from where he leaned against his desk, staring at something in his hand. "A bit."

"Liar."

He gave a lopsided smile and set aside whatever he'd been holding.

"What's that?" she asked.

"Jane Ambrose's locket."

"Ah." She came to hand him the cup. "Here. This is for you. Drink it."

"Yes, ma'am."

"Can I talk you into some breakfast?"

He took a sip of the tea and grimaced. "Not hungry." He pushed away from the desk and went to stand at the window, his gaze on the long icicles that glittered in the cold sunshine. "What in all of this am I missing?" He brought one clenched fist down on the windowsill. "Bloody hell! I still don't know where she actually died, how or why she burnt her fingers, or even who raped her a day or two before she was killed.

Something must tie it all together. And now Vescovi is dead, and it's damnably hard not to hold myself in some measure responsible."

"Why? Because you underestimated the importance of the communication between Princess Charlotte and her mother?"

Devlin nodded. "And yet I can't think of anything that could be in the letters Vescovi carried that would motivate someone to kill over it. What could Charlotte have said? That she regrets allowing her father to trick her into this betrothal? That Caroline is working with her Whig friends to find a way to stop it? None of that is exactly a secret."

"No," she agreed. "But why else would someone kill Vescovi?"

Sebastian drained his tea and set it aside. "Damned if I know."

An hour later, Sebastian received a note from Kat Boleyn telling him she had found Edward Ambrose's mistress.

"Her name is Emma Carter," said Kat as she and Sebastian walked along the stalls of Covent Market. The icy, ferocious cold still held the city in its grip, but the roads from the countryside were finally passable enough that some supplies were beginning to trickle in. "She used to be an opera dancer before Ambrose set her up in rooms in Tavistock Street. Almost no one knows about her. He must be extraordinarily discreet in his visits to her."

"He couldn't afford to have his wife find out," said Sebastian, his gaze scanning the shivering, desperate crowd. "Not when she was the one actually writing his operas."

"Was she really?"

"She was indeed. How long has Ambrose had this woman in keeping?"

"Three years."

"Three years? He has been discreet."

Kat put out a hand, stopping him as she lowered her voice. "That's her there—in the cherry red pelisse."

Sebastian studied the woman who stood at a stall mounded high with carrots and potatoes. She was a tiny thing, surely no more than nineteen or twenty, with a pretty round face and dusky curls that peeked from beneath a fur-trimmed hat. As she turned away from the stall, her pelisse flared open, exposing a heavily pregnant belly.

"Good God," he said softly. "She's with child."

Chapter 39

*E*dward Ambrose buried his wife beside her sons in the crypt of their parish church of St. Anne's, Soho.

He played the part of the grieving widower to perfection, Sebastian thought, watching him. The man's features were drawn and pallid, his shoulders slumped as if beneath a crushing weight of pain and loss. He accepted the condolences of friends and colleagues with a graciousness that impressed everyone who saw him. But if Sebastian's suspicions were correct, the show of grief was all for effect, all false.

Sebastian stood beneath the church's west gallery and watched the funeral service. Built by Wren or one of his associates in the aftermath of the Great Fire, St. Anne's was a classic basilica—broad and spacious and plain, although cluttered with the high, ornate box pews of the parish's wealthier families. He noticed that Jane's brother, Christian Somerset, came in just before the beginning of the service and left immediately afterward, slipping quietly away without attempting to join those who stayed to console his brother-in-law.

Women did not typically attend funerals. But it occurred to Sebastian as he watched Ambrose shake hands and speak quietly to the somber files of men who had come to pay their respects to Jane's husband just how sad and lonely her life must have been. All the members of her family except for Christian Somerset were dead. The real genius behind the operas of "Edward Ambrose" was hers, yet with the exception of the social philosopher William Godwin, all those attending her funeral were her husband's friends, associates, and admirers.

Sebastian waited while the church emptied of mourners and Ambrose paused to speak in low-voiced consultation with the rector. After a moment, Ambrose nodded to the vicar and walked over to Sebastian to say bluntly, "I take it you wish to speak to me?"

"It can wait until you're finished here," said Sebastian.

"No. If you've something you wish to say, say it to me now. Why not? It's only my wife's funeral."

"All right," said Sebastian. "I know about Emma Carter."

It occurred to Sebastian, watching him, that Ambrose had as much control over his expression as any actor on the stage. Sebastian waited while the dramatist absorbed the implications of Sebastian's words, considered denying all knowledge of the woman, then decided simply to say nothing. And none of those ruminations showed on his face.

Sebastian said, "I'll give you this: You've been extraordinarily careful in your dealings with her. But then, you had to be, didn't you, given that your success depended on your wife?"

Ambrose threw an anxious glance over his shoulder at the waiting vicar. "Why here, for God's sake?" he asked in an angry undertone. "Why now? You bring this up at my wife's funeral? Have you no decency?"

"Decency?" Sebastian felt an absurd impulse to laugh. "You know what I think? I think Jane found out about your mistress—your *pregnant* mistress. I think she threatened to leave you, and you flew into a rage and killed her."

"You son of a bitch," hissed Ambrose. "I did not kill my wife."

Sebastian studied the other man's handsome, even-featured face. "I don't believe you."

Ambrose threw another worried glance in the direction of the vicar. "Jane did not know about Emma. She didn't even suspect!"

Sebastian shook his head. "I keep thinking, what would it do to a woman who'd just lost both of her own children to then learn that her husband had got another woman quick with child?"

"I was always careful. Always."

"Perhaps. But that doesn't mean someone didn't tell her. Someone who wished you harm—you, or her."

"You're wrong, I tell you. Do you understand me? Wrong!"

"Perhaps." Sebastian turned to go, then paused to say, "Tell me this: Did your wife have a particular friend? Someone in whom she might have confided?" *Someone who knows the shadowy recesses of her life, which might hold the secret to her tragic death?*

Ambrose shook his head. "No, not really."

"You're certain?"

"Not to my knowledge."

"But then, how well did you actually know your wife?"

"What the hell is that supposed to mean?"

"Think about it," said Sebastian, and walked away.

Sebastian sat for a time in the quiet of St. Anne's churchyard and watched a few lazy snowflakes fall to earth, his thoughts drifting haphazardly from one aspect of Jane Ambrose's death to the next.

He'd been coming around to thinking that the threat to Jane's life had come from outside her home—from someone such as Rothschild, Jarvis, or van der Pals. But like so many women, Jane had lived with a man who had no hesitation in taking his frustration and anger out on her with his fists. Debt, infidelity, jealousy, and rage were a potent brew that all too often could lead to death. The problem was, if Ambrose had killed his wife, why that Thursday? And where? It seemed to make no sense.

Which meant Sebastian was still missing something.

Frustrated, Sebastian walked to Christian Somerset's establishment on Paternoster Row, only to find the bookstore closed and the printing workshop deserted except for a sandy-haired, rosy-cheeked lad of perhaps fifteen who was cleaning dirty type, his arms black with ink up to the elbows.

"Mr. Somerset and the other lads are all at the Frost Fair," said the young apprentice with a grin. "You ought to see our booth; it's ever so grand!"

Christian Somerset had set up his booth midway between Blackfriars and London Bridge, on the Frost Fair's main promenade. It was indeed an impressive structure, painted with craggy cliffs and fairyland castles beneath a pastel sky and stocked with a fine collection of romances, poetry volumes, and packets of feminine stationery. For a penny, fairgoers could also buy a souvenir memento that carried a crude image of the Frost Fair above the Lord's Prayer, with PRINTED ON THE THAMES 1814 FROST FAIR emblazoned in large type below it. Christian Somerset himself was personally working the press.

"Somehow I didn't expect to find you here," said Sebastian, walking up to him.

Jane's brother rotated the press's handle to roll the bed under the platen and gave one of his slow, self-deprecating smiles. "This frozen river is minting money. A man would need to be a fool to miss this kind of opportunity." He paused to turn the screw's long handle. "I even dragged my old wooden press out of the basement for the occasion. I was afraid if I brought one of the new iron-framed Stanhopes out here it would crash through the ice and drown us all." He nodded to a nearby apprentice to take his place at the press, his smile fading as they stepped away from the booth. "I saw you at Jane's funeral."

"Allow me to express my condolences again on the loss of your sister," said Sebastian.

Somerset nodded and had to look away for a moment, blinking. "Have you learned something new?"

"I've discovered you were right: Ambrose does indeed have a mistress—an opera dancer he keeps in rooms in Tavistock Street."

Somerset's jaw tightened. "I knew it. The bloody bastard."

"What would Jane have done, do you think, if she found out? Would she have left him?"

Somerset shook his head. "Not Jane."

"Not even if she discovered his mistress was heavy with his child?"

"My God. Is she?"

"Yes."

Somerset stared thoughtfully at a group of men drinking rum and grog around a nearby bonfire. "I still don't think she'd leave him."

"Even with both her children now dead?"

"She might threaten it in the heat of the moment. But she'd never actually do it."

"The question is, would Ambrose know that?"

Somerset frowned. "Perhaps not."

"Did you know Jane wrote the music for all of Ambrose's operas?"

Somerset blinked. "I always suspected she helped him, although she would never admit it—at least, not to me."

"She didn't simply help; the music was hers."

He blew out his breath in a long, pained sigh. "Poor Jane. To think of the acclaim that could have been hers, had she only been born a man."

"Did she feel it, do you think?"

Jane's brother rubbed his eyes with a splayed thumb and forefinger. "She must have. Growing up, we all knew she was actually more talented than her twin, James—even he acknowledged it. Our father tolerated her playing, but he never actually encouraged her the way he did James. People were always complimenting her for 'playing like a man.' I know that used to anger her. But she never said anything to me about Ambrose's music, if that's what you're asking. She was a very private person, Jane."

"Do you know if she had any close female friends?"

"Our sister, Jilly, was just a year older than Jane, and they were quite close. But Jilly died a couple of years ago. Consumption."

"Is there no one else?"

"Not that I know of. Sorry."

Sebastian watched one of the men drinking rum by the fire stagger to his feet, only to fall flat on the ice. "You say Jane would never have left Ambrose because of the way your father raised her. But even fiercely devout people can lose their faith, particularly after the deaths of two dearly beloved children. She might have changed her mind."

Somerset shook his head. "Not Jane. Liam Maxwell begged her to leave Ambrose right after Lawrence died, and she wouldn't do it. She said she'd made a vow before God, and just because she later realized it was a mistake didn't give her the right to forsake that vow. I can't see the discovery that Ambrose had a mistress—even an *enceinte* mistress—changing that."

Sebastian felt the wind cold against his cheek. "Are you saying that your sister and Maxwell were lovers? Because just a few days ago you insisted Jane would never be unfaithful to her husband."

Somerset looked troubled, as if he regretted what he'd said. "No; I didn't mean to imply that at all. Jane would never have been unfaithful to Ambrose; I'm certain of that. But there's no denying that Maxwell has been in love with her for years. And while she never admitted as much to me, I've often thought Jane felt the same."

"Did Ambrose know?"

"I suppose he might have suspected it, but I couldn't say for certain. He's so wrapped up in himself, it's possible he never noticed. Although if he did—" Somerset broke off.

"If he did?" prompted Sebastian.

Somerset thrust his hands deep into his pockets and shivered, as if suddenly feeling the cold. "A man like Ambrose, I don't imagine he'd take it well, knowing his wife was in love with another man. Even if he didn't believe they were lovers."

Sebastian kept turning Somerset's words over and over in his mind as he worked his way through the Frost Fair's surging crowds. It certainly provided an easy explanation for what had happened. It was an old, familiar tragedy: A woman discovers her husband is unfaithful; they argue; the husband, himself already suspicious of her infidelity, strikes her in anger and accidently kills her.

Could it really be that simple? Could all the dangerous undercurrents in Jane Ambrose's life—her discovery of the financial maneuverings of the Rothschilds and the political machinations surrounding Princess Charlotte—simply be a distraction?

It was possible. It might even seem the inevitable solution if it weren't for the questions raised by the murder of Valentino Vescovi. But if it was true, then why the devil had Liam Maxwell—a man who claimed he wanted to catch Jane's killer—deliberately kept hidden from Sebastian such an important aspect of her life?

By the time Sebastian arrived at the upper end of the Frost Fair's grand promenade, his feet were cold and he was in no mood to tolerate any more of the printer's evasive games. But Maxwell's booth was being manned by three apprentices; Maxwell himself was nowhere in sight.

"He went off a good long while ago," said one of the apprentices, inking the press's text block. "Didn't say where he was going."

"You're certain? This is important."

The two younger apprentices shook their heads, their expressions believably blank. But the oldest lad hesitated a moment, then said, "I think he went off on account of that lady's funeral. But I can't tell you where he went any more than Richard and Paul here."

" I hank you," said Sebastian.

The lad simply stared back at him, his face taut and troubled.

Leaving the river, Sebastian climbed the hill to Maxwell's printing shop in a cluttered ancient court off Fleet Street. It was a far different establishment from that of his former partner: cramped and dirty, with no elegant bookshop and bindery attached. But the workroom was locked up and deserted.

After that, Sebastian tried every public room and tavern in the area, all without success.

Liam Maxwell obviously didn't want to be found.

The whistled refrain of what sounded suspiciously like "Alasdair Mac-Colla," an old Irish rebel song, floated across the snow-filled yard as Sebastian plowed his way to the door of the surgeon's stone outbuilding. He banged on the old warped panels, and Gibson broke off to shout, "Go away. I'm busy."

Sebastian pushed open the door to find the Irishman leaning against the stone slab in the center of the room, a saw in one hand. The only thing on the table before him was a human leg neatly sliced in two just above the knee.

"Ah, it's you," said Gibson, setting aside the saw with a clatter. "Thought it might be someone I didn't want seeing this."

"What is that?"

"And what does it look like, then?" said Gibson, reaching for a rag to wipe his hands. "It's a leg. I've been practicing a new amputation technique."

"Lovely." Sebastian closed the door against the cold. "I won't ask where you got it." He looked beyond the Irishman to where what was left of Valentino Vescovi rested on a low shelf. "Finished with him, have you?"

"I have."

"Learn anything?"

"Nothing you didn't know." Gibson tossed aside the rag. "He was stabbed in the back by someone who either knew what he was doing or got lucky."

"That's it?"

"That's it."

"Bloody hell." Sebastian slapped one hand against the doorframe. "How the devil am I supposed to figure out who's doing this?"

"His clothes are there," said Gibson, nodding to the jumbled pile on a nearby shelf. "If you care to go through them."

Sebastian had checked the musician's pockets last night while waiting for Lovejoy. But he went over everything again anyway, this time examining the seams and linings, as well.

He found nothing.

"His death might not be related to what happened to Jane Ambrose," said Gibson, watching him. "People really do occasionally get killed by footpads in London."

Sebastian carefully folded the harpist's red scarf and rested it atop his serviceable, slightly worn clothing. "This wasn't footpads."

On his way back to Brook Street, Sebastian decided to swing past the church of St. Anne's, Soho.

And it was there he finally found Liam Maxwell, sitting hunched over at the top of the steep stone steps leading down to the crypt, his hands thrust between his knees and his face wet with tears that slid un-checked down his cheeks.

Chapter 40

The church was bitterly cold and filled with shadows, for the morning's weak sunshine had long since disappeared behind a thick cover of heavy white clouds.

Sebastian went to stand with his hands braced against the crypt's iron railing, his nostrils filling with the scent of dank stone and old death. Liam Maxwell did not look up. But after a moment he drew a shaky breath and said, "I can't believe she's down there. I can't believe she's down there, dead, and I'll never see her again." His voice cracked. "How can that be?"

Sebastian shook his head, for there was no answer to give. "Why didn't you admit you were in love with her—and she with you?"

Maxwell squeezed his eyes shut. "I don't know. I didn't want you to get the wrong idea about her—about the kind of woman she was."

It was possible, Sebastian thought. But he could also think of another explanation that was considerably more damning. "Were you lovers?"

Maxwell swiped his sleeve across his wet eyes. "No. I swear to God, no."

"Yet you asked her to leave her husband?"

"Who told you that?"

"Is it true?"

The journalist hesitated, then nodded. "She wouldn't do it, though—for all he made her as miserable as a woman can be."

"How long? How long have you been in love with her?"

A ghost of a smile touched his features. "Since the September I was fifteen. I went with Christian to watch a regatta on the Thames, and she was there. I remember she was wearing a wide-brimmed straw hat and a white muslin dress with little puff sleeves and a blue sash, and I fell hopelessly, irretrievably in love with her—even though she was twenty years old and married and she treated me like her little brother's awkward school friend. Which is precisely what I was."

"When did that change?"

"I don't know. It happened slowly, over time. I think if I hadn't been so much younger than she, and her brother's friend, it never would have come to be. As it was, it simply . . . crept up on her unawares. When Christian and I were in prison, she used to come see us, and we would talk for hours." He drew a deep, shuddering breath. "That's when I first realized Ambrose hit her. One time she came, she had a black eye. She refused to admit he'd done it, but Jane never was very good at lying. He was furious with her for visiting her brother in prison." Maxwell huffed a sound that was not a laugh. "What a bloody bastard."

"Did you know he's had an opera dancer in keeping for the past three years?"

Maxwell entwined his fingers together and tapped his joined hands against his mouth. "I suspected it."

"Did you tell Jane?"

"No."

"Why not?"

"Because I didn't know for certain. And because even if it were true, I knew she still wouldn't leave him. It would only have hurt her, to realize that the man she'd given up everything for couldn't even be faithful to her."

"Could she have found out?"

"No."

"You're certain?"

"Yes. She never would have kept it from me, had she known."

"Yet she didn't tell you about either Rothschild's gold shipments or his threats, did she?"

Maxwell held himself very still. "No. No, she didn't."

"You said you last saw her the afternoon before she died; was that true?"

Maxwell nodded.

"What exactly did she say to you?"

He scrubbed his hands down over his face. "I told you: She talked about Princess Charlotte's betrothal—about what a mistake it would be for Charlotte to go through with the marriage. She said the girl didn't realize how much she would be giving up. And then she said . . . she said our society asks women to give up too much, but nothing's going to change as long as women keep meekly doing what is expected of them."

"That doesn't sound like what I've come to know about Jane."

"No, not at all. I asked her what she meant by it, but she only gave me a strange smile, kissed my cheek, and said, 'You'll see.'"

"'You'll see'? You'll see—what?"

"I don't know."

Sebastian kept his gaze on the younger man's face. "The postmortem showed Jane had been raped a day or two before she was killed."

"*What?*" Maxwell pushed to his feet, his hands curling into fists at his sides.

"She didn't say anything to you about it?"

"No!" He flung away, only to draw up short and whirl to face Sebastian again. "Who? Who did it?"

"We don't know."

"Was it Ambrose?" Maxwell's nostrils flared. "Did he force himself on her? Hurt her? Because if it was Ambrose, I swear to God I'll—"

"Don't," suggested Sebastian quietly.

The journalist thrust a shaky hand through his disheveled hair and swallowed hard.

Sebastian said, "Is there anyone to whom Jane might have confided something of that nature?"

Maxwell thought about it a moment, then shook his head. "I can't think of anyone. She was fairly close to Miss Jones, but I doubt she would have revealed something like that to her. Women don't usually talk about such things, do they? Not if they can hide it."

"Who is Miss Jones?"

"Lottie Jones. She's the Princess's official miniature portrait painter. Jane's known— knew—her for years. She painted the miniatures of Jane's children in her locket."

"Where would I find her?"

"She has a studio in Lower Grosvenor Street." Maxwell slumped back against one of the side aisle's columns, his head falling back as he stared up at the old church's arched ceiling. "I can't believe she kept so much from me—first Rothschild, then this. Why? Why would she do that?"

"What would you have done if she had told you someone had forced himself upon her?"

Maxwell's jaw clenched. "Killed the bastard."

Sebastian nodded. "Then that's why she didn't tell you."

An early dusk was falling over the city by the time Sebastian turned down Brook Street. He could hear Hero playing the pianoforte, a haunting melody that carried clearly in the cold air as he nodded to the lamplighter and his boy working to kindle the flame of the oil lamp near the corner.

Hero had always been a technically proficient pianist. But there was a quality to her playing on this frigid February evening that he'd never heard before. And as he handed his hat, gloves, greatcoat, and walking stick to Morey and turned to climb the stairs, he finally realized what it was: emotion. Hero typically approached her playing as a skill, a task, something she mastered and yet from which she held herself aloof. But not tonight. Tonight she was pouring herself into her music, and the result was both exquisite and heartrending.

He paused outside the drawing room door, not wanting to interrupt her. And so engrossed was she in her music that she remained unaware of him watching her until the piece ended and her fingers slipped from the keys to rest in her lap. Then, as if sensing his presence, she turned her head and saw him.

"A beautiful piece," he said, going to rest his hands on her shoulders.

"It's from *Lancelot and Guinevere*." She leaned back until her head was resting against him. "I keep thinking about all the incredible music Jane gave the world. All that beauty and joy, yet no one will ever know it's hers because she was a woman."

He kissed the top of her head and went to pour himself a brandy before coming to sprawl in a nearby chair. "Are you acquainted with a woman named Lottie Jones?"

Hero swung around on her bench. "You mean the miniature painter?"

"So you do know her?"

"Not well, but yes, I know her."

"Well enough to ask if she has any idea who might have raped Jane Ambrose?"

"Oh, Lord," said Hero, and reached out to take a sip of his brandy.

Thursday, 3 February

It was not easy, being a woman in London's male-dominated art world. Miss Lottie Jones had succeeded on the strength of her personality as much as her prodigious talent and by wisely choosing to focus on the one niche of her profession popularly perceived as being particularly suited to women: the painting of miniature portraits on ivory.

She was now forty-five years old, her appearance striking, her manner deftly calculated to flatter her subjects' amour propre without being obsequious. Hero had known the artist for seven or eight years. And so Miss Jones received the Viscountess in her studio's private parlor with a warm welcome. But her eyes were watchful and knowing, for this was a woman whose gift for capturing likenesses came as much from her ability to see behind the masks her subjects tried to present to the world as from her skill with brush and tint.

They spoke for a time of the weather, of the progression of the war on the Continent, and of an exhibition Miss Jones had planned for the spring. And then, when Hero was still working her way around to the reason for her visit, the artist fixed Hero with a steady gaze and said, "I've heard the palace is suppressing the truth about Jane Ambrose's death. Is that why you're here, my lady? Because the rumors are true and you think I might know something of use to Lord Devlin's investigation?"

Hero met the older woman's gaze and held it. "I understand you and Jane were friends."

Miss Jones gave a sad sigh. "We were, yes. Our backgrounds might have been dissimilar, but we nonetheless had much in common. We both knew what it was like to be female in a profession that is not friendly to our sex."

"Not to mention years of experience in dealing with Princess Charlotte and her father."

A gleam of amusement lit up the older woman's shrewd eyes. "That, as well." The amusement faded. "But the truth is, I don't see how I can be of much assistance to you. It is possible to know someone quite well in some ways and yet remain ignorant of the intimate details of her life. I can tell you that the loss of Jane's two boys last year utterly devastated her, that she loved her surviving brother dearly and still missed her dead siblings and parents dreadfully. But if you were to ask me who might have killed her . . ." Her voice trailed away, and she shook her head.

"When was the last time you saw her?"

Miss Jones frowned in thought. "It must have been a week or more before she died. She came for tea one afternoon, and we spoke of the Prince's gout and this new poem of Byron's, but nothing of any real importance."

"How did she seem then?"

Miss Jones was silent a moment before answering. "Actually, she did her best not to show it, but there's no doubt she was preoccupied and unhappy in a way I don't recall her being before. But I couldn't tell you why. As she was leaving I asked if she were all right, and she simply laughed and said the wretched weather was making her blue-deviled."

"Did she ever say anything to you about someone forcing unwelcome advances upon her? A man, I mean."

The question obviously took the older woman by surprise. "Good heavens. No, never. Although . . ."

"Yes?" prompted Hero.

The artist folded her hands in her lap and looked down at them.

"Miss Jones?"

She drew a deep breath. "I don't know if this is relevant, but I did see Jane one other time recently. I didn't mention it before because I didn't actually speak with her, but I was coming out of Warwick House and she was there, in the small receiving room just to the left of the entrance. I was surprised to see her because it was Tuesday—quite late—and Jane's lessons with Charlotte were always on Monday and Thursday mornings."

"So why was she there?"

"I don't know, but she was engaged in a decidedly heated exchange with Lady Arabella."

"The Duchess of Leeds's daughter?"

"Yes. That was strange enough, given that Jane's opinion of the vile, sneaky little girl matched my own. But what was particularly startling was Jane's appearance. She was still wearing her pelisse, and I could see that the back was horribly smeared with some sort of muck while one sleeve was torn at the seam. Even the flounce of her walking dress was ripped, for I could see it trailing beneath the hem of her pelisse." She paused. "If it hadn't been for Lady Arabella, I'd have gone to her. But given the nature of their conversation, I didn't feel it would be right for me to interrupt."

"What were they saying?"

"I didn't hear much—I was trying not to. But I did hear Arabella say something to the effect of 'You brought this on yourself. How dare you presume to now blame me for your mistakes?'"

Hero leaned forward. "But you don't know what she was talking about?"

"No. It was all so awkward, I doubt I'd have asked her about it the next time I saw her. But as it was, I never had the opportunity. Two days later, she was dead."

Chapter 41

"What the devil do you make of that?" said Devlin when Hero told him of her conversation with the miniaturist.

"I've not the slightest idea. But it sounds as if we need to have an urgent—and brutally frank—conversation with young Lady Arabella."

Devlin frowned. "The problem is, how to do it away from Mama Duchess."

Hero pushed up from where she sat to go thumb through the various invitations on the mantelpiece. "I'd utterly forgotten. What's today?"

"Thursday. Why?"

She swung around as she found the one she was looking for. "We have an alfresco breakfast in Kensington Gardens to attend."

"In the snow?"

"In the snow."

The Duchess of Leeds's decision to give a grand wintertime alfresco breakfast had been risky but inspired. A fresh white blanket of clean snow covered the sprawling lawns and empty flower beds of the royal gardens, while long icicles hung sparkling from the bare branches of the surrounding trees. In addition to tables groaning with food and copious libations of mulled wine, coffee, tea, and hot chocolate, Her Grace had also strewn the snowy gardens with braziers for those most sensitive to the cold. But even the weather cooperated: The day had dawned crystal clear without any wind, and the golden sunlight and dry air made the afternoon surprisingly pleasant despite the actual temperature.

Like all Society breakfasts, this one was held in the early afternoon, since few members of the *ton* rolled out of bed before midday. Most of the guests arrived wrapped in furs, and they came in droves, for invitations to the breakfast were highly coveted. Its very site—the gardens of Kensington Palace—clearly signaled to the world the Dowager Duchess's high standing with the royal family. Not only was the aged Queen herself present, but so were four of her spinster daughters and a brace of Royal Dukes. Even the Prince Regent put in an appearance, still hobbling about with a cane, thanks to his recent attack of gout.

The only royal of any significance noticeably absent was the young heiress presumptive to the throne.

"Charlotte?" said the Dowager Duchess of Leeds when Devlin paused beside their hostess to inquire after the Princess. "Oh, His Highness prefers she not attend such affairs."

Hero had to force herself not to meet Devlin's gaze. "But your daughter, Lady Arabella, is here?"

"Oh, yes," said the Dowager smugly. "She makes her Come Out this year, you know."

"How lovely," said Hero.

"And you almost sounded as if you meant it," Devlin told Hero as they strolled along snowy paths, looking for Lady Arabella.

Hero pulled a face. "Beastly woman."

He stared off across the winter-shrouded gardens filled with laughing, chatting guests. "The other day you compared Charlotte to Rapunzel, but I'm beginning to think a more apt comparison might be Cinderella. Admittedly, no one is making Charlotte sweep out fireplaces. But she certainly is forced to sit home while everyone else is out having fun."

"Except that in Charlotte's case, I fear there will be no Prince Charming in her future to ride to her rescue." Hero frowned as she scanned the crowd. "Do you see her little ladyship?"

"There, at the table by the sundial. Which of us do you think would be most likely to intimidate her into telling the truth?"

"I doubt anyone could intimidate that girl."

"I am larger."

"True. But if she simply refuses to answer your questions? How precisely do you intend to force a sixteen-year-old duke's daughter to be more forthcoming? In the middle of her mama's party?"

Devlin thought about it a moment, then said, "I haven't the slightest idea."

Hero nodded. "I thought not. Leave her to me."

Lady Arabella was choosing between the relative merits of sliced roast beef and bacon when Hero walked up to her and said bluntly, "I'm going to ask you some questions about Jane Ambrose, and you are going to answer me truthfully."

The Duke's lovely young daughter gave a trill of laughter. "Indeed? And if I don't?"

Hero made a show of studying a platter of what must have been hideously expensive greenhouse asparagus. "It's actually quite ridiculous how easy it is to ruin a young lady's reputation," she said in a pleasant, conversational tone. "A little whisper here, an innuendo there, and the opprobrium quickly takes on a life of its own—whether it's true or not, and even when the young lady in question is the daughter of a duke."

Lady Arabella's beautifully molded lips curved into an arrogant smile. "I don't believe you would do that."

Hero met the girl's glittering gaze and held it. "Oh, believe me, I would."

It was the girl who looked away first, her nostrils flaring on a quickly indrawn breath.

Hero said, "Something happened to Jane Ambrose the Tuesday before she died—something dreadful—and you know what it was."

Lady Arabella lifted her chin. She was no longer smiling. "I'm afraid I haven't the slightest idea what you could be referring to."

"Yes, you do. She came to Warwick House right afterward, specifically to confront you about it."

"If you know so much about it, then why bother asking me?"

"Don't," said Hero, her voice low and lethal. "Don't even think about trying my patience any further."

The girl's pointed little chin jerked up higher. "Very well. She came because—or so she claimed—the Dutch courtier Peter van der Pals had forced himself upon her, and she had the ridiculous notion in her head that I was responsible." The girl gave another tinkling little laugh that made Hero long to slap her beautiful, spoiled face. "As if I could somehow be held to blame for her folly."

"You don't think you were?"

"Hardly."

"Van der Pals threatened to make her sorry if she told anyone he'd tried to get her to spy for him. I know you overheard her warning Ella Kinsworth about what he'd done because you later repeated the conversation to Valentino Vescovi. Did you also tattle to van der Pals himself?"

"And if I did?"

"He *raped* her because of you."

"So she claimed."

"Oh, it happened."

The girl simply stared back at Hero, jaw set hard.

Hero said, "Where did the rape take place?"

"I've no idea. Do you seriously think I inquired into the sordid details?"

Hero searched the young girl's lovely, cold face. "Two people are dead, in all likelihood because of you. Don't you even care?"

"I am no more responsible for their deaths than you are."

Hero shook her head. But all she could find to say was "May God have mercy on your soul."

She was turning away when Lady Arabella said, "Mrs. Ambrose actually thanked me, you know."

Hero paused. "For what?"

"She said I'd helped her see something she should have realized long ago."

"And what was that?"

"I haven't the slightest idea. I didn't ask her to particularize."

Hero said, "If you know anything else—anything at all—about what happened to Jane Ambrose or Valentino Vescovi—"

"I've told you all I know." Lady Arabella shook back her dark, beautiful hair. "Now, you must excuse me, Lady Devlin; I see my mother the Duchess looking for me."

And with that the girl slipped away, her head held high and a faint smile curling her lovely lips, secure in the knowledge that her wealth, birth, and beauty would insulate her from the myriad ugly fates that could befall the world's less exalted mortals.

Chapter 42

$\mathcal{P}$eter van der Pals was looking over a tray of snuffboxes in an exclusive little shop on Bond Street when Sebastian came to rest one forearm on the counter beside him.

"Leave us," Sebastian told the slight, fastidious shopkeeper hovering nearby.

The shopkeeper took his tray of snuffboxes and scuttled to the back of the shop.

Van der Pals turned with deliberate indolence to face Sebastian. "I presume you are here as a result of Lady Devlin's conversation with the Duchess of Leeds's daughter?"

"Lady Arabella managed to get word to you about that already, did she? And are you planning to deny what you did to Jane Ambrose?"

The Dutchman gave a low, incredulous laugh. "Hardly. Why should I? I warned her to keep her mouth shut, and she did not."

"You think that justifies what you did to her?"

The courtier shrugged and started to turn away. "I taught the bitch a lesson. She had it coming."

Sebastian caught van der Pals by the shoulder and spun him around to shove him back against the nearest wall hard enough to rattle the contents of the display cases.

"Gentlemen," bleated the shopkeeper, clutching his tray of snuff-boxes against his chest. "Gentlemen, please."

Van der Pals held himself very still. "You are physically assaulting the particular friend of the man who will someday be the prince consort of your Queen, if not king in his own name."

"I'll worry about the consequences when that day comes."

The courtier raised one supercilious eyebrow. "What precisely is it you want from me?"

"Answers. First of all, where did this happen?"

"Savile Row. I believe she was coming back from a visit to her dear uncle Sheridan, but I could have that wrong."

"So you—what? Dragged her into a convenient alley and took her there up against a wall?"

"Something like that. It was, after all, an act of punishment, not pleasure."

Sebastian resisted the urge to slam the man against the wall again. "And then two days later you killed her."

"Hardly. I'd already made my point. Why would I then kill her?"

"For refusing to keep quiet about the rape."

"In my experience, women never talk about such incidents. They understand that for others to know what's been done to them is far more damaging than the initial violation and therefore keep silent for their own good."

"Except that Jane Ambrose wasn't keeping silent. And given your friendship with young Lady Arabella, I have no doubt you know that."

The courtier gave a dismissive shrug. "So she told one sixteen-year-old girl. She wouldn't have told anyone else."

Sebastian studied the man's handsome, self-assured face. "This isn't the first time you've done something like this, is it?"

The courtier shrugged again, his smile never slipping.

Sebastian's fists closed on the man's lapels. "You son of a—"

"*Gentlemen. Please.*"

Sebastian threw a quick look at the shopkeeper, then took a step back and let the courtier go.

Van der Pals carefully adjusted his coat. "If you ask me," he said, his attention all for his clothing, "the husband killed her."

"Oh? And is this wild speculation on your part, or are you actually basing it on something?"

Van der Pals frowned as he studied his reflection in a nearby mirror and swiftly repaired the folds of his cravat. "Call it a logical deduction. You see, I told her about her husband's young mistress—his *enceinte* young mistress."

"How the bloody hell did you know about that?"

"It's my business to know such things. I even gave her the girl's name and address."

"Why?"

"Why what?"

"Why did you do that?"

The courtier gave a wide smile that showed his even white teeth. "Because I knew it would hurt her. Why else?" The smile faded. "In the past, out of respect for my Prince, I have allowed your insults to my honor to slide. But such an outrage will not go unavenged."

Sebastian turned away. "You can try."

Chapter 43

Sebastian's knock at the door of the rooms Edward Ambrose kept for his mistress in Tavistock Street was answered by a young housemaid no more than twelve or thirteen years old. She was a gangly thing, all arms and legs, with a head of rioting dark hair inadequately constrained by a mobcap. She was evidently so surprised to see an unknown gentleman standing at her mistress's door that she simply stared at him, mouth agape.

"Is your mistress at home?" said Sebastian.

The girl closed her mouth and nodded, eyes going wide.

Sebastian handed her his card. "Kindly tell her Lord Devlin would like a word—"

"Who is it, Molly?" Emma Carter came from a distant room, trailing a length of delicate white knitting. At the sight of Sebastian, she drew up abruptly. "Oh," she said, her free hand creeping up to cup her heavy belly. The way she was looking at him told Sebastian she not only knew who he was, but also had some idea as to why he was here.

She wore a high-waisted figured muslin gown with long sleeves and a pink shawl, and she looked lovely, frightened, and very, very young. Her accent was good enough to make Sebastian wonder what had brought her to this.

He said, "If I might have a word with you, Miss Carter? I need to ask you some questions about Jane Ambrose."

"But I don't know anything about what happened to her," she whispered, her nostrils flaring with alarm. "I swear it."

"Did she come here last Tuesday or Wednesday?"

Emma Carter and her housemaid exchanged quick, anxious glances.

Sebastian said, "She did, didn't she? What did she say?"

The young woman's breathing had become so agitated she was shaking with it. Her lips parted, but she seemed to find it impossible to say anything.

"Miss Carter? What did she say?"

It was the housemaid who answered. "She didn't say nothin'. She jist stood there and looked at mistress. Then she whirled around and left."

"That's it?"

Mistress and housemaid both nodded.

"Did you tell Edward Ambrose she had come?"

Emma Carter shook her head *no* even as her housemaid was nodding *yes*.

"When did you tell him?" demanded Sebastian, his gaze hard upon her even as her features crumpled with her tears. "And don't even think about lying to me again."

"The next day. Wednesday," said the young woman in a broken voice. "Wednesday evening."

"And did you see him again that Thursday?"

"No. He was supposed to come in the afternoon, but he didn't."

"Did he ever tell you why not?"

"He said something came up. He didn't tell me what."

"Thank you," said Sebastian. As he turned away, he found himself wondering what would happen to this heavily pregnant young woman if the father of her unborn child were convicted of murdering his wife.

Then he caught the horror in Emma Carter's frightened brown eyes, and he knew the same thought had already occurred to her.

Sebastian walked the icy streets of the city, his thoughts turning over everything he'd just learned and everything he thought he'd known before.

In the last month of a life cut tragically short, Jane Ambrose had inadvertently made some nasty, formidable enemies: Lord Jarvis, Nathan Rothschild, and the courtier Peter van der Pals. All were hard men who wouldn't hesitate to kill a beautiful young pianist if she got in their way. She had moved through a dangerous swirl of greed and palace intrigue that Sebastian suspected he still didn't completely understand. But he was coming increasingly to suspect that her death might actually have been the result of forces that were for the most part considerably more personal.

What would happen, he wondered, if a woman who'd recently buried both her children were to discover that her husband was about to have a child by his young mistress—a mistress he maintained in grand style on money earned from the operas she herself had secretly written?

What would she do?

Sebastian found himself coming back to what Jane had told Liam Maxwell the afternoon before she died: *Our society asks women to give up too much, but nothing is going to change as long as we keep meekly doing what is expected of us.* When Sebastian first heard those words, they struck him as oddly out of character for the woman he thought he was coming to know. But that was before he'd learned all that had happened to Jane Ambrose in the twenty-four hours before that strange conversation, from van der Pals's brutal rape in a Savile Row alley to her discovery of her husband's pregnant mistress. When considered in that context, Jane's statement to Liam Maxwell sounded like the dawning resolution of a woman who'd had enough. Who'd had enough of hiding her talent from the world because of her sex. Who was weary of denying a love that had been slowly deepening over ten long years. Who no longer believed she should endure a loveless marriage to an abusive husband simply because that's what her religion and society expected of a wife.

So what had she done? Sebastian wondered. Confronted Ambrose? Threatened to leave him?

It wasn't difficult to imagine how a man such as Edward Ambrose, deeply in debt and known for hitting his wife, would react. And if he hit her hard enough that she fell and fatally struck her head?

A man like Ambrose would never admit what he had done.

The housemaid who answered the door of Ambrose's Soho Square town house looked less sorrowful than the last time Sebastian had seen her, but more anxious.

"My lord," she said, bobbing a quick curtsy. "If'n yer here t' see Mr. Ambrose, he's in his library. He's been in there forever, but he don't take kindly to us interruptin' him when he's working like this, and I don't dare disturb him."

"That's quite all right," Sebastian said pleasantly as he simply walked past her toward the library door. "I'll interrupt him myself."

"But, my lord—"

She broke off in a gasp and threw her apron up over her face as Sebastian thrust open the door without knocking.

It was the unexpected chill that hit him first—the chill and the ripe smell of blood. Edward Ambrose lay sprawled on his back beside the library's cold hearth, one knee bent awkwardly beneath him, his arms flung out at his sides. His mouth was slightly agape, his eyes wide, as if he were startled by something. But the eyes were already filmed and flattening, and a dark sea of blood stiffened the front of the torn white silk waistcoat from which protruded the handle of an elegant dagger.

The housemaid, who had crept up to peek around Sebastian's side, dropped her apron and began to scream.

Chapter 44

"How long do you think he's been dead?" asked Lovejoy some-time later as he crouched beside the dead man.

Sebastian stood with one hand braced against the nearby mantel-piece. "Quite a while, from the looks of things. Much of the blood has dried, and the fire has burnt itself down to ashes. According to the house-maid, he shut himself in here shortly after breakfast, and no one in the household had seen him since."

"Not even to bring him a cup of tea?"

"She said he didn't like to be disturbed."

"Someone obviously disturbed him." Lovejoy pushed to his feet with a stifled grunt as his knees creaked. He turned in a slow circle, taking in the room's gently worn furnishings and scattered musical instru-ments. Jane Ambrose's basket of mending still rested beside her chair. "There doesn't appear to be any sign of either an altercation or a search."

"No."

Lovejoy sighed. "I'll set some of the lads to going over the house. We might find something."

"Perhaps," agreed Sebastian, although he doubted it.

Lovejoy brought his gaze back to the dagger protruding from the dead man's chest. It was an exotic weapon, the nephrite handle gently curved to fit comfortably in the palm and set with pearls and semiprecious stones. "An unusual piece."

"It looks Indian to me—probably Mughal," said Sebastian, and left it at that.

Dusk was falling by the time Sebastian made it back to St. Anne's, Soho.

Liam Maxwell was not there.

He checked the journalist's printing shop, then his booth at the Frost Fair, and drew a blank both places. Frustrated, he turned his steps toward Tower Hill. As he crossed Gibson's snowy yard, he could see the glow of a lantern shining through the high windows of the surgeon's stone outbuilding to cast a warm pool of golden light into the night. But when Sebastian pushed open the door, the Irishman was just tugging off Ambrose's boots.

"Bloody hell," said Gibson, looking up. "I hope you aren't already expecting me to know anything about this latest corpse you've sent. Lovejoy's men just delivered him."

Sebastian grunted. "Let me see the dagger, at least."

Gibson shifted to carefully ease the weapon from the dead man's chest, his eyes narrowing as he studied the inlaid handle. "Looks Mughal."

"That's what I was thinking."

"It also looks like a woman's weapon."

Sebastian took the knife in his hand and frowned. "Yes." It was an exquisite piece of work, the blade curved with a central ridge and damascene floral decoration near the hilt and a floral motif of inlaid pearls and red and green stones on the pommel.

Gibson was watching him carefully. "Do I take it that means something to you?"

"Maybe. Maybe not."

"Well," said Gibson, exaggerating his brogue, "it's a relief, it is, knowing you've narrowed things down a bit." He tugged off the second boot. "Since you're here, you might as well help me strip the fellow. Your eyes are better in this light than mine anyway."

Whoever killed Edward Ambrose had stabbed him three times.

"Doesn't look like this killer knew what he was doing," said Sebastian, staring at the three jagged gashes in the dead man's now naked torso.

"Doesn't, does it?" Gibson unhooked the lantern from the chain over the stone slab and held it closer. "I'd say this was the first wound," he said, pointing to the lowest slit. "That one got his stomach. Then this one"—he prodded the tip of one finger into the next cut—"hit a rib. Got it right the third time, though: straight into the heart. Unless of course Edward Ambrose's heart isn't where it's supposed to be, which sometimes happens."

Sebastian took a step back as Gibson reached for his scalpel. "Do you still need me?"

Gibson looked up with a grin. "Why? Don't you want to stay and observe?"

The stone outbuilding was cold enough that when Sebastian blew out a quick, harsh breath, the exhalation billowed around him in a white cloud. "Thank you, but no."

A light snow began to fall as Sebastian searched the dark frozen city for Liam Maxwell. Without a wind, it hurtled straight down, big flakes that looked like shadows against the rows of dimly glowing streetlamps on Fleet Street and the Strand. He trailed through a score of taverns and coffeehouses, then worked his way down toward the riverfront again.

The night became a blur of smoky bursts of firelight gleaming on strange upturned faces, of warmth and laughter punctuated by stretches of darkness and bitter cold.

He finally ran the printer to ground in a Frost Fair drinking tent that some wag had christened THE MUSCOVITE, the letters spelled out crudely on a weathered board. A rough shelter concocted of old sails and crossed galley oars, it was crowded with tradesmen, watermen, and fairgoers, all drinking Mum and Old Tom as if there were no tomorrow.

Liam Maxwell sat on a bench at one end of the rough trestle table, hunched over and alone, his somber mood effectively isolating him from his gay surroundings. His cravat was rumpled and askew, his cheeks unshaven, his collar torn. From the looks of things, the man hadn't been to bed in days.

Sebastian walked up to press his hands flat onto the table's boards and lean into it. "Did you kill Edward Ambrose?"

Maxwell's head fell back, his eyes widening and mouth going slack with a credible expression of shock that shifted ever so subtly into fear. "He's dead?"

"Stabbed."

"When?"

"Probably sometime this morning."

"I didn't do it."

"Can you prove it?"

The journalist pressed his lips together and shook his head.

Sebastian said, "Then why the devil should I believe you?"

Maxwell's eyes were bloodshot and puffy. "Why would I kill him?"

"You know why."

He swallowed. "Are you saying he did it—Ambrose killed Jane?"

"Possibly. Maybe even probably. And I can't conceive of anyone besides you who had a reason to kill him."

"I didn't do it," he said again.

"So where have you been all day? As far as I can tell, no one has seen you."

"I've been . . . around."

"Where?"

"No place for any length of time. I wanted to be alone."

Sebastian reached into his greatcoat and tossed the Mughal knife onto the table between them with a flick of his wrist. The jeweled dagger spun around once, then lay still. "Recognize this? It was found in Ambrose's heart."

Maxwell leaned back on his bench, hands braced against the table's edge, his breath coming quick and shallow.

Sebastian said, "You were raised in India, weren't you? As was your mother before you."

Maxwell brought up tented hands to cover his nose and mouth as he nodded. Slowly he raised his gaze to meet Sebastian's. "That's not my knife. I swear to God, I've never seen it before."

"One of two things," said Sebastian. "Either you're lying, or—"

"I'm not!"

"Or someone is trying to frame you."

A burst of laughter from a nearby table momentarily jerked Liam Maxwell's attention away. Then he leaned forward and lowered his voice. "There's something I haven't told you about. Something that might explain all of this."

"Such as?"

Maxwell threw another quick look around the crowded tent and pushed to his feet. "Not here."

Chapter 45

They pushed their way through the throngs of laughing, staggering, wildly celebratory fairgoers. The snow continued to fall; the scent of hot pitch from the torches mingled with the fragrant aromas of roasting chestnuts and spiced wine to hang heavy in the cold air.

"What haven't you told me?" Sebastian demanded, swerving to avoid a woman selling baked potatoes from a barrel.

"First of all, you must understand that I kept silent about this largely because it didn't occur to me that it might have anything to do with what happened to Jane. But also because it betrays a secret that is not mine to tell."

Sebastian glanced over at him. "So why tell me now?"

"I . . . I haven't been reading the papers much lately, which is why I only just heard this afternoon about what happened to that harpist Valentino Vescovi."

Whatever Sebastian had been expecting, it wasn't that. "Vescovi?"

Maxwell's jaw tightened. "You must swear to me that this will go no further. Jane would never forgive me if she were somehow to become the cause of bringing harm on the young Princess."

"This involves Princess Charlotte?"

"You must swear to me that whatever happens, you won't betray the Princess."

"All right. You have my word as a gentleman."

Maxwell nodded, then hesitated as if choosing his words carefully. "About a year and a half ago, the Regent sent Charlotte down to Windsor and made her stay there for months. The Princess always hates it when he does that—it separates her from her mother and all of her instructors, and she doesn't actually live in the castle with her grandmother and aunts, but in a separate house called Lower Lodge."

"That's odd. Why?"

"Who knows why? Because Prinny is a vicious, ugly human being, that's why. Lower Lodge is a damp, isolated place, and this particular time she was there so long she became horribly lonely and depressed. And then she made the acquaintance of an officer whose regiment was billeted in the neighborhood—a Lieutenant Charles Hesse, of the Eighteenth Light Dragoons." Maxwell paused. "Are you familiar with him?"

"Should I be?"

"He's a natural son of the Regent's brother, the Duke of York."

"In other words, he is Charlotte's first cousin."

"Yes." Maxwell squinted into the distance. "He's said to be a very attractive man. Rather short of stature, but then a man's height is not so noticeable when he's on horseback."

"And the Princess saw him largely on a horse?"

Maxwell nodded. "He used to ride beside her open carriage every day, when she drove out with Lady de Clifford—Charlotte's governess before the present one. The Princess has a carriage with a team of lovely grays she keeps down at Windsor and is no mean whip, you know."

"So I have heard," said Sebastian. "Do I take it a flirtation developed?"

"It was inevitable, really, when one considers the way the Regent keeps the girl so isolated. What did he expect to happen the first time she met a handsome, personable young man in regimentals—especially one she was inclined to trust because he was related to her?"

"How long did this go on?"

"That they met daily in Windsor Park? Some six weeks. Then Lady de Clifford moved—belatedly—to put a stop to the growing friendship. Charlotte protested, of course, but eventually Hesse's regiment was transferred to Portsmouth in preparation for embarkation to the Peninsula."

"He's there now?"

"On the Continent? Yes. With Wellington."

"This all occurred more than a year ago. What bearing can it possibly have on what happened to Jane?"

"The thing is, you see, after Captain Hesse—he's a captain now—after he left for Portsmouth, the Princess wrote to him. Frequently. And she continued writing to him even after his regiment was sent to the Peninsula. Some of the letters referenced incidents between them that were . . . not wise."

"How unwise?"

Maxwell stared off across the ice. "Unwise enough to cause the Princess considerable embarrassment, should they become known."

"Enough to cause the Prince of Orange to withdraw from the betrothal?"

Maxwell hesitated a moment, then nodded.

Sebastian said, "Go on."

"For months now Princess Charlotte has been desperately trying to contact Hesse and convince him to return the letters to her."

"And?"

"It turns out Hesse doesn't have the letters with him. He left them in a trunk with a friend in Portsmouth, along with instructions to sink the trunk in the sea, should Hesse be killed." Maxwell paused. "The Princess was thinking she'd finally be able to get the letters back. But then word came a few weeks ago that the trunk had been broken into and the packet of letters stolen."

Sebastian had a sudden vivid recollection of a dying Valentino, his face contorted with pain, saying, *I was coming to see you . . . tell you about the letters.* He'd assumed the harpist was referring to the letters he had carried between Charlotte and her mother. In that, obviously, he had been wrong.

He said, "Do you know who stole them?"

"No. But the Dutch alliance is unpopular with powerful elements both here and in the Netherlands. I can see someone stealing the letters and publishing them in the hopes of embarrassing Orange enough that he'd back out of the alliance."

"When precisely did this happen?"

"That the letters were stolen? I couldn't say for certain. The Princess told Jane about it at her Monday lesson."

"The week she died? Or before that?"

"The week before. It's the reason Jane went out to see Charlotte's mother—to ask if she was behind the letters' theft."

"And?"

"She said no."

"Jane believed her?"

"She told me Caroline was so upset when she heard about it that she spilled her glass of wine. So yes, Jane believed her. The Princess of Wales might be desperate to prevent Charlotte from marrying Orange, but not at the cost of destroying her daughter."

Sebastian wasn't so sure about that. But all he said was "Just because Caroline didn't do it doesn't mean some of the men around her weren't responsible."

Maxwell blew out a long, troubled breath. "That's what Jane was afraid of."

Sebastian stared off across the frozen river. "I still don't see how the death of either Jane or Edward Ambrose could be linked to the Hesse letters."

"I don't either. But I know there were things she wasn't telling me."

Sebastian studied the other man's strained, exhausted profile. "Because she was afraid you'd publish something about the letters?"

"Good God, no! I would never do that! Just because I don't believe in monarchy doesn't mean I'd deliberately destroy an innocent young girl—no matter who her parents are."

"So what are you suggesting?"

Maxwell swiped a shaky hand down over his lower face. "I don't know what I'm suggesting. But you can be sure both Princesses know a damned sight more about it than I do."

"The problem is," said Sebastian, meeting the other man's troubled gaze, "how to get them to admit it?"

Chapter 46

Friday, 4 February

"I t's true, then?" said Hero as she and Miss Ella Kinsworth walked side by side around the high-walled, snowy gardens of Warwick House.

The older woman nodded, her hands gripped tightly together in her fur muff. "Please tell me you understand why I couldn't say anything about the Hesse letters."

When Hero remained silent, Miss Kinsworth looked away, her eyes blinking rapidly. "Dear God, is that why poor Valentino Vescovi was killed? Because of the letters?"

"I think it very likely, yes."

"But . . . why?"

"How much did Vescovi know about Hesse?"

Miss Kinsworth sucked in a deep breath. "After Lady de Clifford realized—belatedly—what was happening between the two cousins, she put a stop to Charlotte's daily drives around Windsor Park and convinced the Regent to allow the Princess's household to move back to London."

"Did the Prince know about Charlotte's growing feelings for her cousin?"

"Not then, no."

Hero kept her gaze on her friend's half-averted face. "What I don't understand is how this correspondence even came about. I was under the impression the Prince had someone read all of Charlotte's letters. So how was she able to write to Hesse?"

"Through her mother."

"Good heavens," said Hero softly.

Miss Kinsworth nodded. "That's how Vescovi was involved. He carried the letters between Charlotte and her mother."

Hero stared up at the bare, snow-shrouded trees. "Why on earth would Caroline do such a thing?"

"Who knows? The Princess of Wales is nothing if not eccentric. Perhaps she did it because she felt sorry for the unnatural way Charlotte has been kept so horribly isolated. But the truth is, I wouldn't put it past her to have done it to spite the Prince—or in a spirit of pure mischief."

"Her own daughter? I can't believe that."

Miss Kinsworth pressed her lips together and said nothing.

Hero watched her for a moment, then said, "There's something you're not telling me."

The older woman drew a deep, troubled breath. "At the time of the flirtation, the Princess of Wales was staying in apartments in Kensington Palace. After Charlotte's return to London, Hesse used to come to the palace's garden gate when Charlotte was visiting her mother, and Caroline would let him in so that the cousins could meet."

"What utter folly."

"There's worse. One evening Caroline actually locked the young couple alone together in her bedroom and told them to 'have fun.'"

"For how long?"

"Hours."

"Dear Lord. Why?"

"Who knows why Caroline does the things she does? Perhaps she'd had too much wine with dinner. But for whatever reason, it was beyond inexcusable."

"And Charlotte referenced this incident in her letters to Hesse?"

Miss Kinsworth nodded miserably. "Charlotte swears nothing happened and that Hesse behaved most gentlemanly. But if it becomes known . . ."

"She'll be ruined," said Hero. "Utterly, irreparably ruined. Princes can get away with such behavior—and far, far worse. But not princesses."

The older woman's lips tightened into a thin line. "Prinny hasn't helped matters, either. He's spent the last ten years and more endlessly accusing his child's mother of adultery, all in a sordid attempt to divorce her. He even paid that horrid Douglas woman to swear the Princess gave birth to one of the little boys she fosters! If word of Charlotte's relationship with Hesse gets out, people will say, 'Like mother, like daughter,' and everyone will believe the worst."

Hero stared out over the snow-filled garden. "When did you learn the Hesse letters had been taken from Portsmouth?"

"It's been several weeks. Word came on a Sunday evening. I remember because poor Charlotte was so distraught she cried all night, so that by the time Jane arrived for their lesson the next morning, the girl was hysterical."

"Jane already knew of the letters' existence?"

"Oh, yes. Charlotte told her about them months ago, when she first started trying to get the letters back from Captain Hesse. You have to remember that Jane taught Charlotte from the time the girl was six or seven, so they were unusually close. It was Jane who offered to go out to Connaught House and ask Caroline if she had the letters."

"But Caroline didn't have them?"

"So she claimed."

"You don't believe her?"

"I don't know what to believe. It's been weeks now since the letters disappeared, yet no one has come forward with them. Obviously I'm grateful that they haven't been published. Yet at the same time, I can't help but worry." The older woman was silent for a moment. "What I don't understand is how the Hesse letters can be implicated in Jane's death . . . unless of course she somehow discovered who has them. Is that possible?"

"Who do you think has the letters?"

Miss Kinsworth's face hardened. "Honestly? I'd say the most likely culprits are the Whigs around Caroline, rather than Caroline herself. Not Earl Grey, but someone such as Brougham or Wallace. They'd do it. They're passionately opposed to the Dutch alliance, and I don't believe either of them would hesitate to ruin Charlotte if they thought it would stop the marriage."

"Yes, I can see that," said Hero. "Who else?"

"There must be forces in the Netherlands who feel the same way, but I know nothing of them."

"You said the Regent didn't know about Hesse at the time the cousins were meeting in Windsor Park. That implies that he does now."

Miss Kinsworth brought up one hand to rub her forehead. "I can't begin to guess how he discovered the truth, but he's said one or two oblique things that made it obvious he found out somehow. He has so many spies. Everywhere."

"Could the Prince himself have sent someone to steal the letters?"

"It's possible, isn't it? He knows Charlotte is furious with him for tricking her into the betrothal to Orange. And she is determined to fight his attempts to set things up so that she'll be forced to spend most of her life outside of Britain."

"You're suggesting the Regent might see the letters as some sort of insurance against the possibility that the Princess could try to break her betrothal? So that he could essentially blackmail her into marrying Orange? Surely even he couldn't be that contemptible and conniving."

"Oh, he's that contemptible. As for being that conniving, perhaps not the Regent himself, but someone determined to see that His Highness gets what he wants."

"Someone like Jarvis, you mean."

"I didn't say that, my lady."

"No." Hero gave her friend a slow smile. "You were very careful not to."

On Sebastian's second visit to Connaught House, he found Caroline of Brunswick seated beside a roaring fire in her rather sparsely furnished morning room. She wore a tattered shawl over a plain gown with a plunging round neckline and was fashioning a crude doll out of wax when he was shown into her presence.

She looked up, her plump face breaking into a wide smile. "I thought you'd be back." She did not give him permission to sit, so he stood with his hat in his hands and watched her work on what he realized was a wax image of her husband, the Prince of Wales. She said, "Do I take it you've learned something new?"

"Jane Ambrose's husband was murdered yesterday."

"So I heard. He vas a nasty man." She used her shoulder to swipe at a loose curl tickling her cheek. "I told Jane she should leave him long ago. But she never listened to me, and now she's dead, isn't she?"

"You think he killed her?"

"You don't?"

"I don't know. The question is, if he did, then who killed Edward Ambrose?"

"Obviously someone who did not like him. I've no doubt there are many."

"Valentino Vescovi is also dead."

"*Ja*. That death is far more *triste*." She gave a heavy sigh that heaved her ample expanse of exposed bosom. "He played the harp like an angel, and now he plays vith the angels."

The sentiment was undeniably maudlin, but Sebastian suspected the tears he saw glittering in her eyes were real. He said, "Several weeks ago, someone stole a packet containing letters Charlotte once wrote to her cousin Captain Hesse. Do you know who did that?"

She focused on draping a doll-sized purple velvet cloak around the wax figure's shoulders. "You think it vas me?"

"No, Your Highness." *Not necessarily.* "But I'm hoping you might have some idea who did."

She smiled faintly as she settled a miniature tin crown on the figurine's head. "Vhen I vas first married, Vales gave me my own rooms at Carlton House and furnished them to his own taste. And then, several months after we ved, he sent servants to take back most of my furniture. He said he could not afford to pay for it. But I noticed none of the furniture in his rooms disappeared." She held the wax figure at arm's length, studying it. "He also took back the pearl bracelets he gave me as vedding presents and gave them to his mistress, the *putain* Jersey. She delighted in wearing them in my presence. And there was nothing— *nothing*—I could do about any of it."

The implication was clear: As a new, young bride she had been alone and powerless, unable to defend herself in any way, let alone strike back. She was not so powerless anymore.

Is that what this is? he wanted to ask. *A game of revenge against your bastard of a husband? With your daughter as the helpless pawn?*

Except of course that one did not say such things to the Princess of Wales.

She took a pin and thrust it into the wax doll's foot, her face twisting with bitterness as she shoved it deep. Then she laughed and said, "I hear he has a bad case of gout. I vonder how that happened?"

She picked up another pin, then paused to look over at Sebastian. "Vhen Vales sent my daughter down to Vindsor for months, trying to keep her avay from me, young Charles Hesse vas kind enough to carry letters back and forth between us. Then, vhen he and Charlotte were forbidden to meet, she came to me in tears, begging for my help." The Princess shrugged. "So I passed correspondence between them and arranged for them to meet in my apartments in Kensington Palace. It vas all intensely romantic and utterly innocent, and I regret none of it."

And locking them alone together in your bedroom? thought Sebastian. *Was that "innocent"?*

Caroline thrust the next pin deep into the wax figure's bowels. "Are you familiar vith vhat happened to Sophia Dorothea, the mother of King George I? Her husband imprisoned her in the castle of Ahlden vhen she was just twenty-seven, and he kept her there for thirty-three years until she died. Then he ordered her casket thrown into the castle's cellars."

When Sebastian said nothing, she continued. "My aunt Caroline Matilda was sister to the present King. She married her cousin, the King of Denmark, who like Orange preferred men and vas all messed up in the head. He had her arrested and strangled at the age of twenty-three."

Sebastian had heard George III's unhappy sister died of scarlet fever, but he also knew that could simply be a tale put out for public consumption. She had most certainly died while under arrest, and her husband was utterly mad at the time of her rather convenient death.

"And you know vhat happened to my sister," said Caroline darkly.

Sebastian nodded. Caroline's sister, Augusta, had married Prince Frederick of Württemberg when she was just fifteen. He beat her so viciously the young Princess was given asylum by Catherine of Russia, only to then die under suspicious circumstances and be hastily buried in an unmarked grave.

Choosing another pin, Caroline thrust it with slow deliberation into the wax figure's groin. "I vill do anything," she said, *"anything* I must, to stop vhat the Regent is trying to do to my Charlotte." She looked up to meet Sebastian's gaze. "But I don't have the Hesse letters, and I don't know who does."

It was a dismissal. Sebastian thanked her and bowed low.

As he backed slowly from her presence, he saw her throw the wax effigy into the flames and watch, smiling, as it flared up and then melted into nothing.

Chapter 47

𝒟evlin was seated behind his desk, a disheveled lock of dark hair falling over one eye, his pen scratching furiously across a sheet of paper, when Hero came to stand in the library doorway.

"What are you doing?"

Looking up, he spun the page—covered with a rough graph of horizontal and vertical lines—around to face her. "Trying to make sense of four very tangled threads."

As she drew closer, she could see that across the top of the page he'd written *Monday, Tuesday, Wednesday* . . . "With a calendar?" she said, coming to lean over the desk.

He nodded. "Of the last weeks of Jane Ambrose's life. As far as I can tell, her trouble started *here*." He pointed to the first Tuesday in January.

"The last day of the Great Fog," said Hero.

Devlin leaned back in his chair. "That's the day Jane accidently overheard Rothschild discussing his gold shipments to France, as a result of which he both dismissed her and threatened her."

"Which had the unintended effect of sending her to visit her uncle Sheridan," said Hero. "The first time."

Devlin pointed to the following week. "This is when Jarvis sent one of his men to pick up Jane from Warwick House and bring her to him at Carlton House. He warned her to shut up and threatened dire consequences not only to her but to anyone else she should tell about the gold."

"And it worked," said Hero. "She shut up."

"She did. She doesn't appear to have told anyone else—not her brother, not Liam Maxwell."

"Because she didn't want to risk their lives," said Hero quietly. "So she kept it all to herself. The poor woman. She must have been so frightened, and with no one to turn to for advice or support."

Devlin pointed to the following Sunday. "It was just a few days after that when Princess Charlotte received word that the packet containing her letters to Hesse had been stolen from his trunk in Portsmouth. By the time Jane came for their lesson on Monday, the Princess was in a panic, and Jane offered to ask Caroline if she knew what had happened to the letters. She went out to Connaught House the very next day— Tuesday. But Caroline said she'd had nothing to do with the letters' theft."

Hero studied the calendar. "Then what?"

Devlin tapped the square representing the day after Jane's visit to Connaught House, a Wednesday. "This is when Jane went to see Lord Wallace. Given the timing, I seriously doubt it had anything to do with piano lessons for young Miss Elizabeth Wallace."

"Jane suspected Wallace was involved in the letters' theft?"

"I think so. And if she was right—if Wallace actually was behind both the theft of the letters and now all these deaths—then how the devil do we prove it? Because you can be certain his lordship isn't doing his own dirty work."

"Something obviously made Jane decide to ask Wallace about the missing letters but not the other Whigs around Caroline—not Brougham, not Earl Grey, but Wallace. Why?"

"Because she knows him for the nasty piece of work he is?"

Hero gave a startled huff of laughter. "Perhaps. Although I can't help but wonder what she hoped to accomplish by going to see him. Surely she didn't expect him to actually admit to the theft, let alone give her the letters?"

"Probably not. Although she might have thought she could convince him not to publish them by appealing to his better nature."

"Does Lord Wallace have a better nature?"

"He must. His belief in everything from the evils of slavery to the need for public education suggests a basic core of decency—somewhere deep down below all that massive self-regard and natural abrasiveness."

Hero frowned as she studied the rough calendar. "Your handwriting is appalling. What happened on that Thursday—exactly one week before she died?"

"That's the day Peter van der Pals asked Jane to spy on Princess Charlotte for Orange—and promised nasty repercussions if she told anyone about it."

"Only, this time Jane didn't keep silent. She felt honor bound to speak up, and so she warned Miss Kinsworth."

"She did. Unfortunately, she didn't realize the lovely Lady Arabella was listening at the keyhole. Which is why on the following Monday—just days before Jane was killed—she and Vescovi had that argument beside the ice-skating pond in St. James's Park."

"That's when Vescovi told Jane about the Prince of Orange's sexual interests."

Devlin nodded. "Jane went the very next day to see her uncle Sheridan and ask him for the truth. It was as she left Savile Row that van der Pals waylaid her and raped her."

"To punish her for telling on him," said Hero.

"To punish her, yes. But it could have been more than that. I suspect he knew Vescovi told Jane about Orange. Van der Pals was familiar with their argument by the canal, remember? And while he claimed he didn't know most of what was said there, I think we can be fairly certain that was a lie."

"So the rape was not only a punishment, but also a warning?"

Devlin nodded. "Jane ignored van der Pals when he threatened her the first time. So the rape was his way of showing her that he was deadly serious. I suspect he warned her that if she made the mistake of telling the Princess about Orange's sexual exploits, he'd kill her. And then, out of pure spite, he told her about Edward Ambrose's mistress."

"After which Jane went to Covent Garden to see the woman for herself. Oh, heavens. Poor Jane."

Devlin leaned forward again. "That's the same evening she was arguing with Ambrose on the steps of the Opera. When I asked Ambrose about it, he claimed they were quarreling about her recent visit to Caroline at Connaught House. But looking at this, I think he lied. I think she confronted him about his mistress."

"Given the timing, it makes sense," said Hero. "It also might explain the strange things she said to Liam Maxwell the next day."

Devlin nodded. "I think she'd decided to leave her husband."

Hero looked up at him. "So Maxwell is lying?"

"Perhaps. Although it's also possible she simply hadn't told him yet."

"You think that's why Ambrose killed her? Because he found out she was going to leave him?"

Devlin scrubbed his hands down over his face. "On the one hand, it seems to make sense. The problem is, if he did, then who killed Ambrose and Vescovi?"

"Maxwell. He realized Ambrose had killed the woman he loved, and murdered him for it."

"He could have. Although if he didn't, I suspect whoever left that Indian dagger in Ambrose's chest wants me to think that."

"So you doubt it? Why?"

"Mainly because Maxwell had no reason that I can see to kill Valentino Vescovi."

"Van der Pals could have killed Vescovi," reasoned Hero. "For telling Jane about Orange. Or his death could somehow be linked to the letters. For a harpist, he was involved with some nasty, dangerous people."

"He was indeed. As was Jane—through no fault of her own."

"As was Jane," Hero said softly, her gaze meeting his.

Phineas, Lord Wallace, was eating a beefsteak in the dining room of Brooks's when Sebastian came to sit opposite him.

His lordship glanced up, then calmly went on cutting a thick slice of meat, merely saying, "And if I prefer to eat in solitary splendor?"

"Answer my questions, and I'll be gone," said Sebastian. "I know why Jane Ambrose came to see you the week before she died."

"Oh?"

"She thought you had in your possession certain letters—sensitive letters stolen from a trunk entrusted by a handsome young Hussar captain to his friend in Portsmouth. She was hoping to convince you to return them to the young lady who wrote them."

A faint smile curled the Baron's lips as he swallowed. "An interesting theory."

"I notice you don't claim ignorance of the letters."

"Oh, no, I am fully aware of the existence of the Hesse letters, and have been for weeks now. As it happens, Mrs. Ambrose did indeed accuse me of being involved in their disappearance. Unfortunately, I don't have them."

"Why should I believe you?"

"Why?" His smile turned into something cold and gritty. "It's rather simple, actually: because if I had them, I would have used them by now to put an end to this ridiculous betrothal. As you so accurately observed the other day, I am more than willing to sacrifice one pampered eighteen-year-old girl for the good of the nation."

"I'm not sure anyone who knows the truth about Charlotte's miserable upbringing could call it 'pampered.'"

"I seriously doubt she's ever gone to bed hungry—which is more than one can say about millions of her grandfather's subjects."

Sebastian watched the Baron cut another piece of his steak. "I can think of several reasons why you might not have used the letters yet."

"Oh? Do tell."

"Timing. Leverage. Second thoughts."

His lordship chewed thoughtfully and swallowed. "Mmm. I suppose all are possible—with the exception of 'second thoughts.'" He paused to point the tines of his fork at Sebastian. "Are you seriously suggesting that I might have killed Jane Ambrose?"

"I am."

Wallace gave a loud laugh. "Why on earth would I?"

"Because the game you're playing—and the individuals you are playing it against—are dangerous. Most men prefer to do their dirtiest work from the shadows."

Wallace was no longer laughing.

Sebastian said, "It would give you a similar reason for killing the harpist Vescovi if he somehow knew you had the letters. And you could have killed Edward Ambrose in a futile attempt to convince me that Jane's death was simply the result of a wretched lovers' triangle."

"Oh? Was Jane Ambrose involved in a lovers' triangle? That I did not know."

"No? In my experience, men like you have a tendency to keep abreast of such things."

"How . . . flattering."

"Someone stole those damned letters, and Jane seems to have suspected you. Why was that? I wonder."

"I've no idea."

Sebastian studied the older man's faintly smiling face. "So who would you have me believe did take them?"

"You credit me with far more knowledge than I possess."

"Then speculate. Surely you've given it some thought."

Wallace leaned back in his chair. "Well, given that they've never been published, suspicion must presumably fall on the Prince—or, rather, individuals close to him. If Brougham or Somerset or anyone else opposed to the betrothal had somehow managed to get their hands on them, the Princess's folly would be splashed all over the newspapers by now."

Sebastian held himself very still. "Are you suggesting Christian Somerset knows about the Orange alliance?"

Wallace gave a rude snort. "Of course he knows."

"You're certain?"

Wallace rested his knife and fork on the edge of his plate. "Given that we've discussed various possible ways to scuttle this damned alliance? Yes, quite certain."

"Does he know about the Hesse letters?"

"As to that, I couldn't say." Then he pushed up and walked away, leaving the rest of his meal uneaten.

Chapter 48

Sebastian found Christian Somerset standing before the side altar in St. Anne's, Soho, his head bowed, his hat in his hands. A weak winter sun had come out to stream a rich palette of green and gold light through the stained glass window above the main altar. But the stones of the church radiated a dank cold that was numbing.

Jane's brother stayed in prayer for several more minutes before heaving a heavy sigh, opening his eyes, and raising his head. His gaze focused on Sebastian standing quietly nearby, and he said, "I take it you're looking for me?"

Sebastian nodded. "Can we talk?"

"Of course."

They left the church to walk along a well-packed path that wound through the churchyard's snow-covered tombs and ancient headstones. Somerset said, "You've discovered something?"

"Perhaps." Sebastian paused, choosing his words carefully. "You said you didn't know about Princess Charlotte's betrothal to the Prince of Orange. But I've now discovered that's not true."

Somerset glanced over at him. "Who told you that?"

"Are you saying you didn't know?"

Somerset was silent for a moment, then shook his head. "No; I knew. I denied it before because—oh, I suppose out of loyalty to Jane. She shouldn't have told me about it, but she was upset at the time and needed to talk. Afterward she begged me to forget she'd ever mentioned it, so it seemed wrong to betray her."

"Yet you discussed the Orange alliance with other Whigs?"

"I did, yes—but without acknowledging that I'd also discussed it with Jane. It's no secret in certain circles, you know. I'm sorry for misleading you, but . . . Are you suggesting this damned betrothal could have something to do with her death?"

"Perhaps. I don't know for certain. When did you say was the last time you saw her?"

"When she brought me the ballads I was going to publish."

"Do you remember what day that was, precisely?"

Somerset frowned. "Let's see . . . I'd been out of town visiting friends in Kent and returned home on a Sunday. I believe she came to see me the following afternoon."

"So, Monday the seventeenth?"

"Yes, I suppose it must have been. Why?"

Monday the seventeenth was the day Jane Ambrose learned from Princess Charlotte that the Hesse letters were missing and the day before she went out to Connaught House to see the Princess of Wales. Was that significant? Sebastian wondered. Or not?

But all he said was "I'm simply trying to understand the sequence of events that occurred in the last several weeks of your sister's life. Did she talk to you that day about Princess Charlotte?"

"Not that I recall, no. But the truth is, I remember very little about our conversation that day. I don't think it was in any way remarkable; we mainly spoke of music."

"Did she say anything to you about a packet of letters?"

"Letters? I don't believe so. From whom?"

"The Princess."

"No." Somerset gave Sebastian a hard look. "You obviously do think Jane's death has something to do with the Princess."

"At the moment it's simply one of several possibilities."

"And Edward Ambrose? How does his death fit into this?"

"I wish I understood."

Somerset blew out a harsh breath. "I won't pretend to feel sorrow at his passing, but I wouldn't have wished death on the man—especially not murder."

Sebastian said, "I've discovered Jane did find out about Ambrose's mistress—just two days before she died."

Somerset drew up and swung to face him. "My God. You think she confronted him and he killed her?"

"You told me the other day you didn't think she would confront him if she found out."

Somerset stared off across the snow-covered tombstones. "I know. But I've been thinking about it some more. There's no doubt that at one time she never would have mentioned it to him—that she would have quietly accepted the pain, humiliation, and betrayal of a husband taking a mistress as one more of the many burdens women must bear. But lately . . . I don't know quite how to put this, but ever since Lawrence's death, I've sensed a change in Jane. As if she were rethinking her beliefs, challenging some of the old assumptions and rules by which she used to live."

"I'm told she'd recently read Mary Wollstonecraft's *The Rights of Women*."

"Did she?" said Somerset with a shaky laugh. "That is radical reading, indeed. Although given her friendship with the Godwins, I'm surprised she hadn't read it years ago."

"Perhaps she was afraid to before, and somehow dealing with her children's death gave her the courage."

"Perhaps." Somerset pressed his lips together. "I still can't believe she's dead. I keep thinking . . . wondering if there wasn't something I could have said—something I could have done—that might have kept her safe. Alive."

"I understand the impulse to believe you might have been able to save her," Sebastian said quietly. "But you need to move beyond it."

"Perhaps." Somerset brought up a hand to rub his eyes with a spread thumb and forefinger. "But still . . ."

The bell in St. Anne's tower began to ring out the hour, the dull clangs reverberating across the still graveyard. Sebastian said, "You know Liam Maxwell—have known him for years. If he found out Ambrose had murdered Jane, do you think he would be capable of killing Ambrose in revenge?"

The church bell gave a final *dong* and then fell silent. In the sudden hush Sebastian could hear a street hawker's distant shout and a melting clump of snow slide from a branch overhead to hit a nearby tomb with a sodden *plop*.

Somerset's face went slack, his nostrils flaring as he sucked in a quick, deep breath. "Surely you don't expect me to answer that?"

Sebastian said, "I think you just did."

There was a freshening quality to the wind that surprised Sebastian as he walked the icy, winding streets of the Frost Fair. Now in its fourth day, the fair was more crowded than ever, the air filled with shrieks and laughter and the roar of thousands of voices. He caught the pungent scents of cinnamon and cloves as he passed a tent selling spices, its exotic odors mingling with the familiar smells of ale and tobacco and roasting meat. "Buy me pies," called a roving pieman, his tin tray slung around his neck by a leather strap. *"Eels! Get yer eels!" "Hot chestnuts!"* The shouts of the vendors rose above the drone of a hurdy-gurdy and the distant wail of bagpipes. But for Sebastian it was all background noise. He walked on, lost in his thoughts.

A sudden outburst of laughter drew his attention to a circle of spectators gathered around a circus comic in a red velvet doublet and blue hose. The clown's improbable yellow hair was curling wildly in the damp air, his white face paint and frozen, exaggerated red grin lending a faintly menacing quality to his pantomimes and pratfalls. For a moment Sebastian paused, his gaze drifting over the laughing men, women, and children of the performer's audience. Their eyes were sparkling with delight, their cheeks rosy with the cold. But for some reason he could not have named, Sebastian found himself noting the subtle differences in attitude and posture that distinguished the men from the women, the boys from the girls.

He had never subscribed to the belief that women were by nature either less intelligent or less capable than men. Yet he now realized he'd never appreciated to what extent an Englishwoman's sex determined essentially every aspect of her life—far more than her wealth or social status or perhaps even her skin color. Simply by virtue of having been born female, Jane had been raised by a father who tolerated rather than encouraged his girl child's amazing talents. As a woman grown, she'd hidden her gifts as both a pianist and a composer in order to conform to the behavior considered proper for a modest gentlewoman of her station. And because of England's civil and religious laws, she'd been forced to bear her husband's unfaithfulness and physical abuse without complaint or possibility of redress.

Yet in the last months of Jane's life, that willingness to conform, to play by the rules, had shattered. Much of it, surely, came from the spiritual crisis provoked by the recent deaths of her children as well as by her growing anger over the Regent's treatment of the young Princess. But Sebastian suspected that the breaking point had come in that fetid alley off Savile Row.

Peter van der Pals had used all the advantages afforded by his privileged maleness to brutalize and hurt her, safe in the knowledge that she would never tell because, for a gentlewoman, the shame of others knowing what had been done to her was seen as worse than the rape itself.

And van der Pals had been right; she hadn't told anyone—with the exception of Lady Arabella, although that was in the form of reproach rather than a confidence. And it came to Sebastian now as he watched the clown pantomime slipping and falling on the ice that the rape had acted as a kind of catalyst in Jane's life. Up until then she had faithfully adhered to all the stringent, unfair rules of their society. She had done what her religion and her class demanded of her. Yet this terrible thing had befallen her anyway, and as a result, something within her had snapped. He wondered if she would actually have broken free if she'd lived. He suspected she would have. Instead, she had died.

How? Why?

It would be all too easy to pin her death on her weak, abusive, conveniently dead husband. But another explanation was beginning to form in Sebastian's mind.

An explanation as troubling as it was tragic.

Liam Maxwell was helping one of his apprentices knock apart his stall on the Frost Fair's grand promenade when Sebastian walked up to him.

"Calling it quits?" said Sebastian, watching the lad pile wooden shingles into a handcart.

The afternoon was warm enough that they'd worked up a sweat, and Maxwell paused to swipe a forearm across his face. "Feel that wind? It's swinging around to the south. When I was a lad, I used to listen to my grandmother tell stories about how fast she'd seen the ice break up in the middle of a Frost Fair. I can't afford to lose my press." He grinned at the boy turning away from the cart. "Or any of my apprentices, for that matter."

The boy laughed and stooped to gather another armload of shingles.

Sebastian nodded toward the growing throng of laughing, noisy fairgoers. "They don't appear to share your concerns."

Maxwell shrugged and swung his hammer at a cross brace, knocking it loose. "Had a couple of constables from Bow Street here a bit ago. They're thinking I killed Ambrose, aren't they?"

"Are they?"

Maxwell let his hand drop, the hammer dangling by his side. "You know they are."

"Constables like simple explanations."

"I didn't kill him," said the printer, his voice low and earnest.

Sebastian studied the other man's haggard face. "Did you ever talk to Christian Somerset about the Orange betrothal?"

Maxwell cast a quick glance at his apprentice, who was now loading the loose boards from the dismantled stall into the cart. "No. Why?"

"Would Jane have told him about it?"

Maxwell looked thoughtful for a moment. "She might have. I couldn't say for certain."

"What about the Hesse letters? Would she have told him about those?"

Maxwell started to say something, then stopped.

"What?" asked Sebastian, watching him.

Maxwell's eyes narrowed. "Why are you asking me about Christian?"

"I'm simply trying to get an idea of what happened in Jane's life the last few weeks before her death."

Maxwell tossed his hammer aside. "I don't think she ever told him about Hesse, no. I remember one time she was in my print shop, talking about the Princess's attempts to retrieve the letters, when Christian came in without her realizing it. She was worried he might have overheard what she was saying. But when she carefully tried to find out if he had heard, he teased her about being involved in some deep, dark secret and laughingly asked if he needed to worry she'd taken to plotting nefarious deeds."

"So he didn't hear?"

"I don't think so."

"When was this?"

The printer looked thoughtful. "Must've been three or four weeks ago now."

"Before Somerset left for Kent?"

"Was he in Kent? I didn't know that. I remember Jane had stopped in to see me that day on her way back from one of her lessons at the palace. It was before the letters were stolen, at the time the Princess was still trying to get them back, which is how we came to be talking about it." Maxwell's brows drew together. "You can't be suspecting *Christian* of all people."

Sebastian shook his head. "Would Jane have told her husband about the letters, do you think?"

"Ambrose?" Maxwell gave a harsh snort. "Not hardly. To be frank, they rarely spoke. And I doubt he would have been interested." He cast another anxious look at his apprentice and dropped his voice even lower. "I didn't kill the bastard. I swear it."

"Unfortunately, you're the only person who appears to have a motive."

"What about his bloody creditors?"

"You know he was in debt?"

"I know."

"How?"

Maxwell twitched one shoulder.

Sebastian said, "Did you tell Jane?"

"I think she suspected it."

"But you never told her?"

Maxwell shook his head.

"Why not?"

"For the same reason I never told her about her husband's philandering: because there was nothing she could do about it, and I knew it would only upset her."

When Sebastian simply remained silent, Maxwell's nostrils flared on a quick, angry breath. "You don't believe me, do you?"

"Should I?"

"Someone is trying to set me up!"

"It's certainly possible. The question is, who?"

"I don't know!"

"How many people were aware of your relationship with Jane?"

"We've been friends for years. That at least was never a secret."

"All right, look at it another way: Who would want to do you harm?"

The printer gave a low, humorless laugh. "Probably too many people to count—starting with your own damned father-in-law."

"Who else?"

"Ambrose, maybe. But he was too selfish of a bastard to ever take his own life."

Sebastian thought about the other dangerous men who had moved through Jane's life in those final weeks: Rothschild, Wallace, van der Pals. All commanded the resources that could have enabled them to learn of the long-standing connection between Jane and her brother's childhood friend. And Sebastian wouldn't put it past any of them to have killed Ambrose in a calculated maneuver to deflect suspicion away from themselves and onto the hot-tempered, radical young journalist.

Or rather, have Ambrose killed, Sebastian reminded himself. The handsome Dutch courtier might conceivably do his own killing—and enjoy it. But with the exception of van der Pals, such men rarely did their own dirty work.

He became aware of Maxwell watching him thoughtfully. The journalist said, "There's something you're not telling me."

"Not really. All I have at this point is conjecture. I'm still missing something—something that's obviously vitally important. I wish I knew where the hell Jane went after she left the palace that last day, and why. You're certain you have no idea where she might have gone?"

Maxwell sucked in a deep breath that shuddered his chest, and the look of soul-scouring anguish on his face was so profound that Sebastian almost—*almost*—believed it genuine. "I—" Maxwell's voice cracked, and he had to begin again. "I lie awake at night, trying to remember every little thing she said to me, something I might have overlooked—something that might explain what happened to her. But I can't think of anything. I just can't."

"Then it must have been something that came up unexpectedly."

"What?"

But that was one more question to which Sebastian had no answer.

Chapter 49

"I spent some time out at Clerkenwell yesterday," Alexi Sauvage told Hero as the two women walked the snowy paths of Berkeley Square. A large private garden the size of several city blocks, the square was maintained by the area's residents and had a high fence of iron palings to keep out the riffraff.

"How is Jenny Sanborn?" asked Hero, looking over at her friend.

"As well as one might expect, I suppose. Although she wasn't the only reason I went there. I was hoping the residents around Shepherds' Lane might be more willing to open up to me than to Bow Street or his lordship."

"And?"

Alexi shook her head, her flame-colored hair curling wildly in the moist air. "I couldn't find anyone willing to admit they either knew Jane Ambrose or had seen her in the streets that day."

Hero stared off across the square's ice-covered clusters of shrubs and soaring plane trees. With the rising temperatures, the snow was beginning to melt, filling the air with a chorus of drips and plops. It was warm enough that Hero withdrew one hand from the new black fur muff she'd taken to carrying and reached up to open the top clasp of her pelisse. "I have the most wretched, demoralizing feeling that we're never going to figure out who killed her. That whoever took her life and left her in that lane for us to find will simply be free to go on living his life as if she'd never existed."

"I know," said Alexi, her voice more troubled than Hero could remember hearing it. "We like to believe the world arcs toward justice—I suppose because it reassures us and makes us think there's some sort of order to our existence. But what if we're wrong? What if it's all meaningless chaos and chance?"

"Even if it is, that doesn't mean justice isn't worth striving for. Less inevitable, perhaps, but not impossible." Hero paused, then added, "Hopefully."

Alexi gave a soft laugh. "Hopefully."

The sound of approaching footfalls drew Hero's attention to a dense clump of shrubs that hid the path ahead, and for some reason she couldn't have named she felt again that vague, uneasy sense of being watched that had troubled her before.

"I think we should go," she said, slipping her right hand back into her muff just as a fashionable man in a caped greatcoat and glossy high-topped boots came around the bend in the path. He drew up a moment as if in surprise, then sauntered toward them.

"Ladies," said Peter van der Pals, touching his tall beaver hat in a casual salute. "This is unexpected."

"Mr. van der Pals," said Hero, inclining her head. "I didn't know you lived in Berkeley Square."

He shifted his grip on the silver-headed walking stick he carried, bringing it up in a way that caught her attention. "I don't."

"Ah. Unfortunately, this is a private garden."

He gave a slow, lazy smile that brought dimples to his cheeks and showed his even white teeth. "I know. And at this time of day all the neighborhood nursemaids have obligingly shooed their little charges home for tea, leaving it quite conveniently deserted." With a flick of the wrist, he released his walking stick's hidden stiletto and drew away the sheath. He was no longer smiling.

"*Mon Dieu*," whispered Alexi, taking a step back.

The Dutch courtier kept his gaze on Hero. "I'm told his lordship is inordinately fond of his ridiculously tall bluestocking wife."

"So this is—what?" said Hero. "Revenge for some insult or imagined slight? Or merely a taunt?" She could hear the ragged sound of her own breathing as she let her left hand fall from her elegant fur muff and shifted its angle. She spoke loudly, hoping the combination of her voice and the hand warmer's thick fur would deaden the telltale click as she carefully eased back the hammer of the small muff pistol she held hidden within it. "You have two intended victims but only one knife."

Van der Pals gave a ringing laugh that sounded genuinely amused. "Do you seriously think two women are capable of fighting off a man my s—"

Hero squeezed the trigger.

The loud report of the pistol shot echoed around the square, sending up a flurry of frightened pigeons that took flight against the darkening sky. A crimson stain bloomed around the neat hole in the chest of the courtier's exquisitely tailored greatcoat. Hero saw his eyes widen, saw the features of his face go slack. For a moment he swayed, his hand clenching around the handle of his dagger. Then he pitched forward to land facedown in the snow, his arms flung out above his head, the knife falling beside him.

Hero leapt to kick it beyond his grasp. "Is he dead?"

Alexi knelt in the snow beside the still body. "Not yet. But he will be soon."

Hero sucked in a deep breath tainted with the stench of fresh blood and burning fur. "Good."

Alexi looked up at her. "Your muff is on fire."

"Drat," said Hero, dropping the flaming fur into the melting snow. "I just purchased it."

Sebastian arrived back at Brook Street to find Hero seated at his desk, once again cleaning her small muff gun.

"I've shot Peter van der Pals," she said calmly.

"Dead?"

She looked up, her eyes cold and hard, her hands admirably steady at their task. "Quite."

Rather than contact the local public office, Hero had gone straight to her father, which was undoubtedly the wisest choice under the circumstances. By the time Sebastian arrived at Berkeley Square, night had long since fallen and Sir Henry Lovejoy was in attendance. But there were no constables, no staff from the nearest deadhouse. Sebastian recognized the men gathered around the courtier's body as belonging to that shadowy network loyal to Jarvis and Jarvis alone.

"His lordship has informed us there will be no inquest," said Sir Henry Lovejoy, his voice pitched low as Jarvis's men lifted the dead body onto the shell they would use to carry the courtier to the Dutch ambassador's residence.

"Precisely how does his lordship plan to explain the Dutchman's rather inconvenient death?"

"He doesn't intend to even try. It will be given out that van der Pals has been called home, and no one will know he left London in a box rather than by post chaise. The Dutch are most anxious to hush this up."

"I should think so," said Sebastian. "Bit awkward, having your Prince's boon companion try to kill a distant cousin of your betrothed."

"Thank heavens her ladyship had a pistol," said Lovejoy, although there was something about the way he said it that made Sebastian suspect he found the idea of a viscountess carrying a muff gun and using it to shoot an assailant highly disturbing—even if it was fortuitous.

Sebastian said, "She began carrying it several days ago, when she thought someone was following her."

"You think that was van der Pals?"

"It must have been, surely?"

Lovejoy's eyes narrowed as one of Jarvis's men kicked at the bloodstained snow, obscuring it. Soon there would be no trace of what had occurred here. "So van der Pals killed them all? First Jane Ambrose, then the Italian harpist, and finally Edward Ambrose? The man must have been mad."

"He was obviously a killer," Sebastian said slowly. "But I'm not convinced he was responsible for all three deaths."

Lovejoy turned to look at him in surprise. "No? Why not?"

It was a question Sebastian had been asking himself. By attacking Hero, Peter van der Pals had shown himself to be capable of plotting to coldly and deliberately take another person's life. And he had a motive to kill each of the three victims: Jane because of her refusal to keep quiet about the rape; Valentino Vescovi for betraying Orange's sexual tastes; and Edward Ambrose as an attempt to shift suspicion toward Liam Maxwell.

And yet, somehow, it didn't feel right.

"I suspect van der Pals did kill Vescovi," said Sebastian, choosing his words carefully. "But I'm not convinced he's behind the deaths of either Jane Ambrose or her husband."

"No?" The magistrate was silent for a moment, his gaze on the mist drifting across the nearest streetlamp. Sebastian knew Lovejoy's continuing but unavoidable ignorance of the palace intrigues swirling around Jane Ambrose's death frustrated him. But when he spoke, all he said was "Did you hear that a section of the ice has given way on the Thames? Down near London Bridge. The three men who were on it when it broke free had to be rescued with some difficulty."

"That should be the end of the Frost Fair," said Sebastian, remembering Liam Maxwell's dire prediction from that afternoon.

"One would think so. But I understand most are convinced the rest of the ice is still sound."

"It won't be for long."

"No, it won't be," said Lovejoy, turning away. "But I suspect it'll take someone getting killed before they're willing to admit it."

Later that night, Sebastian lay awake in bed and held his wife as she slept. She felt warm and vitally alive in his arms, her breath easing quietly in and out, her hair silky soft against his bare shoulder. And yet he had come so close to losing her—would have lost her if not for her foresight and quick thinking and unflinching courage.

Death could come so quickly and unexpectedly. It was a knowledge that filled him with both terror and fury. Some of that fury was directed outward, toward Nathan Rothschild and Jarvis and the bloody royal houses of Hanover and Orange. But he was also angry with himself for his failure to unravel the dangerous, deadly tangle into which Hero had inadvertently stumbled that snowy night in Shepherds' Lane. He wished he could believe the easy explanation, that Peter van der Pals had killed all three victims. But the niggling doubts remained.

A subtle shift in Hero's breathing told him she was no longer asleep. Glancing down, he saw her eyes wide and luminous in the night.

She said, "You might be able to figure it all out better if you got some sleep."

He tightened his arm around her, hugging her closer. "Possibly."

"Why are you so convinced Peter van der Pals wasn't Jane's killer?"

Sebastian ran his hand up and down her arm. "Part of it is because Vescovi's murder looks like the work of a man who has killed before and knew precisely what he was doing—which is why I think the courtier was responsible. But Jane's and Edward Ambrose's deaths were"—he paused, searching for the right word, and finally settled on—"messy. And van der Pals was so bloody arrogant, so cocksure of the mantle of his Prince's protection, that I find it difficult to believe he ever considered himself in serious danger of being charged with Jane's murder. Which means he would have had no reason to kill Edward Ambrose in an effort to divert suspicion away from himself."

"So Ambrose killed his wife, the way you originally thought. And then Maxwell killed him in revenge."

"Perhaps."

"But you don't think so?"

"Consider this: We suspected Maxwell was in love with Jane, but the only reason we know for certain it's true is because her brother told me. Why would he do that? What kind of man deliberately casts suspicion on his best friend?"

"Perhaps he didn't realize what he was doing."

"Oh, he knew. We're talking about someone who uses words for a living."

"So perhaps he suspects Maxwell himself, but felt it was inappropriate to say so."

"Now, that's possible."

"But?" said Hero, watching him.

"This afternoon when I spoke to Lord Wallace at Brooks's, he mentioned Somerset's name as someone who would publish the Princess's letters to Hesse if he had them."

"Except Christian Somerset no longer has a newspaper," said Hero.

"No. But he does write for various journals. And I find it interesting that out of the hundreds of journalists and politicians in this city, Wallace named only two: Somerset and Brougham. He even said he and Somerset had discussed various ways of scuttling the Orange alliance."

"So maybe Wallace was trying to cast suspicion onto Somerset and away from himself."

"Maybe," Sebastian acknowledged. "It's also possible that I'm simply chasing after unnecessary tangents. It's even conceivable that Maxwell accidently killed Jane in a lover's quarrel and then murdered Ambrose when the man accused him of it."

She pushed herself up on her elbow so she could see his face better. "But you don't think so?"

He thrust the fingers of one hand through the heavy fall of her dark hair, drawing it back from her face. "Jane went to see her brother ten days before she died, on a Monday. He says she was there to bring him some ballads for a collection he's publishing."

"Ten days?" She gave a faint smile. "Where is your calendar when we need it?"

"I stared at it enough to know exactly which Monday that was—it's the same day Princess Charlotte told Jane that the Hesse letters had been stolen from Portsmouth. The next day, Tuesday, Jane went out to ask the Princess of Wales about the letters. And the day after that, Wednesday, she paid a visit to Lord Wallace."

"You think the real reason she went to see her brother that Monday was to ask if he had the letters?"

"The timing is suggestive, isn't it? According to Liam Maxwell, Jane was worried that her brother had once overheard her talking about the Hesse letters. Somerset claimed he hadn't. But she must have had a reason to suspect him, if she went to see him that day."

"The timing could be a coincidence."

"It could be," he agreed.

"It also wouldn't explain why Christian Somerset would kill her. His own sister? Over a packet of letters?"

"Maybe it wasn't murder. Maybe it was simply manslaughter. An accident."

"But why would she suddenly decide on that particular Thursday to walk across London—in a snowstorm—and visit her brother again?"

"That I don't have an answer to at all."

Hero said, "I suppose something could have happened as Jane was leaving Warwick House that we don't know about—either then or shortly afterward."

It occurred to Sebastian there was another possibility: that Jane Ambrose had never actually left Warwick House alive that day. That after Miss Kinsworth saw her crossing the courtyard, Jane could have turned around and gone back into the house for some unknown reason. But he wasn't quite ready to voice that suspicion aloud.

Hero folded her arms on his chest and smiled down at him. "You know, sleep might help."

He hauled her up so that her slim, naked body lay long against his and took her mouth with a whispered "I have a better idea."

$$Chapter\ 50$$

Saturday, 5 February

*T*he next morning Sebastian went in search of John Fisher, the officious little Bishop who served as Preceptor to Princess Charlotte. As far as they knew, Fisher was the last person—apart from her killer—to have spoken to Jane Ambrose before she died. He claimed they had merely exchanged "pleasantries." But it struck Sebastian as conceivable that their conversation might have been more important than he'd realized.

It was snowing by the time Sebastian reached Warwick House, big, wet, windblown flakes that melted quickly when they hit his face. As he passed through the old house's weathered gate, he found himself thinking about the day Jarvis had sent his carriage to collect Jane Ambrose and convey her to his chambers at Carlton House, a distance of—what? Five or six hundred feet? But Sebastian understood only too well the significance of Jarvis's gesture. By doing so, he had made certain that Jane would never again walk through this gate without remembering the ominous sight of the powerful man's carriage awaiting her. She

could never again have come to Warwick House without being ines-
capably aware of the palace's looming presence and the very real threat
Jarvis posed to her. And that suggested to Sebastian that when Jane left
Warwick House for the last time on the day of her death, she had not
lingered in Stone Cutters' Alley.

Unfortunately, the Bishop of Salisbury was not at Warwick House
on this blustery Saturday morning. According to the whey-faced footman who answered the door, the prelate typically attended the Princess
only on Thursdays and Fridays. He advised Sebastian to try the Bishop's residence. At the Bishop's residence, a somber cleric who identified
himself as Fisher's chaplain said he believed Salisbury intended to spend
the day in the Reading Room of the British Museum. The staff at the
Reading Room said Salisbury had been there and gone. They suggested
a local coffee shop favored by the prelate.

When he drew a blank at the coffee shop, Sebastian decided on a
long shot to try the House of Lords. The snow was coming down harder
now but still wet, turning the streets and footpaths into an ugly brown
slush.

"It's bloody miserable out 'ere," said Tom through the folds of his
scarf as they plowed their way up Whitehall.

Sebastian kept his head ducked as he guided the curricle around a
stalled brewer's wagon. "Hopefully he'll be here."

The Reverend Doctor Fisher *had* been around Parliament that day—
several people reported seeing him. But it was long past noon before
Sebastian found a harried clerk who said he rather thought the Bishop
had mumbled something about spending the rest of the day in the library of St. Paul's.

The Cathedral Library was reached from St. Paul's southwest tower,
via a grand cantilevered stone staircase that spiraled upward in sweeping
swirls. The door to the library was locked. Sebastian knocked discreetly,
waited, then knocked again. The minutes ticked by. Impatient, he raised

a fist and pounded hard, just as the Cathedral's choir began to sing, the sweet notes floating up from below.

"Stop that racket!" hissed a voice on the far side of the panel as unseen hands worked the bolt.

The door jerked in to reveal a shriveled, white-haired librarian, who glared at Sebastian's proffered card, sniffed, then stood back grudgingly to admit him into the stone chamber. The Cathedral's collection was contained within a single soaring room lined with dark oak cases and smelling strongly of musty old books. Volumes were everywhere: overflowing the shelves, stacked on tables, and cramming the wooden gallery that ran around the entire space overhead.

"What are you doing here?" demanded the Great Up in a harsh whisper, scrambling down a steep ladder from the wooden gallery above. "You're all *wet!*"

Sebastian swiped a crooked elbow across his face. "You're not an easy man to find."

"Shhh! Keep your voice down. And stay away from the books. You are *dripping!*"

As far as Sebastian could tell, the Bishop and the aged librarian were the only people in the chamber, but he obligingly lowered his voice. "I've been thinking about the day Jane Ambrose died. You said—"

"Merciful heavens, you aren't still going on about that, are you?"

"You said you met her in the entrance hall as she was leaving Warwick House and exchanged a few pleasantries."

"Y-yes," said the Bishop, drawing the word out into two syllables. "And that triviality requires you to interrupt my studies and risk ruining a collection that dates back centuries?"

Sebastian held himself very still. "Did you actually see Mrs. Ambrose leave Warwick House that day? I mean, physically walk through the gate?"

"Of course not. I told you: I encountered her in the entrance hall immediately following the Princess's lesson. After we spoke, I continued on my way up the stairs. Why would I watch her leave?"

"And you spoke of—what? The weather?"

"It is an endless topic of conversation these days, is it not? I'd recently returned to London, and needless to say the roads were atrocious."

"So you did speak of the weather?"

"Yes; I thought I'd made that clear. I believe I made some reference to the state of the roads and said I was fortunate I'd decided to return to London when I did, since things had become so much worse. I spent the Christmas holidays with family in Petersfield, you see."

"And did you speak of your trip out of town?"

"Briefly. I mentioned encountering Mrs. Ambrose's brother at a coaching inn there, and as I recall, she expressed surprise, since she was not aware of his having been out of town."

"You saw Christian Somerset in Petersfield?"

"That's right."

"You know him?"

The prelate sniffed. "Let us say simply that I know of him."

"Well enough to recognize him?"

The Bishop tilted back his head so that he could look down his impressive nose at Sebastian. "That is rather implied by what I said, is it not?"

"And when was this? That you saw Christian Somerset in Petersfield, I mean."

"Saturday the fifteenth of January. Why?"

"You're certain of the date?"

"Of course I am certain. It's the day I returned to London."

"And Mrs. Ambrose was unaware of the fact that her brother had been out of town?"

"That is what I said. Seriously, my lord, are you not listening?"

"I simply want to be certain I understand exactly what you're telling me."

"About a trivial, inconsequential weather conversation?"

"I have a feeling it wasn't inconsequential," said Sebastian. "Not at all."

As he guided his horses eastward through the slush-snarled traffic of the Strand and Fleet Street, Sebastian found himself pondering the random incidents that can alter a person's life, sometimes for the better but at other times catastrophically.

What were the odds? he wondered. What were the odds that a superficial exchange of pleasantries between Jane Ambrose and the Princess's self-important Preceptor could have led in just a few hours to Jane's death? Or was that seemingly inconsequential conversation simply the inevitable culmination of a fated series of events that had begun with Christian Somerset overhearing Jane's low-voiced discussion of the Hesse letters with Maxwell and continued through Somerset's chance encounter with Fisher at a coaching inn in Petersfield?

The Hesse letters had been stolen from Portsmouth sometime around the thirteenth or fourteenth of January. Given the weather, anyone traveling from Portsmouth to London at that time would surely have stuck to the main coaching road. And that road passed through Petersfield. According to the Bishop, Jane hadn't known about her brother's trip out of town, while according to Somerset, Jane had come to see him shortly after his return from a visit to Kent. Not Petersfield, Hampshire, but Kent.

The variation could be meaningless, of course, but Sebastian didn't think so. Far more likely it was a clever misdirection wrapped in a truth: The printer *had* been out of town, but he had been careful not to tell his sister, and he had not been to Kent.

It was all too obvious, now, why Jane had not returned home as planned when she left Warwick House that last day. Troubled by her conversation with the Bishop, she must have gone to Paternoster Row to ask her brother if he had been behind the theft of the Hesse letters. Sebastian found it difficult to believe Christian Somerset had deliberately murdered his sister to keep her quiet. Far more likely that the siblings had quarreled, and at some point, Jane's brother had struck her—the same way Jane's husband had struck her so many times in the past. Only this time, when a man who claimed to love Jane knocked her down, she didn't get up.

Somerset's dangerous involvement in the theft of the Princess's indiscreet letters also explained why he had then panicked. Why he had—somehow—carried his sister's body through the snow to leave her in a mean, snow-choked lane in Clerkenwell. Why Clerkenwell? The question had bothered Sebastian from the beginning. But the answer was simple: Unlike Jane's husband, Christian Somerset had known his sister taught William Godwin's daughter. But he had been unsure of the exact day of her lessons.

And so he had made a simple, telling mistake.

Sebastian reached Paternoster Row to find Somerset's workshop once again manned by a single apprentice, who sat perched on a stool sorting type.

"They're all still at the Frost Fair," said the boy Sebastian remembered from before.

"Despite the rising temperatures?"

The boy laughed. "That ice'll hold for days yet. Everybody says so."

"Do they?"

"Oh, aye," said the boy. "Through Monday at least. It's that thick, it is."

"Tell me," said Sebastian, "did you know Mr. Somerset's sister Jane Ambrose?"

"Aye. They say she used to come here all the time when Mr. Somerset was in prison. She helped Mrs. Somerset a lot."

"Do you recall the last time you saw her?"

"Aye," said the lad, his hands stilling for a moment at their task. "She was here the day she died."

"She was?"

The boy nodded. "I told her Mr. Somerset had gone off to see someone, but she said it didn't matter because she just wanted to drop off a couple more ballads for him."

"Do you remember what time she left?"

"I wouldn't know. We weren't busy that day, so Mr. Somerset had given us the afternoon off. I was talking to a friend in the courtyard and just happened to see her as she was lettin' herself in."

"She had a key to the shop?"

"I guess she must've. And Mr. Somerset keeps a spare key to his office just there, behind that picture." The boy nodded to a water-stained lithograph of the old Cathedral of St. Paul that hung on the wall near the office door and grinned. "He thinks nobody knows about it, but we all do."

"Ah," said Sebastian, shifting the print and calmly helping himself to the key. "Christian says he left a book for me on his desk. I'll just fetch it."

With that, he unlocked the office door and let himself inside while the boy shrugged and went back to sorting type. It would never occur to a simple printer's apprentice to question the actions of one of his master's associates—particularly one as grand as a viscount.

Closing the door behind him, Sebastian let his gaze drift around the small room. Somerset's office was the same disorderly jumble he remembered from before, with stacks of manuscripts and books strewn everywhere. But Sebastian was looking at it all with different eyes, for he knew things now that he hadn't known the last time he had been here.

He stood with his back against the door, trying to imagine the afternoon more than a week ago when Jane had come to Paternoster Row for the last time. She could easily have chosen to wait for her brother in the comfort of his house's parlor. Instead, she had come here. Why?

Pushing away from the door, Sebastian tried to mentally reconstruct that stormy afternoon. It had been snowing hard, so she'd probably taken off her wet hat and gloves. But not her pelisse. Why? Because the fire in the stove had gone out and the room was cold?

He found his gaze fixed on the rusty iron stove in the corner of the room. It was a large, old-fashioned piece, probably dating back to the time of the American War or before. Had she decided to light a fire to keep warm while she awaited her brother's return? Was that how she had burned her fingers? It seemed a plausible explanation. Unless . . .

Unless she had found the Hesse letters and burned her fingers in the process of lighting a fire to destroy them. Was that why she had chosen to come here, to her brother's office, rather than to his house? Because she knew instinctively that if he had Charlotte's letters he would hide them here, in this messy, dusty room that no one ever cleaned, rather than in his house?

Had she found them? Sebastian wondered. Had she been trying to destroy the letters in the stove when her brother came in and saw her? What would he have done? Hit her and pushed her away from the stove? Tried to rescue the flaming letters? Had she picked them up again, burning her fingers as she thrust them back into the fire? Had he pushed her away again, knocking her down so that she struck her head? On what?

Sebastian started looking.

If the room had been cleaner, he never would have found it. But it was quite obvious, really, once he realized what he was seeing: a noticeably clean section on the side of the dirty old stove and another on the floorboards below, where Christian Somerset had carefully wiped up his dead sister's blood.

Sebastian stood for a moment, staring at the spot where Jane Ambrose had died. Then he turned and quickly searched the office. He hoped he might find something—Jane's hat, gloves, and reticule, perhaps, or even the half-burned letters themselves. But there was nothing. And as the minutes ticked away, he realized with a rising sense of frustration that he had no evidence that Christian Somerset had accidently killed his sister. And nothing at all to prove he'd then deliberately murdered her husband in the hopes of throwing suspicion onto his childhood friend.

Yes, Somerset's young apprentice had seen Jane enter the workshop the day of her death. But Somerset himself hadn't been there at the time, and the printer could easily claim that she'd been gone before he returned home. Given that afternoon's worsening snowstorm, it was doubtful anyone had seen him. And the cause of the siblings' argument—the missing Hesse letters—could never, ever be mentioned. Hell, he couldn't even tell Lovejoy about them.

Sebastian went to stare out the dirty window, his hands on his hips. The small courtyard was sloppy and wet now with the rising temperatures. But the handcart he'd noticed before was still there, parked just to the left of the workshop door.

That's how he did it, thought Sebastian. *He loaded his sister's body on the cart and pushed it through the snow to Clerkenwell.* It wouldn't have been easy, and the printer must have been beyond exhausted by the time he finished. But fear could drive men to do incredible things. Fear and the instinct for self-preservation. The problem was, how to prove it? Especially without involving the Princess and her stolen letters.

How?

Chapter 51

*I*t was almost dark by the time Sebastian reached the banks of the frozen Thames. The now-bedraggled strings of gaily colored flags and lanterns danced fitfully in the warming wind, but hundreds of fairgoers still thronged the ice, their shouts and laughter mingling with the cries of roving hawkers. The smell of ale and roasting mutton and hot spice cakes hung heavy on the damp air.

"Ye think it's 'er brother what killed 'er, don't ye?" said Tom when Sebastian drew up at the foot of Queen Street to hand him the reins.

Sebastian turned to give the boy a long, steady look. "I do. Although I'm afraid I can't explain my reasoning to you."

Tom nodded, his face flat. He might not know the exact train of Sebastian's thoughts, but he was clever enough to grasp the implications of their movements that day. "'Ow they ever gonna put 'im on trial if it's got somethin' to do with the Princess and they don't want nobody t' know about it?"

Sebastian dropped lightly to the slushy ground. "I don't think they will."

A heavy, wet snow was falling again, big clumpy flakes that hovered perilously close to rain. Sebastian could see gaps here and there in the dou-
ble lines of tents, booths, and stalls, where some of the more prudent
tradesmen had obviously begun to mistrust the ice and withdrawn. But
the crowds were still thick. Half-grown boys with dogs at their heels
mingled with tradesmen and apprentices, stout matrons and merchants
in high-crowned hats, clusters of giggling serving girls and roving bands
of seamen from the ships frozen fast at the docks. There was a raucous,
almost frantic note to the noisy merrymaking, as if most sensed this would
be the Frost Fair's last night and were determined to make the most
of it.

He found a couple of apprentices working Somerset's old wooden
press, turning out souvenir cards while Somerset himself guarded the
piles of books and stationery from possible thieves. "Still doing a good
business, I see," said Sebastian, walking up to him.

Somerset's eyes crinkled with his soft, sad smile. "Can't complain."

"May I speak with you for a moment?"

Somerset nodded to one of the apprentices to take his place. "Of
course."

"I know what happened to your sister," said Sebastian as the two
men turned to push their way down the crowded promenade.

Something shifted behind the printer's eyes, something swift and
calculating and quickly hidden by half-lowered lids. "You do? Well,
that's encouraging. Was it her husband, then?"

"Actually, no."

"Oh?"

"It was you."

Somerset drew up and swung to face him, the light from the torches
flanking a nearby dance tent falling golden across his features. A burst

of shouts and laughter and the high-pitched, urgent screech of a fiddle filled the night. "Is this some sort of sick jest?"

"Hot pies!" shouted a passing boy selling mutton pies from a tray slung by a strap around his neck. "Pies, fresh and hot!"

Sebastian kept his gaze on the printer. "The day she died, Jane discovered by chance that you'd been in Hampshire at the time the Hesse letters were stolen. She went to your print shop, presumably intending to confront you with what she suspected. Only you weren't there. And so she searched your office, looking for the letters. She must have known you well, because she found them, didn't she? Then she lit a fire in your stove so she could burn them. That's when—"

"This is madness! Whatever makes you think—"

"That's when you came in. You realized what she was doing and you struck her, knocking her aside so you could pull the letters from the flames. The way I figure it, she must have picked up the burning letters with her bare hands—singeing her fingers—and thrust them back into the fire. So you pushed her away again. Only, this time when she fell, she hit her head on the side of the stove. And it killed her."

The torches beside them hissed and smoked as a clutch of drunken soldiers reeled past, voices warbling, *"O'er the hills and o'er the main—"*

Somerset swallowed hard. "No. You're wrong. Do you hear me? You're wrong."

"The ironic thing," said Sebastian, watching him carefully, "is that what happened to Jane that day wasn't murder. It was manslaughter. If you hadn't panicked, you could even have passed it off as a simple accident by saying she'd slipped on the wet floor and hit her head. No one would have suspected anything. Except because of those bloody letters, you did panic. You were so desperate to get rid of her body that you hauled her through the snowstorm up to Clerkenwell and dumped her in the middle of Shepherds' Lane. And it might have worked— except you had the wrong day for her lessons there, and one of the women who found her had the medical training to realize that the lack of blood meant she must have died someplace else."

"You're wrong," said Somerset again, breathing so hard and fast his chest was jerking. "It was Ambrose. I can't prove it, but it had to be him. He was a lying, cheating, foul-tempered bastard who beat her for years. Years! Of course it was he."

Sebastian shook his head. "Ambrose was all that and more. But he wasn't a murderer. Unlike you."

"Apples! Hot apples!" shouted an aged, stoop-shouldered woman with a steaming basket she thrust toward them. "Buy me hot apples, gentlemen?"

Somerset's gaze darted sideways. Jaw tightening, he yanked the basket from the woman's arms, threw its contents in Sebastian's face, and ran.

The apples rested on a grate above a pan of coals, and Sebastian squeezed his eyes shut and flung up one crooked elbow to protect his face. He felt the shower of hot embers sting his skin, smelled the pungent reek of burning wool as the glowing coals and hot grate tumbled down the front of his greatcoat. A horde of laughing urchins descended on him to scramble after the fruit rolling at his feet.

"Me apples!"

"Bloody hell," swore Sebastian as one of the children knocked into the old woman and sent her staggering against him.

Steadying her, Sebastian paused long enough to thrust a couple of shillings into the woman's hand, then turned and half tripped over a joyfully barking dog. "Bloody hell," he said again.

Christian Somerset was already seventy-five to a hundred yards ahead, plowing up the crowded promenade like the prow of a ship through debris-thick waters. Shaking off the old woman, the children, and the dog, Sebastian took off after him just as a stout butcher stepped backward out of a nearby mulled wine tent and slammed into Sebastian hard enough to make him grunt.

"Oye! Why don't ye watch where yer goin' there?" the man shouted after Sebastian as he ran on. "Bloody nobs!"

Sebastian kept going, past cook stalls and trinket booths and tents of tattered canvas that flapped in the wet wind. The snow was turning to rain now, and he nearly collided with a pretty woman in a fur-trimmed hat who'd stopped suddenly to look up at the sky and laugh, her face wet in the torchlight. Swerving, his feet slipping and sliding in the slush, he pelted past the Punch and Judy show. The children turned to laugh and point, the puppet master pivoting Judy to call after him in a high-pitched voice, "*Tsk-tsk.* Young gentlemen! Always in a hurry!"

With Sebastian now gaining on him, Jane's brother ducked through a beer tent, pausing just long enough to snatch up a tankard of ale and lob it at Sebastian before streaming out the far end.

"Oye!" yelped the bereft drinker as Sebastian ducked.

Erupting out the back of the tent, he caught his foot on one of the stakes holding up the canvas and nearly went down. "Shit," he swore, stumbling against the mound of icy snow that formed the edge of a nearby skittles alley just as Somerset yanked the heavy wooden ball from the hands of one of the players and threw it at Sebastian's head.

Sebastian feinted sideways, his slush-encrusted boots sliding on the smooth ice of the alley to send him smashing into the skittles. The pins went flying, and a roar of indignation rose from the players.

Jumping the far edge of the alley, he ran on, ducking beneath a young lady soaring high on a swing. Up ahead, he saw Somerset swerve onto one of the Frost Fair's short side "streets." Sebastian raced after him, past a last straggling shoemaker's and a toy stand. And then they were in the open, heading out across the river's ragged, uneven ice toward the opposite bank.

A small rivulet of water still ran down the middle of the river. Farther upstream, the gap had been bridged with planks, with boatmen there to hand fairgoers across for a small fee. But there were no planks or boatmen here, and as Somerset neared the center of the river he was forced to veer right again, running straight toward the looming stone arches of London Bridge.

Sebastian pelted after him, his breath coming in hard gasps, his boots slipping and sliding on the melting ice. Out here, away from the Frost Fair, the world was white: white sky, white ice, white snow, with a thin black ribbon of water surging beside them as they ran on and on.

They'd almost reached the bridge when a loud *crack-crack* cut through the night. A chorus of screams arose from the distant fair as a massive section of the ice sheared off in front of them with a roaring crash. Skidding to a halt at the edge of the ice, Somerset swung around, his gaze darting frantically from side to side as he fought to draw in air.

"End of the line," said Sebastian.

Somerset shook his head, his chest shuddering with the intensity of his breathing. The rain poured down around them. "If you want me, you're going to have to kill me. I've seen men hanged. I'm not dying like that."

"They'll never put you on trial," said Sebastian. From the distance came more shrieks and cries of alarm as another loud crack echoed across the frozen river and fairgoers and booth keepers alike started a frantic rush toward solid ground. "They can't afford to let anyone know about the Princess's letters."

The printer gave a ragged laugh. "So you're saying—what? That Lord Jarvis will simply send one of his henchmen to Newgate to garrote me in my sleep? I suppose that's better than hanging. Marginally."

"Why the hell didn't you just admit what had happened to your sister that day and face the music?"

Somerset took a step back, then another, his gaze never leaving Sebastian's face. "I can't go to prison again. If you'd ever been in prison, you'd understand that."

"So instead you *murdered* Edward Ambrose? Just so you could cast suspicion away from you and onto your best friend?"

Somerset's nostrils flared wide, his eyes wild. "I'm not proud of what I did."

"What about Valentino Vescovi? Did you kill him, too?"

"Good God, no. Why would I?" He swiped the cuff of one sleeve across his face. "I didn't mean to kill Jane. *I loved her.* She was my sister! She was all I had left in this world. Don't you understand that?"

"Yes."

Another series of massive *cracks* sounded, and the ice heaved and buckled at their feet. What had minutes before been a small rivulet in the center of the river was now a wide yawning gap. A chunk of ice with a shack advertising brandy balls went spinning past, a gray-faced man clinging to one of its upright timbers screaming, "Help! Somebody help me!" The air echoed with the terrified shrieks from the ruined Frost Fair.

Somerset took another step back, then another, the ice beneath him groaning as he edged closer to the cold, rushing black water.

"Don't do this," said Sebastian.

Somerset gave him a strange, wobbly smile. "Why not? You think I should fear for my immortal soul? If I have one, it's damned already for what I've done. And if not, then at least I'll end it all at a time and in a manner of my own choosing."

If Sebastian were to lunge forward and haul Somerset back from the edge, he might have been able to save him. But for what? A few miserable days in prison that would end all too quickly in hideous certain death?

Something flickered across the other man's face. "Thank you," said Jane's brother. Then he stepped back off the edge of the ice into the cold, dark water. He made only a small splash and sank quickly, coming up once with a gasp before being carried off on the swirling current.

The screams and shouts of the panicked fairgoers had for one suspended moment faded from Sebastian's awareness; now they came roaring back. Turning, he sprinted for the riverbank, his feet slipping on the slushy surface, the ice cracking and collapsing behind him, the rain cold in his wet face. His world narrowed down to endless ice and wind-driven rain and the ragged rush of his breath rasping in and out. Then hands were reaching out to grasp him, haul him in, steady him as he sagged. Safe. He was safe.

Whirling, his breath a raw agony, he turned to stare out over the heaving, broken ice and black water.

Somerset was gone.

Chapter 52

"*H*ow many people were killed last night?" Sebastian asked as he walked with Sir Henry Lovejoy along the terrace of Somerset House. The ice-churned waters of the Thames raced swift and deadly beside them.

"I doubt we'll ever know," said Sir Henry with a heavy sigh. "I'm told dozens of booths were carried off with much loss of property. But who's to say how many lives were lost with them?" The magistrate paused to look out over the runoff-swollen river. Some of the abandoned booths and tents were still out there, perched precariously on the last remaining stretches of solid ice. But they wouldn't be for long. "Last I heard they'd pulled four bodies from below the bridge. But most will probably never be found."

"None of them was Somerset?"

"No." The magistrate paused, then said carefully, "I'm told by the palace this must all be hidden from the public."

Sebastian nodded. He'd had a short, terse conversation with his father-in-law in the small hours of the night. Jarvis's men had torn Somerset's office and workshop apart, looking for the Hesse letters. But there'd been no sign of them, and Sebastian suspected Jane Ambrose had successfully destroyed them after all. He wondered if the young Princess appreciated that her beloved piano instructor had died trying to save her from the repercussions of her own folly, but he doubted it. Royals were like that. Typically, any sacrifice on the part of their subjects—no matter how great—was simply accepted as their due.

"'Our hands have not shed this blood, nor have our eyes seen it,'" said Sir Henry softly to himself.

Sebastian glanced over at him in inquiry, and the magistrate cleared his throat self-consciously. "The Book of Deuteronomy, chapter twenty-one. It says that if someone be slain and found lying in an open place, then the elders of the nearest towns must behead a young heifer on the spot and wash their hands over it, saying, 'Be merciful, O Lord, and lay not innocent blood unto thy people's charge.' And then the blood debt is forgiven them." Lovejoy shook his head. "I've always found it an odd passage, given that an all-seeing God must surely know the identity of the guilty party."

Sebastian found himself faintly smiling. "True." The smile faded. "Do you ever think that sometimes these things might best be left to fate?"

"'Vengeance is mine, sayeth the Lord'?" Lovejoy studied him with wise, compassionate eyes. "Neither Edward Ambrose's death nor Christian Somerset's is on your hands, if that's what you're suggesting."

"Not exactly. And yet . . . my determination to bring murderers to justice has always been driven by the obligation I believe we the living owe to the dead. Yet I can't believe Jane Ambrose would have wanted to see her only surviving brother die, even if he did accidently kill her. It wasn't deliberate. And my attempts to uncover what happened to her led directly to her husband's death."

"Perhaps. But the fault was all Somerset's, not yours. The Bible also says, 'All things work together for God to them that love him.'"

"You think in this instance things worked 'for God'?" asked Sebastian.

Lovejoy turned his face into the wind, his eyes troubled. "Only God has that answer."

Later that afternoon, Sebastian found himself sitting in one of the worn pews of St. Anne's, Soho. He tilted back his head, his gaze on the gloriously hued light streaming in through the stained glass window above the altar. He was not a religious man; his belief in the teachings of his youth had been swept away by six brutal years at war. Yet he was not immune to the sense of enveloping peace that a church could bring to those in need. And he was in need.

After a while he heard the echo of a distant door opening and closing, followed by soft footsteps. Liam Maxwell came to sit beside him, his elbows on his spread knees and his hat in his hands. They sat in silence for a time. Then Maxwell said, "I heard about Christian's death. He's the one, isn't he? It was Christian who killed Jane."

"Yes. By accident. And then he panicked. He was terrified of being sent back to prison. Or hanged."

Maxwell stared straight ahead, his jaw held tight. Sebastian expected him to ask next about Ambrose's death, but he did not. And Sebastian realized it was because the journalist must already have figured it all out.

He'd obviously known his friend very well indeed.

The sun was slipping lower in the sky, the vibrant colors of the stained glass darkening to somber tones as the light began to fade. "I've loved her nearly half my life," said Maxwell, his voice a raw whisper. "I don't think I know how to go on living my life without her in it to love."

"Yet you will," said Sebastian.

Maxwell nodded, his lips pressed together, his throat working hard as he swallowed.

"I honestly believe she had decided to leave Ambrose for you," said Sebastian. "I don't know if that makes everything easier or harder to bear."

Maxwell's chin quivered. "Maybe both."

Sebastian nodded. This time he was the one who couldn't quite trust his voice to speak.

He stood, his hand resting briefly on the other man's shoulder. Then he turned and left him there, with his grief, and his memories of the past, and his yearning for a tomorrow that would never be.

"Oh, I do so wish I could have gone to the Frost Fair," said Her Royal Highness Princess Charlotte Augusta of Wales. She stood between Hero and Miss Kinsworth at the side of Blackfriars Bridge, one finely gloved hand resting on the stone parapet, her cheeks rosy from the fresh air, her eyes shining as she looked out over the broken ice of the Thames. The wind was warm out of the south, the sun so bright that the glare off the melting snow dazzled the eyes. One of the fair's remaining tents shuddered out on the ice and then tipped sideways as the section beneath it collapsed, and a sigh went up from the crowd gathered on the bridge.

Watching the young Princess gaze longingly at the ruins of the Frost Fair, it struck Hero just how cruel it had been for the Regent to keep his daughter away from what had surely been one of the grandest spectacles of her age. She really was a coddled version of Cinderella—without the promise of a handsome Prince Charming to someday sweep her away from a dark, narrow existence in a gilded cage to which Prinny had doomed her.

"Miss Kinsworth told me how Jane died," said Charlotte, casting a quick stricken glance at her companion. "That this all happened because of those letters."

"I believe they truly have been destroyed," said Hero.

"It was unforgivably foolish of me to have written them," said Charlotte. "And now Jane is dead because of my folly."

Hero's gaze met Ella Kinsworth's, and the older woman looked away, blinking hard. Charlotte stared out over the icy waters. Her features were solemn, but the agitation of her breathing betrayed the extent of her inner turmoil.

"Don't marry him," Hero said in a sudden rush. "Orange, I mean. Forgive me, Your Highness, for speaking so boldly. But without the Hesse letters hanging over you, you are no longer as vulnerable as you were before."

Eyes wide and hurting, Charlotte turned to face her. "But how can I not?"

"Drag out the negotiations over the marriage contract. I've heard Orange's father is anxious for his son to marry and beget an heir. That means it's not unlikely he'll tire of the delay and look elsewhere for his son's bride. This dreadful war will be over soon, and then so much will change—doubtless far more than we can even imagine."

For a long, pregnant moment, the Princess held Hero's gaze. Then she nodded silently and smiled.

It would take courage for a powerless girl of just eighteen to stand against the overbearing will of a selfish, bullying father who was also her prince. But Hero suspected Charlotte had the grit to do it.

"How did two people as selfish and foolish as Prinny and Caroline manage to beget a child as basically good and decent as Charlotte?" Devlin asked later that evening when they gathered in the drawing room before dinner.

Hero looked up from where she sat by the fire with Simon and Mr. Darcy. "I honestly can't imagine."

He took a long, slow swallow of his wine. "Do you think she will indeed stand up to Prinny?"

"I believe she might. In some way I can't quite define, I think Jane's death has given Charlotte the determination she needs to refuse to let her father destroy her life."

Devlin cradled his glass in one hand, his gaze on the flames dancing on the hearth. "I wish I could have met her. Jane, I mean."

Hero watched their son pet the big black cat with studied care, and felt a part of the burden that had weighed so heavily upon her begin to shift. "I'm glad we know how and why she died—and that Princess Charlotte knows, as well. I suppose in the grand scheme of things it makes no real difference. And yet, on another level, it does."

"She was an extraordinary person—steadfast, loving, and brave."

"Yes," said Hero. "Yes, she was."

Author's Note

The Frost Fair of 1814 was the last Frost Fair held on the Thames. It came at the culmination of a horrid winter that included what was known as the Great Fog. Smothering London from late December to early January, the fog was followed by days of massive snowfall that buried the entire Kingdom and then weeks more of freezing temperatures and continuing snow. Food and coal in the city became scarce and prohibitively expensive, and many of London's poorest died. In late January, ice floating down from the upper reaches of the river became caught between London Bridge and Blackfriars; eventually the remaining open water froze, and the people of the city took to the ice for a Frost Fair that lasted until the fifth of February. Then a shift in the wind and warming temperatures led the ice to break up rather suddenly, carrying off booths and people. The exact number killed was never determined since most of the bodies were never recovered. There had been other Frost Fairs on the Thames down through the ages, but with the removal of the old narrow-arched London Bridge in 1831, the Thames has never again frozen so solid.

The verse on Liam Maxwell's souvenir is adapted from one actually printed at the fair and reproduced in John Ashton's *Social England Under the Regency*. Maxwell's "free press" sales pitch was also used at the fair.

The Prince of Wales was every bit as horrid to his wife, Caroline, as portrayed here. He did send his mistress to meet her ship when she landed, had Lady Jersey attend their wedding feast, and took her on their honeymoon (along with a bunch of his male friends who—like the Prince—were constantly falling-down drunk). He also forced Caroline to accept his mistress as her lady-in-waiting. The nasty stories about the furniture and pearl bracelets he took back are likewise true. Through his unsavory personal secretary, Colonel McMahon, he deliberately spread false gossip about his wife and paid newspapers to print ugly rumors about her, and he actually did award a certain Lady Douglas a pension for life after she swore to a tawdry—and easily disproven—pack of lies about the Princess of Wales as part of one of his numerous attempts to secure a divorce. In his preserved letters to friends and family, the Prince comes across as a petty, manipulative, breathtakingly narcissistic pathological liar, and paranoid to the point of being mentally unbalanced. He actually did have a fervent but totally unfounded belief that Caroline was conspiring to destroy the British monarchy.

Caroline of Brunswick is a fascinating, colorful character, although difficult to research because so many lies were told about her at the time and most of her biographers have been far too credulous. She was twenty-seven when she married. Although I do not believe she was as promiscuous as she is sometimes portrayed, it appears likely that when she was younger she fell in love with a certain Irish officer and might have had a child by him. That child would have been taken away from her, which was probably the cause of the intense hatred she exhibited toward her mother the rest of her life. After the Prince essentially took baby Charlotte away, Caroline then poured her maternal urges and considerable financial resources into fostering a string of poor orphans.

Although relatively pretty when young, she was always careless in her attire, blunt spoken, and utterly unsophisticated. Yet she was far from stupid; a polyglot and lifelong enthusiastic reader, she was acknowledged even by those who disliked her to be a well-trained and unusually fine pianist. She was also artistic and continued to study painting and sculpture as an adult. She had a very real and oft-expressed fear of being unjustly accused of adultery and executed for treason. Given how hard the Prince tried to convict her of adultery, including hiring men to hide in the bushes and break into her house to search her bedroom, I strongly doubt she violated her vows while in England. After she left England and moved to Italy, however, she does appear to have made up for all those lonely years by indulging in a torrid affair with a handsome young Italian. And yes, Caroline really did make wax effigies of her husband, stick them with pins, and burn them.

Caroline's daughter, Princess Charlotte, is best known through the memoirs of her subgoverness Miss Cornelia Knight (on whom I have modeled Miss Ella Kinsworth) and through the Princess's touching, intimate, and brutally honest letters to her only real friend, Margaret Mercer Elphinstone. When I first began researching this story, I did not expect to like Charlotte, but she soon revealed herself to be an endearing, engaging, and truly tragic figure. In a later age she would have been called a tomboy; her rather mannish stride and ways, her enthusiastic love of horses and dogs, her open, friendly demeanor and habit of shaking hands with men were all roundly criticized. Given her bizarre upbringing, it is truly amazing she turned out to be such a warm, funny, likable person, with a gift for mimicry and a clever wit. A fervent Whig, she was furious when her father allied himself with the High Tories after becoming Regent, and genuinely believed the Irish were totally justified in rebelling for their independence.

Charlotte was very close to her old grandfather, King George III, and for a time he was able to protect her from the worst nastiness of her father, who used the child to torment his hated wife. Once the old King slipped into madness, however, she was left without a champion. As the crowds in the streets cheered Charlotte more and more, Prinny's resentment of his daughter and his determination to remove her from the country increased. While it was traditional to mark the eighteenth birthday of the heir presumptive to the throne with widespread celebrations, he used "economy" as an excuse to ignore the occasion and simply left London to visit friends in the north.

Charlotte did indeed have a brief, innocent romance with a Captain Charles Hesse. His position as an illegitimate son of the Duke of York is disputed by some, but the fact that Charlotte herself accepted the relationship and was very close to her uncle York makes it more probable. As difficult as it is to believe, the story about her mother locking the young couple in her bedroom at Kensington Palace is true. The possible explanations Hero and Sebastian discuss have all been suggested, but no one knows exactly why Caroline did it. Charlotte did send Hesse letters and trinkets she then desperately tried to get back, and those letters did refer to the bedroom incident. Hesse did leave the letters in a trunk with a friend when he sailed for Spain. But the "Hesse letters" were never stolen, and Charlotte was eventually able to retrieve and destroy them.

Captain Hesse's future exploits are interesting, for he joined up with Caroline and traveled with her for a time after she left England. He later became the lover of the Queen of Naples (a daughter of King Carlos IV of Spain) and was ultimately killed in the Bois de Vincennes in a duel with Count Leon, an illegitimate son of Napoléon. What are the odds?

The story of the circumstances surrounding Charlotte's betrothal to Orange as told by Caroline to Sebastian is based on the accounts left by the various people involved. The Regent did pressure his daughter into promising that she would give him a yes or no answer after her first meeting with Orange at a dinner at Carlton House. Then, when the Prince asked her opinion of the young man and she tried to prevaricate, Wales pretended to misunderstand and immediately announced to both

Liverpool and Orange that she had given her consent. Charlotte was appalled, and when she discovered the next day that Orange intended to require her to leave the country—and that her father had known of this—she was furious. Although the betrothal was arranged in December 1813, the announcement was indeed delayed for months while Orange solidified his position in the Netherlands.

Negotiations on the marriage contracts dragged out when Charlotte—who knew her father well—refused to accept vague promises and kept insisting that everything be put in writing. She became convinced that her father planned to push through a divorce from Caroline once his daughter was out of the country. Along with Charlotte's concerns for her mother was the very real fear that her father might then remarry and produce a son who would take her place in the line of succession. Eventually, in the summer of 1814, Charlotte broke off the betrothal. Her father reacted by firing everyone in her household in a truly hideous scene that ended with Charlotte running out of the house.

While various reasons are given for Charlotte's decision to break the betrothal, I suspect from the subtle things she said in various letters that at some point the Princess discovered the truth about Orange's sexual preferences. But because her friend Mercer was in London at the time when Charlotte's attitude toward Orange shifted suddenly from a determination to make the best of things into an intense, bitter loathing, we do not know for certain. But we do know that because of her experiences with her father, honesty was very important to Charlotte, and she felt betrayed.

The Dutch Republic dated back to the sixteenth-century Union of Utrecht and lasted until overrun by the French in 1795. After the defeat of Napoléon, the Allies decided to turn the stadtholder—who had been an elected head of state—into a king and joined Holland to the largely French-speaking Austrian Netherlands (today's Belgium). The resultant Kingdom of the United Netherlands lasted until the Belgian Revolution of 1830, after which the Belgians were allowed to recover their separate identity, but only as the Kingdom of Belgium under Leopold I (yes, the same Leopold who was by then Princess Charlotte's widower).

The Regent did suffer a well-publicized attack of gout in January of 1814, and he really did hate dogs. Charlotte did have a white greyhound named Toby that had belonged to Napoléon's wife before being seized aboard a French ship and sent to the Prince.

Charlotte Jones (I have called her "Lottie" to avoid the confusion of two characters with the same name) was Princess Charlotte's miniature portrait painter. The daughter of a Norwich merchant, she moved to London after the death of her father to study under Richard Cosway. Appointed Princess Charlotte's official miniature portrait painter in 1808, she also received commissions from numerous other members of the Royal family and the likes of Lady Caroline Lamb. She was dismissed by the Regent along with the rest of Charlotte's household in the summer of 1814.

While Jane Ambrose is fictional, Princess Charlotte did have a piano instructor named Jane Mary Guest, who had a minor reputation as a composer. A pupil of Johann Christian Bach and Thomas Linley, Guest also taught Charlotte's youngest aunt, the Princess Amelia. The Regent fired her along with the rest of Charlotte's staff in the summer of 1814.

The limitations placed on the fictional Jane Ambrose as a female musician were real. Mendelssohn's sister Fanny and Mozart's sister, Maria Anna, were both acknowledged as being at least as talented as their famous brothers. Like the fictional Jane, they were allowed to perform with their brothers while young but forced to retire from the public eye when they reached marriageable age. Maria Anna Mozart did compose music, but it is not known if her brother published any of it as his own; Felix Mendelssohn did publish some of his sister Fanny's works, but since that occurred after the date of this story, neither Hero nor Miss Kinsworth is able to reference it.

Thomas Linley was a famous tenor, music teacher, and composer whose numerous musical children were legendary. The family seems to have had a fatal weakness for tuberculosis, or consumption as it was then called, and most died quite young. One of his daughters, Elisabeth, was the first wife of playwright Richard Sheridan. A noted soprano, she had to give up performing at the time of her marriage.

Princess Charlotte's governess in January of 1814 was the Duchess of Leeds, who was much as I have described her here. The young Lady Arabella is modeled on the Duchess's daughter, Lady Catherine Osborne, who was introduced into Charlotte's household to spy on the Princess. Lady Catherine actually did learn German when Charlotte and Miss Knight began speaking that language to keep her from eavesdropping on their conversations. When the Princess and her subgoverness switched to Italian, Lady Catherine then began taking Italian lessons from Charlotte's harp instructor. And yes, at one point Princess Charlotte did lock the annoying duke's daughter in a water closet (toilet) for fifteen minutes.

William Godwin was a real historical figure, famous at the time as a political philosopher but better known today as the widower of the pioneering feminist Mary Wollstonecraft. He was also the father of Mary Godwin Shelley, author of *Frankenstein* and wife of the poet Shelley. Godwin did live in Clerkenwell, on Skinner Street, and in later life he did write, publish, and sell children's books.

Publishers, printers, and bookstores worked differently in the early nineteenth century than they do today. Printers typically sold their books in plain paper wrappers with temporary sewing; the books were permanently bound by either bookstores or their purchasers, who would have them bound to match their libraries. Many printers had their own bookstores and binderies.

The character of Liam Maxwell is a composite of several radical journalists including Leigh and John Hunt, William Cobbett, Thomas Jonathan Wooler, Richard Carlile, and others. It was not uncommon for journalists to be imprisoned for publishing unflattering truths about the

Prince of Wales or simply criticizing practices such as the pillory or impressment.

The large size of the Royal Navy combined with the brutal discipline, hideous living conditions, and low pay for which it was infamous meant Britain's warships could be kept crewed only by the use of impressment. Armed press gangs roamed ports and nearby villages to carry off able-bodied boys and men; men were also seized off merchant ships, both British and foreign, and from foreign naval ships (the latter played a major role in the United States' declaration of the War of 1812). It is said that at the time of Trafalgar more than half the Royal Navy's 120,000 sailors were pressed men. These men's wives and families were often left destitute.

While I have altered her name and some details, a seventeen-year-old wife of an impressed sailor was hanged at Newgate for theft after walking up to London from Cornwall in search of her husband; her newborn baby was taken from her arms on the scaffold. The description of Amy Hatcher's hanging is an amalgamation of several contemporary accounts of hangings from the period of the Napoleonic Wars. Murderers were typically (but not always) hanged on a Monday morning; prisoners guilty of any of the period's two hundred other capital crimes could be hanged any day of the week. Hangings were usually multiple; the record is believed to be twenty at one time.

Napoléon really did set up a "ville des smoglers." One of the best sources for this strange chapter in history and the role played by Rothschild is Gavin Daly's 2007 article in *The Historical Journal*, "Napoleon and the 'City of Smugglers,' 1810–1814." The claim that Rothschild's January 1814 gold shipments to Paris were then sent on to Wellington is disputed by some; attempts by certain later apologists to further claim that *all* of Rothschild's well-documented gold smuggling ventures had for years been going to Wellington are patently ridiculous. As Hero notes, the Royal Navy had control of the Channel and had no need for such costly and dangerous subterfuge.

Rothschild was only one of many London financiers engaged in activities that aided France. Apart from arranging the loan that enabled the United States to buy Louisiana from Napoléon, London bankers also gave Napoléon the five million pounds he needed to raise an army after he escaped from Elba. Napoléon was what some have called a "bullionist"; he really did distrust paper money and hated bankers and credit. Despite his constant wars, he is said to have left France a credit balance in 1814. (Of course, looting Switzerland and the Vatican helped make that possible.)

Lord Wallace is a fictional character modeled largely on Lord Grey (of Earl Grey tea fame), although I have given him the more abrasive and opportunistic personality of Henry Brougham, one of Caroline's best-known supporters.

Famous for his plays *The Rivals* and *The School for Scandal*, Richard Sheridan was also a Whig MP for more than thirty years. His marriage to Elizabeth Linley (of the musical Linley family) was colorful. He did live on Savile Row, although at the time it was called Savile Street. He lost his seat in Parliament after the Prince moved against him and, ruined by the burning of Drury Lane and Covent Garden theaters, he died in great poverty.